FLAGSHIP

First published in 2007 by

WOODFIELD PUBLISHING
Bognor Regis, West Sussex, England
www.woodfieldpublishing.com

ISBN 1-84683-027-3

Flagship March

The sequel to 'BlueBelles on Parade'

ROBERT C BERTIE

Woodfield

Dedicated to the memory of the late Albert Barrett
who it was my privilege to call a true friend.

Whatever the situation, he was always there
to lend a helping hand.

In Warrant Officer Bill Barrett
I have tried to recreate Albert's admirable qualities
of firmness, kindness and a sense of humour.

Acknowledgements

To my brother Roy, who gave me ideas from some of his National Service exploits.

To Viv Allison (my heroine), who did so much to spread the word of my first book *BlueBelles On Parade* to the numerous ex-RAF and WRAF colleagues.

To Ted Whittaker, ex-National Service, RAF Regiment, Queen's Colour Squadron, for boosting my confidence after reading my effort and giving it his top marks.

The Author

Born in 1921 in the West Riding of Yorkshire Robert Bertie's family returned to Lancashire when he was a babe.

An 8th.Army war veteran, he also served for 23 years in the peacetime Royal Air Force.

He has been married for 57 years to Jean, who was a nurse for 39 years.

They have one son, Robert Ian.

CHAPTER 1

As Station Warrant officer Bill Barrett was making his way towards the guardroom to check on his staff, the Station Commander's car pulled up to a halt. Bill immediately saluted its occupant, Group Captain Wildeman, who wound down the car window.

"Good morning Mr Barrett, a word please!"

Bill approached the car.

"Good morning sir."

"It is time you and I had a chat, Mr Barrett. It has been too long since we had one and I miss our little tête-à-têtes. If we are not careful, we are going to lose contact, due to the fact that I am not as accessible as I was since my promotion. I am on my way to Command to attend a meeting which I have a feeling will concern both you and I. When I return I will send for you to discuss whatever it is. Let's hope it's to our advantage…"

"Sounds interesting sir, I will look forward to it."

"Carry on Pauline," the Station Commander ordered his WRAF Sergeant chauffeur, as he returned Bill's salute.

Bill carried on to the guardroom to see Flight Sergeant Tom Bridges who, along with six police corporals, was responsible for the daytime security of the station, the overnight security being carried out by permanent staff airmen.

"Everything going alright Flight, any complaints?" he asked with a smile. "Are the cells empty?"

"Yes sir, everything is nice and quiet, just as we like it."

The formality between the two was because of the presence of three junior NCOs.

"Fill me in again with your security system," said Bill.

"I have one man on the gate and two patrolling the camp in a Landrover. The other three are here with me, they are the reliefs."

"How are you settling down here? A bit different from airfield duties isn't it?"

"It certainly is. This is what we call a cushy posting. It will do me for a while and the wife likes it here too. She says it is nice and quiet and good to get away from the noisy aircraft, especially when they were night flying. It is a nice part of the country around here and so easy to get to places like the Dales and the seaside. Yes, we are happy enough here."

"Good. By the way, I am going to get the Sergeants Mess back on its feet. It's time things were happening in there; a few functions hopefully will put some life back into it."

"I am all for that," replied Tom.

"Right then, I will be off and have a scout round the place and see if everyone is behaving themselves."

Approaching the front of SHQ he saw the Fielding brothers tidying the gardens.

"Make a good job of them, I happen to work in there," he chided them.

"Good morning sir," they said, beaming at him; they had become very fond of Bill, because he always played fair with them. "Now don't we always do a good job? Tell you what, we wish we were still working for you and Mary Butcher."

Bill laughed. "Only because we were too soft with you both! Would you like me to have a word with Tom Hardcastle and tell him to dangle a few carrots for you?" He left them grinning.

Going round to the rear entrance to SHQ he paused to watch two flights of recruits being put through their paces on the parade ground, then carried on to his office.

"Any messages Ian?" Ian was Flight Sergeant Roberts, the replacement for Flight Sergeant Jim Ball, who was away on a resettlement course prior to his discharge from the service.

"No," he replied, "it has been quiet up to now."

"If I am wanted I will be with Roy Shaw, I want to sort something out with him."

"Come in," said Roy, in answer to the knock on his office door.

"Ah! It's you," he exclaimed as Bill entered. "What brings you here so early in the day? What's on your mind Bill, is it serious?"

"Yes, I think it is."

"Sounds very onimous."

"Don't you mean ominous, Roy?"

"Course I do, I can never say ominous! Now spit it out what you want to tell me."

"The Sergeants Mess"

"What about it?"

"Don't you think it is due a damned good shake up? It is not supported as it should be and I suggest we have a Mess meeting to get the place sorted out with a proper committee who have the ability to make it into an attractive venue by organising plenty of functions, all the usual things that go with a Sergeants Mess. We must do something Roy. When was the last time we held a Mess meeting? The nearest thing to that was when the Commandant, as he was then, told about the role of the station in Operation Smarty Pants. How long ago was that?"

"I see your point Bill and I am in total agreement with you, in fact I will have some print-outs done to the affect that there will be an extraordinary Sergeants Mess meeting giving the day, date and time also stating it is not a request but an order to every Mess member to attend. For any reason anyone who cannot attend must submit the reason in writing to the SWO. I will make sure that each individual gets a copy. I think we had better leave the reason for the meeting until the day, otherwise you will have a postbag of excuses on your desk."

"Excellent Roy! I know I can always count on your support when it is needed."

"That is only because I have no more sense. I shall probably regret it later when I have had time to think about it."

"I agree, that is why I am volunteering myself as Chairman. Is there anything you fancy volunteering for… secretary for instance?"

"It's a thought. I will think about it."

"We will need the help of your Sergeant Page to take the minutes; she is mustard with her shorthand, that I *do* know. So far we have the makings of a good team, me and you. If we can get an enthusiastic entertainments committee together then the jobs a good un', but I do want at least two of the WRAF on it."

"How about sounding Mary Butcher out to head it?" suggested Roy.

"Good thinking, I will have a word with her."

"One more thing…" said Roy. "What timescale are we thinking of before the next re-election?"

"I reckon a six-month stint should be enough," mused Bill. "I mean, in three months the committee is only getting going and more or less getting their feet under the table. No, they need a bit of time to achieve their objectives, three months is neither use nor ornament and I will note the member's reactions to that. I will leave you to it Roy… but let me see the message before you send it out."

>>> <<<

Wing Commander Pilling had only been posted to RAF March recently from RAF Chatworth and had not quite settled in; at present he was in command of the station while the Station Commander was at Command. Until he had sorted out his stall, he was reliant on Helen Fraser, the CO's Personal Secretary. Going to Helen's office he asked her, "Is there an airwoman with some rank on the Station with the qualifications to do secretarial work to a high standard?"

"We have no commissioned officers with those qualifications sir. The nearest one with high qualifications is Sergeant Page, who works in the orderly room. She is well qualified, I can vouch for that. She is also quite a clever young woman with bright prospects. She is the one whose ideas were accepted by the Air Chief Marshal to formulate the rules for the Three Women's Services Drill Challenge."

"That is interesting Helen, thank you. I think I will follow that up. Will you please get in touch with her and ask her to report to me, no time being like the present."

After he left, Helen rang the orderly room and asked for Sergeant Page.

"Sergeant Page speaking."

"Barbara, Helen here, can you come to my office? Wing Commander Pilling would like to see you, so be prepared. He wants to interview you regarding you becoming his PA. I will brief you when you arrive."

When Barbara came, Helen duly put her in the picture and gave her a brief run down on the procedures. "Do you fancy doing it Barbara?"

"I wouldn't mind if I could do a trial period to see if we were compatible."

"I can only say it would give your promotion prospects a hell of a boost. Are you ready to go in now?"

"I am… and thanks, Helen."

"Come and see me when you come out." She knocked on the OC's door and entered, "Sergeant Page sir…"

"Show her in Helen."

Barbara entered, saluted and said "Sergeant Page, sir."

"Come and sit down Sergeant. I will come straight to the point. You know I have been here just a few days and I have yet to settle in. As second in command to the C.O. my responsibilities have increased enormously and I am finding it tough going without a PA to keep me on the straight and narrow. Would you be interested in filling that role? If you are not interested, say so now, then I will have to look elsewhere."

"Thank you sir, you are paying me a great compliment. I would like to accept if I could spend a few days with Helen Fraser to get to know the 'ins and outs' of what my duties will be and will you please give me a trial run to see if we are compatible."

"I understand your logic. This may be presumptuous on my part but I can see us getting along fine together."

"When do you want me to start sir?"

Laughingly he replied. "You make it sound like a job interview, which, when boiled down actually it is. Go and spend the rest of the day clearing your desk, etc. then report to Helen in the morning. In the meantime, I will have a word with WO Shaw to put him in the picture. Thank you Sergeant Page."

Barbara saluted then went to report to Helen to tell her what had transpired.

While they were talking, the OC put his head round the door and said, "Ask WO Shaw to come and see me right away please Helen."

"He is a proper gentleman Barbara, you will like him."

"Roy, Helen Fraser here, the OC would like to see you. Yes, right away… There will be one very unhappy man coming out of that office very soon Barbara."

"I had better go now," said Barbara. "I will see you in the morning and thanks Helen."

As she was leaving Roy entered the office.

"What's going on?" he asked.

"You will soon find out," said Helen. "Come on Roy, he is waiting for you." She knocked on the door and entered. "WO Shaw sir…"

"Come in Mr Shaw and sit yourself down. You will probably need to after what I am about to tell you…" He filled Roy in as to what he had decided, then added, "Mr Shaw, your Sergeant Page is the only person on this station who has the qualifications to fill this position. I appreciate you will be sorry to lose someone you must hold in high esteem, but as second in command of this station, my needs are greater than yours. Now let us talk of a replacement for Sergeant Page. Who would you like, a male or female?"

"I will go for a male, sir… a well-qualified one."

"Good. Have no fear Mr Shaw, I will see you get a good one. How would someone in the Albert Einstein mould do?"

They both had a good laugh. Roy saluted then exited.

"Well?" asked Helen.

"I was quite miffed when he told me what it was all about, but to be fair, I could see his point. In the end I was quite proud he had chosen her and I can see them getting on well with each other, for he is such a nice guy. Besides, he outranks me," he said with a laugh. "I must go and congratulate her now, she deserves a good break."

>>> <<<

Flight Sergeant Ian Roberts was sat at his desk reading the printout appertaining to the Sergeants Mess meeting when the phone rang.

"Flight Sergeant Roberts speaking. Oh hello Helen. No, he is not in at present, but I expect him anytime."

"Tell him to report to the CO at 10:00hours, Ian, and if he does not appear to be showing, send a Tannoy message out for him, it is that important."

"I will make sure he is there, Helen." From then on he was busy answering the telephone from various SNCOs with excuses for not attending the meeting. He told each caller to re-read the printout and follow its instructions.

When Bill arrived he was given the message.

"Good," was his reaction, "I wonder what they have cooked up for us this time?"

"What's that," asked Ian.

"The CO has been to Command to a meeting. He thought it may have something to do with us both. I see you have got your print-out… What do you think about it?"

"Not before time, I reckon. That Mess is the worst one I have ever been in. We would be better off in the NAAFI. By the way, I have had a dozen phone calls with excuses for not attending the meeting."

"What did you tell them?"

"To re-read the print-out and follow the instructions. They call themselves SNCOs! They don't deserve a Sergeants Mess."

"Right then, I am off again, no rest for the wicked."

Away he went, reporting in to Helen Fraser. She greeted him warmly.

"Hello Bill. I don't see much of you these days. How are you and how is Tommy?"

"I am fine thanks Helen and Tommy is as lovely as ever. Have you any inkling as to what this is about?"

"None at all Bill and that is gospel. I may be wrong, but I think he is not quite his usual self, as if he has had some disturbing news."

"I hope you are wrong Helen, for he went to that meeting expecting both of us being involved in something."

"Come on then, I do not want you coming out with bad news." She knocked on the door entered. "WO Barrett sir."

"Come in Mr Barrett." As Bill saluted he continued, "Take a seat. I don't know how you are going to react to what I am about to tell you, for the powers to be at Command have had a change of plans that concerns you. You are to be relieved of your post as Station Warrant Officer… let me finish please." He could see a reaction in Bill's face. "Before you condemn this move, just give it a little thought.

Your new title is to be Training Command's Chief Training Officer. You will still be based here and your role is to do random checks at the other training establishments to keep them up to scratch or if necessary to make sure they improve their standards to your satisfaction, by whatever means you think fit. That means you have the authority to enforce any changes to either the manner in which instructions are carried out or how they are given. Any objectors are to be put on your report to me, you see Mr Barrett, I still have some clout. Now I would like to hear your thoughts."

"I can see the logic in releasing me from SWO – that is a full time job on its own – and so is recruit training, but I am not over keen on this troubleshooting job. Personally, I think that should be the responsibility of a senior officer, because he has the rank to squash any objections, especially coming from commissioned officers. No sir, I am not trying to pass the buck but I do not like the idea one bit, it may have a fancy title, but whichever way you look at it, the clout which I would get from my rank would get me nowhere."

"What do you suggest then, Mr Barrett?"

"That I have an interview with the Air Officer Commanding and have a straight talk with him. We both know he is approachable. It could be that someone is giving him duff gen and he has not given enough thought as to what it entails. What would your reactions be, sir, if I came to your station and told you how to run it? Someone at Command has no idea what Chain of Command is about and should be told it runs from the Station Commander down to the lowly corporal, where the buck always stops."

"You have put up a damned good argument Mr Barrett and I agree with you entirely. I will tell you what I am going to do. I shall go to Command and point out where that system falls down in its entirety."

"There is another thing I would like to mention sir, regarding a new Station Warrant Officer. WO Miller was SWO to Wing Commander Pilling at RAF Chatworth, who will vouch for him. I hear he is at the end of his Cyprus posting and in my opinion he is the right man, already having had the experience of a mixed station."

"What you are really saying, Mr Barrett is that you would like me to see what I can do in that department."

"With respect sir, you are putting words in my mouth."

"Alright Mr Barrett, I will see what I can do."

"Thank you, sir." He saluted and was stopped at the door by the C.O.

"You still are a crafty bugger, Mr Barrett," he said grinning.

On the way back to his office Bill called in to see Roy Shaw and told him what had transpired.

"I don't like the sound of that one bit. If you accept that job, or if it is thrust upon you, your name will stink throughout the Command. According to that idea, you could even over-ride Station Commanders. You would never get a foot past the gates, Billy-Boy! There must be some right idiots up at Command to think of a brainwave like that. I will admit that doing the recruit training and being the SWO does not mix, that makes sense, your job is recruit training that is your forte. Don't get me wrong Bill, but the BlueBelles saga appears to have stirred up a can of worms at Command and the Staff officers there are trying to jump on the bandwagon by thinking up tin-pot ideas to impress the Brass Hats."

"Aye, I think you have got something there Roy, I just hope the CO can make somebody see sense. I have put a word in for an old pal of mine to take over from me, he was SWO at Chatworth, I know the Wingco' would be chuffed if he was posted in. Anyway, I am still going to do the Mess chairman. Ian Roberts told me that since the print-outs were received he has had quite a number of phone calls with a 'sorry I cannot attend the meeting' plea. I will give em' sorry I cannot attend if they don't turn up they will have to have a damned good excuse. Which reminds me I will have to see the Wingco' to tell him we need an officer for Mess President."

"Now you have given me ear-ache with your problems," said Roy. "I would like to return the favour."

"You mean to tell me that *you* the very backbone of this station have got a problem. I could crush a grape in amazement," grinned Bill.

"I will crush your grapes and wipe that grin off your face if I don't get some sympathy from you. Our beloved Wing Commander has commandeered Barbara to be his PA … starting tomorrow."

"That is great news, well done Barbara! Her assessments will go sky high from now on, which will boost her promotion prospects. I am right pleased for her."

"I am looking for sympathy, you miserable wretch! I thought we were good mates."

"Come on Roy, lets face it, she was wasted in here with her talents. She is a very clever lass is our Barbara. So you will be getting a replacement soon, another female?"

"No way! With my luck I would get a dragon. No, I have asked for a male with high qualifications and I have been more or less promised one. Now sod off, I don't want you to come in here whingeing again with your minor problems and NO! you are not getting a brew. Hop it!"

"See you tonight in the bar, pal!" grinned Bill.

CHAPTER 2

Bill stopped at Sergeants Mess reception and greeted the duty receptionist.

"Good morning Jackie, and how is my favourite receptionist this lovely morning?"

"Good morning Bill, nice to see you looking so cheerful. You will want to see Tommy, of course, unless you have come specially to see me."

"Not this time Jackie, although you are next on my list."

"I will go and tell her, won't be a minute…"

Tommy came out with Jackie trailing behind her. "Good morning darling," she said, giving him a kiss, with Jackie smiling in the background. "What can I do for you?"

"It is the Mess meeting this afternoon at 14:00hrs. Will you arrange the seating please, I am expecting a big turn out because no-one is exempt without a valid excuse… and that includes you, my love."

"Ooh you are so masterful, isn't he Jackie?"

"But so wonderful with it," Jackie sighed, to a roar of laughter from the other two.

At exactly 14:00 Bill opened the meeting with a count of those present. Barbara was the only other person sat with Bill; she was taking notes of the proceedings.

"Good afternoon Ladies and Gentlemen. If you are wondering why this meeting has been called, we are here to form a Sergeants Mess Committee and like it or not you are all going to be involved. I have had it likened to a

NAAFI instead of a Sergeants Mess but from this moment that image goes right out of the window. At present we are short of a figurehead, a President. He or she will be detailed by the OC. In the meantime we will go ahead and choose a committee and we will do that right now and I tell you that no-one will leave this meeting until one has been chosen. I will start the ball rolling by submitting my name as chairman; can I have a proposal and someone to second it please?"

Roy Shaw said, "I propose you."

Jock Webster said, "I will second that."

"Can I have a show of hands in favour please? Anyone against? Thank you, that was unanimous, I hope the rest of the voting goes as smoothly. The post of Mess Secretary is now up for grabs, any volunteers?"

Roy raised his hand and was voted in, and so it went on. Flight Sergeant Jock Webster from Pay Accounts was voted in as treasurer, that post being only open to the rank of Flight Sergeant. WO Mary Butcher, three RAF Sergeants and two WRAF Sergeants were voted onto the entertainments committee.

"The barman's duty will continue to be carried on by the rank of Sergeant and will be for a period of one month and is presently held by Sergeant Jones.

"When does your duty finish Sergeant?"

"In one week's time sir."

"Has your replacement been nominated yet?"

"Not to my knowledge sir."

"Right then, your replacement will be notified tomorrow. Flight Sergeant Roberts, make a note of that will you? Monthly subscriptions will be paid in to the secretary religiously you will quickly get a reminder if it just happens to slip your mind! Now here is the good news. I suggest the committee stay in situ for a period of six months. The reason being, what can a committee do in three months? Think about it, they will have hardly settled down to doing the job before some eager beavers want to take their place."

That caused howls of derisive laughter from the floor.

"Please could I have a proposal and someone to second it?" When it was duly carried Bill remarked. "There you are committee members you are now safe for six months." That brought a few ironic cheers.

"I would like you to know my aim is to hold dances, discos, dining-in and dining-out nights and games evenings. There are plenty of things we can do, please, if you have any ideas let us have them, obviously we must draw the line somewhere, but we will listen. I would also like put in the minutes the debt we owe to those very few members who have for some months now voluntarily kept the books up to date and stopped the Mess from getting into one big hell of a mess. Ladies and gentlemen, I would like someone to propose a vote of thanks to them and someone to second it. A vote less than unanimous will not be accepted". A unanimous vote was given plus a generous round of applause.

"After the meeting will the elected committee please stay behind for a few minutes? One last thing I would like to stress, support your Mess; lift it up from the mess it is in now, non-supporters will be noted and will be reminded of it in no uncertain terms. Thank you for your attendance and co-operation. See, it didn't hurt. I now bring this meeting to a close." He asked Barbara. "Have you got everything down?"

"I have Bill I will let you have it when I have typed it out from shorthand into something you can understand. When I start my new job I may not get the chance to attend future meetings the O.C will have priority."

"I understand Barbara, we will cross that bridge when we come to it. I wish you all the best in your new job; you should be all right for he is a good man. If you need a reference I will give you a good one." To which they both laughed.

Bill now addressed the committee. "I would like to personally thank you all for your support, we have as you will realise some hard graft facing us to bring this Mess up to a really good standard and it is now our task to build a firm foundation and make it like a Phoenix rising from the ashes. We need to have committee meetings to decide where we are going in respect of entertainments, so when we call a meeting WO Butcher will let you know and give you the details. Has anyone any questions or not sure of anything?"

Jock Webster spoke up. "Before we can make any plans Bill I will need to check the books to see how solvent the club is."

"Precisely Jock, we are more or less starting from scratch, those are the things we need to check on. Once we get your sums Jock we can then cut our cloth to size."

I would like to ask you entertainments committee could you start the ball rolling by trying to get the families interested, you know how the ladies enjoy a game of Bingo, try to find out which would be more popular a Saturday or Sunday night and could you get that off the ground please? Once we get the families interested enough to want to come to the Mess that will be half the battle. Has anyone else got anything they want to add? No? Shall we call it a day then? Thank you again there is now a light at the end of the tunnel."

Barbara Page spent a couple of days with Helen Fraser learning the do's and don'ts and felt quite confident when she was allocated her own office adjoining that of the O.C. and felt quite proud when her name and title was fixed to the door. In the next few days she soon found how busy a P.A. could get and felt very satisfied now she had taken the job.

>>> <<<

It was more than a week since Bill had the interview with the C.O. when his phone rang and Helen Fraser informed him "The C.O. would like to see you."

When he entered Helen's office he asked. "What mood does the prophetess say sir is in today?"

"If you cross my palm with silver O' sceptic one, all will be revealed." When they stopped laughing, she said. "I think you will find him in a very favourable mood, I even heard him humming to himself a little while ago."

"Then lead me to him I have got a gut feeling it may be catching."

Helen knocked on the door, entered and announced, "WO Barrett sir."

"Show him in Helen. Come and sit down Mr Barrett," he said as he acknowledged the salute.

He looked at Bill and smiled. Bill automatically returned the smile. "I am smiling Mr Barrett because you have done it again. You have not only got the full support of the AOC but I have left one or two Staff officers with very red faces. When I told the AOC your version and the implications he was furious because he had not been told the full extent of what your duties would involve, that had been glossed over. What he had sanctioned was you being relieved from SWO to concentrate on training."

"Thank you very much sir for all your help, you have helped me out of a few tight situations in the past and you are still doing it."

"Mr Barrett, we have helped each other and I have a lot to thank you for, so long as we can carry on doing that nothing will please me greater.

One final thing before you leave, your replacement as SWO will be WO Miller."

Bill could hardly hide his reactions, his face lit up with pleasure.

"Apparently," said the C.O. "He is on disembarkation leave at the moment but a signal has been sent to him telling him his posting has been changed to here. His original posting was to a flying station in Scotland. I expect him here in about two week's time."

Bill stood up and said. Thank you sir, you have certainly made my day and it will make WO Butcher's day when I tell her. He saluted and turned to go.

"Mr Barrett, I do not know how you get away with it.

Another Yorkshire saying, "If you fell in a midden you would come up smelling of roses."

On leaving there he went to see Mary to give her the good news.

"Come in Bill, it is always a pleasure to see you, what news have you got for me today? I could do with a nice surprise."

"It is a bigger one that you would expect Mary. I am being relieved of the SWO job to concentrate on the training."

"Well that makes sense although I will admit you have been a damned good one. I wonder who your replacement is. If he is as daft as you and Roy

Shaw I think I can put up with it but if he is a martinet I would not like to commit myself."

"He has already been appointed and joins us in a couple of weeks but I am unsure of your reactions."

"Come on Bill spit it out, tell me the worse."

"It is somebody by the name of……George Miller!"

"Mary gave a scream of delight, "Bill Barrett you are a darling, the three of us together once more plus Wingco' Pilling, wait until *he* finds out. I'll bet you had something to do with that you little devil. That is the best bit of news I have had for a long time, thanks Bill, come here while I give you a kiss and a big hug. Won't we have a lot to tell him Bill, I should imagine he will have heard about the BlueBelles, news like that would travel like wildfire throughout the RAF but he will not know the nitty-gritty of how the success came about, gosh I am looking forward to seeing him again."

"Me too Mary, he has been a good friend to us."

When Bill got back to his office and told Ian the story, Ian said, "In the short space of time I have known you it has been a pleasure working with you Bill. Right from the start you made me feel welcome and I appreciate that. I hope I am not being out of order by saying in that time we have become friends."

"Thanks Ian it has been a pleasure working with you and I know that you and George will get on well together."

"You know Bill, the name George Miller rings a bell, I have never met him but isn't he the one who had a run in with some officer?"

"You mean the time when he broke the officer's swagger cane and threatened to shove it up his stupid arse, then ordered him off the parade?"

"That's it, it was numero one topic throughout the service for long enough. Everyone said he should have got a medal."

"I was there on that parade with George so was Mary Butcher and our Wing Commander Pilling was the O.C at the time."

"So is RAF March the venue for a family reunion?" asked Ian.

"You could say that," laughed Bill."

That night in the mess bar Bill, Roy and Derwent were having a quiet drink and talking over events. The new Duty Barman was John White, who, like most with the surname of White inevitably got called Chalky.

Bill told about his interview with the C.O. and his replacement as SWO. "You will get on fine with George he has the same type of humour as us."

"Do you mean," asked Roy, "we are to get another nut case for SWO?"

"For your sins, yes!" replied Bill. "Unfortunately he is married so he will not be a barfly like wot' we are, although he does like the odd gargle especially when someone upsets him.

Fill em' up Chalky and get one in for you. I tell you what, we have a very quiet barman on duty."

"He won't be quiet for long," spoke up Derwent, "we will soon get him out of his shell. We haven't seen Fred Fox in here since he was replaced behind the bar, do you think he is under the thumb?"

"No, I don't think so," said Roy, "once we get things moving in here he will bring his wife in for a game of bingo while he has a jar in the bar with the lads."

"Have you made any progress towards organising bingo Roy?" asked Bill.

"We have had a meeting and are going to advertise it by sticking a print-out in the member's mail boxes. We have also found the original bingo game that was used in the past. Sandwiches, tea and coffee at the interval will be provided and could turn out to be a crowd puller! We will do our best to make the Mess a good place for a night-out and we are getting some good ideas from the committee members."

"Have you had any word from Jock about the financial situation?"

"Not as yet but I will give him a buzz tomorrow."

"Right Chalky, what do you think of this job?" asked Bill.

"There is more to it than you think," he replied, "but like anything else practice makes perfect, so they say."

"Do you ever see anything of Fred Fox?" asked Roy, "he is the lad to give you some good tips on 'My stint as a Sergeants Mess Barman'. Rule one, take good care of the three Crackpots, that is us three and do not make any bets with them you will be the loser. Rule two, keep your ears tuned in to conversations, surprising what you hear then do a trade with information. I think that is a good start for you Chalky."

"Thanks, I will bear that in mind especially the one about the bets."

"He is learning," exclaimed Derwent.

CHAPTER 3

The next day Bill paid a visit to the ops' room for the training staff where Flight Sergeant Viv Anderson was in charge. She had a staff of six who relieved instructors on leave, sick or duties other than instructing. When not instructing they worked in the ops' room keeping the documentation up to scratch appertaining to the training programme. The office walls were covered with wall charts bearing the names of all the recruits and what stage of training they were at, the instructors and their details. Every little detail appertaining to the training programme was there in black and white and was meticulously kept up to date, each and every day.

"Hello Viv he said as he sat himself down at her desk, how are things going?"

"Everything is fine Bill we have no problems and each flight is keeping up with the schedule."

“That is good, have you had any visits from our beloved leader Flight Lieutenant Curtis?”

“Not in here I don’t think he knows where we are but I hear he has been snooping round the flights and not been making himself popular with the instructors.”

“I wish I had been told about that for I have been so busy with other things I feel I have been neglecting this part of my job. Not for long though Viv, I am being replaced as SWO so that I can concentrate more on the training.”

“I like that Bill, it is not the same not having you around I think all the instructors will welcome that. Then this will become your office.”

“Our office Viv.”

“It appears I am going to be needed to keep tabs on our Mr Curtis, nobody is going to come upsetting my staff and getting away with it. Are you satisfied with the instructors we have, are they doing their job to your satisfaction?”

“I am none too keen on Sergeant Battle he is far too short tempered for my liking and Sergeant Alders has somehow gained a superior attitude since we became the Flagship you would call it more of a cocky attitude which I think is spreading to his corporals. Sergeant (w)Bell, when she went on detachment to Chatworth she found herself a boy friend and since she returned her mind has not been on her job. I have had words with her but there is no improvement.

I am also keeping my eye on her two Corporals ; one is doing her best under the circumstances while the other one Corporal Harrison appears to have got the Sergeant Bell syndrome, love sickness.”

“Well I need to do something about it; thank goodness I am being relieved of being SWO.”

“Who have we in ops’ Viv that can take over from Sergeant Bell and Corporal Harrison?

“Sergeants Roper and North, of the two I would give Sergeant Roper and Corporal Peters the first chance.”

“Right get them in here Viv one at a time we will make their day.” Viv went to the door and called in Sergeant Roper.

Bill addressed her. “Sergeant Roper how does having your own flight strike you?”

“It would be wonderful sir, give me the chance and you will not regret it.”

“Good, you will take over Sergeant Bell’s flight as from now. Tell me, how do you get on with Corporal Peters?”

“Very well indeed sir, she is a bright girl and quite intelligent, she often tells me she wishes she could get out there instructing.”

“That is good to know because she will be replacing Corporal Harrison. When you both have cleared your desks report back to Flight Sergeant Anderson and she will do the official change over. Will you ask Corporal Peters to come in please?”

When she came in Bill said. “I understand Corporal You want to get out there to do some instructing.”

“Yes sir I do, if I don’t I will get rusty and probably have to be sent back for a refresher course.”

“Not this time Corporal. With immediate effect you will be instructing with Sergeant Roper, you will be replacing Corporal Harrison. Go and clear your desk then report back to Flight Sergeant Anderson who will escort you to your flight.”

“Thank you very much sir,” her delight was written all over her face.

“There go two happy people Viv, now to deal with two unhappy people when you bring them back here.”

“What do you intend doing with them Bill?”

“First I will tell them why, then I will refer them to Mary Butcher telling her I want to be rid; she in turn will refer them to Flight Lieutenant Adams who should put the wheels in motion for replacements. Do you want to sit in while I give them the good news?”

“Yes I would, it will be good experience for me.”

“Very well, send those two back and I will hold them here until you return after you have introduced their new instructors. Here they are, off you go then.”

When Viv arrived at the flight the only activity was the girls standing around just laughing and talking. “Sergeant Bell!” she called. Bell came over with a smile on her face.

“Something wrong Viv?”

“Don’t you Viv me Sergeant. You are on duty and you know better than to be familiar in front of recruits.”

“Sorry Flight Sergeant I did not realize you were so touchy.”

“Sergeant Bell, I am relieving you as i/c of this flight, now go to the flight office and report to WO Barrett NOW!. Get FELL IN!” she shouted to the recruits. “You are a shambles! Corporal Harrison…”

“Yes Flight Sergeant.”

“Report to WO Barrett at the Flight Office at once.”

“But I have done nothing wrong Flight.”

“GO! NOW!”

“Viv then addressed the recruits. “You have been set a bad example and it is only natural you would take advantage of it; I want you to get it out of your system right now. To help you do this you will get the help of Sergeant Roper your new instructor and by your present Corporal Briggs with Corporal Peters your other new instructor. Between the three of them they are going to work your socks off to make sure you make the grade as well trained recruits. At present you are sloppy; that was not all your doing, but that is going to change with a vengeance. Not only are you sloppy in your drill but also you are also sloppy in your appearance and turn out, that *is* your fault. To remedy that I will personally hold an inspection on your turn out tomorrow morning and be warned, it had better be good… Right you are then Sergeant Roper, they are all yours."

When she returned to the office she saw the pair of them waiting in the ops' room. Ignoring their presence she walked straight into her office and reported to Bill what had happened.

"Okay Viv, wheel the Sergeant in and we will see if she has become less belligerent."

Viv went to the door and called Sergeant Bell in.

"Sergeant Bell," Bill began, "I understand that you are not very happy here at RAF March, consequently your instructing ability has dropped, which is the reason your flight is in such a state both in their drill and more so in their appearance. They are sloppy on both counts and you just could not care less. What is your excuse Sergeant?"

"I have personal problems sir."

"Have you spoken to your Flight Sergeant or your Warrant Officer? They both have sympathetic ears and your W.O especially has great shoulders to cry on."

"No sir."

"And why not?"

"It is too personal a thing and I do not want to confide in anyone."

"Can I ask you a very personal question Sergeant Bell?"

"Yes sir."

"Are you sure? Because it is a very personal question."

"Go ahead sir."

"Are you pregnant Sergeant Bell?"

She blushed, broke into tears and nodded her head.

"Sit down. Would you like a glass of water?"

She regained her composure. "No thanks, I will be all right."

"Well that explains everything. You have nothing to be ashamed of about your condition but you do realise that it will be the end of your service career. What I want you to do now is see WO Butcher, explain everything to her you will find she will be a great comfort to you."

"Thank you sir for your understanding and I am sorry about this morning Flight Sergeant."

When she left, Bill phoned Mary Butcher. "Mary, its Bill here. I am sending Sergeant Bell to you; her problem is your department… No, I am not passing the buck, she is pregnant and needs your guidance and your sympathy… Yes of course she is distraught wouldn't you be? Watch your language over the phone! I will tell George Miller about how your endearing personality has changed into an old battleaxe. Ta-tTa love."

Viv was killing herself laughing. "I don't know how Mary puts up with you."

"You wait till George Miller arrives, then there will be some banter. Right then Viv, shall we have Corporal Harrison in now?"

Viv called her in. Bill looked at her. "What are you chewing Corporal?"

"Chewing gum."

"I will ask you again Corporal, what are you chewing?"

"Oh yes, chewing gum sir."

"Well get rid of it outside and when you return I want you to enter as an NCO should."

A knock on the door and Bill called "Come in"

The Corporal entered, walked towards his desk and said. "You sent for me sir?"

"How long have you been a Corporal drill instructor?"

"A year sir."

"Have you got an aversion to discipline?"

"I don't know what you mean sir."

"I will rephrase that to a language you understand. Does discipline bug you?"

"It certainly does."

"Then how can you mete out discipline to the recruits you train, in other words, how do you make them do what you want?"

"The first time they do anything wrong I give them a good rollicking, the second time they get a rollicking and a few press-ups."

"What if they do it a third time?"

"I make them clean out the bogs!"

"Are you aware that you have not got the authority to deal out punishment? No, don't answer. This is what I am going to do. I am not taking disciplinary action against you, you are the most nauseating WRAF junior NCO I have ever come across. How you got through our vetting procedure I do not know. With immediate effect you will no longer be a part of my training staff. I want you here at 09:00hrs.tomorrow morning scrubbed clean with your uniform pressed your hair tidied to regulations and some polish on those shoes. Now get out of here, you are a mess."

After that dressing down she never even blinked an eyelid.

"What a little madam." Said a shocked Viv "You dealt with her brilliantly and she never turned a hair, inwardly she was laughing at us."

"Not for long Viv, she will be out of the service very quickly. I really think that is what she wants, if so we can oblige her, anyway her days on this station are numbered.

Now we have to sort out the RAF NCOs, namely Sergeants Battle and Alders. I think I will have a little stroll round and see these two in action. Can you manage for a short time having two staff less in the Ops' Room?

"That will be no problem they are not exactly over worked."

"I will see you shortly Viv."

He found Sergeant Battle's flight that was in their first week of training and he made sure he was unobserved while he took stock of what was going on. The recruits were being taught the basic movements from the position of attention and naturally a few could not quite grasp the orders they were to perform. The Sergeant stood facing them giving the orders and the two Corporals were going round the airmen correcting their stances at the same time bellowing in their ears the mistakes they were making. The Sergeant carried on shouting his orders while the Corporals moved up and down the ranks correcting the mistakes and sometimes pushing or pulling the unfortunate airman around. Bill was about to intervene when he saw the Sergeant approach an airman, grab him by the front of his tunic and pull him to the front of the flight. He thrust his face into the airman's and snarled. "Now show your pals your fancy footwork." The airman was petrified as the Sergeant kept bellowing orders in his face and the more he bellowed the more frightened the lad became.

Right said Bill to himself, enough is enough. He made himself known by moving towards the flight. When the Sergeant realised who it was a look of shock appeared momentarily on his face.

"Hello Bill he squawked through a dry mouth."

"My office NOW Sergeant "

"My office NOW I said."

As he left Bill looked at the two Corporals You two, out here on the double." The two Corporals ran round to where Bill was standing. He now addressed the recruits. I have just witnessed something which is never taught in the RAF and that is bullying that is a punishable offence I apologise for you being victims of it and you can rest assured you will never see anything like that again on this station.

He turned to the young lad who was the victim of Sergeant Battle's wrath and asked. "Are you all right son?"

"Yes sir." said a very relieved lad.

"Go back and rejoin the flight then."

"You two Corporals – to my office and wait for me. He turned to the airmen. "Now for the bad news… you have got the rest of the day off and tomorrow you will have new instructors. Flight Atten…tion. Dismiss!"

He returned to his office and asked Viv to stay. "You may be needed again as a witness. Call Sergeant Battle in please?"

When he entered he said, "Bill I…." He was stopped speaking by Bill.

"I want an explanation of this morning's episode."

"Can we discuss this in private sir?"

"No! Flight Sergeant Anderson is my witness and furthermore she outranks you Sergeant! Now I want that explanation."

"It was a mistake, I lost my temper, I do not know what came over me."

"That was not the first time you have lost your temper with those recruits, that I do know and through it you have begun bullying those kids. They are in their very first week of training how can you explain away the treatment you have been handing out to them like they were something stuck to the soles of your shoes. Your evil tactics even brushed off on to your two Corporals and you even encouraged their behaviour. What went on this morning and most likely in the past was tantamount to bullying and you know as well as I do that is a punishable offence and that is not tolerated in the service. Therefore I am taking disciplinary action against you for bullying and manhandling airmen recruits in your charge. You are relieved from your post as from now. I will see you tomorrow to find out what is to be done with you."

"Thank you very much sir, I don't think."

"Get out of my office!

Send the two Corporals in Viv please."

They came in and stood to attention facing him.

"You know why you are here don't you?"

"Yes sir," they answered.

"Tell me about it."

"It is to do with the treatment of the recruits, sir."

"Exactly."

"It was Sergeant Battle's orders sir he told us to be tough with them."

"Was manhandling included in being tough?"

"Yes sir to a certain extent."

"If I need you as witnesses to what you have just told me will you testify to that effect?"

"Yes sir."

"Now that does not exonerate you from your part in the bullying but I cannot allow you to carry on instructing here. I realise you were instructed to do what you did so I am not going to take any disciplinary action against you instead I will have you posted."

"Thank you sir," they happily replied.

"Until you are posted you will work in the Ops' Room here. Now go and wait outside and Flight Sergeant Anderson will assign you to a task.

Right Viv, we want a Sergeant and two Corporals to take over that flight tomorrow, what are the options?"

"We have one RAF Sergeant one WRAF Sergeant two RAF Corporals and two WRAF Corporals "

"Who is the RAF Sergeant?"

"Sergeant Franks."

"Bring him in please."

"Sergeant Franks, tomorrow morning you will take charge of Sergeant Battle's ex-flight. You will also need the two remaining Corporals "

"Thank you sir, they are Corporals Bates and Powell."

"Call them in please."

When they came in Bill addressed them. "Due to circumstances which I do not intend to disclose, you will find out soon enough. You will now be under the command of Sergeant Franks instructing the recruits in their first week of training. All I ask is you do a good job and above all treat them as you would like yourselves to be treated. Remember, you only need to shout to make your voice carry to the airman not to abuse them. For the rest of the day hand over whatever you were doing to the rest of the staff and take over the flight tomorrow morning, I have already stood them down for the rest of today. Any questions gentlemen? Okay then, do a good job and we will get on fine, any problems see Flight Sergeant Anderson. Thank you. Now comes the paper work Viv and the enquiries, but it has got to be done."

Sergeant (w) Bell and Corporal (w) Harrison were discharged from the service.

Sergeant Battle was discharged from the service with ignominy.

The RAF Corporals were posted with warnings of their future conduct.

>>> <<<

Flight Lieutenant Curtis called Bill to his office to explain the drastic steps he had taken in disciplining the five instructors.

"Bullying needs no explanation sir and neither does a junior NCO who despises discipline and metes out unauthorised punishment to raw recruits."

"I have never seen any signs of bullying when I have watched the instructors."

"That is because they saw you watching them we were always on our best behaviour when we knew our superiors were watching."

"Hmm, yes I take your point Mr Barrett.

There is another point I would like to bring to your attention. I don't like you going over my head to see senior officers, if and when you want to see them you will first come to me and I will decide if you can proceed. Do you understand Mr Barrett?"

"I understand alright sir." The word "Pisspot" immediately came to mind.

"Very well Mr Barrett return to your duties and go and put some snap in the flight Sergeant Battle had, they were a shambles."

That remark got right up Bill's nose he thought I am not going to let this sod get away with that.

"Can I ask you something sir?"

"Yes of course but be quick about it I am rather busy."

"What were you like as a brand spanking new recruit in the first week of recruit training? That is what those kids are you say are a shambles. This time and without your permission I am going over your head to see a more senior officer." He saluted, walked out of the office and went to see Barbara Page and asked her. "Can you fix me up with an interview with the Wing Commander?"

"When do you want it for Bill?"

"Yesterday will do Barbara," he said with a smile.

"Sorry Bill, he is away for a few days."

"Look can you ask Helen if she can fix me one with the C.O.?"

"Hang on I will see what I can do.... Helen, Barbara here I have W.O Barrett here who wanted to see the Wing Commander but he is away for a few days, he has asked me if you can get him to see the C.O. He says it is rather important. Yes, I will tell him to wait a few minutes thanks Helen. You heard that Bill, she is trying. How are things Bill have you got problems?"

"Yes – Flight Lieutenant Curtis."

"Oh *him*," she said, as she curled her lip. "He is a right creep. Between you and me, the Wing Commander can't stand him."

"Really?" said a surprised Bill. "Then hopefully I will get a good reaction from the C.O. because he is sure to have been told by your boss."

"Good, I like the sound of that."

The phone rang. "Hello Helen, he can? Lovely thanks ever so much, Bye. You can go right in now Bill."

He leaned over her desk gave her a peck on the cheek. Thanks Barbara."

Helen was pleased to see him. "Come on Bill I will take you right in he is waiting for you, a couple of old rogues together. WO Barrett sir."

"Come in Mr Barrett and sit yourself down." Bill saluted and sat down.

"Methinks you have something on your mind, somebody has been upsetting you Mr Barrett, I know the signs."

"It is something I do not like doing sir, I feel it is unethical but I cannot brush it to one side."

"Come on then, let me have it and get it off your chest."

"Before I start, I did try to see the Wing Commander first but he is not available."

"Fair enough," said the C.O.

"I have been ordered I must get permission from Flight Lieutenant Curtis before I can see the Wing Commander or yourself." He then told the C.O. the whole story.

"Now that is not what I expect from one of my officers but between you and me Mr Barrett I am not surprised. That kind of attitude is detrimental to the well being of this station and the recruits and it needs to be rectified sooner rather than later. Do not feel guilty about reporting this to me I thank you for doing so; I will not tolerate a bad apple in my barrel, rest assured Mr Barrett you will have no more trouble from that source and thank you for ensuring our standards are not lowered. One last thing before you go, the only person who can refuse you permission to see me is Helen Fraser just bear that in mind. I will put Wing Commander Pilling in the picture when he returns."

"Thank you, sir. He saluted and as he got to the door he turned and asked. "No comments sir?" They both laughed.

"Not today Mr Barrett, not today."

CHAPTER 4

"Next week at this time you will have a new SWO sat in this chair, Ian."

"I hope we can work together, Bill, or it will be awkward for us both."

"If you cannot get on with George Miller I will eat hay with a donkey; he is a good man. He has a lot of experience under his belt and you will learn a lot from him. He comes from this part of the country and like most Northerners he talks straight."

The phone ringing interrupted the conversation. Bill picked it up.

"SWO's office… Hello Roy, yes I will come right away. I am wanted at the orderly room as you heard. I don't know what it is this time… See you in a bit Ian."

"Come in," Roy called in answer to the knock on his door. "Come and sit down Bill."

"Get on with why you brought me here, I have been here too long, I know when I have overstayed my welcome."

"Hand me a tissue from that box to wipe my eyes and stop being a blooming martyr."

"I will wipe your nose with my fist if you don't get on with it."

"Patience dear boy… I have been informed officially when your replacement personnel will be arriving."

"Good, I am glad I came after all Roy, it is always a pleasure to come here."

"Bloody creep. In two days time a Sergeant Fell will be arriving."

Bill interrupted very excitedly. "Is it Alan Fell Roy?"

"It is. You know him then?"

"Yes, I had him at Chatworth; I could not have picked a better man. Somebody up there must love me."

"With the amount of bodies you have got rid of from here and got away with it does it surprise me? Can I carry on? Also coming from Chatworth is Corporal (w) James. You will know her as well, I suppose."

"Do I? She was one of Ann Wilson's Corporals. I will welcome her with open arms."

“Steady on Casanova, don’t get yourself in a lather. Do carry on Roy, oh thanks Bill I will.”

“You forgot to say please Roy.”

“Look, do you want me to carry on or not? If so, shut your cake-hole. Sergeant (w) North is coming from RAF Camberly and so are both the RAF Corporals Harris and Lucas. WO Miller arrives on Monday. I have heard a little whisper you will also be getting a new officer i/c Training. That would not have anything to do with you, would it?”

“My lips are sealed Roy.”

“I thought as much, I certainly would not like to get on the wrong side of you it would be the kiss of death!”

“Thank you for the information, I will now go and brief my staff.”

>>> <<<

Flight Lieutenant Curtis was standing before the Station Commander and not feeling too happy.

“I have received a very disturbing report from my Station Warrant Officer that he has to obtain permission from you before he is allowed to see me, is that correct?”

“I am working on the chain of command sir, I am not going to have him going over my head to simply barge into your office as and when he feels like it”

“I will stop you right there Curtis before those chains of command drag you down further than you already are. Mr Barrett does not barge into my office willy-nilly, he comes to my office when I summon him or, because I think very highly of him I invite him and that is something that you will never get Curtis, an invitation. Furthermore your attitude and interest towards the trainees leaves much to be desired and it has no place on my station. This station is the Flagship of Training Command and I will not allow you or anyone else whatever their rank to besmirch the reputation it is getting for turning out recruits to a high standard. I shall get in touch with Command to have you removed from my station as soon as possible. In the meantime I am relieving you from your post and remember to leave everything up to date for your replacement. There is one other thing I would like you to know about Warrant Officer Barrett before you leave. The RAF has a lot to thank him for, among many other things he is sole responsible for this station becoming the Number One of Training Command and when the highest ranks in the RAF show him respect, that Flight Lieutenant Curtis is an achievement you will never reach as long as you have a hole in your ear. That is all, dismiss.”

>>> <<<

“I have come to give you the good news about our replacements Viv.”

"Is it good news Bill?"

"Definitely, Sergeant (w)North is coming from RAF Camberly, Corporal (w)James is coming from RAF Chatworth along with Sergeant Fell. He was one of my Sergeants and he is good so is Corporal James, she was one of Ann Wilson's Corporals she knows her stuff. The RAF Corporals are also coming from Camberly. What I suggest if you are agreeable is to put the two new lads with Alan Fell he will teach them instructing to how it should be carried out. We will withdraw high and mighty Sergeant Alders and his two Corporals for sure as eggs are eggs his attitude will have rubbed off on them and replace them with Alan Fell and his team, you will see the difference from the word go. As for Corporal James, with her experience you must find a slot for her. Put Sergeant North in the ops' room for assessment, I will break the news to Sergeant Alders."

"Sounds all right to me Bill, if we can keep getting these quality replacements it will be great for the station."

"They will all be arriving within the next two or three days. What I am going to do now is to go and have a shufti at Sergeant Alders, do you want to come along then we can compare notes?"

"I would like to, thanks."

They went to the drill area and tried to be inconspicuous to watch Sergeant Alders and his Corporals performing. The Sergeant was stood a little way off from his flight having a smoke, the Corporals were having a great time. One had his face just a few inches from one recruit's face bawling into it. When the recruit fished a handkerchief from his pocket obviously to wipe away the spittle, the Corporal knocked it from his hand and made him do press-ups where he stood. The other Corporal had his knee in one recruits back, hands on his shoulders and as he was pulling his shoulders back he was yelling "Straighten your bloody back Quasimodo!" Bill and Viv walked towards the flight; as soon as the Sergeant saw them he threw away his cigarette and came to meet them.

"You have a lot of explaining to do Sergeant "

"You know how it is Bill…

"Stop right there Sergeant this is not a social call we are on duty."

"Sorry sir."

"While you were having a fag when you were supposed to be on duty you were actually watching your Corporals breaking every rule in the book and doing nothing about it. How do you explain that?"

"I can't."

"Right, I will tell you what you can do now. Get off this site, you are suspended and report to my office at 09:00hrs tomorrow." He then called Corporals Smith and Rogers to him. "At the double!" he shouted.

"What are your explanations for your disgusting and brutal behaviour? "You," he pointed to one of them, "assaulted an airman."

"I was only helping to get him to stand up straight sir."

"With a knee in the small of his back, pulling his shoulders back and yelling in his ear insulting him. Is that what you call help? Do you realise that if an NCO lays a finger on a junior rank or anyone for that matter it constitutes an assault. Your assault was out and out bullying."

He turned to the other Corporal. Before he could speak, the Corporal pleaded, "I never touched him sir."

"You, you disgusting piece of low life, assaulted that lad by spitting in his face. Then, when he tried to wipe off your germs, you knocked his handkerchief from his hand then made him do press-ups. How disgusting can you be and how long have you been practising this sadism? I will find out… He faced the recruits and asked "How long have these creatures been mistreating you?"

The answers came back fast and furious.

"Calm down, I just need one man to speak for you."

A few hands were raised. He picked one out.

"They have been bullying us for some time sir and that includes the Sergeant, sir."

"Thank you. I want to apologise for the treatment you have been receiving. You will not see these three again it will be their turn to be on the receiving end of some severe punishment for a change. Right you two I am placing you both under close arrest."

He addressed the recruits. "Tomorrow morning you will have two Corporal instructors on a temporary basis for a few days. Now for the bad news, Flight, Attention! You have got the rest of the day off. Dis…Miss."

"Viv, go and pick one Corporal from two of the other flights and put them in charge of these lads as from tomorrow morning and explain to them and the Sergeants, the reason. I will march these two to the guard room. Single file you two, to the guard room, Quick March."

On arrival at the guard room he filled in the relevant paper work then handed them over to Flight Sergeant Bridges of the station police. When the two Corporals had been put in the cells Bill explained to Tom what had gone on and the action he was taking with Sergeant Alders.

"You are certainly weeding them out Bill."

"It is catching them red handed Tom that does the trick. What these rogue Sergeants are thinking of I don't know, they have so much to lose, what makes them throw away a good career?"

"It beggars belief Bill," agreed Tom.

Within a few days all the replacements had arrived on the station and Bill made it his business to give them a very warm welcome. Alan Fell and Corporal (w).James were delighted when they saw who their boss was. After they all had officially arrived on the station they reported back to Bill in his office, he then escorted them to the Training Staff Office where he introduced them to Flight Sergeant Viv Anderson.

"The Flight Sergeant will explain our system and show you ladies to your duties. Sergeant Fell and you two Corporals come with me I am shoving you in at the deep end. You are taking over a flight, where at present two Corporals are running it waiting for you to arrive to take over."

As they approached the flight, it was brought to attention.

Bill went to the two Corporals shook their hands and thanked them for doing a good job. He then addressed the recruits. "This is Sergeant Fell, Corporals Harris and Lucas, who are now officially in charge of this flight. You are in good hands and before long you will agree how lucky you are to have such good instructors." He shook hands with Alan Fell and the Corporals. "They are now all yours Sergeant Fell, I will see you in the Mess tonight and we will have a good chin-wag."

Meanwhile Viv was showing the newcomers the Ops Room.

"We have only Corporal Banks and myself running it due to being a Sergeant and two Corporals short, it should be only a matter of a few days before we get replacements and with the status this station has we get replacements much quicker than most. Obviously, you will be conversant with the set up and you will until you can get your own flight act as relief for any of the SNCOs and Junior NCOs. We have just lost one Sergeant (w) and one Corporal (w) who I have already replaced that is the reason Corporal Banks will be working with us. We are also waiting replacements for one RAF Sergeant and two Corporals. Are you both happy with the situation?"

They both said they were.

"Come on then," said Viv "let us go and meet Corporal Banks and help her out in the Ops' Room."

Sergeant Alders was discharged from the service with ignominy and the two Corporals were stripped of their ranks and sent to detention before being discharged from the service.

CHAPTER 5

"A message for you from the Mess manager, will you see her as soon as possible?"

"Thanks Ian I had better get over there right away it sounds as if it is important."

At reception Jackie said. "You want to see Tommy! I will bring her, not be a minute Bill." Tommy followed her out almost immediately.

"Glad you came love I have some bad news. You will have to move out from your room straight away."

"Why?"

"You are occupying the SWO's room, it is the only one wired for a telephone and WO Miller will have to move in there."

"You are right I completely forgot about that, in fact I never gave it a thought. But just a minute, George will need married quarters. Can I use your phone to ring Roy?"

"Of course you can."

"Roy, Bill here, can you tell me if there is a married quarter available for George Miller to walk straight in to?"

"Yes Bill, there is always one ready for an incoming SWO if he needs one. But he will have to officially arrive on the station before he can March-In. In the meantime he will need a room in the Mess."

"Thanks Roy, I have to vacate my room to accommodate him."

"No need Bill, just stay put, I do not want you moving down the corridor nearer to me, I have heard you snoring too often as I have passed your room."

"I can stay where I am love, there is a quarter ready for him, and he will need a room only for a night or two."

"That is one big problem solved," said Tommy, "we will make a room ready for him coming on Sunday. You are looking forward to that aren't you?"

"I certainly am and so is Mary Butcher. That reminds me I must see her to find out what is happening about the Bingo session she was trying to arrange."

"You are behind the times Mr Mess Chairman there is one arranged for Saturday, we have to arrange tables and chairs in the big room and Chef is making nibbles and tit bits. So if you are at a loose end you can take me there for an evening out, I will get to work on Viv and Barbara to drag Roy and Derwent there. Would you like to come as our guest Jackie?"

"Thank you Tommy," she replied, "but I go every Saturday night to the one in the Village it is like a family affair, if someone does not turn up one of the players will call at the house to see if you are all right, I would not like to miss it."

"Okay then Bill, I must be off and detail the stewards to get a room ready for George, of course the room will be ready it will only need to be titivated up but it will be nice to come in to, all our rooms are." She gave him a kiss and teasingly asked,

"Are you looking forward to Saturday night and a game of Bingo dear?"

"No, I am not."

"Oh yes you are! It was your idea my love you must show interest on the first evening, what would your Entertainments Committee think if you did not show your face? Besides you will have moral support from Roy and Derwent."

“That is if they go,” he replied trying everything to wriggle out of it but deep down knowing he did not stand a dog’s chance.

“They will go alright, what they want and what we girls want are two different things. Would you like a little bet on whether they play or not? You can tell the other two reprobates if they do not play I will have the three of you barred from the March Hare.”

“You are a wicked woman Jean Atkins,” as he gave her a kiss.

“I agree with him,” said Jackie supporting Bill.

“See here madam, we will have a bit less of this hero worship if you don’t mind,”

“Ah! But he is lovely Tommy,” said Jackie sighing.

“Well just keep your hands off him! He is spoken for.”

They both had a good laugh at themselves.

>>> <<<

That evening the three crackpots met in the bar exchanging the events of the day.

Bill said. “I am expecting Alan Fell in tonight, I would like to know how he has gone on today I have teamed him up with the two new Corporals he will be very good for them.”

“Have you finished weeding out your undesirables now? You have got rid of eight in a matter of two or three weeks,” Roy pointed out. “I will admit after reading their charge sheets they certainly deserved it but why is it that you have only just found them out?”

“There are three ways to look at it. One, I have been too busy being SWO; I don’t have to tell you what that entails. Second is catching them red handed, remember we used to be on our best behaviour when we knew we were being watched. Third, the recruits were too scared to complain.”

“That explains it,” agreed Roy.

“I think you have done the station and the RAF a service getting rid of them,” added Derwent, “I applaud you for it Bill.”

“I do not understand them at all,” added Bill. “Before they went on detachment they were as right as rain but on returning they had changed, there never was a hint of bullying before then.”

“Forget em’ they got what they deserved,” said Roy. ”Fill em’ up again Chalky and put one in for yourself.”

“Are either of you two coming to Bingo on Saturday night?” asked Derwent.

Bill spluttered in his beer.

“What’s up with you?” asked Roy, “there is nothing wrong with that, Barbara and I are going.”

“Viv and I are going as well,” said Derwent. “Why don’t you come with us Bill? Ask Tommy if she would like to go.”

"I don't know, I am not a Bingo fan, I don't know about Tommy she may prefer going to the March Hare."

"Would you like us to try and persuade her, if she knows Viv and Barbara will be going she might want to come along?"

"I will see what I can do," Bill said with tongue in cheek and inwardly splitting his sides laughing.

Just then Alan Fell came in.

"Chalky! Get a drink in for Alan Fell our new member, what are you having Alan?"

"Just a beer please Bill."

"You have already met Roy now meet Derwent the third crackpot and of course Chalky White our duty barman." They all shook hands.

"How have you got on today Alan with your new flight? How are your Corporals shaping up?" asked Bill.

"Come on Bill give him a chance to have a drink and why don't you leave your work in the workshop?" objected Roy.

"Alright, point taken, replied a deflated Bill. "Sorry Alan I should know better I suppose it was because I was so pleased you were posted here."

"Forget it, as a matter of fact I like the set-up here and once I have settled in it will do me fine."

"How is he fixed for a married quarter Roy?"

"I think he will be having one or two offered him this next week."

"That is great the wife will be pleased I don't know about the kids they will not fancy leaving their pals."

"They will soon make new friends children always do," said Roy. By the way are you coming to Bingo on Saturday Alan?"

"Fraid not I will be motoring back to Chatworth to see the wife and to tell her the good news."

Tommy had told Bill they were all to meet at reception 7:40pm which would give them time to settle down and get the drinks in ready for the 8pm start. "There will be no stampede to the bar either, I have got the services of three of my stewards, one will be behind the bar helping Chalky and the other two will be waiting on at the tables."

"Do you think many will turn up," asked Bill.

"The feed-back I have been getting points to that, apparently the wives are really looking forward to it, they say they have been socially starved for too long and are also looking forward to when the bigger functions materialise."

Bill deliberately made himself be last at reception and what a welcome he got from Roy and Derwent. "Here comes the Macho Man, chickened out did you, or was it the rule of the 'Thumb'?" Of course everyone had a laugh at Bill.

Tommy interrupted the laughter by saying. "To make amends I propose he buys the first round of whatever you want. Now come on let us get in there."

When they entered the room they were amazed at the number of people who were already present, they found themselves a table where they could all sit together. From all sides of the room came greetings and before Bill could take his seat he had to be introduced to many of the wives, foremost was Fred Fox and his wife who gave him a kiss and a "thank you for all you did for us." Jock Webster's wife not to be outdone followed suit with a kiss and, "thanks Bill you were very kind to give us tickets for that marvellous show, I will never forget it and you."

Roy went over to see Mrs. Fox. "Hope you have still got me on your Christmas card list Mrs. Fox."

"Well, you only just managed to get on in time, but you are on there. It was touch and go for a little while."

When they returned to the table the steward was waiting for the drinks order, which Bill duly paid for.

When all the punters had got tickets the game commenced. There were the usual laughs that go with the game and it went very smoothly the lucky winners enjoying it more than the rest. When it came to the break period everyone trooped into the dining room where Chef and his helpers had laid out quite a tasty looking buffet for which they received many pleasantries and thanks from the players.

The second half got very hilarious probably because the stewards had been busy taking orders. At close of play Bill as Mess Chairman gave a short address.

"Ladies and gentlemen, thank you for turning up in such great numbers; it does give our Entertainment Committee a lot of encouragement. You will be or should be aware of what we are trying to do to make this Mess somewhere to come for an evening out. There are plans in the pipeline to hold functions, dances, dining-in nights and so on. If you carry on supporting us as you have done tonight then this Mess will be worth dragging the old man out to. Finally, will you please show your appreciation in the usual way for the committee who ran the Bingo, the Chef who provided us with a lovely buffet and not least by any means our stewards who have done a great job for us all evening. Thank you." He returned to his table where he stayed chatting to Tommy and their friends. Gradually everyone said their Good Nights then drifted away.

>>> <<<

Early Sunday evening, a message came through to the Mess from the guardroom for Bill informing him George Miller had arrived. He immediately went to the guardroom and met him. They greeted each other warmly as old friends do.

"I never realised you were the SWO here," said George greeting Bill, "until an old friend told me about you and what you had been up to. So I am replacing you am I? What's up is the job too much for you?" he said with a laugh.

"Come on, let me get you settled in then we can discuss it over a pint later on. It is going to be like old times with you, me and Mary."

"Don't tell me Mary is here too?" said George with surprise.

"She certainly is and is looking forward to seeing you, it made her day when I told her you were being posted in and she has been looking forward to it ever since."

"How is the old Battleaxe?" George asked with a grin, "is she keeping everyone in their place? It will be grand to see her again."

"By the way," added Bill, "there is a fifth member to be added to the reunion."

"Who can that be?" queried George "and who is the fourth?"

"Alan Fell, he joined us last week and the fifth you will be surprised to know is your old friend Squadron Leader Pilling who is now a Wing Commander and our O.C!"

"Well I'll be blowed," George exclaimed how the 'L' has that happened? It is unbelievable."

"It is a long story George, when you have settled yourself in you will be told all the details, you might say it is like a fairy story and nobody will be more pleased to tell you all about it than Mary. Here is the Mess car park, park over there where the SWO sign is. Right then, let us get you booked in."

Tommy was at reception waiting to greet them. Bill then introduced them. "George, this is Flight Sergeant Atkins known to the Mess members as Tommy and she among other qualifications is our Mess Manager."

"I am very pleased to meet you Tommy," he said as he shook her hand.

"The pleasure is mine," she replied, "I have been looking forward to meeting you for quite some time now."

"Have you bai' gum'?" replied a bewildered George.

"Oh yes," said Tommy, "I know quite a bit about you."

"Is being a clairvoyant one of your qualifications? You know I have had nothing but surprises since I entered this station."

"You are now to receive the biggest surprise of them all," interrupted Bill.

"It is my pleasure to introduce you to my fiancée Jean Atkins."

George's mouth opened in amazement not believing what he had just heard.

"Say that again and say it slowly you bloody dark horse." He turned back to Tommy, leaned across the desk, grabbed her arm and pulling her as close to him as possible, gave her a kiss. Then pumping Bill's hand he said with a great big smile on his face. "Now that is the best bit of news I have heard in years, congratulations to you both that really has made my day, wait until I phone the wife to tell her I have arrived and she will certainly have something to say about this surprise."

"Are you ready for signing in George?" asked Tommy, "we have a room ready for you it will be only for a few nights for there is a Quarter ready for you. Do you want anything to eat; can I tempt you to a brew? I know you like your brews."

"Go on then, twist my arm, I will have a brew and a sandwich if it is not too much trouble for you."

"No trouble at all, it will be my pleasure. You show George to his room Bill while I rustle up something for him."

"It is a nice clean room Bill."

"Oh yes, they certainly look after us here."

"How long has this romance been going on Bill?"

"It happened as soon as I arrived here, we saw one another and we just clicked."

"She seems a grand lass."

"Look, I will leave you to sort yourself out and if you fancy a drink later I will be inthe Mess bar with my two pals, they are both WO.s you will like them George they are great guys and they both live-in"

"All right Bill, I will see you later".

He took stock of his surroundings as he began his unpacking and was pleased with what he saw. Soon a knock came on his door it was Tommy with a cloth covered tray. George thanked her saying. "I like the service here!"

"It is my pleasure George, Bill has told me so much about you he has great respect for you."

"We have always got on well together and I have always counted him as a very good friend, you have got yourself a good man Tommy and I do wish you both all the very best."

"Thank you George, he is a good man and he is well thought of throughout the station, you will not hear one single wrong word said`against him and believe it or not that goes from our Commanding Officer right down to the lowest airman. You will understand when you are told the saga of Bill Barrett."

"Not more surprises Tommy?"

"Only Mary, she is simply dying to meet you. In the meantime, enjoy your sandwiches and your brew."

"Thanks Tommy, you are a good un'."

After enjoying his tray meal he finished unpacking then strolled to the public telephone box near the guardroom and phoned his wife to ease any worries she may have had then surprised her with news of Bill Barrett, ending by telling her it would only be a matter of days before she would be joining him. He then had a little stroll around noting the layout of the station was a typical RAF Training Establishment.

He returned to his room and made sure his uniform was neatly pressed ready for his interview with the Commanding Officer the following morning. When he was satisfied he carried his tray back to the dining area and proceeded to the Mess bar, returning the greetings of some mess members and their wives who were sat at tables enjoying an evening out.

"Good evening George," called Bill. "Come and meet WO.Roy Shaw and WO Derwent Waters." They all shook hands and exchanged the usual pleasantries.

"This is Sergeant Chalky White our duty barman who is now going to serve you with a beer."

"Howdo Chalky," said George, at the moment you are the most popular man here, well you will be when I get my beer."

"Here you are sir, pulled especially for you with that extra touch of finesse, enjoy your first pint here it is on the house."

"You little creep," exploded Roy. "What are we supposed to do to get some of this finesse?"

"Treat me like a human being. There are times when I feel like handing in my resignation the way you treat me."

"Come round to the Orderly Room," continued Roy and I will show you how to fill in the form. Failing that I will call an extraordinary mess meeting and have you removed from behind that bar."

"Is that a promise?" asked a delighted Chalky. He turned to George. "These guys are known as the three crackpots don't get mixed up with them."

"I will tell you something Chalky, you serve a damned good pint and if they try to shift you, come and see me."

"Groans came from Bill, Roy and Derwent. "Just when we thought we had him trained," said Derwent. "Fill em' up all round again Chalky!"

"Now you see the kind of company you will be keeping but you won't find better anywhere else." Said Bill

"I think you are right," replied George I must admit I am feeling quite at home here and I am sure we are going to get on very well with one another. Anyway, if you will excuse me I will turn in and have an early night for I know I am going to be very busy tomorrow."

"Yes." Said Roy, "I am the man you will see first; I will be giving you the gen on your itinerary etc. By the way, at breakfast the top tables are reserved for Warrant Officers only, it has become a kind of tradition in this Mess."

"Give me a knock when you are ready for breakfast I will walk in with you and show you the lay out," Bill told George.

"Will do, thanks Bill. Goodnight all."

"He appears to be a good man Bill I think we will get on well with him. What do *you* think Derwent?" Asked Roy.

"I can get to like the guy."

"He is one of the best," added Bill.

CHAPTER 6

George Miller duly reported to the Orderly Room and was shown into Roy Shaw's office.

"Morning George," Roy greeted him with, did you have a good night's sleep?"

"After a while I did, my brain was a bit too active to start with but I soon dropped off."

"This morning, you will be having an interview with the O.C. at 10:30; I believe you know Wing Commander Pilling."

"Aye, I served with him at Chatworth, he is a good officer."

"Then at 11:00 you will have an interview with the C.O. Group Captain Wildeman, I can tell you that he is one of the best, he and Bill Barrett have great respect for each other so much so you could say his office door is always open to Bill. That might sound strange to you but when you hear the full story of Bill Barrett and the BlueBelles you will understand why Bill is a VIP in his own right but you will never hear him admit it."

"I saw what he did with the BlueBelles at Chatworth," said George, "I know his capabilities but the little bits I have heard about him since then seem a bit exaggerated."

"I'll tell you what I will do George, you have quite a wait for your first interview, I will take you to see your friend Mary Butcher, she is the one to tell you everything you will want to know but I must have you here by 10:15."

They went to Mary's office, Roy knocked on the door to hear a "Come In."

"In you go George," said Roy taking his leave.

"When he entered Mary gave a squeal of delight and came to him with arms outstretched. After giving him a kiss and a bear hug she said, "I am so glad to see you George."

"It is nice to see you too Mary."

"After a preliminary chat to catch up with each other's news, George said.

“I understand you have a story to tell me Mary about our mutual friend and from the little bits of information I have been given it sounds like some story.”

“It certainly is George and we are so proud of him settle yourself down because it is a long story.” She then began from the very beginning and began to recount the events phase by phase right up to George’s posting to RAF March.

“There you have it George, he has the respect of the highest rankers in the service to the lowest and believe me he has earned it but you will never hear him boast about it, he is the just same Bill Barrett we knew at Chatworth but a lot wiser.”

“I don’t know what to say Mary, what a story, what a man and I am proud to call him my friend. As I said before, I heard various stories from time to time but I took them with a pinch of salt because you know how they get exaggerated but well done Bill, every damn one of them was true. What a story to tell the wife when she comes down, she always had a soft spot for him.”

“Well haven’t we all George?”

“I have got to go now I have to report to Roy Shaw to take me for my interviews, I will see you later Mary.”

“Come on George we are going to the O.C’s PA’s office, incidentally she is my lady friend.” He knocked on her door and entered on command. Barbara this is Warrant Officer Miller our new Station Warrant Officer.”

She shook his hand, “I am very pleased to meet you sir I am Barbara Page. I will tell the O.C you are here.” She buzzed the intercom Warrant Officer Miller is here sir.”

“Send him in Barbara.”

“This way sir,” as she guided him to the connecting door then ushered him in and announced “Warrant Officer Miller sir!” George saluted.

“Welcome to RAF March Mr Miller,” he said as he shook his hand. “I am very pleased to see you again and have you as my Station Warrant Officer, it is like old times. Sit yourself down and tell me what you have been up to since we last saw each other. If I remember rightly you went to Cyprus, how did you enjoy your tour?”

“That’s right sir, I enjoyed it but the wife took some getting used to the heat, she liked it better during the winter months.”

“When you settle down here you will find it a very good station and the staff are excellent they need to be with it being the Flagship of Training Command, they were hand picked by the C.O, myself and Warrant Officer Barrett who you will know from his RAF Chatworth days.

“Indeed I do sir actually we are very close friends.”

“I thought as much when he recommended you for the SWO’s post he is a very good judge of character and has never failed us yet with his recommendations. Then of course we have our mutual friend Warrant Officer Butcher."

"It is like a family reunion sir and I am really pleased with this posting."

"We are very pleased to have you Mr Miller. I believe you now have an interview with the Station Commander." He buzzed for Barbara. "Take Mr Miller round to the C.O's office please Barbara."

"This way sir," she said as she led him to Helen Fraser's office. "Helen, this is Warrant Officer Miller for the C.O."

"Thanks Barbara." She held out her hand. I am Helen Fraser the C.O.'s PA. I will just give him a buzz to see if he is ready for you. Warrant Officer Miller is here sir are you ready for him?"

"Bring him in Helen."

She ushered George in. "Mr.Miller sir." George saluted.

"Sit down Mr Miller and welcome to RAF March. I see from your records you have just completed a tour in Cyprus how did you like it out there?"

"I liked it but the wife struggled with the heat, she preferred the winter time."

"That is understandable. I also notice with pleasure that you have an excellent record but I did not need your records to tell me that, Wing Commander Pilling did a good job of boosting your character and assuring me we had got an excellent SWO. Warrant Officer Barrett backed that up and his word is good enough for me. You see Mr Miller; we have a great working partnership which resulted in this station being given the status it now holds. Furthermore the RAF in general owes a great deal to him and that includes myself if you follow my drift and I must add, that working partnership still exists. Between you and me Mr Miller, he could have become a Staff Officer immediately but he would not accept a commission. I am telling you this as his friend, he will not tell you, so when you hear many people singing his praises you will know why. To his credit he is totally unaffected by it all.

"Right then, Station Warrant Officer Miller, Welcome to RAF March, he shook George's hand."

George saluted and said. "Thank you for taking me into your confidence sir."

He then returned to the Orderly Room. "Did you have good interviews George?"

"I did and they were very enlightening, I learned quite a lot about our friend this morning and all to his credit I might add and now taking over his post as SWO it appears I have got a lot to live up to."

"He has been a first class SWO but I know he would expect you to be the George Miller SWO as he knows you, he has a great deal of respect for you George. Don't you be surprised when he comes to you for advice, mark my words he will. Come on let me take you to your office it is only a couple of strides away. This room here between us is my stock room and where the brew tackle is kept and here we are your domain."

He knocked and they entered. Bill was at his desk but got up to shake George by the hand and direct him into the SWO's chair. "There you are old timer, that chair could not be sat upon by a better SWO man. It is a pleasure for me to introduce your second in command Flight Sergeant Ian Roberts."

"I pleased to meet you Ian."

"It is a real pleasure to meet you sir, I was stopped from putting down the red carpet for you by his nibs here."

"Ian, do me a favour and call me George, you are an old hand and I would not insult you by telling you the score. The red carpet bit does not surprise me in the least, he never would accept the fact that I am better looking than him." They all had a good laugh.

"Bill interrupted by telling Ian. "Beware his Pearls of Wisdom; he is murder Mary Butcher will vouch for that."

"Right then," said George. "Shall we get our priorities right, what about a brew?"

"I will go and tell the runner to get cracking with one," said Ian. How do you like your brew George?"

"Sergeant Major style with milk and two sugars please."

When Ian had left the room, Bill told him. "You have got a good man there George, he knows his job and nothing is too much trouble for him, I think you and him are going to get on well together. He has no time for the moaners he soon puts them in their place, he is summat like you, firm but fair."

Ian returned followed by the runner carrying the three mugs of tea on a tray.

"Now then!" who have we here?" asked George. "What is your name lad?"

"Adams sir."

"Well Lac.Adams, you present yourself well, smart creases and shiny footwear and you look very neat and tidy. What is your duty here?"

"I am the SWO's runner sir."

"How did you qualify for the post?"

"The airman with the smartest turn out on work parade gets picked for the job on a daily basis sir."

"How do you like the job?"

"It is great sir all the lads try their best to get picked now."

"That sounds good, tell the lads you have just met the new SWO and I will soon be having a look at you all. If they all turn themselves out like you have done I will be more than pleased." He turned to Bill. Have we any more jobs today for this young man?"

"No, it looks like being a quiet day."

"Good, then you can knock off at lunch time Adams."

"Thank you sir," the lad replied with a huge grin on his face.

After he left, Ian looked at Bill when George said. "Treat em' right and they will respond!"

"Now I know who you got *that* 'Pearl of Wisdom' from Bill."

That brought a big smile from the two WO's

"It is lunchtime," Bill pointed out. "Shall we shut up shop while we go and feed our faces?"

>>> <<<

Bill was walking along the corridor of SHQ when he heard a voice shout, "BILL" It can only be Roy he said to himself. He went into his office and asked. "How did you know it was me? You had your door closed."

"There are not many footsteps in SHQ that I do not know and yours are the easiest of the lot."

"How?"

"They are the heavy plod, plod, plod of a typical Drill Instructor."

"How would you like one of those plods rammed up…

"Steady now or I will report you to Tommy for threatening me."

"Why did you call me?"

"To give you my good news of course."

"That you are posted?"

"Now would I call that my good news to leave you my very best friend?"

"It can be arranged!"

"Oh no it can't, you are no longer the SWO."

"But I have still got friends in high places so less of the sarcasm or I will cast one of my magic spells on you."

"Mercy, I shall throw myself at your feet in supplication."

"And I will throw up! Now, what is it you want to tell me?"

"My Sergeant clerk arrives tomorrow, Frank Thomson, he is married."

"Perhaps you will be able to concentrate on your work now seeing he is a male!"

"What are you up to at the moment now you have got rid of one job?"

"Actually I was on my way to take George a stroll round the station and fill him in as to what will be going on around him. I had better get back to the office or he will think I am skiving off, see you later Roy."

"Do you fancy a stroll round the station George?"

"I wouldn't mind Bill I could do with a bit of fresh air and exercise to walk that good lunch off. You have a good Chef in the Mess he serves up some good grub."

"I think I will start you off by introducing you to Sam Brown, he is the civilian head gardener of the station's market garden. Before you ask, his father was a regular army officer with a sense of humour. Sam grows a lot of vegetables for the three Messes, it supplements the service rations, he also grows flowers for the Messes as well and the married families are allowed to buy his produce the money going into the station funds. He has an airman working with him, SAC Bond he is by trade a qualified horticulturist between them they do a great job for the station. I have excused Bond from all station duties to enable him to work full time with Sam. When I arrived Sam was working by himself almost for most of the time relying on any spare GD bods. Young Bond puts in a lot of off duty hours which includes weekends he puts in more hours than any of us, he is a good conscientious lad and we cannot afford to lose him otherwise that would be the end of the market garden. Anyway let us go and meet Sam.

"Where are you Sam?" shouted Bill when he could not see him around.

"Here in the potting shed Bill."

"Come on out I would like you to meet somebody."

Sam came out wiping his hands on a grubby piece of rag.

"I want you to meet George Miller who has taken over from me as Station Warrant Officer. He is a very good friend of mine from way back and you can breathe easy for you will be in very good hands."

"I am very pleased to meet you sir," said Sam offering his hand, which George took and shook. "If Bill says you are a good friend of his then that is good enough for me."

"You can start off on the right foot Sam by calling me George, Bill here has given me your case history and I can see no reason why I should change anything."

"Thanks George that is good to know and it certainly takes a load off my mind. Would you like a look round the place or have a brew first then a look round?"

"You have touched my weak spot Sam I think we will have a brew."

While they were enjoying Sam's brew he told George the history of the Market Garden and how it was run.

"That was a good brew Sam I know where to come when I am feeling thirsty."

"You are more than welcome George, come on I will show you around the place."

George was impressed especially with the flowers grown under glass.

"When your wife moves down to your married quarter George come and see me and I will fix you up with some Welcome to your New Home flowers."

"Thanks Sam, I will appreciate that."

"Now what do you fancy doing?" Asked Bill, "How about a look at your staff in the bedding store I don't know where the rest will be, or a look at my training staff? No, that will be better in a morning when they are drilling and not in the classrooms. We will go and give the bedding wallahs a surprise. Corporal Brown is in charge there, he was a skiving little sod until I showed him the light, now you would not think he was the same bloke, he is good at his job and you can rely on him. When things were pretty hectic I excused him from station duties and it paid off, he is still excused them. Here is the bedding store but I have to knock now after I put him wise about leaving it open for me to catch him on the hop."

He then gave a loud knock and waited, they both grinned knowing there was a mad scramble to make them look busy. An airman opened up for them.

"Bill asked. "Is Corporal Brown in situ?"

"No sir, he is in here!"

The two WOs looked at each other, Bill grinned and George just shrugged his shoulders.

Bill addressed Corporal Brown. "This is Warrant Officer Miller your new Station Warrant Officer and as from now you answer to him."

George was looking around the bedding store, peering under the racks containing the bedding. Looking at the two young airmen who were stood to attention he told them, "Stand easy lads this is not an inspection. What is your name lad?" He asked the one who was wearing spectacles.

"Lac. Jones sir."

"Are you the famous Tom Jones I have heard about?"

"I don't think so sir."

"What is your job here?"

"I help to keep the place clean I help out on sheet changing day. I help to bundle all bedding for the laundry and help with the stock taking."

"You are kept busy then it seems. Do you attend work parades?"

"Yes sir."

"Have you managed to get picked for stick man as the SWO's runner?"

"No sir I have not," he replied.

"What about you?" he asked of the other airman.

"No sir I have not either."

"I hear from other airmen it is a great job with plenty of free time for yourselves, they all want to be the SWO's runner, don't either of you want it?"

"No sir. We prefer doing this job besides Corporal Brown would be short staffed and the other airmen who would stand in for us would not know what to do in here."

"I admire your loyalty to Corporal Brown, what happens when one of you go on leave?"

"I ask you the same question Corporal what happens when one of them goes on leave?"

“There are two airmen on the staff who stand in when that happens sir, they have attained some knowledge of the workings of this department so we manage alright.”

“That is what I wanted to hear but there will be no let up on the standard of dress and turnout just because they don’t want to be stick man. If I find the standard slipping I shall be breathing down your necks constantly. On the other hand, if you keep to my standard all will be well. Corporal Brown, I am impressed with the standard you are keeping this store in, well done. As for you two airmen, keep up the good work.”

George turned round at the door as he and Bill were leaving and said. “A word of advice for you, in future when you hear a knock on the door make sure you camouflage that bed up there on top of those blankets you don’t know who wants to come in.”

When they got outside they had a right good laugh. “They can’t teach us any tricks or skives, we could write a book Bill. What say we go back and see what Ian has been up to?”

“Roy Shaw rang he wants a word with you Bill.”

“Thanks Ian.”

>>> <<<

“You are to have a new Flight Commander in a couple of days time old lad, this one has wings. He is an ex-flyer, been grounded for medical reasons and will be flying a desk for the foreseeable future, he will be chuffed about that, I don’t think. He has just completed a course on General Duties plus a few days with the Mouth and Trousers Squadron.”

“That is a new one on me,” said Bill.

“It will be,” smirked Roy “I just made it up. The Drill Instructors who else? So you had better be on your toes when he runs his beady eyes over your little set-up.”

“Looks like he will be starting from scratch Roy, if he is willing to learn we will get on famously, if he is a know it all we shall have fun. Has he got a name?”

“Flight Lieutenant Cody”

“You are now going to tell me he is called William aren’t you?”

“No! His name is Winston! George might know him for his last posting was in Cyprus. He may know of him but I don’t think he will know him personally.”

“Thanks for the info’ Roy, I will have a word with George and thanks for the offer of a brew but I am too busy to accept at the moment, sorry to disappoint you.”

“Get out of here Bill Barrett and don’t come whingeing to me when Buffalo Bill ropes you in”

When he returned to the SWO's office he asked George. "Did you know Flight Lieutenant Cody in Cyprus?"

"No! why?"

"He is posted in as O.C. i/c Training. Apparently he has been grounded for medical reasons he will be my new boss. I wonder how he will take to flying a desk."

"These flying bods normally do not take doing a desk job too kindly, maybe he will be all right if he has come to terms with being grounded. If he is only a youngster there may be problems you know what these whiz kids are like."

"I hope for his sake George he has accepted it, we do not want another Chambers-Jones on our hands."

CHAPTER 7

Bill was in the training office he now shared with Viv Anderson. Everything was going smoothly, the new staff had settled themselves in, one Sergeant and two Corporals were expected very shortly to make up the full quota of staff. He had just returned from his rounds of inspecting the Flights along with Viv and they were both pleased with the progress being made when the phone rang.

"WO Barrett."

"Ah Mr Barrett, Flight Lieutenant Cody here, can you come to my office please I would like to meet you, say in an hours time?"

"Very good sir I will be there. That was our new boss Flight Lieutenant Cody," he told Viv. "He wants to meet me in an hour. Good, I hope he is one who will work with us and not against us but that I will soon find out."

He was told to enter when he knocked on the Flight Lieutenant's door. Bill saluted a young looking fair-haired officer. He stood up from his seat behind his desk, offered his hand and said. "I am very pleased to meet you Mr Barrett, do sit down. I have heard so much about you and now that we will be working together I am looking forward to learning a lot from you about the job which I have had thrust upon me. You see Mr Barrett I am now what is commonly known as flying a desk as opposed to actual flying. The reason for that is because I failed to maintain the medical qualifications. The options I got were, take a desk job or a discharge. I like the RAF Mr Barrett and I shall try to carry on and make a career in the service."

"Thank you sir for being so frank with me and I think you have made the right decision to stay in the service. I know you will find it tough coming down to this level from flying but you can be assured I will help you all I can to make a success of this job. With respect sir, all I ask of you is to play fair with my staff and not to take the hump if at any time I should need to point you in the right direction. I will probably be firm at times but it will not be in a manner of disrespect, if you can accept that it will be half the battle with you being the pupil for a little while and me the teacher."

"Mr Barrett, you have outshone my expectations of you, thank you I will try my best to be a star pupil, sir!"

They both had a good laugh over that remark.

"Have you met your opposite number Flight Lieutenant (w) Adams?"

"Only socially in the Officer's Mess, we have not got into any conversation over my taking over this job."

"Confidentially sir, from my observations she knows just about as much as you do now. I will make sure that in a very short time you will be 'Top Gun'."

"When do we make a start Mr Barrett?" He asked, giving a big grin.

"First I will give you a run down of how I run the training programme and what I expect and demand from my training instructors and then tell you of the few sad incidents we have had just lately. Then when you can fit it in I would like you to pay a visit to *my* office where we map out the training programmes and monitor each individual's progress in the ops' room. That is where you will make your start, then when you have to show some brass-hats round who asks awkward questions you can baffle them with science."

"Excellent, I am already beginning to warm to the prospects. Fire away Mr Barrett but should we have a cup of tea for starters?"

"Now you sir are my kind of officer but can you make it a mug of tea please? That is what you will get over at my place, you will not get tea you will get a brew. Also a little tip for you, the Station Warrant Officer likes his brew"

"I like it he grinned I will go and order a brew."

"Well? What is he like?" asked Viv

"He is a right grand lad I am pleased to say, I could not have wished for a nicer boss. He openly admitted he knew nothing about recruit training but he is willing to learn and wants me to teach him the ropes by becoming my number one pupil. You will like him Viv; I took to him straight away. You know what I even converted him from having a cup of tea to having a brew. He is eager to make a start and here in the ops' room is where he takes his first lesson. He will stay in here until you or I are satisfied he knows what it is about and is capable of running it himself. Do not namby pamby him, correct him where necessary and tell it to him straight that is the way he wants it. At last we have a winner, he is approachable, he will listen and learn and I will make darned sure he will turn out a good officer who is good at his job."

"He *has* made a good impression on you Bill and you are a good judge of character. It will seem a bit weird bossing the boss around but from your appraisal of him. I am sure we are all going to be of a similar mind. Is there any news of the replacements yet?"

"Thanks for reminding me Viv, I will chase that up and there is no time like the present." He then rang Roy Shaw. "Hi Roy it is me Bill, have you had any word about the Sergeant and two Corporals replacements for me?"

"Why? Are we getting rid of you at last and is that the best offer we can get for you?"

"Roy, I am rolling about in hysterics listening to your wit, now do try your best to be serious for once in your life."

"What is it worth?"

"Can I tempt you with a pint tonight in the Mess?"

"I did not know you had come into an inheritance ask away old pal, old buddy."

"Well have you heard owt'?"

"As a matter of fact I have received a signal, I rang Ian to tell you to contact me but I forgot you have been sacked from the SWO's Office so I decided to tell you at lunch time because I got so busy, you know how it is here at the very hub of the station. Your three replacements are due to arrive tomorrow. I will fill you in with their details when you come to see me is that all right with you sir?"

"Thanks Roy, that is good news see you later."

"They are due in tomorrow Viv; it will be great to get back to full strength. Shall we stand the staff down then lock up and go to lunch? I will walk you to the Mess."

As they were walking, Bill asked. "I never see you in the mess of an evening is there a reason for you not coming in?"

"I do come in when we have an entertainment meeting and I can tell you we are having quite a few of those because we are arranging functions to please the members and it is not easy I can tell you."

"What about refreshments? I know from experience that those meetings can last most of the evening."

"Tommy usually sees we get fed and watered, nobody gets drinks from the bar or we would get nowhere with the arrangements."

Bill stopped at reception on his way to lunch and asked Jackie if Tommy was available?

"II will go and see."

She soon returned with Tommy in tow. "Hello love." She said giving him a kiss.

Jackie looked on face beaming as usual when she saw them together.

"Have you come to tell me anything special?"

"Not really I have only come to see you it will make me enjoy my lunch all the more."

A big sigh and an "Ahhh! how lovely," from Jackie.

"I had a meeting with my new boss, Flight Lieutenant Cody this morning. He is a grand lad, I took to him straight away I am taking him under my wing to teach him the ropes and he is chuffed to bits."

"If you are doing that for him then he must be a nice man and it does not surprise me one little bit Bill Barrett but he cannot be as nice as you," giving Bill another kiss much to the delight of Jackie.

"Good, then I will leave you light of my eyes and get myself some lunch." He gave her a kiss that brought another sigh from Jackie and a smile to the lovebird's faces.

In the bar that evening Chalky was serving drinks to Bill and Derwent when Roy appeared.

"Get him one in Chalky and don't forget yourself," said Bill. "How are you Roy and what is the news from the sharp end?"

Roy took a slurp of his beer. "Well done Chalky that is as good a pint you will find anywhere, cheers. Not a great lot apart from what I told you on the phone this morning only you were too busy to come and see me. You will now have to wait until you can find time to visit me to find out about your new staff, end of story."

"Sorry Roy I was indeed very busy today and I apologise."

"Too late to agolopise."

"Don't you mean apologise Roy?"

"I can't say apologise!"

Derwent and Chalky were laughing their heads off at the banter between these two great friends.

"I have something you all may be interested in," said Bill. I had an excellent meeting with my boss Flight Lieutenant Cody. He is a right grand lad, if he was a SNCO instead of an officer he would mould very nicely into our little group. He has put himself entirely in my hands to teach him the ropes because he wants to make a success of the job. I have told him he will have to play it my way because I will not be pulling any punches and he accepts that. In addition, I have been thinking; we cannot keep using his full title every time we mention his name. I think 'Wings' would be appropriate and it is not disrespectful."

"It is as good as any and better than most agreed Roy. I will second that."

"I will third it," said Derwent.

"Can I fourth it?" asked Chalky giving a cheeky grin.

"I hope for his sake Wings does not upset you or you will be giving *him* the elbow," said Roy. Go on then put him a pint in Chalky I don't want to get on the wrong side of him and yes you are right, I *am* looking after numero uno, I am not daft! Go on fill em' all up and one for yourself."

"From what you tell us Bill," remarked Derwent, he is one of the young officers that can earn respect which are few and far between especially when it comes to the whiz kid fliers they are on a planet of their own."

"They are brilliant at what they do," exclaimed Bill, "they deserve credit for that. By the way does anyone know why George is not in tonight?"

"Gone home to bring his wife down, they are moving into Quarters. Alan Fell has just taken over a Quarter as well so he will be sloping off to bring his family down, he will be seeing you in the morning to tell you," Roy informed Bill.

"Are there any functions coming up?" asked Chalky.

"I do believe," spoke up Roy, "there is a Disco and a Dining-In night on the cards but I don't know in which order."

"I had better be getting some extra stock in for the Dining-In night especially," said Chalky, "plus extra staff to wait-on tables."

"Tommy will arrange the staff have no fear, she will recruit some of the WRAFs and her stewards and don't you go and forget the Port Wine Chalky that would be sacrilege."

"We will need Sherry in Reception to greet the guests on entrance," added Roy, "I will have a word with the entertainments committee to book a dance band that can play a variety of music to please all tastes. Have you done a dining-in night before Chalky?"

"No I haven't and I'm not looking forward to it either."

"There is nowt' to it," said Bill, trying to alleviate any tension, "we will guide you. Remind me Roy to get an officer nominated as Mess President."

"Everybody comes to Roy. Roy, will you do this? Roy, will you do that? Roy, can you show me how?" While Roy was putting on his martyrs act, the other three were playing imaginary violins.

"Chalky," said Derwent, "will you please get Roy a pint? His glass is empty and he has nothing to cry into… Then fill the rest up while you are at it."

>>> <<<

"I have taken over a married quarter Bill and I would like a few days off to bring the family down."

"No problem Alan, I know you have to hand over your quarter at Chatworth, will a week suit you?"

"It should be fine if the MOD there marches us out quickly."

"Right get your skates on then go and see Roy Shaw he will get your leave pass organised, by the way the replacements are due in today so I will have the new Sergeant standing in for you until you get back."

Bill went into the ops' room to see Viv.

"I am off to get the gen on our replacements Viv; I will be with Roy if I am wanted."

"Okay sir, we will hold the fort."

"Didn't I tell you last night that everyone comes to Roy for something," was the greeting Bill got when he walked into Roy's office. "I have just sent your Sergeant on his way with his pass in record time that is the service you get here. Now it is your turn to want something, come on and spit it out."

"The gen on my replacements."

"I wish they were replacing you maybe I would get some peace."

"C'mon Roy what is biting you? You are getting all bitter and twisted these days, you need a spot of leave, get yourself off to Spain or the French Riviera and laze in the sun, pamper yourself. You have not had a falling out with Barbara have you?"

"You are right Bill I have been a bit nowty lately. No, we have not been falling out but I don't see much of her these days when she has to go with the OC for special meetings to take shorthand notes for him, sometimes it is an overnight stay. It sounds a bit selfish but I do miss her a lot."

"Look Roy, why don't the pair of you put in for some leave and go off together, it will do the pair of you the world of good. When you see her put the proposition to her, I am sure she feels the same way about missing you."

"You have got something there Bill thanks, I like the idea. Now let us get down to business. The Sergeant is Peter York posted in from the D.I School of Training, he should know his stuff."

"That is a different world Roy, training people to be instructors and teaching recruits basic training are totally different I am a bit wary of postings from there but I hope he is the type to accept the difference. What about the Corporals?"

"Corporal Evans is coming from RAF Camberly and Corporal Harper is coming from…he was interrupted.

"RAF Chatworth," grinned Bill. He was on my staff there and I put him in Alan Fell's team who brought the best out in the lad, Alan will be chuffed when he sees him."

"They should be arriving some time today. The Corporals will be sleeping in transit until we find them accommodation, I don't know if any of the three are married. I will let Ian Roberts know then his staff will be ready to give them a bed in transit."

"Have you told Tommy about Sergeant York?"

"I have, you forget how organised we are here at the sharp end."

"How are you getting on with your new Sergeant?"

"He knows his job backwards and is very methodical and everything must be 'by the book' but he does not appear to have any sense of humour Bill which I do find offputting. I will tell you one thing, he could never join The Crackpots."

"Not daft like us Roy?"

"No, he keeps himself to himself, I still know nothing about him he may come out of his shell one of these days. Has Buffalo Bill showed his face at your ops' room yet for his first lesson?"

"No but he will be doing so very soon. From what I can gather his opposite number Flight Lieutenant (w)Adams is not very sociable I must have a word with Mary Butcher to hear her views."

CHAPTER 8

"Come in" shouted Bill in response to the knock on his office door. Sergeant York entered.

"Ah, you must be Sergeant York," said Bill holding out his hand in greeting, which was taken and shook.

"Will you sign my arrival chit Bill, it is Bill isn't it? I have heard a lot about you."

"Yes it is Bill Sergeant and until I give you permission to call me by my Christian name you will address me according to my rank, do I make myself clear Sergeant?"

This outburst shook the Sergeant rigid so much so he could only manage to stammer,

"Yes sir."

"I must congratulate you Sergeant York, you are the first stranger to walk into my office and greet me like a bosom pal. You have started off on the wrong foot with me and it could be a long time before you are back on the right one. Tell me is your rank a substantive one or are you still an acting Sergeant?"

"I am acting sir."

"And you have the audacity to walk in here and show no respect to my rank. Now listen to me and listen good. Here you will have to prove your worth, we are training youngsters who have the potential to do well in the service that is why they are sent here. You will, I repeat, you will treat them like human beings and not like something the dog has dragged in. In easy to understand terms you will have to prove to me that you have earned the right to wear those chevrons, if not, I will have them off you in a flash. Have I made myself clear as to how we stand with each other?"

"Yes sir and I would like to apologise for my actions."

"How old are you?"

"Twenty eight sir."

"How long have you been in the service?"

"Seven years, sir."

"Married?"

"Yes sir, with two children."

"You will want married quarters I presume."

"Yes sir."

"When you get a quarter come and see me right away and I will give you the necessary time off to move your family in without any delays. I will see to it you have a quarter very soon. Now give me your Chitty," which he promptly signed then handed back and said. "One more thing you should know, I do not bear any grudges, if that makes you feel any better."

"It does sir and thank you, I only got what I deserved. You will have no further trouble from me."

"Report here, for duty in the morning."

When the Sergeant left, Bill rang Roy. "Roy it is Bill here your best mate."

"Oh hello, what do you want this time?"

"How do you know I want something? Old pal."

"Because you never say anything nice or complimentary only, will you do me a big favour Roy? Am I right?"

"Well I wouldn't put it like that exactly Roy," he said grinning.

"You can wipe that stupid grin off your face Bill Barrett or I will not do what you want me to do what do you want?" he said all in one breath.

Bill could not help but burst out laughing over the phone. "You have got me well and truly taped haven't you?

"That is why we are buddies," said Roy. "Now c'mon tell me what you want."

Bill told him about Sergeant York. "I really did lay into him Roy but I get the impression he is going to be a good Sergeant and I want to help him do this.

He is married with two kiddies and would you please use some of your influence to get him a quarter quickly?"

"Of course I will but there is something I think you should know in advance. It is Corporal Evans, I hope I am wrong Bill but I sense he has got an attitude"

"Thanks Roy on both counts, I hope he is a good Corporal and knows his job that is all I want from him. You say he is from RAF Camberly; do you have a contact there that can give us some background on him?"

"Will do what I can Bill, see you in the Mess tonight."

Corporals Harper and Evans entered Bill's office and marched to his desk. Bill stood up. You are Corporal Evans" he held out his hand to him and said. "Welcome to RAF March and to my staff."

Evans shook his hand and thanked him.

"Corporal Harper, welcome, I am delighted to see you again. He offered his hand which Harper shook and thanked him.

"I have some good reports about you from a mutual friend of ours Sergeant Fell; you do know he is here on my staff."

"Yes sir it will be grand serving with him again, he is a great instructor."

Bill looked at Evans. Are you chewing Corporal?

"Yes sir, gum."

"Then go and dispense with it outside this building."

Evans turned on his heel slamming the office door behind him.

When he returned Bill asked him. "Have you got a problem Corporal?"

"No."

"No what?"

"No sir."

"You come into my office showing little respect by chewing in my face then you have the audacity to slam my office door after I gave you an order. Now before we proceed I want to know if you have got a problem against authority and are satisfied with this posting?"

"I can take it or leave it."

"What does that mean Corporal?"

"I feel that at times I do not fit in,"

"You mean you feel that you are not being accepted by authority?"

"That's right sir."

"But the authority promoted you to Corporal if you had not been accepted you would not have been given those stripes."

"What do you to say to that Corporal?"

Evans just shrugged his shoulders.

"Tell me your thoughts on instructing raw recruits in basic training?"

"They will have a shock coming to them if they expect any kid glove treatment from me."

"Will you explain to me of your intentions when you get a flight of new recruits who have never seen a parade ground before never mind foot drill?"

"The first thing I will show them is who the boss is."

"How will you do that? By shouting them down and punishing them if they do not conform to your teaching?"

"You have hit the nail right on the head sir."

"Thank you Corporal Evans for being open and forthright with me. What I want you to do now is go back to the transit block and you will stay there until you are called for which will be in just a short while."

"What about signing my arrival chitty?"

"You have not arrived yet and you are not likely to do either. Now get out and back to transit and if you have any other ideas the station police will be ordered to keep you under observation at all times. Now get out of my office."

He left, slamming the door angrily.

"Let me sign your chitty Corporal Harper. Not a nice scene and not a nice guy."

"I have only just met him sir and I saw at once from his attitude that he was trouble."

"There is a possibility Corporal you may be called as a witness to what the dialogue was all about, a pity because I was hoping we could have made something out of the lad. Anyway, it is good to have you on my staff

Corporal Harper; by the way does Sergeant Fell know you were posted here?"

"No sir I have not seen him."

"He has gone to Chatworth to bring his family down into quarters, somebody there may tell him. I will see you here tomorrow when you have finished arriving."

Bill rang Flight Lieutenant Cody. "Sir I would like to see you see you on a very urgent matter concerning one of the new Corporals?"

"Certainly, come over right away."

When he arrived he told the whole story word for word.

"It certainly is serious Mr Barrett, we cannot have someone with an attitude like that instructing raw recruits, we shall have to get rid of him he will be detrimental to our training methods. Who promoted the lad? Surely he could not have been vetted properly unless something has sparked him off to change his attitude. It is too hot for me to handle so I will go and see the Wingco'. Where can I contact you Mr Barrett?"

"I will be in WO Shaw's office in the Orderly Room sir."

"It looks like we have a serious problem on our hands Cody," said the Wing Commander. I will have a word with the CO. and I will contact you at your office on what steps we will take."

Bill told Roy the sad tale.

"I knew there would be trouble with that lad his whole attitude gave him away and we cannot take any disciplinary action against him because he has done nothing wrong. All they can do is relieve him of his rank because of his attitude.. I imagine the OC is now in with the CO. and very soon you will be getting a phone call telling you to escort Evans to the CO's office."

"Are you a mind reader or summat' Roy?"

"I am in the right place to know about these things old lad, I have seen it happen before but under different circumstances."

"I've just thought of something Roy; I may need Corporal Harper to verify my story. Will you send a tannoy message out telling him to report here immediately?"

"Roy picked up the phone and rang the guardroom asking them to announce the message. By the time he had put the phone down the message was being broadcast. Five minutes later a breathless Corporal Harper arrived.

Sergeant Thomson called through the hatch, "He is here sir."

"Keep him there until he is wanted Sergeant "

After a short while the phone rang. Roy looked at Bill. "This is it!"

"Flight Lieutenant Cody here I would like a word with Warrant Officer Barrett please."

Roy gave Bill the phone. "WO Barrett speaking."

“Mr Barrett, will you bring Corporal Evans to the CO’s office immediately please.”

“As soon as I can get hold of him sir.”

“Roy, ring the guardroom and asked them to escort Evans here, he should be in the transit block, tell us when he is on his way, we will keep the line open.”

Roy rang and explained to Tom Bridges, he then heard him order one of his Corporals to go and find Corporal Evans.

“Is there some trouble in t’ mill Roy?” Tom asked.

“You could say that Tom, it looks like being a dodgy bit of trouble too if it is not handled carefully.”

“He is on his way Roy.”

“Thanks Tom.”

“He is on his way Bill.”

“Right I will pick young Harper up and wait for him outside here. “Thanks a lot Roy I will see you in a bit.”

“C’mon Corporal, come and stay with me while Corporal Evans arrives, he has to see the CO. You will stay in his secretary’s office just in case you are needed you will be all right there. Ah, here he comes, thanks Corporal, stay around until he comes out, you may still be needed,” he said to the police Corporal.

“Corporal Evans, we have a date with the Station Commander so let us go and not disappoint him. He knocked on Helen Fraser’s door and entered when he heard “Come in”.

“We have an appointment with the CO Helen.”

“Yes I know, I will give him a buzz. Warrant Officer Barrett is here sir.”

“Show him in Helen.”

Bill told her Corporal Harper would stay with her in case he was called for.”

She knocked on the door, “Warrant Officer Barrett and Corporal Evans sir.”

They both entered and Bill saluted. He saw both the OC and Flight Lieutenant Cody stood behind the CO who was seated at his desk.

“Do you not salute senior ranks Corporal?”

Quite unconcerned, Evans replied, “I thought he was doing it for both of us.”

“You sound a very bitter young man, are you averse to officers?

He just shrugged in reply.

“It is quite obvious you have no respect for anyone who is senior to you. I have your service record here and I find it interesting yet puzzling. You have been in the service five years and there is no blemish in that time on your records until the assessments from your last station. Something or someone during your stay there was the cause of a complete change in your character. You became disobedient, insolent, and lost all respect for seniority and discipline. On top of that you received a caution in respect of your bad attitude. I cannot understand why a young man like you who has done so well to reach the rank of Corporal in a relevant short period of service should suddenly change, I call that a Jekyll and Hyde syndrome. Something tells me there is more to this than meets the eye. Deep down under that mask of indifference you are portraying I think you are an honest lad. Are you?"

"Yes!"

"Then give me an honest answer to this question. Are you trying to work your ticket?"

"Yes!"

"Thank goodness for that young man, your wish will be granted. RAF March is the end of *your* line. I cannot allow you to mingle with the rest of the RAF personnel on my station with such a bad attitude you have now adopted."

Beckoning the OC to him he whispered, "Get Flight Sergeant Bridges here with a police escort immediately."

The OC left the room to carry out his instructions.

The CO continued. "With the powers invested in me as Station Commander of RAF March I am demoting you with immediate effect to Leading Aircraftsman and to safeguard my personnel I am placing you under close arrest. You will be held in the guardroom until I receive your discharge papers.

"Is there anything you would like to say?"

"I will be glad to get away from you lot and this rotten service."

"Not as pleased as the service will be to see the back of you, God help society when you get out there. Which character will you assume then, Dr. Jekyll or Mr Hyde? Perish the thought. If Flight Sergeant Bridges is out there send him in please."

Tom came in and saluted smartly.

"Flight Sergeant, I am placing this person under close arrest until I receive his discharge papers, the first thing I want you to do is ensure those chevrons are removed from all his uniforms his rank now is Leading Aircraftsman. I will sign the relevant documents later confirming my decision."

"Very good sir."

"Take him away Flight Sergeant."

"Mr Barrett, once again you have upheld the standard of this station, thank you, you can certainly pick out the wrong ones."

"I cannot take all the credit for this one sir it was Warrant Officer Shaw who tipped me off that he thought the lad had an attitude."

"Well spotted Mr Shaw. Never the less Mr Barrett you handled it very well. Now you will want us to find you a replacement, this time we will make sure he fills the bill.

Flight Lieutenant Cody, I had you witness this sad affair to show you how we operate here at March, we work as a team, remember that."

"I certainly will sir it has been a great experience for me."

"Righto Mr Barrett, I will send for you when we need another chat."

Bill saluted. "Thank.you sir."

He then went into Helen's office and told Corporal Harper. "He has been stripped of his rank and will be dismissed the service as soon as his discharge papers arrive. In the meantime to protect the station personnel from his bad attitude he is being held in the guardroom under close arrest, that is a precautionary measure.

Seeing that you have had a harassing day go and see WO Shaw give him my respects and ask him to make out a day pass for you dated tomorrow and I will sign it shortly and I recommend you go and get some fresh air have a walk to the village and pop into the March Hare Pub you will meet an old friend of ours who is the landlady. Do you remember Sergeant (w) Ann Baker who led the BlueBelles to victory in that drill competition? Go and see her she will be so pleased to see you again."

"Thank you sir for the pass and I certainly will go and see Ann, she is a lovely lady and was well thought of."

"You do that Corporal, and tell her the gang will be coming to see her soon. By the way, are you married?"

"Not yet sir."

After the lad had left, Helen said. "Bill Barrett, you are the only Warrant Officer I have ever met who has a heart of gold."

"Helen, my favourite saying is.....Helen said it along with him. "Treat em' right and they respond." They both ended up laughing.

"Helen, would you mind having a woman to woman chat with Barbara? Roy is getting right down in the dumps because he is seeing so little of her, he realises her position and it just boils down to the fact that he is lovesick. I have put an idea into his head for them both to take a spot of leave together and go somewhere nice and peaceful where they can just enjoy each other's company, or even taking a trip out to the Costa's where they can just laze in the sun."

"I see what you mean Bill, I do know she needs to go and support the OC at important meetings quite a lot. I will have a woman's talk with her as you so put it. Roy should have no worries about her cooling off for she thinks the absolute world of him."

"Thanks Aunt Helen."

"You are welcome Uncle Bill. Do you think we should start an RAF March Aunt and Uncle agony column?"

He left in a fit of laughter and proceeded to the Orderly room to see Roy.

"Hello Bill," welcomed Roy. "Have you come to give me the grisly details?"

"First things first Roy, is the pass for Corporal Harper ready for my signature?"

"It is did you expect it not to be? How many times do I have to tell you that speed and proficiency is our motto? Here you are you big soft ha'porth, you spoil your staff, I know your little saying, treat em' right and... Bill stopped him.

"Okay Roy I have had that already thrown back at me today. That Corporal was ready and willing to stand by me if needed and that pass is my way of saying thank you, give it me here and I will sign it, is he waiting next door?"

"Sergeant Thomson, is Corporal Harper still there?"

"Yes sir he is."

"Give him this pass please with WO Barrett's compliments."

"Thanks Roy. Did you manage to sort out a quarter for Sergeant York?"

"Bill, what can I say, when you ask me to do you a favour I drop everything else to comply with your request, I like it here I don't want a posting!"

"Stop it Roy my sides are aching which only a brew can cure."

"I knew it, that is the only reason you come to see me just because.....

"It is the best brew on the station." interrupted Bill.

"Precisely, tomorrow first thing your Sergeant York will be taking over a married quarter and you never saw such a happier man when I told him. He shook my hand and he was profuse with his thanks."

"It was only what you deserve Roy."

"Thank you Bill, two teas with biscuits please," he shouted through the hatch. "You can tell me your saga when the brew comes, I am looking forward to it, and it should be interesting. Ah, here it comes, thank you young man," he said to the airman who brought it.

"Right Bill, you have my full attention."

To Bill's credit he was able to recount the whole incident almost word for word.

"You have got to give the CO credit; he knows exactly how to deal with any situation and in the best possible manner. He could have had that lad in all sorts of trouble, he knew the lad was putting on an act but it was too dangerous an act to ignore. I take my hat off to him. No, that is the wrong ternimology I salute him."

"Don't you mean terminology Roy?"

"Of course I do you, know very well I can't say terminology."

"I put a good word in for you Roy old friend, best mate, bosom pal."

"Pass me a tissue out of that box I think I am going to need it."

"O ye of little faith, how could I pass up a good chance to put you in the CO's good books?"

"Go on Bill, make my day."

"The CO said to me," "Thank you Mr Barrett you can certainly spot the wrong ones."

"I replied, I cannot take credit for that sir it was WO Shaw who tipped me off, he suspected Evans had an attitude".

"Well spotted Mr Shaw."

"He is the best officer I have ever served with," said Roy glowing with pride. Andy Warhole said everyone has fifteen minutes of fame in his lifetime. I have just had thirty seconds of mine."

"Congratulations," said Bill, "we must celebrate that tonight."

CHAPTER 9

"Hello Mary," Bill greeted as he entered her office, "how are you?"

"All the better for seeing you Bill, I do not see you for a chat nowadays since you left the SWO's office."

"I have been very busy lately Mary a lot of things has been happening and many of them not to my liking."

"I hear you have been going through your staff with a fine toothed comb and got rid of all the undesirables."

"We are getting there, I have just got rid of a Corporal who is now reposing in a cell in our guardroom waiting for his discharge papers. We have got some good replacements, you know Alan Fell is now with us; he has gone to bring his family into married quarters. Our latest addition from Chatworth is young Corporal Harper, do you remember him he was in Alan Fells team at the time they lost to the BlueBelles"

"Wasn't he that fair haired boy that Chambers-Jones said would soon need a haircut?"

"That's the one Mary. There is something I want to ask you. What is your opinion of your Flt. Commander Flight Lieutenant Adams?"

"That is a sore point with me Bill. She has no interest in the girls whatsoever, we rarely see her and when she does show her face everyone and I mean everyone is out of step except her. I think she has modelled herself on Chambers-Jones; she is a real pain in the backside. Why do you ask?"

"We have got a new Flight Commander by the name of Cody, he is ex-aircrew got grounded for failing his medical. You know Mary he is one of the nicest officers I have met, he is only young and he has put himself entirely into my hands to teach him the job. We are teacher and pupil and he accepts that. I told him he would start at the bottom in the ops' room then proceed from there, any day now he will start his first lesson. I asked him if he had met Flight Lieutenant Adams and he replied only briefly in the Mess.

To me that sounded like she wanted nothing to do with him, you would think she would want to help him out with being opposite numbers in our training."

"That is her all over Bill she is a proper little madam it sounds like you have a winner in your man, lucky you."

"Are we to play a waiting game for when she trips herself up Mary, is history going to repeat itself?"

"If it is it needs to hurry up."

"Did you know George has gone for his wife, they should be here any day now I just wish I new what day he is due to arrive because Sam has promised him some welcome flowers for the house. I am hoping George remembers that and phones in to tell us he is on his way. I tell you what Mary, ring Ian and ask him if he knows when George is due back." She rang Ian and asked him. "Thanks Ian that is what I wanted to know. He will arrive just after lunchtime tomorrow."

"Brilliant, all we need now is the duplicate key for the house, I will see Roy he may be able to help us, if so I will come and tell you then will you ring Sam and ask him about the flowers he promised? And to have them ready by ten o'clock then you and I will pick them up and you can do the flower arranging, tell Sam what flowers you want, okay?"

He went round to Roy and explained everything.

"No problem Bill, I will have keys here for you by nine thirty and you return them to me when you have finished."

"Thanks Roy. I will go and tell Mary to get to work on Sam."

"Everything is sorted out Mary, I pick up the keys at nine thirty then we pay our respects to Sam. Now get cracking on the phone and use your charm."

"I don't need to use charm with Sam, we are good buddies."

"I guessed that Mary."

"Now none of your cheek Bill Barrett you are still not too big to be clattered around the ears. Now get off with you I don't want any eavesdroppers when I am sweet-talking" she said with a big smile"

"Ask Sam if he has any flower containers to loan us in case there are no flower vases in the house, we will see they are returned."

"Good thinking Bill."

>>> <<<

"You have done it again, got rid of an undesirable" said Viv to Bill when he arrived back at the office. "Was it a nasty business?"

"Actually it went very well. The CO had the measure of him straight away, he knew the lad was working his ticket and got him to admit it. He stripped him of his rank then placed him under close arrest to wait for his discharge papers knowing that was the best option. There was no way Evans would change his attitude whatever punishment he received so the CO decided it would be better for the service if he was discharged. He is a wise man is our CO he could foresee a lot of trouble with that young man otherwise. We are still one Corporal short but we will be getting a replacement very soon.

"How are Corporals Harris and Lucas getting on without their Sergeant?"

"I took one of the more experienced Corporals from another flight and swapped him with Corporal Harris and it is working, Harris is now getting the benefit of working with another Sergeant and Lucas is getting the benefit of working with a very experienced Corporal so they are not losing out on instructing and the flight is not losing out either."

"Well done Viv. I have been doing a bit of thinking. Why don't we rotate the four teams of instructors every six weeks? That means that on the conclusion of every passing out parade that team of instructors will take up post in the ops' room!"

"I think that is a good idea; it means everyone will be more conversant with running the training programme, plus it being a nice little break from instructing. Why have we not thought about that before now Bill?"

"Exactly, it is so simple we just did not see it, we will put it into practice Viv after the next passing out parade, I will get all the teams in here after training and put them in the picture of what we intend, that of course goes for your WRAF too. Bring in your two Corporals will you please?

I want you two young ladies to do an errand for me. Go to the Sergeant (w) Instructors and the other to the RAF Sergeant Instructors with a message. WO Barrett sends his compliments and will you please assemble in the ops' room after training today?

How are things with the WRAF training flights, have you any problems there?"

"No, touch wood, everything is fine and would be a lot better if Madam would take time out to find how the training programme works and get to know her staff."

"You do mean Flight Lieutenant Adams?"

"Sorry Bill, I do not mean to be disrespectful but she is not the officer for us."

"That is alright Viv, I have already been put in the picture as to her lack of qualities."

"I just wish I could do something to help but my hands are tied she is out of my jurisdiction.

Sergeant York is taking over a married quarter today so he will be away a few days to collect his family and will be coming for authorization to be absent from place of duty, I think he has the makings to be a good Sergeant. Corporal Harper I have given the day off for services rendered and in the morning I will be leaving you about nine thirty. Mary and I are collecting some flowers from Sam Brown to put in George Miller's married quarter to welcome his wife to the station. I would like to do that with all my newcomers to married quarters. On second thoughts why shouldn't I, it is not going to break the bank and it will start us off on the right footing with them what do you think?"

"All I can say Bill, you are a very nice man and I love being part of your team, you are a big softie at heart!"

"Thank you for coming Ladies and gentlemen. I want to tell you of a new system that concerns each and every one of you. Viv and I have gone into it deeply and have come to the conclusion it will work in your favour. After the next passing out parade the team of instructors will not automatically be assigned to the new intake of recruits instead they will come here to work in the ops' room. The present ops' room staff will then be assigned to the new intake, this will work on a rotating system I am doing this for two reasons. One, to keep you up to date with the training programme and secondly, it will give you a break from Square Bashing. I will tell you here and now this is not an option but I would like your views and please speak freely."

"Yes Sergeant Williams, you are one of the old stagers and should be good to listen to."

"A break from training from my selfish point of view is something I will look forward to with great pleasure."

"What about the spell doing office work Bill?"

"That goes with the job."

"Has anyone got other thoughts?"

"Yes Sergeant Roper?"

"I think I can speak on behalf of my female colleagues. I think it is a very fair system and has been well thought out you understand our feelings because you have been there yourself."

>>> <<<

"Good morning Roy how are you this lovely morning? You look very bright and cheerful. I did not see you in the Mess last night, Derwent and I wondered where you were."

"I had a right good night Bill, I met Barbara and we went for a drive round."

"Down lover's lane?"

"Well you could say that. We had a good chat and you will never guess what she suggested."

"If you are going to embarrass me Roy I don't want to know."

"Give over you daft beggar, what do you think I am?"

"Go on then, surprise me."

"She said we should take some leave together; I could not believe my ears."

‘Thanks Helen,’ Bill said to himself. “Go on, tell me more then…”

“We are going to get some holiday brochures and have a good browse through them then put in for leave together then it will be ‘Adios Amigos’.”

“You fancy a trip to Spain then?”

“Either that or the Algarve, anywhere where the sun shines and not too touristy.”

“Well that *is* good news Roy I am pleased for you both, there is a snag though, when Tommy gets to know she will be getting ideas.”

“We could do a foursome Bill.”

“Not on your Nellie, this is one time when you two want to be on your own, forget RAF March put it out of your mind and enjoy each other’s company. Whatever you do Roy, do not mention a foursome to Tommy she would be on to it in a flash. Look, I will see you later, can I have George’s key? Then Mary and I can get cracking with the flowers.”

He and Mary went to see Sam.

“Good morning Mary, Bill, I have the flowers all ready for you, come on into the greenhouse.” He showed them two bunches of mixed flowers in containers.

“There you are Mary,” he said. “Are you satisfied with what you asked for? and these containers will show them off a treat.”

“You have done us proud Sam,” said Mary, “they are beautiful, aren’t they Bill?”

“Indeed they are and are a credit to your green fingers Sam, now what do we owe you?”

“Not a thing” replied Sam, “it is as much a pleasure me giving you them as much as you have appreciated receiving them.”

“I’ll tell you what then,” said Bill, will you accept a donation for your brew-ups and don’t say no because whether you like it or not you are getting it with our thanks.”

“Okay then, if you put it that way.”

Mary then got hold of him and kissed him on the cheek. “You are a very nice and generous man Sam Brown and I think Bill has something he wants to ask you.”

“Sam, I want to do something similar for my new staff, they are away at the moment bringing their families down into quarters. At present I will only need two bunches I will leave you to choose them, but I will let you know when I will need them which will be in a matter of a few days. Is that all right with you?”

“Of course, that is no problem anytime you want some just let me know.”

“Are you ready then Mary? Let us go and deliver our little surprise. As he was leaving he slipped a five pound note into Sam’s apron pocket. “Thanks old timer.”

On the way to the house he asked Mary. "What is the gen on this dining-in night you are organising?"

"All will be revealed soon, we are just tying up a few loose ends then a notice will go up in the Mess in plenty of time for the members to get organised especially for the ones with families. I must ask them how many will want baby sitters because I can organise them from the young girls who would like to earn a bit of spending money."

"That is great Mary you certainly sound very organised and I can see it going down a treat. I am not as organised I am sorry to say because I have yet to get an officer to be our Mess President. I would like Wings to do it he would enjoy mingling with us."

"Who the heck is Wings?" she asked.

"Flight Lieutenant Cody, we can't keep calling him by his full title and Wings fits him perfectly."

"You fellows, what are you like?"

"Here is the house, let us get the job done then I will try and get to see the Wingco'."

"It is a good job Sam had these containers because I cannot find a single flower vase Bill, we must tell George to return them to Sam when they have finished with them. I have made out a little card saying 'Welcome to RAF March' George will know where they have come from."

"Okay, let us lock up and return the key to Roy.

"Mission accomplished Roy, thanks for getting the key for us. Now, another favour which you will like doing, will you ring Barbara and ask her if I can have a few minutes with the OC.?"

"But of course; you have come to the right man. I will do it immediately. Hello Barbara pet, it's only me… how are you? Busy? Is there any chance of Bill Barrett having a few minutes with the Wing Commander? Yes I will hang on. Okay I will do that. Thanks, luv you. Yes I know, bye. You can go straight away Bill."

"Thanks Roy" then with a big grin, "luv you too"

"Get out you ungrateful sod and stop taking the Mickey!"

"Come in Mr Barrett." Bill gave him a smart salute. "I am sorry but I can only spare you a couple of minutes, now what can I do for you?"

"We need a Sergeants Mess President sir I am turning the Mess into a proper Sergeants Mess and the finishing touches is a President. I have just had a Mess meeting and as chairman I had to adopt the Presidents role. Very soon we are starting with a dining-in night where as you well know sir a President is a must."

"Indeed he is, now you have given me the problem of who to nominate."

"Do you mind sir if I can make a suggestion?"

"I would be very happy for you to do so Mr Barrett it will save me a headache, who have you in mind?"

"Flight Lieutenant Cody sir."

"Why do you want him?"

"He is a young officer who is very keen to learn by starting right at the bottom, my opinion sir he has got the makings to become a fine officer and I want to help him all I can. Making him President will not only add another string to his bow but it will give him a boost in confidence."

"I think you have taken him under your wing Mr Barrett, I approve of that and I wish you every success, he is a lucky young man. Very well, you have got your President and I will break the news to him gently which initially may be quite a shock but I will soften the blow by informing him that you are the Mess Chairman."

"Thank you very much sir. I will take good care of him."

"I have no fear of that Mr Barrett and thank you."

Bill saluted then made his exit.

He returned to tell Roy his news.

"I just do not know how you do it Bill Barrett, one way or another you always get your own way in the end, when you were born you must have been blessed with the Good Sign. Anyway we now have a President and of our own choosing too, I hate to think who we would have got had we left it to the Wingco'. Mind you he would not have trusted a plonker with that position."

"Mary tells me the entertainment committee is doing well organising the dining-in night with just a few loose ends to tidy up then she can put the information on the Mess notice board even to organising baby sitters for the families. *They* will have to pay the baby sitters of course."

"I am looking forward to that Bill it is such along time since we had one and I am sure the families are too. You know, the entertainments committee are really doing a great job they are so enthusiastic about their responsibilities."

CHAPTER 10

Flight Lieutenant Cody knocked on Bill's office door and entered. "Good morning Mr Barrett I am reporting for my first day of tuition."

Bill stood up, "Good morning sir, this is a pleasant surprise, come and sit yourself down, can I get you a brew?"

"Not at the moment thanks I just want to get started on my training course first."

"Very well then let us go and meet your instructors, do you want to leave your hat in here sir? You don't want to be prancing about the ops' room with that stuck on your head all the time."

"Good idea Mr Barrett."

When they entered the room, everyone stopped what they were doing and stood to attention.

“Carry on please” Wings said.

“Sir, I would like you to meet my second in command Flight Sergeant Viv Anderson.”

Wings went to Viv and shook her hand warmly. “You led the BlueBelles in that famous victory in the Millennium Dome I saw the recording, you are still the toast of the RAF it is a real pleasure and an honour to shake you by the hand. That victory is still a good topic in Officer Messes especially from WRAF officers; we men have certainly got something to live up to.”

“Thank you sir that is very kind of you but so many people who were involved in it shares the credit.”

“This is the rest of the ops’ staff sir.”

He nodded to them and said, “Hello, I will be working with you all hoping your expertise will rub off on me.”

“The Flight Sergeant will be your main instructor in here but as you progress she will farm you out to the other staff, it is all hands-on learning from now on.”

“Good” he said enthusiastically. Before we start can we now have that brew?”

>>> <<<

“Welcome back Sergeant Fell, how did you get on with your flittng?”

“It went really well, the MOD up at Chatworth was very co-operative and the move into quarters here went very smoothly. The wife seems to like the environment she likes the pretty little village as she calls it.”

“What about the kids Alan?”

“As you could expect, loads of tears, you know the usual parting promises, don’t forget to write etc. They will soon find fresh friends then all the promises will be forgotten.”

“Did you know you will be having a reunion with one of your ex Corporals?

“No, who will that be Bill?”

“Corporal Harper.”

“Well that is great, we did form a very good team in the end who is he teamed up with?”

“Sergeant York a new man we have got, he has also gone off to bring his family into quarters. Young Harper is in the ops’ room now working, we had another Corporal he is now waiting his discharge in the guardroom, you will hear all about it later. Look Alan it is too late for you to get back in harness today, go and have a chat with young Harper but don’t leave just yet and will you ask Viv to send one of the WRAF Corporals in? He then got on the phone to Sam Brown. “Sam, Bill Barrett here, will you make me a bunch of welcome flowers up please, I am sending a Corporal (w) to collect them, no, just wrap them in paper please, thanks Sam I will see you later.”

A Corporal (w) knocked and came in.

"You wanted to see me sir?"

"Yes, will you go and bring me a bunch of flowers from Sam Brown at the Market Garden please. You know where it is."

"Oh yes sir."

"Very good, now take your time there is no rush."

"Here you are Alan take these for your wife to welcome her to RAF March."

"Why thank you Bill, that is very kind of you, she will be delighted and it will put me in her good books too."

"Is Sergeant Dixon still at Chatworth?

"He is but now feeling more unsettled after I told him what life was like here. He says he would give anything for a posting here and would I please ask you if you had room for one of your old trainees?"

"I wish I could Alan, I have great respect for him but as you know I have my full quota of staff. If you are still in contact tell him I have him in mind and at the first opportunity I will have him join me and that is a promise."

"Thanks Bill he will be delighted to know that, I had better get these flowers home I don't want them wilting on me or I will be in the dog-house."

A couple of days later when Sergeant York reported back for duty Bill went through the same ritual of presenting him flowers for his wife. Not expecting such treatment he was dumbstruck. "Thank you very much sir, what a lovely gesture, the wife will be over the moon when she sees these and we also owe you a big debt of gratitude for using your influence in getting us married quarters so quickly."

"I hope you and your family settle down quickly and I hope your stay is a happy one... One thing you should know. You have now only one Corporal; there is another one in the pipeline who will make up your team. I will leave Corporal Harper to fill you in with the details you have had a lucky let-off in that respect. Take the rest of the day off and report for duty tomorrow morning."

"Thank you very much sir."

"How is our star pupil doing Viv?"

"He is doing very well and picking the system up pretty quick."

"How are the rest of the team getting on with him?"

"They all are working well together, give them their due they show their respect and he is trying his best to be that little bit informal. At the same time he does listen and take notice of them when he is being corrected. You know Bill I am right proud of that team in the way they have approached working with their training officer and he is enjoying every minute of it. What is his next assignment when he has finished in here?"

"I will place him with one of the drill teams they can put him through his paces. When he has finished his schooling he will know what it is all about you can be sure of that and it will be much sooner than even he thought."

>>> <<<

Later that morning Bill's phone rang.

"Hello Bill, Helen Fraser. Tomorrow morning you are to attend a meeting with the Station Commander in the Conference Room at 10:00am and you must be seated by 09:55."

"What is going on Helen?"

"I only know it is very important; all the heads of the training staff have to attend."

"Do you know who will be in the chair Helen?"

"The Station Commander."

"If you trying to contact Flight Lieutenant Cody to tell him? He is here with me doing a training course."

"Oh good, thanks Bill, I wondered where he had vanished. Yes please, put him on will you?"

Bill called, "Sir, telephone for you."

He then waited outside the office.

"Okay Mr Barrett"

Bill went back in. "It sounds quite serious don't you think? You have no idea what it is about have you?"

"Not a clue sir, I could not even hazard a guess, the more I think about it the worse it gets obviously it is a training problem because all the heads are to attend."

"We shall just have to wait and see," said Wings I hope it is not going to interfere with my personal training. Hey Ho, back to the grind, I will learn nothing standing here."

Bill's phone rang.

"Hello Bill, Mary here, have you been summoned to the big meeting tomorrow?"

"Yes Mary and I have no idea what it is about."

"I don't like the sound of it Bill, I have a gut feeling that we are not going to like whatever it is."

"Mary don't get yourself worked up it might just be something and nothing and have little or no bearing on us, just leave it and see what happens and Mary, do not lose any sleep over it."

"Okay Bill. By the way George came in to see me a little while ago to thank us for the flowers, his wife was thrilled to bits. He will thank you when he sees you. "I know it was you two who did the honours who else would it have been," he said.

"Thanks Mary, I'll be seeing you."

When Viv came into the office he told her all about it.

"Oh dear," she said that does not sound so good but whatever it is I hope it is in our favour."

"So do I" replied Bill, "we will find out soon."

By five minutes to nine Flight Lieutenant Cody, WO Barrett and WO Butcher were seated at the conference table. At ten o'clock the Station Commander and the Officer Commanding entered the room.

Everyone stood as a mark of respect.

"Sit down please. I have called this meeting to tell you some sad news. Statistics show there has been a severe drop in the recruitment of both airmen and airwomen in the last twelve months, it had been hoped the victory by the BlueBelles would boost……

He was interrupted when the door flew open and Flight Lieutenant Adams burst into the room. She was full of apologies for being late. The CO glared at her then pointed to an empty chair.

He continued. "Would boost recruitment, sadly that did not happen not in the numbers that were expected."

"Sir," said Flight Lieutenant Adams interrupting, "I am afraid I am lost, I do not understand what is going on."

"Madam!" barked the CO. "You were lost when you could not find this room on time and I do not intend to start at the beginning just for your benefit. You must try and pick up the thread as I proceed."

He continued. "There are no signs of any increase in recruits in the foreseeable future. Against all advice from our top brass the Lords at the Ministry in their so called wisdom have decided that in the present circumstances one Training Establishment will be sufficient to meet the present demands for recruit training."

This statement brought gasps of disbelief from everyone.

"In my manifest it states that two establishments will be closed down and placed in 'Care and Maintenance' and their training personnel will be dispersed to various units throughout the RAF. The one remaining Training Establishment will be responsible for training four flights of recruits. Two flights of airmen, one flight of airwomen and one specialised mixed flight of airmen and airwomen who show officer potential. The drill instructors for that particular flight are to be hand picked and to be of the highest integrity. I see you are more than eager to know which of the three has been chosen. RAF Chatworth is to close, also RAF Camberly along with the Instructor Training School based there. That leaves RAF March as the only remaining candidate and from the smiles I see on your faces you have guessed right, we are the chosen one."

"Brilliant" and enthusiastic applause greeted this announcement.

"Apparently it was no contest, all our top brass were unanimous in that decision.

"Ladies and gentlemen we can thank Warrant Officer Barrett for getting RAF March that decision, he has worked tirelessly with dedication to get this station to this status and by golly it has paid off. Mr Barrett, you have three months in which to reshape our training programme and to hand pick the personnel of *your* choice, not an easy task for you but an essential one."

"Are there any questions?"

"Yes sir," spoke up Flight Lieutenant Adams. Am I to presume I will keep my position as Officer i/c WRAF Training?"

"You presume wrong Madam," replied the CO. "Mr Barrett has the sole responsibility and carte-blanche' in choosing the training staff. As far as you and Flight Lieutenant Cody are concerned he will approach me with his recommendations and I alone will make the final decision on that count."

"You expect me a commissioned officer to accept the decision of some Senior NCO? That would be insulting and an affront to my rank and character it could jeopardise my career, I would appeal to the highest authority."

"Madam, you are in a hole and I strongly recommend that you stop digging. Now kindly leave this room and wait for me in my secretary's office."

She jumped to her feet and stormed out.

"I do apologise for that outburst. If there are no more questions then you can take those happy smiling faces back to your staff to tell them the good news. Thank you.

Mr Barrett I would like a word. You know what is going on training wise I would like you to give your honest opinion to the Wing Commander and myself in confidence of course of Flight Lieutenant Adams."

"That is easy sir she is a liability to the WRAF. She shows not the slightest interest in anyone below her own rank. She is incompetent as far as training is concerned and very self opinionated; her chief asset is talking down to people. She definitely tops my unwanted list sir."

"Thank you Mr Barrett that is all I wanted to know, you have made life easier for me once more."

"That goes with the rank sir." He saluted and left.

"There goes one of the finest men I have ever met Eric."

"My sentiments entirely sir, we are lucky to have him."

"Come on let us go and sort this silly woman out."

"Send Flight Lieutenant Adams in please Helen."

"You may go in now Ma'am," Helen informed her.

She bounced into the office and made her way to a chair.

"You will please stand Madam this is not a social visit, furthermore as Station Commander I do merit a salute from my subordinates."

She immediately saluted.

"You are here primarily because of your disgraceful display of bad manners and lack of respect at my meeting. You have opened my eyes to your real character which I find in the present circumstances intolerable. For that kind of behaviour I will not accept any apology from you.

We will now proceed to your post of i/c WRAF training. Tell me what staff you have and their names please."

"I have a Warrant Officer, some Sergeants and Corporals."

"Let us start at the beginning. What is the name of your Warrant Officer?"

"You mean that woman in the meeting sir?"

"If she is your Warrant Officer indeed I do require her name."

"I will have to think for a moment sir, I am almost sure she is my Warrant Officer, I am sorry sir but I am feeling rather fuddled."

"Could it be Anderson by any chance?"

"That is the one sir it was on the tip of my tongue."

"Do you have a Flight Sergeant by any chance?"

"Oh no sir only Sergeants."

"How many Sergeants have you and can you remember *their* names?"

"Only two their names escape me for the moment." She was getting herself deeper and deeper into a quagmire.

"I think you had better sit down Madam."

She did as she was told.

"Now I shall start again at the beginning. Your WO is Warrant Officer Butcher. Your non-existent Flight Sergeant is Flight Sergeant Anderson, don't you remember? She is the one who led the BlueBelles to victory. How could you not know she was a member of your staff?"

"Oh my God," she shrieked.

"You also have *FOUR* Sergeants Roper, Price, Dean and North.

I am the Commanding Officer and even I know their names. You have shown by your attitude and incompetence you are no longer fit to hold the post of Recruit Training Officer. Therefore I am relieving you of that post with immediate effect."

She broke down in tears and sobbed. "Who will replace me then?"

"Warrant Officer Butcher."

She screamed. "What! That woman, what does she know? She is only a SNCO."

"Madam! Warrant Officer Butcher was wearing the RAF uniform when you were wearing a gym slip!"

"What will happen to me now?"

"First I suggest you see our Medical Officer, if you are capable you will clear your desk and vacate your office. You will then confine yourself to the Officers Mess to await me contacting you. In the meantime I will send a report of my findings to Command. You may leave now."

She got up from the chair and walked to the door to leave.

The CO called after her. "Haven't you forgotten something Flt.Lt? A salute would be in order."

"Go to hell," she mouthed.

"What a nice woman!" remarked the Wing Commander.

"Yes indeed!" replied the CO.

He buzzed Helen. "Ask Warrant Officer Butcher to report to me please?"

When Mary arrived she saluted.

"Warrant Officer Butcher, how do you feel about taking over the post of Officer i/c WRAF Recruit Training on a permanent basis?"

Mary was gob smacked. When she regained her composure she replied with a great big smile. "It will be my pleasure and privilege sir."

"You will take over with immediate effect but if I were you I would delay until tomorrow before taking over the Office if you follow my drift?"

"I do sir, but could I not stay in my office in SSQ it will suit the purpose just as well?"

"Very well if that is what you want but do not forget to change your title on the door," he said with a smile. He held out his hand and congratulated her, so did the Wing Commander saying, "I think we have made the right choice."

"Thank you gentlemen." she saluted then made her exit, albeit on cloud nine.

The first thing she did when she returned to her office was phone' Bill Barrett.

"Hello Bill, I want you to be the first to know that I have just come from the CO's Office as Officer i/c WRAF Recruit Training on a permanent basis." She heard a yell of delight.

"Brilliant Mary and congratulations do not go away I am coming over to give you a great big kiss."

He went into the ops' room. "Attention please, I have some breaking news; Warrant Officer Butcher has been appointed Officer i/c WRAF Recruit Training."

Immediately there were cheers and applause from the staff.

"Flight Lieutenant Cody, will you and Flight Sergeant Anderson come with me please?"

He took them in his office and asked them if they would like to accompany him to SHQ to congratulate Mary?

They both said they would be delighted to.

Bill knocked on Mary's door. "Come in she cried." When the three of them came forward and each kissed her with their congratulations her eyes filled up with emotion.

"Thank you so much, I am sorry I have nothing to celebrate with but if you all care to come in the Mess bar tonight I will buy you a drink. They chatted for a little while and when Bill left the room they assumed he was going to the toilet. He went to tell George and sent him to Mary's office then carried on to the orderly room to tell Roy who accompanied Bill back. Mary was showered with best wishes and kisses.

"I feel like a VIP she said."

"And so you are was the reply." Then began the singing of "For She's a jolly good Fellow."

CHAPTER 11

Bill called Viv into his office and asked Flight Lieutenant Cody "Will you take charge in here sir? Flight Sergeant Anderson and I are going to be very busy for some time,"

"No problem Mr Barrett, I will have a guard standing at your door."

"We have another comedian with us Viv!"

"Don't you think we have enough with you three crackpots on the station?"

"Viv, we are going to have a few headaches, I have to do some whittling out of our training staff now that we will have only four flights to contend with. This is a part of my job I do not like but the responsibility rests on my shoulders, I just hope my judgement will be right even though I will have to make some people extremely unhappy that is why I need your help to make sure I do the right thing."

"It will be horrible when we have to tell our friends sorry but you are surplus to requirements then go and replace them with someone else. Bill, we must rule out sentimentality or we will let down the people who entrust us with providing the best training for young people coming into the service with high hopes of a good career. That is what the RAF want and we have to make sure we give it them."

"Thanks Viv you are talking sense, if we let it worry us we would have sleepless nights and we would be ripe for a medical discharge. It is our job, right; let's get on with it then. The first thing I suggest we do is figure out how many training staff we will need in total? Once we have reached that decision we can then decide who to part with.

I reckon we will need eighteen in total, twelve for on the job training and six in the ops' room for reserves and we have twenty-three, we now have to sort out which five have to go. There is one special RAF Sergeant I want called Dixon and I will have to replace one with him, but who?" I have been thinking about this special flight Viv, the Sergeant will have to be RAF and what do you say to an RAF and a WRAF Corporal in his team? The reserves for them would have to come from the float."

"What is so special about Sergeant Dixon?"

"Dixon and Fell have worked as a team under me before and I know their qualities I rate them both in my top three Sergeant Drill Instructors. Now do you agree to an RAF Corporal and a Corporal (w) for No.1 flight?"

"I like that especially with WRAF involved but who is the third in your top three?"

"Joe Franks! And the reason I am not giving him the No.1 flight is because I don't think he can handle women as good as he does with the men. That is the only way I can do it I cannot have a reserve team just for No.1 flight, Command would not allow it. Are you happy so far Viv?"

"I am not happy but I agree with what you are doing."

"Ours is not to reason why, ours is to do or get thrown to the wolves! Have you got any paracetamol tablets handy? Because this is where we are going to need them. First of all I must phone Roy Shaw… Hello Roy, Bill here, can you stop the posting-in of the Corporal who was to replace Corporal Evans, I have now got my full quota of RAF Corporals thanks Roy. What's that? Bill Williams has got an overseas posting? No, I don't know if he will be pleased or not but I am, it solves a big problem for me. Do you want me to send him down to see you? Immediately, No problem, thanks again Roy you have saved some headaches at this end, see you later.

Will you send one of your Corporals to tell Sergeant Williams he has to report to WO Shaw please Viv?"

When she returned to the office, Bill told her. "That was a life saver for us Sergeant Dixon will now replace Sergeant Williams. We now have two WRAF Sergeants and three WRAF Corporals who are surplus to requirements. Shall we go through the list to choose them on their merits?"

"I am afraid we have no option Bill," she said with a deep sigh.

"I feel the same way Viv but it has to be done. Come on old girl and guide me if you think I am making the wrong choice."

They knuckled down to the task until it was finalised.

"I think they would have been my choice Bill but isn't it sad?"

"We will keep this to ourselves for the time being, you never know what can turn up. No.1 flights of both airmen and airwomen pass out in two weeks time and only the airmen's flight will be replaced by a mixed flight. Two weeks after them, both No.2 flights of airmen and airwomen pass out. The airwomen will not be replaced the airmen will. Two weeks following that both No.3 flights of airmen and airwomen will pass out, both flights will be replaced and that is how it will go Viv. Shall we go right through it from the beginning? Just to make sure we are satisfied?" "Right come on, back to the grindstone."

After one or two doubts and assessments they decided to stick to the original choice.

"Thanks Viv you have been a great help, now we can relax for a bit."

As he said that there came a knock on the door. "Come in," he called.

Bill Williams came in with a big smile. "I have come to hand you my notice sir I will be leaving you soon."

"Why?" asked Bill in mock surprise? "Have you got another job?"

"No, it is just me being a bit daft, I have got an overseas posting to Cyprus, I am chuffed to bits and the wife will be when I tell her."

"Tomorrow morning instead of reporting in here, your Corporals will look after the flight for a little while you go and see the SWO, he has just returned from Cyprus he will be able to give you some useful tips for yourself and your family"

"Thanks Bill I appreciate that although in a way I will be sorry to leave this set up it is a good posting."

After he had left Bill rang the SWOs office. "Hello Ian, Bill Barrett here, is George handy? Put him on please. Hello George will it be alright if I send one of my Sergeants to see you in the morning for a chat?"

"Why, what's he done?"

"Only got a posting to Cyprus I told him to come and see you for some tips will that be alright with you?"

"Aye, tell him to be here at nine o' clock, if he is any later I will find him a job."

"See you later, and thanks."

"Is Bill out there nattering Viv? If he is, tell him to get himself in here."

"You wanted to see me boss?"

"Yes, nine o' clock at the SWO's office in the morning and don't be late or he will find you a job if you are?"

"Thanks again Bill."

"Don't mention it Bill!"

"Now that is over and done with let us get back to sanity. How is our star pupil Viv, is he ready for the second stage?"

"He has certainly picked the procedures up pretty quick, give him another two days then I would say yes he is ready to move on."

"Good, I will place him entirely in charge of the ops' room for the next two days and we will keep out of his way and let him get on with it. I will have a word with Alan Fell when I see him I will be placing Wings in his care. Anyway it is now lunch time, let us shut up shop and see what culinary delight the chef has put on for us."

At lunch he sat with Roy and Derwent who asked. "Has anyone got any news worth mentioning?"

"I have had a very busy morning in the office," spoke Bill; "Viv has been upset because we are trimming down the staff in readiness for the big change. I can understand because we have got a damned good staff and they are all nice people but there is nowt' we can do about it only do as we are instructed. I think you had better do a bit of consoling tonight Derwent I do not know what she will be like on the day they have to leave."

“How many are you losing?” asked Roy.

“Five and they are all WRAF. Bill Williams was a turn up for the books If he had not got his posting I would have had to lose an RAF Sergeant to make room for the Sergeant I want who will fit in very well in the mixed flight, he will now replace Bill. Can I come and see you in your office after lunch Roy I need your advice on a little matter.”

“No problem Bill come and pour your heart out to me, everybody else comes to me with their problems, come and take your place in the queue.”

“Do you mean I have to queue up with the rest? Don’t I have a priority?”

“It will cost you for the privilege.”

“How much?”

“A pint tonight.”

Bill gave a sharp intake of breath. You drive a hard bargain do you think Chalky will accept a credit note?”

“Do you hear that Derwent, when was the last time you heard of a WO being skint?”

“Right now Roy, Bill makes two of us.”

“I am going to leave you two paupers to scratch each others backs would you like me to pass the hat round as I go out?”

“No way,” exploded Derwent. “You would pocket the takings!”

Roy stormed off with loud laughter following him the rest of the diners looking to see what the noise was about. Barbara said to Viv. “When will those three crackpots grow up?”

“Give them their due Barbara they have certainly put some life into the Mess and that is what it has needed for too long. “But they are still daft!”

“Can I come in?” asked Bill poking his head round the door of Roy’s office.

“Why, do you want a loan?”

“No oh wise one, advice.”

“I am too soft hearted with you lot, come on pour your heart out but make it quick I go to dinner in four hours time.”

“These five WRAF I have to lose. If I submit their names for posting now would they stand a better chance to get the better postings if the other two stations have not submitted theirs yet?”

“I cannot answer that Bill. It will depend on how much service they have left to do, their experience and their assessments. It is up to Records Office to make the decisions of where they are to be posted. As for submitting them for postings now, I would not know if that would make any difference. I will tell you what, being a kind hearted person that I am who nobody appreciates I will contact my friend at Records Office and ask his advice.”

“Roy, I shall now think very seriously of nominating you for a knighthood.”

Bill then went round to see Mary.

“You are a sight for sore eyes Bill Barrett, what have you been up to?”

“Had a very difficult and unpleasant task this morning Mary, Viv and I have been compiling the list of the staff that will be surplus to requirements under this new scheme.”

“Oh dear, I had forgotten about that,” said Mary. “I am not envious of you having to do that job Bill we had just got a good staff together and now it has to be decimated by how many Bill?”

“Five”

“Five?” she exclaimed loudly. “Thank goodness I was thinking there would be many more than that”

“Unfortunately Mary, they have to be all WRAF.”

“I am not going to argue about that Bill, you were authorised to make the decisions and that was final it must have been hard but knowing you, you will have been fair and no one will dispute that. Thanks Bill, you are still the best in my book, give me their names before you go.”

“Have you made any progress with the dining in night Mary?”

“As a matter of fact Bill I am ready to put up the notice for members to submit their names. You do realise we can only put a certain number of bums on seats. I must phone Tommy and ask her the number that can be accommodated. Hang on I will call her now. Tommy? Mary Butcher here, how many do you seat for a dining-in night not counting the top tables? Fifty, a comfortable fifty okay thanks Tommy. Hear that Bill? The first fifty to put their names down get the seats and that includes a guest each.”

“No Mary, the first twenty five each with a guest will cover the seats. That is not many is it? Don’t do anything yet I will go and see Tommy perhaps it is a shortage of tables that is the problem, we could always borrow some from the airmen’s mess if possible.”

He saw Jackie at reception.

“Hello Bill, you want to see Tommy?”

“Yes please Jackie.”

When she came out she greeted him with a kiss and “Hello love, I have just been speaking to Mary.”

“I know, that is why I am here. About the dining-in night, is the room too small or you have not enough tables?”

“Not enough tables my love.”

“How many more can you get in there?”

“Four which would seat another thirty two.”

“I think that would be ideal because as you know the families have not had social functions for a heck of a long time and I have a feeling they will all want to come.

Can you sweet talk Harry Jackson the catering officer for the airmen’s Mess, tell him the fix we are in and ask him if he can loan us four tables?”

“I will do what I can, stay here I will let you know in a minute or two”

She returned smiling. "No problem, his condition is I have a dance with him."

"Good old Harry. So the first forty one with a guest get seats."

"No Bill, it is the first eighty two bums that get the seats, remember not all will be bringing guests."

"I stand corrected. Mary will be really chuffed so many will get the chance to attend."

"What do I get for that sir?"

"He gave her a kiss, must go and report back to Mary."

"Four more tables Mary, that gives you another thirty-two seats, how is that?"

"Very good we should have no problem now any names or numbers below the maximum eighty two will be on stand-by."

"When is it to be held?"

"In ten days time a week on Friday."

"Why not hold it on a Saturday?"

"Because some go home for the weekend and they will certainly not want to miss out on the first function they have had in Donkey's Years! Now clear off, I have a lot of organising to do."

"Are you ready for your next phase sir?" Bill asked Wings.

"If you think I am ready for it Mr Barrett."

"Good, than I am putting you in at the sharp end with Sergeant Fell, you will be in good hands with him come on I will introduce you."

As they approached the flight Allan called the airmen to attention then saluted the officer.

"Sergeant Fell, meet your OC recruit training." They shook hands. Bill continued. "Sir is in his second phase of training after passing his first phase in the ops' room. You are to be his instructor until you are satisfied he can handle a flight of recruits on his own from scratch. He is doing this voluntarily because he feels that as our OC he should be able to talk to us about the various aspects of recruit training at our level. One important thing I want you to remember Sergeant, sir has asked he should not be mollycoddled. Grant him his wishes." He then saluted Wings and wished him "Good Luck sir."

CHAPTER 12

"Bill, Roy here, I have heard from Record Office and I am informed it does not matter when you submit those names they will all be selected to fit their respective slots."

"Thanks Roy."

"Viv! I would like you to come with me to Alan Fell's flight; Wings is going to do his practical test for us he does not know it but he soon will when we arrive."

"Why do you call him Wings?"

"Because giving him his full title is long and drawn out, Wings is short but still a mark of respect as opposed to the other names we could call him."

"Oh yes, I never thought of that and it suits him, he would be chuffed with it if he knew."

When they arrived they saluted Wings then called Alan fell over and asked him about sir's progress. "Is he ready for a test run Alan?"

"Definitely, he is a natural."

"Well we will soon see."

He called Wings over. "Sir, this is your big day, the moment of truth, now is the time for you to show us we have not been wasting our time, you have got ten minutes!"

Alan came forward, saluted and said. "Number three flight Sir"

Wings returned the salute and replied. "Thank you Sergeant Fell, I will now take over."

Bill, Viv and Alan retired some way back to watch.

Wings took the airmen through all the basic drill movements they responded to his firm and authoritative commands. He did not shout or bellow but appeared to have the knack of making his voice carry.

Alan remarked. "He is certainly making a difference to those lads they did not show that marching rhythm for me."

"I am impressed," said Bll. "What do you think Viv?"

"He is good, now we have someone in command that can speak our language and know what we are talking about regarding recruit training. Well done Wings."

At the conclusion Wings stood the flight at ease then thanked them. The three judges applauded him and even the airmen joined in. The judges marched towards him and saluted, then announced. "You are now our Honorary Chief Drill Instructor congratulations," they each shook his hand. After thanking them and beaming all over his face he called. "Sergeant Fell! Take over number three flight," adding "please" in an undertone in respect.

Alan saluted him and replied. "YES SIR!"

>>> <<<

Bill rang Barbara Page the OC's PA. "Hello Barbara, Bill Barrett here, yes, everything is going well can you get me an appointment with the Wingco' please? Whenever he can fit me in, I will be in my office, thanks Barbara."

Half an hour later Barbara rang to say he could be seen now.

When Bill entered her office she buzzed the Wingco' saying. "Mr Barrett is here sir."

"Send him in Barbara."

Bill saluted. "Sit yourself down, have you a problem Mr Barrett?"

"No sir I wanted to report to you that I have selected my staff except for just one."

"Carry on then and tell me about it."

"I have chosen two WRAF Sergeants and three WRAF Corporals to be surplus to requirements."

"Why have you chosen all WRAF?"

"Because we will have only one flight of the WRAF to train now that we are losing two, even the mixed flight of airmen and airwomen only warrant one WRAF Corporal.

We lose only one airmen's flight but not their instructors; who will then become our reserve team. Now one of the RAF Sergeants has just got an overseas posting which makes me one RAF Sergeant short that is very fortunate for me because I have been waiting to get hold of a Sergeant who I have personally trained and would like to head the mixed flight. That is the main reason I came to see you sir."

"You want me to get him posted here, right?"

"Yes sir."

"You have worked this out very carefully Mr Barrett; the Station Commander certainly knew what he was doing when he gave you what must have been a very onerous task. Tell me what is your plan of action for the change over?"

"In two weeks time one flight of airmen and one of airwomen will be passing out. The airwomen's flight will not be replaced but the airmen's flight will be replaced by a mixed flight. Two weeks after that a flight of airmen and a flight of airwomen again will pass out. The airwomen's flight will not be replaced but the airmen's will. Two weeks after that two flights pass out and both airmen's and airwomen's flights will be replaced. So in a matter of six weeks we will have, two flights of airmen, one flight of airwomen and one mixed flight of both airmen and airwomen and the two weekly pass out cycle carries on."

"Mr Barrett you have sent my head spinning. I must congratulate you on working that puzzle out, to me it is just that, a puzzle and I am sure it will all work like clockwork. Give Barbara the Sergeant's details and I will send it on its way. Thank you Mr Barrett, it has been very puzzling but very informative, if I could only understand it. The problem is, how am I going to explain that to the Station Commander?"

"It is tough at the top sir."

"Indeed it is Mr Barrett."

Bill then saluted and left the office.

He went to see Barbara and gave her all the details appertaining to Sergeant Dixon.

On his return he made a point of seeing Alan Fell. "Do you still keep in touch with Bob Dixon, Alan?"

"Oh yes, I call him now and again but mostly he calls me to ask for news from here, he is so eager to get down here Bill."

"Ring him tonight and tell him to expect a posting to RAF March any day now, I have just come from an interview with the Wingco' and he has just sanctioned it."

"Alan was so delighted he grabbed Bill's hand and shook it very warmly. Thanks Bill that will really make his day and thank you for our families are very close."

"Only too happy to help Alan it will be worth it to me having him on my staff."

The following morning Alan Fell came to see Bill. "I phoned Bob last night Bill and he nearly deafened me, "Brilliant" he shouted, please thank Bill for me Alan, his wife butted in, "Thank him from all of us Alan" I could swear she was crying with happiness. Even my wife got into the act; thank him from all of us too and our kids are delighted their friends are coming."

"I want him here and settled down in married quarters within the next two weeks. He will have a day or two to get conversant with the training programme in the ops' room. Then he will take charge of the first intake of the airmen and airwomen's special flight. His two Corporals will be Harper and WRAF James. That flight has to be special because the recruits will have been chosen for their qualities to be potential officers. So you can tell Bob Dixon what his role will be here. Do you remember at Chatworth when I told him, "Your turn will come? Well it finally has."

"He deserves that break Bill and you know that he will never let *you* down."

The phone rang. "WO Barrett speaking. Hi Roy, that is great, well will you do me the usual favour please, yes please and can you let me know soon, I have his pal here he would like to be able to tell him tonight then he can begin sorting things out without wasting any time. Yes I do realise how much I rely on you but you will get a pint tonight with pleasure, see you Roy and thanks."

"Bob will be here on Sunday and Roy will try to get him a quarter as soon as he can he is going to ring MOD right away and find out what the chances are and when. If you would like to hang on for a little while we may get a result soon."

"Thanks Bill, I keep thanking you but that is the only way I can tell you how grateful I am, I will let Bob speak for himself."

"You know this mixed flight is to be a special flight Alan I am putting Bob in charge of it because like you said he deserves a break and remember it is his turn, you were first choice for that flight at Chatworth. Whenever he is absent for any reason you, and you alone take over until he returns then you go back to your own flight you know one another's style therefore the recruits will not suffer any change in the method. What do you think of that Alan? Be honest with me if you have any doubts at all."

"Doubts! I would not have complained if one of the others had got that privilege, honestly I will admit I am chuffed to bits Bob has got it, you have made a great team there Bill with us two and the two Corporals The only results you will get will be good ones, I promise you that, for you certainly deserve it."

The phone rang. "WO Barrett, Hi Roy what news have you for us? Bloody Nora! That is quick, is it a record? I must make my way to go and thank Tom Hardcastle personally, you will get your thanks tonight, and you have already made one family happy the other one will be when he gets the news tonight, thanks Roy.

There is a Quarter ready for him to take over first thing Tuesday morning Alan and as far as I am concerned he can leave for Chatworth when the take-over has been finalised so tell him to get organised with the MOD there to do a quick March-Out. Now here is the icing on the cake. He is moving in next door to you!"

"That is unbelievable," gasped Alan. "Where in this Air-Force could you equal that? There is going to be some whooping and cheering on that phone tonight and at my house when I go home and tell them."

"When are we to break the bad news to the girls?" asked Viv.

"I think we should leave it until after the dining-in night, we do not want to spoil their pleasure. Incidentally I have decided Bob Dixon will take over the mixed flight. How are things in the ops' is everything going alright need I ask?"

"Funnily enough Bill it seems very quiet now that Wings as gone, I think we all miss him."

"Seeing that it is pretty quiet around here I will take a trip to the Mess and see how Chalky is coping with his ordering of the beverages etc. I fancy he will be a bit nervous with it being his first one and he will welcome all the help he can get."

His first stop was at the Mess reception desk. "Hello Mr Barrett do you want to see Tommy?"

"Yes please Jill if she is available?"

"When Tommy came out they kissed. "What have you come for this time love?"

"Just to check on how you are doing with the preparations for the big night and if you have hit any snags or need help?"

"No, everything is under control thank you."

"Have you given Mary a list of the number of helpers you want from her?"

"Yes, anything else sir you think I may have overlooked?"

"When will you get the tables from the airmen's mess?"

“After the airmen and women have finished their meals!”
“Who will be sitting at the top tables?”
“There will be a seating plan on display, Sherry and soft drinks will be served at reception, the guests will take their drinks into the bar and await the call to dinner.

Your responsibility will be to ensure the men do not take beer into the dining room and please inform our guests that the waiters and waitresses are there to serve the meal only and not to run personal errands for the diners. They will have enough work to do waiting on tables, you must emphasise that Bill, I have seen it happen all too often where diners have been too demanding on the staff.”

“Don’t worry love I will see to that, you have got it all organised haven’t you?”

“I *have* done it before my dear.”

“I had better go and have a word with Chalky to see how he is coping.” They kissed.

“Hello Chalky how are getting on with your ordering etc?”

“Hi Bill it has been a ruddy headache. What Fred Fox ordered and what I have had to order is mind blowing, I hope I get everything.”

“If you have any problems with the suppliers tell Roy Shaw, as secretary he will sort them out, he will stand no nonsense, do you know how many helpers you are getting?”

“Not yet, the Mess Manager is seeing to that and she knows what she is doing.”

“Well you will need at least three behind the bar a little tip is to keep one end of the bar free for ‘Waiters Only Service’ and detail a steward with the most experience to take charge of that.”

“Thanks Bill I will remember that.”

As Bill turned to leave he said. “Don’t forget your ‘Dickie’.”

Chalkie looked at him with a quizzical expression.

Bill laughed. “Your ‘Dickie Bow’ Chalky.”

“Oh! Yes.” Chalky replied with a little giggle.

>>> <<<

Alan Fell was at the guardroom Sunday afternoon waiting for his pal to arrive then he could show him the Mess car park and then take him to reception. It was planned that when he had settled himself in Alan would take him home where his wife would have dinner waiting for them. When Bob got through the security check he and Alan greeted each other warmly. After the guardroom procedure Alan gave Bob directions to the Mess. At reception Jackie welcomed him to the Mess and signed him in, she then gave him his room key and said. “The dining room will open in half an hour Mr Dixon.”

“Thank you,” he replied but I will be dining out shortly with Alan here and his family.”

“That is nice, If there is anything you want please let me know, I think you will find your accommodation up to scratch and if WO Barrett comes asking for you I can tell him you have gone out to dinner.”

“Please do,” answered Bob, “I will see him in the morning and looking forward to it. Thank you for everything. Come on Alan let us not keep your wife waiting I am looking forward to one of her dinners.”

After unpacking and a wash and brush up off they went to meet Mrs Fell and family.

There was great joy when he walked in, hugs and kisses from the family who were so delighted to see him again.

“Dinner will be ready in half an hour which will give you men time to have a beer then we can all have a chat about RAF March and our fairy godfather WO Barrett.”

“Before I forget,” said Alan, after you have taken over your Quarter leave us the door key then we can do what ever needs doing it will need a good dusting that is for sure and maybe odd little jobs we will make sure it is spick and span for you to walk into. How did you go on with the MOD for handing your married quarter back?”

“They were great, when I go back on Tuesday they will take it over Wednesday morning and we have practically everything boxed up. I have brought a big load down with me so there will be room for the four of us and the rest of our gear in the car.”

“After dinner,” said Alan “I will take you to the phone for you to ring home then we will store your gear in here.”

“Dinner is ready!” was the call from the kitchen.

When Bob reported to Bill to have his official arrival chit signed Bill greeted him warmly then introduced him to Viv. “I want you to met Flight Sergeant Anderson who is my second in command. This is the young man Viv who I have been trying to get for quite some time now.”

“I am very pleased to meet you Flight,” I have heard of you for you are quite a celebrity with the WRAF. When you led those girls to victory the girls at Chatworth went absolutely berserk, the whole station joined in remembering the original BlueBelles had been formed there. It is a privilege to be part of your staff. Thank you Bill and I must pre-warn you, my wife is going to give you a great big kiss when she meets you for all you have done for us and don’t be surprised if Alan’s wife follows suit.”

“Who is going to become the station’s pin-up boy then?” laughed Viv. You know Bob all the women on the station are dying to get their hands on this man.”

“Would you like to rephrase that Viv, you may be giving the wrong impression? I suppose Alan has told you the score. After taking over your

Quarter get your skates on back to Chatworth and tell Alan when you expect to be back."

"Thanks again sir, it has been a long time but you did say "Your turn will come" remember? It has been a long wait, but well worth it."

When Bob and his family finally entered their married quarter, a vase of flowers greeted them along with a Welcome to RAF March card.

CHAPTER 13

There was a hundred per cent turnout for the dining-in night. The stewards and airwomen serving at the tables did a great job of serving the meals and making sure no one went short of wine etc. Due to the excellent organisation everything went without a hitch. At the end of the meal and when the dishes had been collected came the time for speeches.

Bill, as the Chairman got to his feet and asked for the Chef and all the serving staff to come back into the dining room. "On behalf of everyone here I would like to express our thanks and gratitude for the excellent service you have provided for us this evening. To our Chef. our appreciation showed on the dinner plates, any leftovers were miniscule and if that is not a sign of excellent food I do not know what is. Thank you so much and can we book you again?"

A big "YES" was the reply.

"Ladies and gentlemen, will you please join me upstanding to show your appreciation?

"We have an hour to spare," he said as he looked down the tables after hearing groans from the men folk. "It is no good you men looking at your watches because the bar is not open yet." That brought more groans from the men and cheers from the ladies. "You know I think I will ask the committee to ban all watches from future dining-in functions". That brought loud applause from the ladies and lots of laughter all round.

"Seriously, if the rest of the evening goes as well as it has up to now it will be a great achievement for our committee and their helpers. This is our first function with many more to follow and because you good people have turned out in such large numbers it is giving our committee the encouragement they need. I want to thank Flight Lieutenant Cody for becoming our Mess President many of you will not know what his status is on this station. He is the O.C. of recruit training. By a cruel turn of fate he had to discontinue flying but it turned out to be our good fortune. He came to us and openly admitted he knew nowt' about recruit training but to his credit he decided to start at the bottom and work himself up to a position where he could talk to us about the training in our language and on an equal footing. He has done that and we the Training Staff are proud of him therefore Flight Lieutenant Cody it gives me great pleasure on behalf of your training staff to present you with this Honorary Chief Training

Instructor Award." It was an inscribed silver plated six-inch high replica of a Pace-Stick on a silver plated plinth.

"Thank you Mr Barrett this is some surprise you have given me I have never heard of anything like this happening before. It is a great honour and privilege and I am absolutely gob-smacked! Thank you everyone most kindly.

I would like to say a few words about my posting here. I was sent here not just to fly a desk but also to command personnel already very expert in the field of recruit training. How was I an ex Whiz-Kid expected to teach a grandmother to suck eggs?" That phrase brought applause and laughter from the diners. "I invited Warrant Officer Barrett to come and see me for an introduction and I put my cards on the table by telling him my situation and that I knew 'nowt' about recruit training. Ladies and gentlemen. I was then interviewed for the job!" Another burst of laughter and shouts of "Well done Bill."

"Fortunately for me I was accepted but with the proviso I did a mini-course in recruit training starting at the bottom with no holds barred!" I was accepted in the bosom of this little family with kindness and respect and receiving this award is the proudest day of my life. I am also honoured and privileged to have been chosen to be your Mess President. Thank you all so much."

When the applause had died down Bill announced. "When we leave the room will you please give us five minutes to avoid the stampede? In addition Gentlemen, please do not hassle the bar staff, as good as they are they can only serve one person each at a time. Enjoy the rest of the evening ladies and gentlemen."

As the top table filed out the diners stood in respect for the President as he left the dining room.

The little group got drinks from the bar and stood discretely in a corner having a chat until the President excused himself. "Thank you very much for a delightful meal, company and this little beauty holding up his award, wait till I show this in the Officers Mess," he said, "it may give some of them ideas, Goodnight ladies and gentlemen."

Bill showed him out.

"Thanks again Mr Barrett, this award means a lot to me."

"You have earned it and with it our respect. Goodnight sir."

The rest of the evening was a success the band played for all tastes; Bill did manage to have a dance with Tommy in between her supervising the clearing up of the dining room. Bill and Viv were in great demand from the wives who wanted to hear first hand of the great BlueBelles victory. Alan Fell introduced him to his wife who said. "Come here you darling man and let me kiss you."

Alan said "Bob was unable to come being so busy just moving into quarters besides he could not get his name on the guest list it was full in no time at all."

At midnight the band played the last waltz then the revellers began to drift away. Chalky's helpers collected all the glasses then they were stood down. The dining room was back to normal with the help of extra willing hands. The airwomen had been stood down earlier.

"There are only the tables to be returned to the airmen's mess," Tommy told Bill. I will now leave you my love I am really jiggered, a hot shower a brew then into bed."

"I will see you tomorrow or I should say later today," said Bill as he kissed her goodnight. "You did a fabulous job for us tonight."

He went to the bar where there were still a few drinkers; the main topic was the success of the evening and how everyone had contributed to it.

"It looks like we may have turned this mess into a Sergeants Mess at last," said Roy. "I will drink to that said Jock Webster we could not have had a better start."

Their little group then bade Chalky goodnight.

"No doubt I will see you crackpots tonight, or will I?"

"It could be the 'Hare' of the dog," laughed Roy.

"What on earth are *you* on about?" asked Chalky.

"Hare, H.A.R.E. the March Hare, Get it?"

"Will somebody take this guy home? He is doing my head in," exploded Chalkie while everybody else curled up laughing.

"Come on Roy let us get you home," Bill said still laughing. "Goodnight all."

>>> <<<

Bill rang Wings "Hello sir, WO Barrett here, can I come and see you please?"

"Of course come right away."

Bill saluted. "Good morning sir."

"Good morning Mr Barrett what can I do for you, are you an instructor short and you want me to stand in?" he said laughing.

"Not exactly sir we are about to lose five of them."

"Oh dear, tell me more."

"I have to lose five of the WRAF because we are losing two flights of airwomen under the new directive. I have chosen the five who will be surplus to requirements: two Sergeants and three Corporals. At the next passing out parade we lose one flight of airmen, which will be replaced with that special mixed flight. We also lose one airwomen's flight, which will not be replaced. The instructors who are surplus cannot be used for anything while they are waiting for a posting. Two weeks after that we lose another

WRAF flight and once again three instructors on my hands with nothing to do."

"We are in a bit of a dilemma aren't we? Have you any suggestions Mr Barrett?"

"I have sir and I will be landing it in your lap to take to higher authority."

"That is what I am here for, a bit of action, carry on Mr Barrett this is getting exciting, for the wrong reasons of course."

"I suggest the five WRAF be sent home on leave to return when we get their postings. I can see no alternative to that sir, what else can we employ them doing?"

"I see your point and I think it is a sensible solution."

"I explained to the Wingco' a little while back what the situation was and how it was going to work, it puzzled him when I gave him the details, I'll bet he had quite a job trying to explain it to the C.O."

"Well that is half the battle, if they both know the situation then they will understand this latest development. I will go and see the Wingco' and will let you know the result."

Bill saluted, "Thank You sir."

Later in the afternoon Wings came to Bill's office.

"Would you like a brew before you start sir?"

"Of course thank you, need you ask, we instructors are well known for liking a brew anytime."

"Can the Flight Sergeant come in and hear what you will have to say sir."

"Certainly she can."

Bill went to the door. "Viv, can I have a brew for two, I will want you in the office so if you want a brew make it three."

She ordered the teas then came in the office and greeted Wings.

"We will wait until the teas come in sir. Ah! Here they are."

"I went to see the Wingco' and explained the situation. You know he is still puzzled about the system of change over you gave him. However he said protocol prevails and I must put it to the C.O., which he did and came back with a huge grin on his face. He said the C.O. is as much puzzled as I am and I have to tell you that if Mr Barrett has worked it out then it will be right. Sending them on leave is the best way out and you Cody will use your discretion in conjunction with Mr Barrett. There you are all done and dusted."

"The Flight Lieutenant and I Viv have decided to send the five WRAF on leave until their postings come through."

"What a good idea, I hope it will help to soften the blow when we tell them, when will that be sir?"

"I thought about tomorrow because after the passing out parade on Friday they can go on leave. Do you want to be the one who tells them sir?" asked Bill.

"I am not passing the buck Mr Barrett it is my duty as their officer to inform them of my decision. Shall we say 9:30 in the ops' room?"

"That will be fine, sir I shall ask WO Butcher to be present and the Flight Sergeant of course."

"Of course, see you in the morning then and thanks for the brew, pop down to my office sometime have one of my specials, it rivals yours." He left laughing.

"How are you going to work the leaves when there will be a two week gap between them?" asked Viv.

Send them all together, the reserve flight you have in there can take over for two weeks. Besides, Alan Fell and his lads will move in there next Monday."

"You have it all worked out to a 'T'."

"I have to Viv it comes with the rank, wait until you become a WO you will find out what it is like. I had better ring Mary and tell her about tomorrow. "Hello Mary, Bill Barrett, fine thank you. Tomorrow morning will you come to the ops' room for 9:30? Wings is going to tell the five WRAF instructors the bad news and he would like you to be here to witness it with you being in charge of the WRAF training." He then told her about the leave plan.

"That solves the problem of how to keep them occupied, I must congratulate him for that. Yes I will be there Bill, thanks for letting me know."

>>> <<<

George Miller was on duty as Station Orderly Officer. He and the Orderly Sergeant had just completed the ten o'clock inspection at the guardroom. They were on their way to the Sergeants Mess when they heard such a din of yelling shouting etc. coming from one of the airmen's accommodation. They immediately made their way to see what it was all about and as they arrived a group of airmen ran out yelling and cheering. George stopped them in their tracks. "Get fell in here he shouted. Watch them little sods sneaking away Sergeant. The Sergeant called them to halt and made them return and fall in with the rest.

"Which flight are you lot from?" asked George.

"The senior flight sir," was the reply.

"You are passing out on Friday?"

"Yes sir."

"Is this your accommodation block?"

"No sir."

"Then what were you doing in there?"

"Visiting some of our friends sir."

"That was very friendly of you, I think I will go and pay a little visit to your friends myself."

He went into the room where he could hear loud voices and swearing and saw it was in a complete shambles. Beds were overturned; bedding thrown about it had been thoroughly trashed. When the occupants saw who it was they immediately shut up and came to attention.

"Relax lads I am here to investigate what the disturbance was about. Which flight are you?"

"We are the new intake sir."

"Is your Corporal around?"

"No sir, the Corporals are at the Corporals' Club; there is a competition on or something."

"Right then, would you like me to bring that lot back to help you clean up or do you want to do it yourselves and leave me to deal with them?"

"You deal with them sir," they all answered grinning.

"I was hoping you would say that, Goodnight!"

"Goodnight sir," they all answered cheerfully.

"Are all you gentlemen from the same room?" he asked the miscreants.

"Yes sir," they answered.

"Which room is that?"

"Number one on the bottom floor sir."

"Good, then I suggest you return there right now, change into your 'jimjams' say your Prayers then get into bed. You have half an hour to do that then turn your lights out. I will personally be round to see if your lights are out and if they are not I will come in and put *your* lights out. Dismiss on the double!" They fled, feeling very relieved they had got off lightly.

Little did they know what George had in store for them…

He asked the Orderly Sergeant if he could get hold of one of the Physical Training Instructors. "One the recruits love to hate would be fine."

"I know the one who eats recruits for breakfast and I can get hold of him for you sir."

"You do that and bring him to the guard room I will be there waiting for you."

When they arrived and introduced George apologised for bringing him out so late.

"Are you an early riser Corporal?

"I am, sir I usually go for a little run first thing in the morning before breakfast."

"Good, I would like you to do a little job for me. Are you conversant with our assault course?"

"Yes sir it is part of our curriculum."

"It gets better," said George. "Instead of doing your normal morning run tomorrow will you take some lads over the assault course? I will make sure they are out of their beds at 6am and on parade outside in their PT kit, that is when you will take over. How long will you have them Corporal half hour, forty minutes?"

"Forty minutes sir."

"Good, when you bring them back hopefully in one piece I will be waiting to give them their final instructions. By the way, this is their Armageddon for trashing the new recruit's dormitory. They think I have let them off lightly. What time is it now?"

"Nearly ten thirty, said the Orderly Sergeant "

"Shall we go and see if they have blown the candles out?

"As they walked within viewing distance the lights went out.

"Thanks very much Corporal for your help, it will be a pleasure to see the state they are in when you bring them back. Goodnight Corporal "

"Goodnight sir."

"I like it sir," said the Orderly Sergeant I might come and have a shufti at them myself in the morning."

George was standing outside the airmen's room and as soon as Reveille sounded he entered the room shouting, "Out of bed you lazy lot, Wakey, Wakey, hands on socks!" as he hit the iron rail at the foot of the bed with his stick. The movements were so sluggish he gave them one minute to get their feet on the floor or their feet would not touch the ground all the way to the guardroom.

When they realised who was doing the shouting they leapt out of bed and stood to attention at the foot.

"That is better gentlemen I have come to wish you a Good Morning. Surely you did not think I had forgotten you I thought a little fresh air will help to unfuddle your brains. This is what I want you to do. You have got five minutes to get into your PT kit and to get fell in outside. The time starts NOW!"

The Corporal was waiting outside sporting a big grin. "Good morning sir, would you care to join us."

"Me? In my state of health? Hey up! Here they come."

"Come on, come on get fell in smartly. Flight, Atten..Shun. The Corporal here is taking you for a little exercise and some fresh air. On your return you will be washed, shaved showered, bed packs made up then you will fall in here properly dressed at 7:30. I will then escort you to breakfast. Do you understand? I said, Do You Understand?"

"Yes sir," they shouted.

"Take them away Corporal "

As George marched away he heard the sound of cheering, on looking round he saw the cheering faces of the younger airmen at the windows of the room that had been trashed.

He laughed to himself and thought, given the chance those little buggers will do the very same.

He was waiting outside their accommodation at 7:25, the lads came down in dribs and drabs but at 7:30 they were all present and correct on parade.

"You young men are supposed to have the potential to become officers, more likely in my eyes to become 'Plonkers! You must now be starving for something to eat after that little exercise. What we will do is take a little stroll past all the Accommodation Blocks for you to receive the cheers or jeers you so richly deserve then we will end up at your Mess for breakfast and if Cook is feeling benevolent he may even serve you boiled eggs with 'soldiers'. Now smarten yourselves up and Quick March."

CHAPTER 14

The five airwomen were in the ops' room along with Bill, Mary and Viv waiting the arrival of Wings wondering what it was all about, the Sergeants sensed it was not to be good news. Bill brought everyone to attention when Wings walked in.

"Good morning everyone thank you for coming. What I have to say does not come very easy and being your immediate Officer Commanding it is a cross I have to bear which goes with my appointment. You are aware of the big change in recruit training where the other two stations are being closed down. RAF March has built up such a good reputation that in a very short time and with your help it has become *The Number One* training establishment for training recruits. The personnel from RAF Chatworth and Camberly are to be posted throughout the RAF. We here at RAF March are to lose two of our WRAF flights consequently we have to lose you but you can appreciate the position this change has placed us, we have to lose someone. Of course we would love to keep you but I am sorry I had to choose you. You are probably thinking, why me? Whoever was in your position would say the very same thing and where would it end? Is there anything you would like to say?"

Some were in tears but one of the Sergeants said. What is the point sir? The decision has been made, when do we leave and where are we posted?"

"I cannot answer that because I do not know! But this I *can* tell you, after the passing out parade on Friday you all are being sent on leave until we get your postings then you will be recalled. This leave however will not affect your annual entitlements and to enable you to get as much leave in as you can, I am not submitting your names for posting until Monday, then it is pot luck whether you benefit from it or not but at least I am trying to soften the blow."

"Thank you sir I think we all understand. Che sera' sera'."

"Please leave your contact addresses with WO Butcher."

"Come and see me first thing tomorrow morning then I can proceed with the paper work." Mary told them.

Wings shook hands with each and wished them "Good Luck and hopefully someday you may get the chance to be posted back to us and we will look forward to that."

When they had left the office he said. "I hated having to do that."

"You did very well sir," said Bill, "nobody likes to do it but as the Sergeant said, che sera' sera'."

When Wings and Mary returned to SHQ, Bill and Viv went into the office to sort out the itinerary for the four flights for when the new schedule becomes operational.

"We will have to liaise with the other sections who take them for other training classes," said Viv. "They have been informed about the change I presume?"

"Oh yes they know about it alright but I will give them a ring to see if they have made out their itinerary because we will need them to programme them onto our boards.

"Hello, WO Barrett speaking. Have you made out your itinerary for the trainees under the new scheme, you have? Good. Can I send someone over to pick up a copy please? Right, thank you." He rang each one with the same result. "Send one of your Corporals to go and pick them up will you Viv please? In the meantime we will sort out the teams of instructors, Friday morning's passing out parade will see two flights off in the afternoon and I want all the remaining instructors in here to be put in the picture of what the routine will be and what the teams will be. We are going to have a busy time getting those boards sorted out with the new programmes. One good thing about it there will not be as many names to contend with. What say we shut up shop now and go to lunch?"

At lunch Bill, Roy and Derwent always sat together; Mary Butcher liked to sit alone for her meal to eat it in peace.

"Anybody got any news worth mentioning?" asked Derwent.

Bill told them about the morning incident with the WRAF.

Roy said, "*I* am going on leave!"

"Great, let us hear all about it and when are you going? Asked Derwent.

"Barbara and I are flying from Leeds to the Algarve on Saturday morning for two whole weeks."

"That is good news," said Bill, are you staying in a hotel or having a villa?"

"A hotel of course, we want to be waited on as opposed to a villa where we would have to fend for ourselves. We want all the time to relax and do what we want; Villas are all right for families. Barbara was fortunate because the Wingco' is going on leave at that time that is why we are going now."

"I can just picture you two on the beach, you with your trousers rolled up and Barbara with her skirt tucked up in her knickers paddling in the shallows holding hands and without a care in the world," said Derwent wistfully.

"If I was you Derwent I would move your dinner plate out of Roy's reach." Bill advised.

"That is you struck off our 'Wish You Were Here' post cards." Roy replied with a vengeance.

"How are you getting to the airport, by taxi?" asked Bill.

"I don't know whether to or go in my own car and leave it at the airport."

"Don't do either, advised Bill, I will take you and pick you up when you return, I will also check with the airport on your ETA. For easy identification will you wear a flower in your button hole and ask Barbara to wear a rose in her hair because I may not recognise you both wearing a glorious sun tan?"

"Thank you Bill that is kind of you I accept with the greatest of pleasure. You will recognise me all right I will be the one with the rolled up trousers and a knotted hanky on my head; I cannot vouch for what Barbara will be wearing."

The three of them had a good laugh at Roy's retaliation.

"Touché Roy, I deserved that," conceded Derwent.

"Anyway Roy, let me know the time you want me Saturday morning. I will have a word with Tommy she might like to do some shopping in Leeds on our way back."

When he told Tommy she got all excited about it. "That will be a nice day out for us I have not been to Leeds for ages. What a pity your car will not take Viv and Derwent as well, or will it Bill?"

"It would at a pinch but going any distance would be a bit uncomfortable. But there is nothing to stop them going in either of their cars. I think you have given me an idea love, what if Derwent and Viv drove to the airport unknown to Roy and Barbara and met us inside the airport at the entrance to Departures then the four of us can see them off. Look, you have a word with Viv and I will with Derwent, Viv might like a look round Leeds Shopping Malls. Alternately, you and Viv go shopping while Derwent and I go to a football match that is only a suggestion, talk it over with Viv."

"I will when she comes out from lunch. I will see you later love," they kissed then Bill went to his room.

Derwent and Viv came out from lunch with Roy and Barbara. Tommy called them over and told them of Bill's idea.

"What do think Derwent? I know I would love to do some shopping in Leeds the shops are great and it has been a long time since I was last there," enthused Viv.

"Do you fancy going to a football match or would you prefer to take *me* shopping?"

"I am not a great fan of football, besides there are one or two items of clothing I could do with."

"Oh Bill won't mind Derwent, I think he could do with smartening his wardrobe up a bit, we will not go shopping as a foursome, instead we can choose a nice restaurant where we can meet up at a given time, that would finish the day off perfectly. How does that appeal to you both?"

"Sounds alright to me," said Derwent, "I have never been to Leeds."

"I like it," said Viv. "I am feeling excited already."

"Good, all I need to do is tell Bill, give him a knock as you go by Derwent and tell him I would like to see him but stand well back when you do tell him or you will get trampled in his rush to get here."

"What kept you?" asked Viv as Bill arrived, it has taken two minutes since Derwent left us to give you the message." She and Tommy just giggled at him.

"I'll leave you to break the news to him Tommy, bye for now. Bye lover-boy."

"What is she on about?" Asked a puzzled Bill.

"We have just sorted Saturday out between us, you and I my dear are going shopping together and so are they, Derwent prefers doing that than going to a football match, he has never been to Leeds and he wants some items of clothing. We go our different ways but find a nice restaurant to meet up again at a set time. Is that alright with you?"

"No problem, we should have a nice day."

"Come on, give me a kiss I have work to do," said a very pleased Tommy Atkins.

Roy and Barbara checked in then along with Bill and Tommy they found seats and were having a short chat before the holidaymakers entered Departures.

"I don't believe it," said Barbara. "It is Viv and Derwent, what on earth are they doing here?"

"They are coming to see you off," Tommy told them, afterwards the four of us are going shopping in Leeds."

When all the greetings were over Derwent said. "I had to bring something you had forgotten Roy."

"I don't think I had forgotten anything that would have been so important for you to make that journey."

"Here you are," said Derwent presenting him with a knotted handkerchief."

"That was definitely worth the journey," said Roy as he joined in the laughter. He and Barbara were still laughing as they walked into Departures with Roy waving the Hanky to their friends.

>>> <<<

The passing-out parade went off without a hitch relatives and friends who had come to see the ceremony gathered round their individual offspring or friend ready to whisk them off home on leave before they had to report for their Trade Training. RAF station transport was laid on to take others to the railway station. Station Warrant Officer George Miller stood outside the guardroom with Flight Sergeant Tom Bridges of the RAF Police watching the exodus.

"I find it very gratifying Tom to see that I am getting farewell waves with *all five* fingers."

"Aye, I can see that George but they are all coming from the WRAF!"

"Don't forget lads," Alan Fell reminded his two Corporals after the parade. "We have to report to the ops' room after lunch for a briefing."

Bill went to the orderly room and saw Sergeant Thomson. "Sergeant, can you tell me when the next intake of recruits are due to report in?"

"Wednesday sir, they will be picked up by our transport from the railway station at about 14:00hrs, if the train is on time."

"Thanks Sergeant."

He then went to see Mary. "Have you been told when the next batch of girls is due to arrive Mary?"

"Wednesday afternoon Bill, why?"

"I have only just found out and I had to go and enquire to do that. How did you find out?"

"It was the Corporal (w) from the orderly room. She came here to ask me something then said. "We have more WRAF coming in on Wednesday Ma'am are they the ones who will be training with the airmen?"

"I wonder why Frank Thomson did not inform us?" pondered Bill. "I cannot understand that because Roy says how super efficient he is. I will take that up with Roy when he comes back."

"Why, where has he gone?" queried Mary.

"He and Barbara have gone to the Algarve for a couple of weeks."

"Why the sly little devil, he never said anything to me."

"You were in the dining room the other day when Derwent was pulling his leg about it."

"Bill! I go in there for a meal not to listen to you three crackpots taking the Mickey out of each other."

"Is there anything fresh on the entertainments front Mary?"

"For a start, Bingo is to be a regular function for Saturday nights that is the feed back we are getting from the wives in married quarters and our committee members are willing to run it. A Darts league has been mentioned where different sections on the station form a team of SNCOs to play against each other. Quiz teams, Snooker competitions. If the Mess members show the same enthusiasm as they did in coming to the dining-in night we should have some very good games evenings."

"That sounds good Mary, your team are coming up with some good ideas that will appeal to the members, you are doing a fine job."

"I must be off now to get some lunch I have all the instructors in for a briefing afterwards."

Bill told his staff. "We are still working the rotation system, that has not changed, as each flight passes out the instructors come into the ops' room and keep the data up to date plus filling in as a reserve when one of the instructors has to be absent for any length of time from his or her flight. The exception to this is the mixed flight of Sergeant Dixon, Cp.Harper and Corporal (w)James they are permanent instructors to this flight. Sergeant Dixon's relief will be Sergeant Fell, when he has to stand in, the reserve Sergeant will take over Sergeant Fell's flight until such time as he returns, the relief will then return to ops' and revert to his role as a relief. Are you all clear on that point? Good. Now we come to you ladies. For the next two weeks you both will have the two remaining WRAF flights. You are wondering who will be your relief. Flight Sergeant Anderson will and if both of you are absent at the same time she will amalgamate your two flights and carry on."

A quiet voice was heard to utter. "Thank you sir!"

"Are you happy about the arrangements or does anyone want to throw a Wobbly?"

"Yes Sergeant Franks."

"I am not trying to be vindictive but can you tell me why you chose Sergeant Dixon for the special flight, when he is just a newcomer on the staff. I have nothing against him but I am curious about your decision?"

"I will explain your very cleverly worded query in plain language. You want to know why you have been passed over as a senior Sergeant to give a newcomer the flight you thought would automatically be offered to you."

"That is unfair sir, the way you have put it is I am complaining about the choice."

"Well aren't you?"

"No sir!"

"Then why did you bring the matter up? I tell you what is unfair Sergeant Franks; you are sowing seeds of doubt in the other NCOs minds with your single mindedness.

Very well then, I will tell you why I made that choice and if you had not brought the matter up no-one would have been any wiser and no-one would have felt hurt."

"I would like you to tell me in private sir."

"But you wanted them to hear my explanation and I am sure they will want to know now more than ever."

Sergeant Franks shrugged his shoulders resigned to the fact that he had dropped a huge clanger.

"In my opinion you have not got the aptitude to teach airwomen!"

"There is nothing wrong with my instructing or you would have got rid of me long ago," he said angrily."

"Sergeant Franks, you are instructing airmen not airwomen."

That deflated the Sergeant he had no answer to that. "Then I will take it further," he said still in anger.

"Sergeant you have two choices, you can redress me or ask for an immediate posting, I will not stand in your way. Has anyone else got a question about the arrangements, please speak up. Very well then, seeing that you have finished with your flights for the day you may as well stand down until Monday morning when I expect to see you here all bright eyed and bushy tailed. Have a good weekend. Stay behind Sergeant Franks I will get you an appointment to see Flight Lieutenant Cody." He went into his office and phoned Wings. "WO Barrett here sir." He then told him the tale concerning Sergeant Franks.

"I will see him first thing Monday morning Mr Barrett and please make yourself available."

Bill called Sergeant Franks. "First thing Monday morning report to Flight Lieutenant Cody's office."

"Look Bill, I want to apologise, I was completely out of order and I know you have always treated us fairly and I had hopes of getting that flight. Honestly I just do not know what came over me. it must have been the disappointment of being passed over."

"Knee-jerk reactions are not exclusive; we all have been guilty of that sometime during our career and we have had to pay the penalty for doing so. It is now in the hands of our OC and whatever decision he makes I will accept. You can stand down now Sergeant "

"Well, that was unexpected," said Viv, "I never expected that from Joe, it looks like we are going to need a replacement for him now."

"Indeed we are," answered Bill. "Pity, he is a good instructor Alan Fell will have to take over his flight on Monday until we get a replacement. It has upset the system a little but we will manage even if I have to do a bit of relief work myself, of course if need be we can always give Wings a bit of experience."

"Now that I would like to see," giggled Viv. "I think he would jump at the chance Bill he is that kind of person why don't you suggest it to him, I'm sure he would welcome a break away from his desk."

"I think you have got something there Viv, it would be more experience for him I will sound him out."

>>> <<<

Saturday night saw Bill, Tommy, Derwent and Viv at the March Hare. As they walked in they got the usual good welcome from the local people. "Not seen you for a week or two," was the comment. "We thought you had deserted us."

"No fear of that replied Bill it was the pressure of work."

"Pressure of work? You young uns' don't know what pressure is. Get behind yon bar on a darts night then you will know what pressure is!"

"Well you lot are not putting Tim under any pressure the rate you are drinking." He went to the bar and was greeted by Tim.

"Hi Bill, are they giving you a hard time?"

"There is only one way to keep this lot quiet Tim, give em' all a drink."

When the locals heard that they gave a cheer and shouted. "Good old Bill you're a good un'."

When Ann came into the bar she asked. "Now what's with all this shouting?

I will have no unruly behaviour in this hostelry!"

She got the answer. "It is not us landlady it only started when yon' mon' walked in," pointing at Bill.

Bill spluttered in his beer. "You lot of turncoats, you need sorting out."

"How? Are you going to serve us with our calling up papers?"

"No, Lord Kitchener has enough troubles of his own than having to cope with you lot."

He joined the other three at their table and admitted. "I don't know why I bother I always without fail come off the worse."

"I know dear," said Tommy, but they like you for it."

Ann came over and sat with them. "I don't know who is worse, you Bill or them?"

"Don't you give me a hard time as well landlady! Anyway we had a good laugh."

"They do miss you all when you are not here," said Ann. "They think a lot about you."

"What is the news from the station anything exciting going on?"

"There is plenty of that," said Viv. The whole training structure has changed we are the only station left now to train recruits."

"No! I can't believe it; you mean to tell me Chatworth and Camberly have closed down? Gosh, your training programme will suffer."

"Apart from one or two minor hic-ups it is just the opposite."

They told her what was happening and how it affected them at RAF March.

"That certainly comes as a shock I never in this wide world thought that would happen it would have been a big blow to this community if March had closed. Thank goodness for you two and the BlueBelles you have saved the day."

“Tom Hardcastle was in here the other evening he was saying he was chatting with you the other day and how well you both get on with each other.”

“Aye, Tom is a good man, he has done me some good turns since he has been with us.”

“Where are Roy and Barbara tonight, have they got a heavy date on?”

“You could say that,” answered Derwent. “At present they are sunning themselves on the Algarve, we saw them off today then did some shopping in Leeds.”

“Ohooo! That sounds nice, I wouldn’t mind a bit of that myself.” Ann said wistfully.

“If you all went as a party they would have to close the station down.”

“Then you and Tim would get *your* calling up papers to keep the flag flying.” Bill said with a laugh.

“Then this lot here would mutiny.” She turned to the locals, “Wouldn’t you?”

“YES!” they all shouted.

“I would clap the lot of you in irons.” Bill said with the pretence of a snarl.

All he got in reply was a concerto of “Boos!” and “Captain Bligh.”

“Oh give them another drink Tim to shut em’ up.”

“Three cheers for Captain Bligh!”

Everyone was having a good laugh.

“Ann said, I can see you leaving here penniless Bill.”

“Ann, they are enjoying every minute of it, the old people do not have a lot to make them happy these days only what they can make themselves. That gives me an idea. What do you think about the Sergeants Mess putting on a Christmas dinner for the Senior Citizens of the village? We could put it on before the station closes down for the Christmas break and get volunteers from the airmen and airwomen to help out; these old people would love to be fussed by young people.”

“What a wonderful thought,” said Tommy.

“That would be lovely,” joined in Viv.

“Tim and I would love to contribute somehow, for instance, vouchers for a free drink in here, we will come up with something for them.”

“That would go down a treat with them,” added Derwent, it might even make them forget Captain Bligh!”

“Shall we propose that at the next Mess Meeting asked Bill?”

“Definitely.” agreed the other three.

CHAPTER 15

Monday morning saw Sergeant Franks stood before Flight Lieutenant Cody trying to explain his actions. “I have nothing against Sergeant Dixon sir it was the thought of him being a newcomer to the staff and getting the very flight I was hoping for, it hurt being a senior Sergeant and getting passed over. When I realised how stupid I had been I immediately apologised to WO Barrett."

"Did he accept your apology?"

"He did not say sir but he did point out to me the precarious position I had put myself in and also he would accept whatever decision you made."

"Would you like him to come in and for you to ask him anything?"

"No sir but I will say he is a very fair man and treats his staff with respect."

"It is a pity you did not remember that when you challenged his authority! I have here your assessments and from what WO Barrett says in them you are a very good instructor. Not a nice way to repay his confidence in you is it?"

"No sir that is something I will always regret."

"Right Sergeant, wait outside and ask WO Barrett to come in."

Bill came in and saluted.

"Sit down Mr Barrett and let us talk about this incident."

"I have tried to put myself in his position and thought what would I have done? To be honest I would have queried it too. The difference being he spoke his thoughts out loud and in public when he should have asked for an interview in private with you, that was a very bad blunder. However, I am convinced he has done some soul searching and will regret it for many years but deep down I am sure he is an honest man and I would like to hear your thoughts Mr Barrett."

"I agree, he is an honest man, he is a fine instructor but he challenged my authority albeit in a moment of letting his tongue do the thinking. Will this rush of madness rear its ugly head again? I admit it would be a pity to lose a good Sergeant in this manner but what options have I when he challenged my authority in public?"

"We both know what a bloody fool he has been and nobody more so than himself but don't you think he deserves a chance to make amends? You just said it would be a pity to lose him."

"I did sir and I meant it. He is not the first and will not be the last to make a mistake I told him I would abide by your decision, I never thought I would agree with it but I do."

"Thank you Mr Barrett," then shook his hand. Shall we have him in to make his day?"

"Why not sir"

Bill went to the door and called him in.

He saluted and stayed at attention.

"Relax Sergeant we have had a deep discussion and Mr Barrett says that every man is allowed one big mistake in his service career and this was yours, just make damned sure it is your last!"

"Thank you sir and thank *you* sir."

"Come on Joe," said Bill slapping him on the back. "Let's get you back with your flight."

They both saluted and as Bill got to the door he turned with a smile on his face to Wings who gave him a wink and a nod as if to say. "We did make his day."

>>> <<<

Bill went to his door that opened into the ops' room and called out. "Sergeant Dixon,

Corporal Harper, Corporal James." They came into his office. "Relax," he said. "Do you know what time the train is due in with the new intakes?"

"It is expected in about 2pm sir," said Corporal Harper."

"Good, that gives us plenty of time for briefing, you two Corporals know you are to meet the train and shepherd the intakes onto the buses. You know my views on shouting and bawling and literary frightening them to death and you know how they will feel coming here for training, it will be like a different world to them. You have experienced that yourself, treat them like you wish you had been treated. You will also find there is always an awkward one to deal with and even someone who needs to be lead by the hand but do not lose your patience with them. The buses will pull up on the parade square where Sergeant Dixon will be waiting, usher them into three ranks keeping the sexes apart of course remember they are carrying full kit they do not know how to handle yet. Once you have got them sorted out Sergeant Dixon will take over to give them a brief introduction to the station, when he has finished he will hand them back to you who will then see them safely to the dormitories. Give them time to chose their bed spaces and who they want to be sleeping next to, then when you are satisfied they have settled themselves in you take over. Introduce yourselves and lay down the law as to what you expect from them. You know the routine so it is no use me rabbiting on about it. Are you all clear on what is needed? Good. Then I suggest you two Corporals find out from MT what time the transport will be leaving here for the station then go and get yourselves an early lunch. Off you go and spend the rest of the day with them."

"Are you happy with everything Bob?"

"I see no problems."

"Okay, get yourself off home and get your lunch you know what time to expect them then tomorrow you take over, you know the ropes you have done it often enough."

>>> <<<

"I wonder how Roy and Barbara are getting on out there in the sunshine, I feel a bit envious of them, I could just do with two weeks relaxing in the sun and being pampered in a nice luxury hotel. You can spare me for a couple of weeks can't you Bill?"

"Any time you want to go, just say the word Viv. it would do you good to wind down and charge up those batteries. You have had no leave for sometime so do think about it and make it soon before the weather changes," he said with a grin.

Thinking to himself, I will have a quiet word with Derwent.

"What do you say we go after lunch and discretely watch the new intake arrive?"

"Yes, I would like that Bill, we could observe how the Corporals handle them as well, they are a couple of bright NCOs I can see them doing well for themselves if they stay in the service for any length of time. You have a good team instructing that particular flight."

After lunch Bill and Viv strolled over to the parade ground and saw George Miller standing outside SHQ so they went over to join him.

"Hello," said George, "have you come to run your eyes over your new intake?"

"We have," Bill replied, "also to see how the two Corporals shape up, those two and Bob Dixon are the permanent instructors for training the special mixed flights and being special ones they have got the best instructors."

"I will be very interested in seeing how that works out," said George, "a mixed flight and with mixed instructors? Hmm! It is going to be interesting. I will make sure I watch that developing you won't mind me strolling around when they are performing do you Bill? I will be very discreet."

"George, I will be grateful for your comments."

"Here come the buses," interrupted Viv.

After being briefed, the first airman to step off the bus was taken by the Corporal to a point and told him to stay there and make sure the rest form up on his left as they de-bus. He then returned to the bus and helped some of the airmen who were having difficulty in manhandling their kit. Everyone had alighted and formed up in three ranks without a hitch and were gazing about them and chatting with each other until Corporal Harper shouted. "Quiet" The chatting stopped instantly.

Corporal (w)James rebuked the airwomen. "That also means you too; now pay attention to what is being said!"

Corporal Harper then continued. "You will be waiting here for a short while so I suggest you remove your back packs until we move off and I do not want to hear any talking. This they did in complete silence.

"Sergeant Dixon came and stood in front of the recruits. "I am Sergeant Dixon and I along with Corporal Harper and Corporal (w)James are your drill instructors. We welcome you to RAF March. You may not know it but this is the Flagship of Recruit Training and you are privileged to do your training here. Something else that is of great importance to us, this is the station where the famous BlueBelles were trained and we still have here the Warrant Officer and Flight Sergeant (w) who trained them If none of you have heard of the BlueBelles you will be seeing the training film of their great victory in beating both the Royal Navy and Army Women's Drill Teams. That is what we are famous for, our drill, we uphold that standard of drill and we mean to keep that standard. All we ask of you is a one hundred percent effort and if you can squeeze a bit more percentage on top of that we will be delighted. I will now hand you back to your Corporals who will guide you to your accommodations listen to what they tell you and if you want to ask them any questions do so by all means. Good Luck to you all and let us have a flight to be proud of."

They were then ushered to their accommodations under the supervision of their Corporals

"What do you think of that George?"

"I am impressed especially with the Corporals they handled them just right, you have two bright young people there Bill."

The next two days the recruits were kept busy with medical and kit inspections, bringing their webbing and packs up to standard with Blanco and Silvo to polish the brasses and especially bulling up of their boots and shoes until they could see their faces in them. Corporal Harper was always on hand to give tips even a short cut or two. They were introduced to the 'Bumper' for polishing the floor and how to keep the floor consistently polished by sliding about the room on two felt pads, heaven help anyone who did not use those pads. With the right kind of help they would soon settle into service life. Although they were off duty at the weekend they were confined to camp and spent most of their free time looking to their kit, the NAAFI and the Astra cinema.

Monday morning would commence with early morning physical training, shower, breakfast then their initiation to drill.

That evening when Bill entered the Mess Bar he was pleasantly surprised to see quite a few of the Mess members with their wives sat at tables and even stood at the bar all enjoying an evening out. After the greetings he joined Derwent at the bar.

"The usual Bill?" asked Chalky

"I will get that," spoke up Derwent, "put one in for me and one for yourself Chalky."

"Nice to see it so busy Chalky," commented Bill, does this suit you getting more custom?"

"This is how a Sergeants Mess should be, it has needed sorting out for a long time and I will take my hat off to the committee they are doing a real good job. Have you seen the notice they have put on the board? Inviting names to form inter-section dart teams, quiz teams and snooker competitions. I tell you this Mess is going to be the *in* place for fun and entertainment and the families are all for it."

"I couldn't agree more," Derwent added.

"You will soon be ready to be relieved as barman," queried Bill.

"Spot on sir, I hand over on Monday, in one way I will be sorry because you crackpots have made it easy for me and now things are happening I am looking forward to which I can enjoy from the other side of this bar. On the other hand it is not fair on the wife and kids but big do's and little do's it is a duty."

"We will miss you won't we Bill?" stated Derwent I hope your relief will be as good to get on with. Who is he?"

"Harry Gordon from Station Workshops!"

"AND?"

"You will have to suss him out for yourselves he is a quiet sort and keen on his sport, he plays football for the village team and he is teetotal!"

"Then they will be short of a player for a month," voiced Bill."

"That is service life for you, full of disappointments," Derwent sympathised. "He is not going to be a very happy man stuck behind the bar here on a Saturday afternoon."

"He can always get a stand-in for that period," said Chalky, "it will cost him though."

"Happen he will get a grant from the FA," continued Derwent.

"That is exactly what he will get….FA," laughed Chalky.

You know being a barman can be very profitable," confided Chalky, "take you wealthy Warrant Officers for instant, you are very generous by including me when you are buying a round of drinks naturally I cannot pour myself a drink every time, I am duty barman and what I do not drink goes into Chalky's benevolent fund. When the bar is busy like it is tonight I do very well thank you."

"When you weigh up the other little perks that the barmen get it is not a bad duty. I know I used to do all right but I earned it the hard way you lot today don't know you are born!" reminisced Bill. "And you can put that imaginary violin down," pointing his finger at Chalky. "Or I will Banjo you with it."

"Roll on Monday," pleaded Chalky.

The members standing at the bar joined in laughing. "Is it always like this in here?" one of them asked.

"More or less," responded Chalky, "it is even worse when the other crackpot is here. He will have a shock when he returns to find his favourite barman is not here any more."

"Shall we send him a signal Derwent? "Return at once, Barman gone AWOL."

"I know what his reply would be," said Derwent. "And bloody good riddance!"

"Come Derwent, sup up, I want a word, Goodnight Chalky you can go in your counting house now and don't keep me awake rattling your coins. Good night all," he said to the other members.

"I'll be back soon Chalky to help you in your counting house." laughed Derwent.

"Sod off you two and leave me in peace, I don't know why I try to be pleasant when I serve you."

They both left laughing with the other members joining in.

>>> <<<

"I want a word Derwent because I am a bit concerned about Viv. I think with Roy and Barbara going on holiday it has unsettled her and made her realise she is tired. She now wants to do the same, lie in the sun and be pampered at a luxury hotel I think she is showing signs of being run down, she has had no leave for some time and it is beginning to show. I wanted you to know because you both are very close and you would be concerned."

"Thanks Bill, I think we should follow Roy and Barbara's example."

"If you are thinking of doing anything about it tread cautiously, you don't want her thinking I have been talking out of turn."

"Don't you worry I will not give the game away, thanks a lot Bill I appreciate it. Goodnight."

"Derwent!" he called. What are you doing tomorrow night?"

"I haven't a clue Bill, why do you fancy going to the March Hare if the girls agree?"

"Well I don't fancy playing Bingo. we can ask the girls in the morning. Goodnight Derwent."

As Derwent was leaving the dining room after finishing his breakfast, Viv who was sat alone beckoned him to come and sit with her.

"Derwent, I have got a yearning to go to the seaside, what do you say to us going to Whitby for the day?"

Thinking of what Bill had told him. "What a good Idea I have never been there I have heard it is a nice place and it would be a shame for us to stay on camp a nice day like this."

"Good, shall we get ready now? We can have our lunch there." She said getting excited about it. "We will take my car because I know my way around these parts."

"Right we will meet at your car, say in fifteen minutes?"

"Yes! Come on let us get moving then."

When they parted to go to their separate rooms Derwent went to see Bill.

"Viv wants to go to Whitby, she wants to go to the sea side and we are going in a few minutes."

"Just what the doctor ordered," said a delighted Bill. "Better still with it being her idea it is the opportune time for you to mention a holiday break discretely of course we do not want her to smell a rat. Will you still be going with us tonight?

"Of course but if we stay longer than we anticipate we will meet you at the pub."

"See you Bill and thanks."

"Have a 'Nice Day'."

When Viv parked her car she suggested they have a nice stroll along the promenade before going for lunch. "Afterwards we will hire a couple of deck chairs have a paddle then just laze on the chairs, we may even get a little suntan," she said excitedly. As they strolled along the Prom' they eyed the various restaurants to see which one attracted them the most.

"What do you fancy for lunch?" asked Derwent.

"Don't you know that Whitby is famous for its fresh fish?" replied Viv. "You know what I would really like Drewent? Fish and chips, you do not get them any better than here in Whitby."

"That would suit me fine," said Derwent, "it is a long time since I had them."

"Then you are in for a treat." They ordered Fish, Chips, Mushy Peas and tea.

"That was really, really good, the best I ever tasted we must come here again Viv."

"I remember," she said, "as a child coming here with my parents and eating fish and chips wrapped in paper eating them with our fingers as we walked on the Prom', they tasted better than having them off a plate."

They found a nice spot where they could hire deck chairs and sit quietly. After a little while she said, "Are you coming for a paddle."

"No, I will sit here and watch you and keep guard over our belongings."

"Okay, I will be off then although I cannot tuck my skirt in my knickers because I am wearing slacks."

On her return, she wiped her feet on a towel she had brought and then as she settled down they held hands.

"You know love," she said. "I could just do with a spell somewhere on a beach where I can relax to my hearts content and where the sun shines all day. I have had that in my head ever since Barbara and Roy went to Portugal."

"Is there any reason why we can't go?" asked Derwent

She squeezed his hand. “That would be wonderful I was hoping you would agree.”

“I tell you what we will do,” Derwent said enthusiastically. “Before we leave here shall we look for a travel agent, get some brochures then find somewhere private where we can have a good look through them.”

Viv gave his hand another squeeze. “Can I tell you something Derwent Waters?”

“Go ahead, I am a good listener.”

“I love you”

“He got up from his chair and gave her a kiss. “I love you too Viv Anderson.”

Monday morning in the dining room, Bill asked Derwent, “Can we talk now? Saturday night we couldn’t even though Viv was in a much happier frame of mind, I might even say to the point of glowing and I did not see you at all yesterday, where were you both, hibernating?”

“We did a Greta Garbo act, ‘I want to be alone!’ We picked up some brochures on Saturday and we were having a good shufti at them.”

“And…?”

“We have not made our minds up, Viv fancies the Algarve and I fancy Tenerife. That is going to be the most difficult decision but we are going to check the small print before deciding.”

“Did she suspect anything when you started fishing?”

“I did nothing, she brought it up about what she would like to do and I saw my opening. I just said what is to stop us both from going and it snowballed from there. When I suggested getting brochures there and then she could not get to a travel agents quick enough.”

“Good, all you have got to do now is keep her interested do not let her grow cold on the idea.”

”There is no fear of that Bill, when we are together she talks of nothing else.”

“I will not say anything I will let her bring the subject up, it will probably be about some leave when she does.”

>>> <<<

Sergeant Dean and her Corporals took charge of the instructorless WRAF flight and Sergeant Fell and his team moved into the ops’ room.

Sergeant Dixon and his team took command of the special flight and began introducing them into basic training.

“You will now be sized off, the drill movement for sizing will be taught to you later as we progress but for now the Corporals will move you around until we are satisfied it is where we want you to stand when you ‘fall-in’. Look around to see who the persons are who are standing next to you in line and in file. In future you will fall in on parade in exactly those positions. I am going to give you a trial run now; he spoke to the tallest recruit, which was an airman. You will be known as Right Marker, when I call you, you will come to attention then march smartly towards me where I will designate a spot where you will stand to attention. Now fall out and stand over there in groups and when I call "March On" you will come to attention and march on smartly and line up in threes on the left of your marker then stand to attention.

"Right Marker." The airman did what he had been instructed to do, the Sergeant praising him for encouragement. "March On!" he ordered. The rest of the flight came to attention in a haphazard sort of movement and trying to line up on their marker and finding their appointed positions was pathetic.

"STAND STILL!" yelled the Sergeant "Now just take a good look at yourselves. You are supposed to be the pick of the recruits the 'Bright Ones' and wipe those silly grins off your faces. Right Turn." Some did, others turned left. "Sort yourselves out and if you are not sure you have my permission to ask anyone to point out your left from your right. Now that we all are facing the same way I want you to run round this parade ground twice then fall out in groups as you did before. I will then call you on parade again and each time you make a mess of it you will go round the parade ground three times and it will be increased each time you make a mess of the simple task of falling in on parade until I am satisfied. Now on the double MOVE!"

George Miller was watching this performance and having a good laugh. If that lot is officer material, bring on the dancing girls! You have got your hands full there Sergeant Dixon. "KEEP OFF THE GRASS!" he shouted as one or two strayed on the grass which bordered the parade ground. He stood watching as they doubled round the parade ground three times then a fourth time, after which he had, had enough. Give me strength he muttered as he walked back into SHQ and to his office. "ORDERLY!" he shouted.

"SIR!" was the reply.

"Get me a brew lad, do you want one Ian?"

"I don't mind if I do George."

"MAKE IT TWO!" he shouted.

When it arrived he asked. "Is it a Sergeant Major brew?"

"Yes sir it is a Sergeant Major Special."

"Good lad, I'll remember you in my will."

He took a drink. "Bai Gum Ian the lads right it is a good brew, we'll have him again I really needed this, I have been watching the new intake the so-called officer material, the lasses have more idea than the lads, they are prancing about like a load of bloody fairies. Bob Dixon has got his hands full with yon lot I can tell you."

"Don't tell me that surprises you George? You did say they were officer material."

“I’ll not argue with that,” George said laughing.

CHAPTER 16

“I have got a card from Barbara and Roy this morning Bill.”

“That’s nice what have they to say for themselves?

“Barbara wrote it and says it is absolutely wonderful, for the first few days they did nothing but laze about, swimming in the sea and sun bathing. Roy is watching over her like a mother hen making sure she does not get too much sun. The hotel is very good, comfortable and the food is really good, she is keeping tabs on Roy’s intake then taking him for long walks to work it off.”

“That won’t please Roy he likes his grub”

“He has added a P.S. It’s like being on bloody jankers!”

“That is Roy alright; it does sound like they picked the right spot by the sound of it!”

“I can’t wait to show this to Derwent,” she said excitedly.

“Why, do you think he will be that interested?” he said trying to draw something out from her regarding her holiday.

“Oh yes, he certainly will.” She said, unwittingly falling into Bill’s trap. “He might change his mind from Tenerife now.” She then gave a scream. “Oh heck! I was not supposed to say that. Ah well, there is no harm in telling you now. Derwent and I are going on holiday he fancies Tenerife and I fancy the Algarve, I am hoping when he reads this he will change his mind. There is one problem though; I do not know which hotel they are staying at.”

“That is no problem,” said Bill, “just hold your fire.”

He picked up the phone and rang the orderly room. “Sergeant Thomson, this is WO Barrett, can you give me WO Shaw’s contact address in Portugal please?”

“Sorry sir I cannot do that.”

“Why not”

“Regulations sir”

“What do you mean Regulations!?”

“I am not allowed to divulge private and personal information without the proper authority.”

“Who is this authority Sergeant?”

“The Commanding Officer.”

“Well, well, well, Sergeant Thomson I am now on my way to escort you to see the Commanding Officer, so stand by.”

“But sir I am only doing my duty.”

“Then it will be my pleasure to nominate you for the Blue Peter Badge.”

“Have you got problems Bill?” asked a concerned Viv.

“No, I haven’t but I will make sure he has.”

He picked up the phone. “Helen, Bill Barrett here could you please get me an interview with the C.O.?”

“Hi Bill, hang on for a minute I will ask him. Hello Bill, come along now he is free.”

“Thanks Helen, I am on my way.”

He then made his way to the Orderly Room. “Are you ready Sergeant?”

“Look sir perhaps I was being a little too officious, I can give you the address now.”

“You are right you are too officious full stop. You are too late to change that now Sergeant because you and I have an interview with the Station Commander in a few minutes. Now follow me.”

The rest of the orderly room staff were watching and listening with glee, it was obvious Sergeant Thomson was not their flavour of the month.

When they entered Helen’s office she showed surprise to see who Bill had brought with him. “I will take you in now sir,” she said to Bill.

“You wait here Sergeant until you are called for,” he snapped.

Helen looked at him quizzically.

Bill gave her a wink.

“Warrant Officer Barrett sir,” she announced.

“Come in and sit yourself down Mr Barrett. You are either going to tell me some good news or I am afraid it is not so good news, am I right?”

“There is no fooling you sir, you know me too well.”

“Come then lets have it and I will see if I can sort it out for you.”

“It is a silly little problem sir which I should not be bothering you with but it was forced on me. I have waiting outside Sergeant Thomson of the orderly room. I asked him for Warrant Officer Shaw’s address in Portugal where he is on holiday. You may or may not know sir that WO Shaw is my best friend.”

“Yes, I am aware of that, carry on.”

“He refused to give it me, saying that regulations forbade him to divulge a persons private information and the only person authorized to divulge that is you sir the Commanding Officer. Now when it struck home that he would have to face you he offered to give me the address but that was too late I had already asked for this interview. I do not know if he is wrong or right but I cannot understand why the holiday address is put under wraps. If it was a service address yes, I could accept the security angle.”

“Mr Barrett, Sergeant Thomson appears to be carrying out his duties to the letter which is very commendable but this time he has got hold of a wrong letter. He is obviously wearing his official hat constantly and never taking it off. If you will excuse the pun which I cannot resist in using Mr Barrett, the official hat has gone to his head.”

They both had a good laugh over that.

“Bring him in I will have a word with him.”

"Shall I wait outside sir?"

"Yes, then go to the orderly room, when he comes out, you will get your address."

Bill saluted and said. "Thank you sir.

As Bill got to the door. "Mr Barrett," Bill turned. "Mountains out of Molehills!"

"You can go in now," he said to the nervous Sergeant

"What was that about?" asked Helen.

Bill told her.

"What a silly man, in all my service I have never heard of anything so ridiculous."

"Roy says he is super efficient and sticks to the book but how do you change someone with an attitude that only upsets people, it does not help them or himself. Maybe he has a thing about always being right, I expect his wife loves him if nobody else does. I am going to bend Roy's ear when he returns from his holiday."

"I am sure he will appreciate such a welcome home present Bill," laughed Helen.

"Here he comes."

"If you will come with me to the orderly room I will give you that address sir."

"Thank you Sergeant, lead the way."

He gave Helen a wink as they left her office.

"They never spoke on the way to the orderly room. The Sergeant went behind the counter and produced the address then handed it over still without a word.

"Thank you Sergeant Thomson, that is very kind of you." On his way out he could have sworn he heard a muffled titter from the rear of the office.

"Here you are Viv, the name of the hotel you wanted."

"Thanks Bill how did it go with the C.O.?"

"He just laughed, he did not say it but he thought Thomson was a bit of a Plonker he came from the office a very subdued man. Roy will be none too pleased when I tell him. Anyway, I think when you show Derwent that card and you turn your charm on him he will be a push over, actually that hotel appeals to me but I will hear your verdict when you return whenever that will be. Now don't go telling Tommy I said that."

"I won't Bill, I promise."

"What were the reactions from your female staff after we had to let their friends go?"

"They were sad; there were a few tears which was only natural but relief because it was not one them who had got the chop."

"Are Alan and his lads coping alright in ops'?

"Oh yes there are no problems, actually they are a very funny team we have some really good laughs in there."

"Have you had any feed back from Bob Dixon or his Corporals?"

"Yes, they are finding the airmen are hard work and wish they were all airwomen."

"We will have a look at them tomorrow, discretely of course, that okay with you?"

"Certainly."

"Talk of the devils, here they come, I never realized it was that time. Let's go next door and hear what they have to say."

"Have you had a good day training the elite?"

"Elite! Is that what you call them?" asked Bob Dixon. I am not kidding you; most of those lads are as thick as two short planks. Where the hell did the assessors get the idea that they were officer material from? I will rephrase that, they could be right you know but they would make very poor airmen! We have kids out there who do not know they have a left and right arm and leg never mind knowing which is which. This could only happen to us with our first special flight. We also have got two bods who swing the same arm with the same leg when marching."

Everyone in the room burst out laughing.

"It is no joke," said Bob Dixon even though he was laughing with the rest, it is not fair on the rest of the flight can you come up with a solution sir?"

"As a matter of fact I can. Corporal Harris, Corporal Lucas, I have a job for you."

"Oh no sir," they groaned, anything but that."

"You should be thankful this problem has arisen, just think of the experience you will gain and how relieved Sergeant Dixon will be to get them off his hands. Think of the pleasure it will give him when you return two fully trained, well lets say two bods who can now march properly. He will welcome them back with open arms and perhaps he might even treat you to a brew for your efforts."

"Make that brew singular, they can join at one," said Sergeant Dixon as he showed the lining of an empty pocket.

"Wow!" was the spontaneous reply, when do we start sir?"

"Tomorrow morning after prayers!"

Every one of them in the room clapped and laughed their heads off.

"Come on, it is home time. He went back to his office singing, 'It's a Lovely day Tomorrow, Tomorrow is a lovely Day'.

"What is that man like?" someone said in answer to the singing.

Bill was having his meal when Derwent arrived and sat with him.

"I am given to understand that Viv has let the cat out of the bag!"

"She has told you then?"

“Yes, it was very funny actually how it happened but so easily done. She was telling me about the post-card I suppose you have already seen it?”

“Yes, she showed it me a few minutes ago and told me about the slip-up.”

“It came out so easy. She was saying she would like to stay there but you prefer Tenerife. That was it, she then told me the whole story, mind you I made her none the wiser that I knew all about it and that is when the trouble started.”

“What trouble?” queried Derwent; “she never mentioned anything about there being any trouble!”

“Bill told him the tale.”

“I do not believe it, what is he trying to prove? Roy says he is very efficient but strange, he will do his nut when you tell him.”

“Forget him, have you and Viv sorted out yet where you are going and when? And before you say anything I will bet you a pint it will be the Algarve.”

“I know from past experience you have the knack of betting on the winner. No, we have not decided yet, but…..

“You are going to accept defeat like a gentleman,” interrupted Bill.

“Is there anything good on the Telly tonight?” asked a grinning Derwent.

>>> <<<

“Will you be all right left on your own to hold the fort while Viv and I go and run our eyes over the flights Alan?”

“No problem Bill, I will keep the door locked then I will feel safe.”

“The RAF News is on my desk if you want to have a read there is an article in it about March we get a favourable report.”

“Thanks I will have a look at it.”

“Come on Viv, we will start with Sergeant York.”

From a respectful distance they watched the recruits being put through their paces.

“I am impressed with Sergeant York he has the makings of a damned good instructor do you see how he is manipulating his Corporals bringing out the best in them? Have you ever seen that program on TV One Man and his Dog where one handler works two dogs to reach the one objective? That is what he reminds me of, total control of his Corporals at work and I thought he was a bit cocksure of himself when he first arrived.

Now to see how Joe has settled down after that silly hic-up. There he goes, quiet and efficient but the recruits know who is in charge and his Corporals respect him. Now why has he brought them to a halt? Ah, I see he has just admonished that lad in the rear rank for talking.”

“How do you know that?” asked Viv.

"Joe moved his fingers across his mouth denoting, keep it zipped. Give Joe his due nothing escapes his beady eyes. He knows we are watching too."

"How on earth do you know that he has never turned his head in our direction?"

"He saw us out of the corner of his eye when he approached that lad and when he recognised who it was he braced himself up and squared his shoulders."

"Hmm! I know someone else with beady eyes," snorted Viv.

"Joe and I are of the old school we were trained properly.

Right then, let us go and see how your Sergeant Dean is shaping up, this time you do the assessing."

"Here we are and it looks like she is giving them a pep talk."

"How do you figure that out?" asked Bill.

"They are still stood to attention and she is doing quite a bit of pointing to individuals. It must be something to do with the co-ordination of head and arms when carrying out the eyes right/left routine because she is using a Corporal to show how the movement is carried out."

"That is indeed what she is doing," said Bill with approval.

"What is she like as a person?"

"Very dependable she knows her job and she is well liked, quick to retaliate if someone upsets her but she is in full control, I have never seen her lose her temper but she has a wicked sense of humour. Margaret Roper, a very experienced instructor. I am surprised she has not been considered for promotion before now. I do not know why she has been passed over she has been a Sergeant for quite some time now and I know she has a clean record. Very dependable, she knows her job inside out she reminds me very much of Mary Butcher firm but fair. If ever I got posted she is the one who would fill my place and nobody would know the difference, providing she got the rank to go with the job."

"Thanks Viv, I will look at her in a different light from now on. I wonder if she has any inkling that she has a good friend in her corner."

"Last but not least by any means, Sergeant Dixon and his performing fairies."

"Bob told me," said Viv, "it took him a full day and a lot of circuits round the parade ground carried out on the double before they could fall in on their marker to his satisfaction."

"Then that is why they are still only at the stage of turning at the halt. Just look at those airmen, they are not a patch on the airwomen. No wonder Bob Dixon is frustrated who wouldn't be, I am going to have a word with him."

He walked behind the flight so the recruits could not see him then beckoned Bob over. Bob had a word with Corporal Harper to keep them facing front.

"Hi Bob, I see what you mean about those airmen, they *are* a bunch of fairies and I know about you doubling them round the parade ground and it worked. Now what is your next step because they are holding the airwomen back?"

"I have something up my sleeve and if it does not work you can kick me off your staff."

"That sounds a bit dramatic Bob, are you going to tell me what it is or have I to wait to see you come into ops' with a big smile on your face?"

"Give me a couple of days and you will see a difference Bill."

"Right then I will leave you to it, but don't let them drag those girls down."

When he got back to Viv he said. "I think those lads are the worse recruits I have ever seen and what I cannot understand is there are so many of them. Anyway Bob has something up his sleeve he is going to hit them with, I hope for his sake it works."

When Bob got back to his flight he remonstrated with them about their lack of commitment. "You have one hour to show me you are trying and if you do not convince me, do you know what I shall do? At 6pm you will fall in outside your accommodation and I personally will drill you for an hour and this will happen every evening until I am satisfied. Corporal James march the airwomen away from here and continue with their drill, they will not be on the 6pm parades that is exclusive for this bunch of fairies."

There were a few suppressed giggles from the girls but he pretended not to hear it.

Bill and Viv met George Miller as they were walking away.

"Hello Bill," he said, then with a big grin. "Have you been to see that lot in action? Bob Dixon has got summat' on his plate trying to teach them, honestly I do not know what has got into youngsters these days, and to think that some day we may have to salute some of these."

"It does not bear thinking about George, what we have to suffer for our Queen and country! Anyway, Bob tells me he has a secret weapon he is going to introduce he says it is guaranteed to produce results."

"Would that be a medical discharge? Got to go Bill, it is getting brew time."

"It is nearly knocking off time replied Bill."

"That makes it taste all the better, I'll tell you something, my lads can make a good crafty brew now after a few tips from the Master. Ta ra, Bill, Viv."

"He is some character," remarked Viv.

"They don't come any better than George. By the way Tommy and I will be picking up Roy and Barbara late afternoon on Saturday so it will be too late to go shopping in Leeds unless Tommy wants to go early to shop in the morning have lunch then go to the airport."

"I am looking forward to getting a first hand report about that hotel, we will not book until I have spoken with her and I can't wait!"

"Did you decide or Derwent on the Algarve?"

"It was a joint decision did you think it could have been otherwise?"

"Yes!"

"Well actually it was....Bill interrupted her.

"No! Don't tell me I will ask Derwent and hear what he has to say."

CHAPTER 17

Friday afternoon and training was over for the day the flights had been dismissed and the instructors made their way to the ops' room to report. Bill wanted to see if Bob Dixon was smiling. When Bob reported in Bill asked him "What kind of a day have you had and have you anything to report? How are those lads shaping up and are you still having problems with them?"

"Problems, what problems?"

"You sly devil, you have cracked it. Where is that smile of success then?"

"How will this do?" he said as he put a finger in each side of his mouth and pulled outwards.

"Okay, okay, don't overdo it. Now tell me about it."

"For two evenings running I had them on parade from 6pm till 7pm and believe me they hated every minute of it, they did not want it a third time. You should see the difference in them now; their leisure time is too valuable for them to lose anymore there will be no more problems I can guarantee that."

"Well done Bob, wait till George Miller sees them now, he felt right sorry for you when he saw what you were up against, how are the Corporals getting on with those two awkward bods have they had any luck yet?"

"Oh yes, they brought them back today completely cured, they did a grand job for me, which reminds me I owe them a mug of tea to join at." he said grinning.

>>> <<<

"What do you want to do tomorrow love?" Bill asked Tommy. Do you want to make a full day of it by going shopping in Leeds in the morning, having lunch then carrying on to the airport?"

"Now you really are coming round to my way of thinking you darling man, that would be very nice because I do not know when we will have the chance to go again."

"Very soon pet, we will be doing the same for Derwent and Viv as soon as they make their minds up when Viv gets the gen from Barbara about the hotel."

"Now that has got me thinking Mr William Barrett."

"Oh hello, I have a good idea of what is coming next."

"If you are so psychic. When?"

"Look, can we talk of this some other time?" he said looking at his watch. "I really have to go and see George Miller; he will be waiting and wondering where I have got to?"

"I can tell you where George will be right now, sat opposite his wife at the dinner table and if you want me to keep you company tomorrow going to Leeds then you had better start coming up smartly with some answers. I will tell you what I am going to do. I am leaving you to think about it overnight then at breakfast you can make my day by telling me if we are or not. If the answer is no then I will give you my engagement ring back."

"But you haven't got an engagement ring!"

"Ah, so you *have* noticed have you? That is another problem you have got, poor darling."

Bill did not wait to hear any more he took to his heels and fled to his room. He did not see or hear Tommy laughing.

All the following day neither subject was mentioned again much to the relief of a very concerned Bill and inwardly a very amused Tommy.

The aircraft was on time arriving and half an hour later the holiday makers came trundling their trolleys to run the gauntlet of taxi drivers with placards bearing the names of their passengers and people waiting to meet and greet someone, but there was no sign of Roy and Barbara.

"I wonder if they have missed their flight?" said a worried Bill, or something has happened to stop them?"

"There they are," said an excited Tommy waving her hand frantically, look Bill they have seen us."

After kisses and a handshake, Bill said. "You had me worried what kept you?" He took control of the trolley and steered them to their parked car. Viv and Barbara trailed behind arm in arm and Roy walked with Bill.

"Have you enjoyed it Roy?"

"It has been great Bill, loved every minute of it, it was spoiled though at this end by the bloody customs."

"So that was the reason for the delay, wait until we get in the car Roy then you can pour your heart out to Uncle Bill."

The two girls were engrossed in woman's talk and even stopped while Barbara made a point.

"Just look at them two said an impatient Roy they can't wait to talk scandal."

”Why, was there any?” asked an inquisitive Bill. “Are you going to tell me the juicy bits?”

“There was NO scandal and there were no bloody juicy bits, so wind your neck in!”

Bill chuckled. “Come on ladies this man is anxious to get home.”

The two girls were sat in the back seats chatting away and ignoring the men.

“Have you been upsetting Her Majesty’s Customs Officials Roy?”

“Customs, what do they know about our customs? I was heading for the Green Channel when one of them who had been leaning on a table looking bored, beckoned me.”

“Are you and the lady together sir? Then would you mind stepping this way please?”

“But we have nothing to declare that is why we were going through green.”

“This way please.”

He went behind a table and told me to put the cases on it.

“Have you anything to declare sir?”

“I told you out there I had not.”

“Open the cases please.”

“He literary emptied the two cases and the hand baggage and found nothing.”

“Thank you sir you may repack your cases, you are free to proceed.”

“I was about to give him a mouthful but fortunately Barbara saw the danger signs, she got hold of my arm and said. “Leave it Roy, he is in charge here.” Yes, I know I should not have got irritated but it was his attitude that got right up my nose.”

“So there you are Bill, now that I have got that off my chest I feel better. What exciting news have you got for me?”

“I have plenty for you Roy but this is not the time and place.”

“Serious stuff then?”

“You could say that but it will have to wait, what I can tell you now is Derwent and Viv are planning a trip and Viv cannot wait to get hold of Barbara, she wants to know everything about the hotel you stayed in. Derwent wanted Tenerife and Viv the Algarve but when she received your card that was it as far as she was concerned, you can bet *she* has kicked Tenerife into touch. She is ready for a good holiday I think she is looking a bit weary and no wonder she has had no leave for yonks’.”

“Well she won’t do any better than there, it is a really good hotel don’t you fancy it Bill?”

“Shush, keep your voice down,” then in a low tone he said. “Tommy has got the holiday bug but for goodness sake do not say a word about it.” Then in a louder voice he asked. You will not feel like doing much tonight will you Roy?"

"I dunno' I will leave it up to Barbara." Speaking over his shoulder he asked. "What are we doing tonight pet?"

"As far as I can tell there is only the Mess or the March Hare, there will be Bingo on in the Mess and I do not really feel like going to the village. What say we go into the Quiet Room in the Mess and have a drink and a chat?"

"A chat? You have never stopped since we left the airport."

"Can you come up with a better suggestion Master Mind? Viv and Derwent will want to join us so what is better than having our little family get together? Remember we have not seen them for two weeks and there is so much us girls have to talk about."

"We must tell Derwent to bring his ear-muffs tonight Bill."

"Barbara retaliated with. "I should have left you with that nice customs man, Roy Shaw!"

When they arrived at the camp and were off-loading the cases, Bill said. "I will see you at dinner then Roy."

"Yes alright Bill. I tell you what, why don't we all sit at one table for dinner it is weekend and we may be the only ones in."

"On yer' bike Roy Shaw," said Tommy we have more woman's talk to get through especially with Viv being there as well and we are allowed some privacy from the City Fathers."

"Hear, hear," said Barbara in support. "Bye Bye, boys."

At dinner the three crackpots were sat together. After welcoming Roy back Derwent said. "Viv and I are hoping to go to the Algarve soon, she has been eagerly waiting for Barbara to get back then she can get all the information about the hotel you stayed in and the area."

"Well they are having a good chin-wag right now I see," said Bill. "By the way Derwent I understood you wanted to go to Tenerife, what happened did you change your mind?"

"More likely Viv changed it for him," laughed Roy. "You know what these women are like once they get a fixed idea in their heads, you can't shift em'."

"I'll hold my hand up there, Viv had the last word although that card you sent us Roy finalised it."

"I would like to thank you two for dropping me right in it," complained Bill. "You have passed this holiday bug on to Tommy; she is starting to twitter about holidays now and giving me a hard time. I know what will happen; I can see myself falling in the same trap as you two guys."

"Serves you right," smirked Roy. "Why should you be any different to us?"

"I couldn't agree more," piped up Derwent. "Welcome to the Hen Pecked Club."

"Are you going to tell me this so called bad news now Bill."

"Roy, I do not want to spoil your weekend, let it lie until Monday but there is one bit of bad news you will be interested in that I *can* divulge. Chalky has finished as duty barman."

"Who has replaced him then?"

"Harry Gordon from Workshops."

"Oh,No! Not 'Appy Arry? The Prima Donna of the village football team that is his sole interest. If you are a football fan you will be his pal for life, anything else and he does not want to know. "I will have a bet with you, when we enter the bar tonight he will either be sat down or stood at the bar reading a football magazine providing he is not serving anybody."

"You are on," said Bill, a pint!"

"Me too," said Derwent. "If Bill has a pint bet he always wins."

"Right gents I am off, I am going to have an hour on my bed and I advise you both to do the same for we are going to get ear-ache tonight when the three girls get together," warned Roy.

"That makes sense agreed Bill, come on lets go."

As they passed the girls who still had their heads together, Bill said. "Don't stay there too long the stewards may have dates tonight."

That evening they all met up at reception. At the entrance to the bar room Roy stopped them outside, he said to Tommy. "Will you poke your head round the door and tell me if anyone is being served at the bar?"

She did as Roy asked, when she reported back she shook her head. "There is nobody there, what is that all about?"

"He is trying to win a bet," said Derwent. "He said the barman would be reading a football magazine if he was not serving someone."

"Come on, come on before somebody comes in," said an anxious Roy.

When they arrived sure enough Harry was sat reading a magazine.

"Evening 'Arry," greeted Roy, I thought you would have been playing football and got a stand-in barman?"

"Evening Roy, evening all. No not this time I am on the injured list, what can I get you folk?"

Bill ordered for everyone, after being served he and Derwent went to take a drink when Roy asked. "What are you reading there 'Arry?"

"A Travel Magazine."

Immediately Bill and Derwent spluttered in their beer and gave themselves a bout of coughing.

"What is the matter?" asked the girls who were curled up with laughter, "has it gone down the wrong way?"

"Have I said something wrong?" asked Harry.

"It is alright 'Arry," answered Roy, "it is these two silly sods taking the Mickey out of me, come on let us go and get a table for four," he said to the girls, "leave these two here to get over their silliness."

When they all got settled down at the table, Derwent thanked Bill.

"What are you thanking him for?" asked Viv.

"He has just won me a pint, good old Bill."

"When you two boys have settled down shall we start a sensible conversation or have we to drink up and leave?" Demanded Tommy.

"Sorry, we apologise," they said after that reprimand.

After that the evening went well, Roy and Barbara took centre stage talking about their holiday to an interested threesome,. Bill's interest was elsewhere he was trying to shake out of his head jewellers and rings and when would the subject be brought up in conversation again when he and Tommy are alone? He looked across at Tommy and she caught his thoughtful look. She guessed with that woman's intuition what was on his mind. The 'I know what is worrying you look' she gave him only brought a wry smile from him. She is reading my bloody thoughts he said to himself, I can tell by that look.

"Penny for them Bill," she smiled rubbing it in. He is not going to wriggle out of this she said to herself and he knows that I know what is worrying him.

"I was just trying to remember what the round of drinks were, are you ready for another everyone?"

"I will come and give you a hand with them Bill," offered Derwent.

When they had left the room Derwent said. "That was some laugh at the bar did you see Roy's face when 'Arry told him what he was reading. Poor old Roy I'll bet he wished the floor could have swallowed him up."

"No, I was too busy choking," laughed Bill. "God knows what his reactions are going to be when I tell him about his super efficient Sergeant I think I will leave off telling him until Tuesday just to see if Thomson does confess to Roy what had happened. I have a gut feeling he will keep quiet about it, if he does not tell him he will find himself right in the ess aitch one tee."

>>> <<<

Monday morning Bill and Viv went to see Bob Dixon's new look flight. On the way they met George Miller.

"Are you going to see the same as we are asked Bill?"

"If it is to see 'The Dance of the Sugar Plum Fairies' yes I am. I heard he has been giving them some overtime for an hour in the evenings I hope he has cracked it. You know as well as I do Bill if you take an airman's off duty away it is like the end of the world to him. Fine him, punish him, give him extra duties and he will moan like the clappers but to interfere with his free time that is sacrilege."

"Well, there they are George, what do you think?"

"I would not believe that was the same flight well done Bob tha's cracked it lad, he will have no more trouble with that lot Bill."

"Right then, we will be off, work to do, be seeing you George."

"Aren't you both coming for a brew?"

"No time thanks George, pop round our place sometime and sample ours."

"There has been a call for you from WO Shaw, he wants you to ring him," reported Sergeant Fell.

"Thanks Alan." Then to Viv he said. "I will leave it for a while I am going to put him in the picture about his Sergeant but I want to leave it today to see if he tells Roy what has happened. I have a feeling he will not say anything, if he is so proficient he should report it to Roy. If the phone rings again will you answer it please? If it is Roy tell him I am sorting some problems out in the field."

At dinner that evening Roy came in and sat with Bill and Derwent. "I have been trying to get hold of you all day Bill, have you been in hiding?"

"It has been one of those days Roy when I have had to be in too many places at once to sort out problems."

"I thought you might be fobbing me off about this serious chat we are supposed to be having."

"Not at all Roy, look, I promise to come and see you about the middle of the morning tomorrow, you have my word on that and I will expect your usual hospitality."

"I thought so there is always a catch to it when you come to see me. I see you have had big changes in your staff while I have been away."

"Yes, the big change over has started and I have lost five of the WRAF. At the present time I am struggling along with the staff I have got, that will last for another couple of weeks or so then it is all systems go. How are things at your end is everything as you left it, no problems to greet you on your return?"

"None at all Bill, I have a good Sergeant. Efficiency is his middle name and he has done a great job while I have been absent you will not find many like him these days. Have there been any more developments from Tommy?"

"Not yet Roy but I am sure she is cooking something up, she has been quiet about it far too long."

"Hello, am I missing out on something here?" asked Derwent.

"Okay I will tell him Roy. Tommy has caught the holiday bug from you four, she is trying to put me on the spot to take her and I am trying my best to wriggle out of it."

"But why?" asked Derwent.

"Simple, I do not want to go on holiday, not for some time anyway."

"You will not get away with it Bill," added Roy "once these females get their teeth into something their jaws clamp tight, very tight. You have not a cat in hells chance of getting out of it, bet me a pint and it will be the first time you will have lost."

"I will bet on that as well," added Derwent, "you will not win this time Billy Boy!"

"Thank you gentlemen for your vote of confidence but I do accept I have not got a leg to stand on regarding Tommy and the holiday, it is now a case of when!"

"Will you be coming in the bar tonight Roy to pay your respects to 'Appy 'Arry?"

"No, I have a bit of home work I want to catch up on."

"I'm just trying to be sociable Roy."

"I know and it always costs me."

"Did you pal up with anyone in the hotel?"

"Not really we just passed the time of day with one or two, they were mostly all foreigners." When he realised what he had said he let out such a loud laugh that startled the rest of the diners. "No, we kept to ourselves it is much better that way."

Tuesday morning Bill said to Viv. "I must go and break the news to Roy he is certainly going to be disillusioned with his Mr Perfect."

"I bet Roy will wish he had stayed in Portugal, nothing has gone right for him since he came back. I wonder what he will do to his Sergeant?" asked Viv.

"Right, here we go and once more into the breach dear friends, or summat' like that. He picked up the phone. "Hi Roy, its Bill, are you free for me to come and see you? Okay I am on my way."

"Now what is this big mystery you have kept putting off?"

"The reason I have delayed in telling you Roy was for a very good reason.

I had hoped the person concerned would have reported to you immediately you were back in office."

"Sounds very onimous Bill"

"Don't you mean ominous Roy?

"You know I can't say ominous!"

"It is and it concerns your Sergeant Thomson. Because I had no prior notification when the new intake was due to arrive I went on Friday afternoon to find out and your Sergeant told me they would arrive Wednesday afternoon."

"It must have slipped his mind Bill being so busy while I was away."

“I went to see Mary Butcher to tell her and she replied that she already knew but only by accident. Apparently your WRAF Corporal went to see Mary for some reason or other and off hand she asked, if the new intake coming on Wednesday were the mixed one? Now I don’t think your super efficient Sergeant would have forgotten twice.”

“I take your point Bill I will definitely take that up with him. Is that it then?”

“No! This is the serious one Roy.”

He then told the tale in detail. “But what the C.O. said to him I do not know I was not present.”

“Bloody Nora Bill, that is bad, you know having such faith in the man’s ability and efficiency it comes hard to believe. He has really let me down, not just me but the rest of my staff what will the C.O. think? He will wonder what sort of an orderly room I am running. Bloody hell Bill that *has* hurt.”

“Don’t put too much in thinking what the C.O. thinks about your orderly room, he has a wise head on his shoulders and he will know the score and also take into account you were on leave at the time.”

“I will find out what his game was and what he was trying to prove and I will wring every word out of him what the C.O. said. Thanks Bill, I now realise why you spared me all this until now it would have been a very disastrous homecoming for me. Thank you, you indeed are a really good friend” He then shook Bill’s hand warmly.

“Well aren’t we like a couple of book ends you and I Roy? I had better leave you now but a friendly word of advice, give yourself time to calm down then attack him with a firm but clear head. Good Luck and I will see you later.”

He went to have a word with Mary Butcher. “It is kind of you to drop in now and again to see an old friend Bill Barrett, where have you been hiding and why?”

“I do not know Mary I have less staff but seem to have less time to myself. Since I lost the SWO job I have more troubles than ever, hopefully when this new system really starts things will improve. I have just left Roy after giving him the bad news about Superman; he is ready to literarily tear him to bits with his bare hands. I have advised him to calm down before confronting him and I am looking forward to the result.”

“I think Roy will make things so uncomfortable he will ask for a move.”

“You are right, that is what I would do except I would not give him the option.”

At lunch Bill and Derwent were eagerly waiting for Roy to show, they had just finished eating when he arrived.

“Before you start asking questions would it be too much to ask if I could eat my lunch in peace?”

"No problem Roy, we will just sit here and be very quiet while you feed your face."

"Aye, like two bloody vultures, I would go and sit with Mary but she does not like company while she is eating, beggars can't be choosers as they say."

"I did not realise what a slow eater you are Roy," said Bill.

"If you do not like it you may find that I will do a Sergeant Smith on you and let you finish it off."

"Touchy touchy, are we, you are eating slowly on purpose aren't you?"

"*YES*!"

When he had finally finished Derwent asked. "Shall I go and get you a cup of coffee Roy?"

"No, but thank you for asking I will go for my own I want to go for a little walk." Off he went, got his coffee then walked out of the dining room with it. The other two could not see the big grin on his face and they could not believe what they saw. Then suddenly they both realised what Roy had done and began to laugh out loud much to the consternation of the other diners.

They caught up with him in the TV room.

"It is not often I can pull a fast one on you two but it was fun. Suckers! And before you ask, NO! I have not seen him yet I have carried out what you advised me to do Bill; now I am ready for the fray, so if you will excuse me I would like to watch the News programme. On your way out would you mind dropping this cup off in the dining room please?"

CHAPTER 18

When Roy was entering SHQ after his lunch he saw his orderly room Corporal Graham waiting at the entrance. "Hi Corp'" he greeted him with, taking a breath of air before we make a start."

"No sir, I would like a word with you in private somewhere where we cannot be overheard."

"It is serious then?"

"Very serious sir."

"Come with me then."

He took him to Barbara's office and told him to wait outside.

When he entered Barbara looked up in surprise. "What are you doing here sweetheart?" They kissed.

"I have my Corporal outside and he wants to speak with me on something serious and wants to be where we cannot be overheard and I was wondering if the conference room is free for a little while?"

"It is free and will not be used today. Here is the key."

"Thanks love, I have got a gut feeling about this that I am not going to like.

Come on Corporal we will not be disturbed in here, is it all right by you if I lock the door?"

"Please do sir I will feel better for it."

"Very well, sit down and get it off your chest whatever it is."

"It concerns Sergeant Thomson sir. Of late when one of the duty clerks including myself have gone to do a security check we have found Sergeant Thomson in the orderly room with the special filing cabinet open. He said he was doing some after hours checking-up while it was quiet and he would see to the locking and security of the orderly room when he had finished. To obtain the key to that special cabinet he would have needed the safe key. Last night he was disturbed by the duty clerk SAC. Barton who heard him speaking in a foreign language as he opened the door and he then spotted a hand held recorder, which the Sergeant had not hidden fast enough. The clerk by the way did not imagine hearing a foreign language because he happens to be bi-lingual himself and he placed it as Eastern European but did not know its origin."

"Bloody Nora Corporal that is red hot, come on we have to take this to higher authority immediately." They both went into Barbara's office, as Roy handed back the key he asked. "Is the O.C. in?"

"Yes but I am afraid he is busy can I book an appointment for you sir?"

"NO! Definitely not, we must see him right away."

"But sir…"

"Right away, tell him it is of a very high security nature, please do as I say."

"She buzzed the O.C. please can I come to see you sir we have a security alert." Not saying a word she dashed into his office and told him what Roy had said.

"Send them in immediately Barbara."

As she returned through the door she waved them in to the office.

They both saluted.

"Security alert Mr Shaw?

"Yes sir, right under our very noses. I will ask Corporal Graham to tell you what he told me."

"Relax Corporal and tell me in your own time and words not the official brisk jargon we have to put up with."

The Corporal feeling very much at ease told him everything.

"Thank you very much Corporal you are right Mr Shaw we do have a very serious security problem on our hands, now we have to go a stage further and report it to the Commanding Officer. It looks like you are just at the beginning of repeating your tale Corporal " He buzzed Barbara, "get me the C.O.'s office please Barbara."

"Hello sir, can I come to see you right away it is a matter of security, thank you I will be bringing Warrant Officer Shaw and Corporal Graham with me."

When they entered the C.O's office they saluted.

"Now Mr Shaw what is all this about, a security breach?"

"Corporal Graham will explain sir."

"Hello Corporal I do not think we have met before, what is the section you work in?"

"Orderly Room sir."

"Right then, tell me clearly and in your own words, nothing fancy mind you but straight to the point and goodness sake lad relax I am here to hear what you have got to say not to bite your head off. When you are ready fire away."

The Corporal was very surprised at the easy-going attitude of the C.O. and his attempt to put him at ease.

He repeated everything he had told the other two.

The C.O. looked at the O.C. "Well, we have certainly got a hot one in our lap here. You two, go and wait in my PA's office. This is very serious Eric, we have to call in the S.I.B. on this one." He buzzed Helen. "Helen, get me the S.I.B. HQ please. That was very commendable of that Corporal and it has certainly stirred up a hornets nest." He picked up the ringing phone. "Hello is that S.I.B. HQ? I would like to speak to your Commanding Officer I am Group Captain Wildeman, Commanding Officer of RAF March… yes I will hold the line…. Hello Wing Commander… yes, RAF March, the very ones who trained the BlueBelles… thank you that is very kind of you. The reason I am ringing you is because we have just had what I think is a very high breach of security which sounds like it could be very serious indeed." He then explained what had happened. "Yes, we will do that, right, we will see you soon and I would like to be present when you interview my men and be put in the picture of the action you will be taking, thank you."

"They, whoever they are will be here in an hour or so. In the meantime Mr Shaw and Corporal Graham must carry on as usual and to treat it as top security. Will you bring them in Eric?"

"Gentlemen you are now sworn to secrecy, it is Top Secret and is now in the hands of the S.I.B. You Corporal Graham will have to repeat your story I do not know how many times yet and thank you for bringing this matter to our attention." He stood up and shook the Corporal's hand much to his amazement.

"What you have to do Mr Shaw is carry on your routine as normal, I can see it being awkward for you Corporal because as soon as the S.I.B. arrive they will want to interview you and of course the lad who reported it to you. How can we work round that?"

“I have an idea sir,” said Roy. To cover his absence this afternoon I found him feeling very ill coming into SHQ. I took him to Sick Quarters where they are keeping an eye on him. The Corporal asked for SAC Barton to come for his room key and bring him something he wants. In the meantime the two of them will be in the guardroom waiting for the S.I.B. All it needs is the co-operation of Sick Quarters in case of any phone calls.

“Excellent Mr Shaw, do you read Agatha Christie by any chance? What do you think of that Wing Commander?”

“It certainly solves the problem and as you say sir, it is like something straight out of an Agatha Christie novel, well done Mr Shaw.”

“By the way sir I was having Sergeant Thomson before me this afternoon to explain that little matter with WO Barrett, do you think I should go ahead? It would seem like normal routine if I did.”

“Go ahead Mr Shaw, that is the best thing that could happen he will be too concerned about that to think of anything else, I thought when I interviewed him he seemed a strange fellow. However, go ahead and give him rice.”

“Thank you sir,” they both saluted then left.

“Now we have to get you to the guardroom unseen by anyone Corporal You did very well in there I will send SAC Barton to the guardroom when I get back. Come on we will sneak out through the front entrance of SHQ.”

When they arrived at the guardroom Flight Sergeant Bridges was just coming off the phone. “I have just been briefed by the C.O. so I know what I have to do. It sounds serious Roy is it?”

“Very serious Tom but I cannot say anything, sorry but you will soon find out when the cavalry arrive I dare not even confide in my best mate. Here I go, now for the next phase.” Roy went back to the orderly room and spoke to Sergeant Thomson. “Corporal Graham will not be in for the rest of the day I had to take him to Sick Quarters. I met him coming in to SHQ and he was feeling pretty ill. They are keeping an eye on him but do not think it is anything serious. Oh yes, SAC Barton go over to Sick Quarters the Corporal wants to give you his room key for you to take some things over that he needs. Come on lets be having you.”

“What, now sir?”

“Yes now and get your skates on and do not come back this afternoon it would be too late for you to do anything. You are duty clerk today aren’t you?”

“Yes sir.”

“That will not interfere with your Florence Nightingale visit.”

Roy walked out the door with him then said quietly. “Forget all that, report to the guardroom Corporal Graham is there, he will explain everything and good luck. Come, I will show you out the front entrance.”

He returned to his office and sat awhile his head churning with the afternoon's events. He asked for a brew feeling he needed one to clear his head for the interview to come. When he felt ready he opened the hatch and called. "Sergeant Thomson, will you come round please?"

When he arrived he went to take a seat.

"No Sergeant I want you to stand."

"Why, is there something wrong sir?"

"There is and I am not pleased with what I hear. Can you explain to me why you omitted to inform WO Barrett and WO Butcher about the pending arrival of the new recruit intake?"

"I did not think it relevant, they would have found out soon enough."

"How? Through the grapevine? This is a recruit training establishment and they are the people who do the training. Did it not occur to you they may want to know the number of airmen and the number of airwomen to be accommodated instead of waiting until they arrive then begin counting heads not knowing how many there should be then getting them put into accommodation. You Sergeant Thomson are not as efficient as I first thought. What have you got to say about that?"

"Whatever I say will mean nothing, everyone makes mistakes but you are in no mood for an apology so I am not giving you one. You have got your knife in me now and you are about to start twisting it."

"You bet I am and it is going to hurt like hell. There is something else I did not pick up about you, which you have just shown me. You are full of arrogance and there is no room for that in my team."

"Can I go now Sir?" emphasising the sir.

"No you bloody well can not; I have not finished with you yet. When I returned from leave you told me there had been no problems, that was as far away from the truth as it could be. Why did you not tell me the Commanding Officer had you on the carpet?"

"That was just a triviality, a difference of opinion between WO Barrett and me."

"It was not trivial enough to be brought to the attention of the Station Commander."

"Look, if I let little things like that upset me I would be a nervous wreck by now, go away and be a good boy was the message I got."

"Well get this message from me I do not want you in my orderly room corrupting my staff with your arrogance and irresponsibility longer than is necessary, I will do my utmost to get you posted out of here as quickly as possible. Now get out of my office you make me sick and get your head stuck into the work you are here to do."

Roy thumped his desk in frustration muttering "IF ONLY!" When he had calmed down he smiled to himself thinking of what was in store for the Sergeant.

In the guardroom the S.I.B. had taken control, they had taken over a cell and had it temporary furnished with a table and chairs. There was a Squadron Leader, a Warrant Officer, two RAF Sergeants and two WRAF Sergeants The Squadron Leader immediately phoned the Station Commander to tell him the interviews were ready to begin. When the C.O. arrived the S.I.B. party were introduced and then began the interviews. Corporal Graham was first then SAC Barton was questioned for a long period, making sure about him seeing the recorder and hearing the foreign language. They asked the Corporal how often the Sergeant went to the orderly room after hours?

"He has increased his visits to three nights a week but I do not know in which order."

Tom Bridges was called for and was told by the Squadron Leader to post someone indiscreetly to watch SHQ after the building has been closed down. "I will post the Duty Clerk with him, he will identify Thomson then both he and the watcher will report back here as soon as Thomson enters SHQ. Who is Duty Clerk Corporal?"

"I am sir," said SAC Barton."

"Splendid, it could not have been better," said the Squadron Leader He then addressed the Station Commander. "This is my plan of action sir. Myself my Warrant Officer and the two Sergeants will accompany the Duty Clerk to the orderly room. He will open the door as he normally would on his security check, naturally the Sergeant will have something to say which the clerk will go along with then as he leaves we rush in and take him by surprise. We then bring him back to the guardroom while the Duty Clerk remains on guard in the orderly room until your Warrant Officer arrives to make sure everything is in order and nothing is missing. I would also like your Medical Officer to be present when we strip and search Sergeant Thomson. When that is completed my two Sergeants will stand guard over him and he will remain handcuffed. Myself, my Warrant Officer, my two WRAF Sergeants and the Medical Officer will then proceed to his Married Quarter and take his wife into custody. After a quick search of the premises I require the house to be sealed and will remain so until a release order comes from National Security HQ. They will go through the house with a fine-toothed comb. One final thing sir, National Security will need a written statement from all your personnel who have been involved."

"Thank you Squadron Leader, that was very informative, I would like to be here when you bring that wretched man in, I promise not to interfere."

"That will be no problem sir, I would like that."

"Thank you I will now go home, have an early meal and will return about 6pm."

"Talking of meals, Flight Sergeant Bridges will you get a good dinner sent from the Airmen's Mess for Corporal Graham?"

"What about meals for your staff sir?" asked Tom.

"We cater for that by bringing a snack with us, if we went into any of the Messes we would only draw attention to ourselves which we do not want. SAC Barton, you can go to the Mess for your meal, carry on as you normally would but when you have finished your meal and done what you normally do in your accommodation do not linger but go to your position to join the watcher. Flight Sergeant Bridges will tell you where he is in hiding and do not forget, as soon as Sergeant Thomson enters SHQ you both return here to report. Got it?"

"Yes sir."

"Good lad, off you go.

Yes Corporal?"

"Can I make a suggestion sir?"

"Of course go ahead."

"I suggest you use the front entrance of SHQ you can make a quieter approach to the orderly room with less chance of being discovered, also it is hidden from the accommodation area where there are bound to be many people about."

"Good thinking Corporal Thank you."

"Ah, here comes your meal go and enjoy it."

About 6pm The Station Commander arrived dressed in his civvies. "I changed into these so that I would not look conspicuous, there may be some puzzled looks seeing me come to the guardroom at this time of day dressed in my uniform."

Warrant Officer Shaw arrived in uniform; he did not draw any attention because it would be thought he was on duty, which in a sense he was.

The Squadron Leader informed him of what he would be expected to do when they had completed the mission.

About 6:30pm the watcher and SAC Barton reported back at the guardroom. "The target entered SHQ about four minutes ago sir."

"Action stations everyone, you all know your instructions, you two Sergeants grab him and ground him quickly yelling at him as you do so, it will put the shits up him. We will give him five minutes for him to set his stall out. Check the safety catches of your firearms are in the 'Safe' position let me see them, good, then let's go gentlemen."

They quickly moved across to the front entrance of SHQ SAC Barton unlocked the door entering very quietly and guided the team to the orderly room.

The SAC opened the door to see Sergeant Thomson there who hurriedly hid something out of sight.

"Working late again Sarge'?"

"Hello Barton, just checking up on something I cannot do during normal hours."

"Will you be long Sarge'?"

"No, about half hour or so, I will see to the locking up."

"I will come round again in about an hour then to make sure everything is Okay.

Goodnight Sarge."

"Goodnight Barton."

Barton got out of the way very quickly as the two Sergeants burst in yelling and throwing the terror stricken Sergeant to the floor as the WO covered him with his revolver.

"Search him," was the order given. They emptied his pockets and found bits and pieces of personal possessions and a bunch of keys containing skeleton keys. On the desk was a mobile recorder, a notebook a small camera and files from the open security cabinet.

The Squadron Leader addressed Sergeant Thomson. "What explanation have you for all this Sergeant?

He made no reply.

The recorder was switched on and Sergeant Thomson's voice was heard speaking in a foreign tongue.

"What language is that?" Thomson was asked.

Again there was no answer.

"Very well, take him in," said the Officer to the two Sergeants

"I want you to stay here until your Warrant Officer arrives," he said to SAC Barton. He then shook his hand. "Thank you for what you did son, you acted naturally and he suspected nothing, you made our job what you might call a doddle. I will make sure the right people will hear of your part in this scenario."

"Thank you sir."

On his return to the guardroom WO Shaw was sent to the orderly room to tidy up and to make sure none of the files were missing.

The prisoner was stripped and searched with the Medical Officer present. When he got dressed he still had nothing to say and remained unco-operative. He was placed again in handcuffs and put in a cell with the two Sergeants to guard him.

"The Station Commander was a witness to what had gone on and offered his congratulations to the S.I.B. team.

"It is those two lads of yours who deserve the congratulations sir for being responsible for us to sort this out with the minimum of fuss. SAC Barton did an excellent job, he was a natural, Thomson never suspected a thing thanks to the common sense that lad showed. I intend to mention that in my report. Are you ready team, shall we go and pay a visit to Mrs Thomson?"

Mrs Thomson answered the door and the Squadron Leader introduced himself and his team. "We have your husband in custody Mrs Thomson for a serious breach of security and I am taking you into custody for suspected aiding and abetting your husband."

He then gave her the official warning.

"Come in," she said resignedly.

"Has your husband got anything hidden away relating to his activities Mrs. Thomson?" the officer asked.

"He has a locked metal box but I do not have the key." She replied.

"That is no problem I have his keys with me." He fiddled with the keys until he found the right one. When it was opened he drew breath in surprise, besides a radio transmitter there was a sheaf of papers in a foreign language.

"What language is that?" the officer asked. When she told him he pursed his lips and gave a whistle of surprise. "Right Mrs Thomson go and pack a case of what you will need, these ladies will accompany you."

The box was relocked then he and the Warrant Officer made a search of the house finding one or two interesting items including an address book which was thought may be of interest. When they had finished and were waiting for Mrs Thomson the officer apologised to the Medical Officer. "Sorry to have brought you out for nothing Doc' but we never can tell in cases where women are concerned."

"I fully understand I thought you were very gracious to Mrs Thomson."

"We never get heavy handed with women Doc' although we have had cases where we could not afford to be too gentle."

"We are ready sir."

"Take her to your car and stay with her she has to have no contact with her husband or anyone else."

"Right then, take the Doc' back to the guardroom Warrant' then return here with our vehicle to pick up this box. Stay at the guardroom Doc' your job will be finished when we leave the camp with the prisoners."

When the box was loaded the house was locked up and they returned to the guardroom the house keys were then handed to the Station Commander who in turn handed them to Tom Bridges to be locked away. The Squadron Leader phoned National Security to inform them they were about to start off to deliver the prisoner and his wife to their HQ, giving the route they would take.

"We will be off now sir, thank you and your staff for all the help in making our job an easier one, it has been a pleasure working with you."

The C.O. shook his hand and said. "It turned out better than I expected and on behalf of RAF March thank you and God speed." The officer saluted and away he went giving orders. "You Warrant Officer will drive the car holding the prisoner with one Sergeant escort. The other Sergeant will drive me in my car and the Two WRAF Sergeants in the other car with Mrs Thomson, one driving the other an escort. I will lead, you second and the other tail-end Charlie."

"Right," said the C.O. "You can now all stand down and thank you very much for the help and dedication, what you did today was a credit to you all. I will go and check with WO Shaw and see how things are in the orderly room, would you care to come with me Corporal Graham?"

"Yes please sir."

"How is it going Mr Shaw, any damage and is everything accounted for?"

"We have got everything sorted out and back to normal, there is nothing missing and certainly no damage, they did a good clean job I must say."

"Yes, they were very efficient and you young Barton have made a big hit with the Squadron Leader he was full of praise of the way you carried out the task you were set, he said it was due to you the job was made an easy one. I endorse everything he said and I add my congratulations, you are a credit to RAF March as indeed you all are. I will now leave you with the good news. We all have to make out a written statement." That brought some groans.

"My sentiments entirely, Goodnight."

"What a day," exclaimed Roy, I am glad that is over. You are alright now are you Barton and back to normality?"

"I am fine sir I think it will be some time before I will get to sleep tonight my head will be buzzing and my brain will be in top gear going over the happenings."

"I think that will happen to all of us," said Corporal Graham. "If we turn up late in the morning sir you will know we have overslept."

"I'll tell you what," said Roy with a grin. "The first one in tomorrow is a sissy!"

The lads roared with laughter hearing the boss come out with that.

"Goodnight lads, I am proud to have you on my team."

"Goodnight sir."

"Are you sure you are going to be alright?"

"I will be Okay sir," said a confident SAC Barton, I am still excited that is all, I can always call on Corporal Graham here to come and read me a bed-time story,"

"By the way Corporal you are in charge of the orderly room until we get a replacement."

"Then I had better not be late tomorrow sir, I will be expected to set an example to the troops!"

"Come on then sir I will let you out as I lock up."

Roy entered the Mess threw his hat into his room and made a beeline to the bar.

Bill and Derwent were sat there and when they saw him Bill said to Harry. "Get him a pint in quick 'Arry he looks like he can murder one."

Roy held up his hand to stop them saying anything, grabbed his pint and took a huge drink. "Phew, I really needed that, thanks lads."

Bill said. "You have something of importance to tell us I have been trying to get hold of you since just after lunch."

"Just let me get my second wind Bill and finish this then we will get another in then we will go and sit somewhere where we will not be disturbed."

"You two go and grab a table, I will bring the drinks over," volunteered Derwent.

When the three of them had settled down Roy began his story.

"You will not believe this it is like something out of an Agatha Christie mystery, I am only just coming to terms with it myself."

He began with the meeting of Corporal Graham outside SHQ then he went through every little detail ending with the locking up of the SHQ by the Duty Clerk."

"Everybody knew there was something serious going on after seeing civilians around the guardroom" said Derwent.

"They were the S.I.B. said Roy and they were pretty nice guys too, but weren't they efficient. Our Station Commander was thrilled to bits with our lads and the parts they played, it will not surprise me to see those two lads got some recognition."

"You played a good part in pushing it through to the top, you realised the seriousness of it instead of Pooh, poohing it as some imagination. I say well done you for setting the ball rolling," said Bill.

"I agree with that said Derwent, you are *our* hero! I wonder what it really was all about."

"I think we all would like to know," said Roy. But the arrogance of the man when I gave him a rollicking, he was laughing at me as if to say you can't touch me I'm fireproof. I cannot get over that but what eases it is, I have had the last laugh."

"Come on back to the bar, said Bill and we will drink to that."

CHAPTER 19

Viv picked up the ringing phone. "Flight Sergeant Anderson speaking can I help you? Oh hello Corporal Graham yes, right thank you very much, have you informed WO Butcher? You have that's great thank you, bye. The new intake will arrive at the station ETA 2pm. Bill."

"A smart lad that Viv he has taken control of that office very well Roy could not do any better having someone else in charge than him. So we lose another flight of your girls on Friday, it will feel strange having just one flight of girls to contend with. Sergeant Roper and her girls come into ops' on Monday along with Sergeant Franks and his lads. It will be back to old times again, two reserve teams in ops'."

"We will just have to get used to it again," said Viv "I am not complaining."

A knock on the door brought a "Come In" response from Bill. He jumped to his feet when Wings entered.

"Sit down Mr Barrett and Good morning to you both. I am glad I have you both together he took off his hat and sat himself down. "How are things at the sharp end Mr Barrett are there any complaints?"

"No sir we are gearing ourselves up to receiving the new intake of airmen on Wednesday."

"Ah yes, it is passing out parade on Friday for two flights, airmen and airwomen."

"So you do keep tabs on what is going on in your domain."

"Indeed I do Mr Barrett, I have my own ops' board in my office now, a legacy from your ops' room not as big as yours by a long chalk but you can say I have my finger on the pulse. I have my own mini ops' room in my office, you want to come and see it you may pick a few tips up from it," he said laughing. "You know I get a bit cheesed off at times, I want to do something useful to make me feel I am earning my salt.

I thought of when I was a raw recruit and what kept me on my toes. Barrack Room inspections and the odd kit inspection, what do you say to that suggestion, Mr Barrett?"

"Yes, I am all for keeping the recruits on their toes and giving them something to moan about. It is good for their morale because when they are all in the same boat it draws them closer together in comradeship."

"Flight?"

"Oh yes, I am very much for it, where it comes natural for a woman to keep everything around her clean and tidy, it works just the opposite with young girls especially when they are all crowded together. Now is the time for them to learn about Domestic Science because when they have a family of their own they will need to know."

"I have had a word with WO Butcher and tomorrow morning at 9am you Flight Sergeant and she will inspect the WRAF's accommodation. You will release Corporal (w) James from drill to do the rounds with you."

"You and I Mr Barrett along with Corporal Harper will inspect the airmen's accommodation at the same time. Have either of you got any other commitments or not able to do the inspection?"

"No," they both said.

"Good, then I will be off and bring my board up to date."

"Well the lad is trying I'll give him his due." Bill said.

"Those girls are in for a shock," said Viv, "Mary will go through them like a dose of salts."

Mary did just that, she went through the accommodation blocks like a whirlwind. "Enough is enough," she said. "A glance is enough for this mess, they are like Doss Houses, where has self pride and personal hygiene gone? Out through the damned window and looking around I see they are all shut. Which room are you in charge of Corporal James? Show me."

"This is the only room I have Ma'am."

"I don't believe it," said Mary, "what do you think of it Flight Sergeant? You would think it was a different Air Force. Excellent Corporal tell me what do you do to get your girls to this standard?"

"I just do my job by telling them what I want and with a bit of push and shove they respond or I lean on them."

"Come on then I have seen enough, you rejoin your flight Corporal, you and I Flight are going to have words with some scrubbers."

Over in the airmen's accommodation things were a little better. "What is the daily layout Corporal Harper?"

"There is a chart on the room notice board showing how the room should be left sir."

Wings went to the board to have a look. "It shows here bed packs and spare shoes and plimsolls should be shown at the foot of the bed. Why are the beds not made according to that chart?"

"I do not know sir the beds in my room conform to regulations."

"This lot are not very tidy are they Mr Barrett?"

"That only reflects on the Corporals sir, it looks like we need to have more, many more of these inspections."

"Right, we will check the other rooms and to see if we can find a tidier one, that includes yours Corporal "

"I think you will find mine up to standard sir." He was proved right.

"Okay Corporal rejoin your flight and keep up the good work. What are your thoughts Mr Barrett?"

"Every morning, Monday to Friday and before coming on parade, they will stand by their beds and their Sergeant Instructors will inspect them. The Corporals will be told in no uncertain terms they will suffer the same fate if they leave their rooms untidy because they will not be exempt from a snap inspection. They will accompany the Sergeant on his inspection. I am going to get moans from the Sergeants but tough! they are in charge of them."

"I like it Mr Barrett but it is still not a patch on when we were recruits I will come back to the office with you, it is thirsty work this inspection lark don't you think?"

"Why don't you leave a mug here permanently?"

"Not a bad idea," he chuckled.

They arrived at the office to find Viv and Mary enjoying a brew.

"Ah ha, we are just in time Mr Barrett, don't get up Ms Butcher, they make a good brew here, I was saying to Mr Barrett, barrack block inspections makes one thirsty."

"According to what I hear sir, you don't need any excuses to come here for a brew."

Everyone laughed. "I see you have got me weighed up as well Ms Butcher."

"Very little misses old eagle eyes here," added Bill.

"I have told you before Bill Barrett, less of the old!"

"You know something, ah here comes the brews, thank you I was ready for this. As I was about to say, this is the best posting I have ever had and it is thanks to you for making it so." He held up his mug in salute and said. "Cheers everyone."

They compared notes about the inspections Bill told Mary what they intended to do.

"What a cracking idea," she said. "We will do the same Flight that will shake them up only Corporal (w) James came out with flying colours".

"What a coincidence," said Bill, "Corporal Harper was our star."

"Thanks for the brew," said Wings. "I will now leave you to sort out your merry men and women."

"They will not feel very merry by the time we have finished with them I can assure you," snorted Mary. "Come on then Flight, let us go and make their day, I for one am going to enjoy seeing their faces when they hear the good news."

"I will follow your example Ms Butcher. Ms. doesn't that sound posh?" said Bill as he gave Mary a bow.

"It is only what I am entitled to *and* deserve, just remember that in future."

Bill saw his Sergeants and told them to get the flights together. He then addressed them. "The O.C. and I did a snap check on your barrack blocks this morning, not a pleasant sight I can assure you. It was a toss up between your bogs and your dormitories which of them were the cleanest and tidiest. I would like to congratulate you all on your dormitories coming in second place! Consequently, starting tomorrow morning and every morning Monday to Friday before work parade and until you pass out from training, you will stand by your beds and will be inspected by your Sergeant Instructors who I am sure are going to be very happy with the extra burden you are putting on their shoulders. At the end of each week if any of the Sergeants is not satisfied with your efforts I personally will carry out an inspection on a Saturday morning. You have not only made a rod for your own backs but you are also leaving a legacy to the recruits who will follow you. Will all Senior and junior NCOs fall out on me please?"

He walked out of earshot of the airmen with the NCOs following him.

"You Corporals are worse than those airmen because it is your responsibility to see to discipline in the Barrack Blocks. You are in individual rooms which you can lock and we cannot see what is behind closed doors. I am sure we would not be surprised to see an even worse mess than the dormitories. I suggest you start to lead by example or you could find yourselves living in a dormitory, your private bunks are a privilege that goes with your rank but abuse it and I will see that you lose that privilege. For your sins you will accompany your Sergeant on his inspection. You can keep your doors locked but be warned we can make a snap inspection on your little hideouts anytime. Remember also if I have to come in on a Saturday morning you will be there too. Now march your flights off while I have a word with your Sergeants.

I am sorry about this chaps but you can tell from what I said it needs to be clamped down on, it has got out of hand and I blame the Corporals but I think the Saturday morning threat has put the wind up them all. We will carry this out for two weeks, that is when we have the complete change to the new training schedules. You can bet the Corporals will have got the message especially when it interferes with their own free time, then they get the frighteners. What I do want from you is your full support; if you do not agree with me I will come and inspect your Married Quarters on a Saturday morning."

They all had a good laugh, one said. "Then you will have to face our wives and God help you! We will support you because we would not wish that on anybody."

Mary had got all the WRAF flights together. "All NCOs fall in behind me," she ordered. Then she addressed the airwomen. "I have been right through your accommodation and it was not a pleasant sight, there was not a single window open and the smell hit me as I went through the front door. Do you realise what the smell of deodorants, scents and other smellies you use to cover up whatever you need to cover up is like? Of course you will not smell it because you live with it and you cannot get rid of it because your windows are shut. You are young ladies who should be taking pride in how you live, to all intent and purposes you are living in Doss Houses that what comes to mind as soon as one enters and sees the mess you leave the place in. Now we come to the ablutions, you have certain facilities being females for disposal of certain things and the lavatory pans are not they. I would imagine your mothers would have given a sigh of relief when you told them you were leaving home to join the WRAF. They may even have thought thank goodness; perhaps *they* will knock some sense into you. Well, we will give it our best shot and believe me we do not fail, you may not pass out from here as ladies but you will definitely not pass out as scrubbers!

Now for the good news. As from tomorrow and each week Monday to Friday until you leave this station, you will, before parading for training stand by your beds for morning inspection carried out by your respective

Sergeants I can assure you they will now look forward to the extra duty you have forced upon them with great pleasure."

She turned and faced the NCOs.

"I hold you Corporals responsible for the state of these accommodations you with your rank are privileged to have a room of your own but be warned you are not exempt from a snap inspection. You will accompany your Sergeant on her morning inspection and at the end of each week if the Sergeant turns in an adverse report then further disciplinary action will be taken and will be carried out in your own time. Now march your flights off while I have a chat with the Sergeants. I will not ask you to go and see for yourselves because believe me it is not a pretty sight. I am not knit picking but the Flight Sergeant here will testify to that and I do not want you to go over the top on your inspections, just make sure they are clean, tidy and well ventilated. I understand this may only last for two weeks but long enough for everyone especially the Corporals to get the message. Alright ladies you can return to your flights and thank you. I hope the Corporals don't decide to become vindictive towards the girls because when all is said and done they were the cause of it by not doing their job. I am off now for my brew, thanks Viv."

When Viv returned to the office she told Bill what Mary had said.

"That was more or less the line I took except I threatened them with a Saturday morning inspection if they did not pull their socks up.

Have you and Derwent come to any decision about holidays yet?"

"As a matter of fact we intend to stay in the hotel Roy and Barbara stayed in on the Algarve, we have the chance of a cancellation for Saturday but getting leave at such short notice is asking a lot."

"As far as I am concerned that is no problem I can get you the leave but what about Derwent?"

"I don't know can I phone him and tell him that if he can get leave we can go? The deadline for this offer is tomorrow."

"Go ahead phone him."

"I would like to speak to WO Waters please, Flight Sergeant Anderson yes, then will you ask him to call WO Barrett's office please it is urgent. Thank you."

"That was Sergeant Jones, he will tell him."

"WO Barrett speaking. Hi Derwent, Viv wants a word hang on till I get her; she is in the ops' room.... Flight Sergeant Anderson!" he shouted, "telephone!"

As she came in Bill went out to leave her in private. After a few minutes she came out. "He is all excited and he is now going to see his O.C straight away, keep your fingers crossed Bill."

Half an hour later the phone rang and Viv who had been sat waiting for it to ring answered it. "She gave a little scream of delight, you have got it?

Brilliant, we will nip down during lunch time and get it booked, I will ring them up to tell them we are confirming it and will be there at lunch time to pay up, alright? Yes of course I do too, Bye."

"WO Barrett," she called. "He has got it."

"Right, get your leave pass made out and I will get it sanctioned."

When she had done the necessary he initialled it then went to see Wings who signed it straight away.

"Is she going off by herself Mr Barrett?"

"No sir with her fiancée WO.Waters from Stores."

"Oh yes, a nice chap I have dealt with him, they make a nice couple, good for them. "Did you get the troops sorted out?"

"Indeed we did. WO Butcher really gave those girls some stick. All the Sergeants are carrying out an inspection with the recruits standing by their beds before reporting for training. I have given the Sergeants two weeks to sort them out that is when the new training system starts from scratch."

"That is good we do not want to make it a permanent daily inspection, you can bet the Corporals will see to that. I say, that 'Catch a Spy' episode was quite something the orderly room staff were certainly on their toes there Mr Barrett all credit to them I hope those two lads receive some recognition."

"They do that sir, I wonder when or if we will be told what it really was all about and the consequences. I hear their Married Quarter has been given a right going over but it has now been cleared and handed back to MOD."

"It will be some time before we get to know anything the interrogation may take some time unless the guy tells what he knows, we may even read all about it in the press first. No doubt the news will have leaked somehow, do not be surprised if we have to increase our security to keep the press out I can see it coming Mr Barrett the troops are going to be happy if we have to mount extra guards."

"Well I must get this pass to the orderly room for them to process, thanks for signing it sir and not putting up any obstacles." He saluted and left to go to the orderly room.

"Good to see you Bill how are things? I was going to say at the sharp end but everyone knows this is the sharp end of the station."

"Okay Mr Spycatcher, what is your next assignment?"

"What can I do for you my friend?"

"I have Viv's leave pass here for you to process."

"So they are going then? That is good leave it with me I will see to it myself."

"She only told me a little while ago that if they could get leave they had an offer to book into the hotel you stayed in this coming Saturday and the Travel Agent was keeping the offer open only till tomorrow. Tommy and I are on the airport run on Saturday, will you and Barbara fancy doing a bit of shopping in Leeds? If so you will have to use your own car."

"That's a thought Bill; I will have a word with Barbara later I cannot see her turning down the chance to go shopping in Leeds of all places. You realise what that means, you are going to get some earache from Tommy talking holidays."

"Don't I know it and I know who the winner will be. I am going to have to face up to it Roy, you had better have that brochure handy for when Tommy wants it."

"We have not got it Bill."

"Well done old lad that will spin it out a bit more. I will buy you a pint tonight for that little snippet."

"We gave it to Viv and Derwent!"

"Cancel that drink. It is lunch time Roy, are you coming?"

"Yes I am feeling a bit peckish."

CHAPTER 20

A car pulled up at the gates of the entrance to the station. A civilian got out and approached the RAF policeman who was on duty.

"Can I be of help sir?" the policeman asked.

"Yes, I would like to see your Station Commander please."

"Have you got an appointment sir?"

"No I haven't but you see....he got no further.

"Then I am afraid you cannot be admitted sir."

"I am a Press reporter and....

"Excuse me for a moment." He went to a box and pressed an emergency button. Immediately Flight Sergeant Tom Bridges came striding out.

"Problems Corporal?" he asked.

"A press reporter here wants to see the Station Commander."

"Tom addressed the reporter. "If you have no appointment there is no way you will see the Commanding Officer and I advise you to climb back in your vehicle and return from where you came."

"As a member of the free press I have a duty to report to the public the goings on behind these locked gates."

"And what are the goings on?"

"That is something I would like to discuss with your C.O. and I demand to be admitted."

"Do you really? Well don't go away and I will see what I can do about that." He went into the guardroom and phoned the local police telling them of the situation. Then he phoned the Duty Officer.

Tom returned to the gate. "I have been in touch with our Duty Officer who is coming to see what he can do for you so be a little patient he will not be long."

"Thank you very much."

When the Duty Officer came he listened to what the reporter had to say then when he told him he could not be admitted the reporter began to be abusive. As he was mouthing off a police car pulled up and two local policemen one of them a Sergeant got out.

"Oh it is you," the Sergeant said, "up to your old tricks again trying to make a name for yourself. Well I can tell you here and now there is no scoop for you here, so climb back in your car and get the hell out of here before I place you under arrest."

"But there is something going on here that the public should know about and it is my duty to report it."

"This is a Military Establishment and you are dead right, there is something going on, you are trying to enter it without authorisation and my duty is to arrest you. Put the cuffs on him then park his car out of the way where it will not be an obstruction. Everything will be alright sir," he said addressing the Duty Officer, "if any more of this lot turn up just give us a bell and we will send in the Cavalry."

"Thanks for your help Sergeant," the officer said laughing.

"Come on Scoop," the Sergeant said as the protesting reporter was led away.

"Enter it in the diary Flight, it looks like we may have more of these reporters trying it on, it is obvious the word has got around I can see us having to increase the security because there are ways to get on the site without coming through the main gates."

"We could do with a team of dog-handlers sir?"

"I will suggest that to the C.O. call me if we get any more incidents."

Later that day there was a Tannoy message from the Station Commander.

"Pay attention everyone. Due to the recent security incident everyone has to be alert for unauthorised personnel trespassing on this station. Today we have had an incident where a newspaper reporter tried to gain admittance but was arrested by the local constabulary requested by our security staff. You are not, I repeat, you are Not permitted to speak with the press on any matter relating to the military. If you see an intruder keep him or her under observation, while you are doing so it is essential you have one of your comrades report it to a person of authority immediately. That is all!"

>>> <<<

"Did you get booked?" Bill asked Viv.

"Yes thank you, we are going to be busy now getting the bits and pieces together for that climate. You should have heard us singing 'We are going on a Summer Holiday' on the way back, just like a couple of kids."

"It is going to do you a power of good, I want you back here with your batteries fully charged and feeling on top form and before I forget, will you give the brochure to Tommy with my compliments. I saw the writing on the wall when you two decided to go I know when I am beaten."

"Poor thing, Derwent told me about it, you did not have much choice did you?"

"Tommy and I will drive you to and from the airport. Roy is going to ask Barbara if she would like to do what we did when we saw *them* off?"

>>> <<<

George Miller after hearing the broadcast went to see Tom Bridges in the guardroom. "What's been going on Tom?" he asked.

When he was told he muttered. "It looks like we could be in for some 'keeping everyone on their toes' for a little while. I will tell the ones who are on duty tonight to be extra vigilant when they fall in for the guard mounting. The word has got round and those reporters will be like bloody leeches, they cannot be shaken off if there is a chance of a story especially with it being a security matter."

"I told the Duty Officer we could do with a team of dog-handlers, they would sort out any intruders I would give anything to hear squeals of fright from somebody getting his britches arse ripped out, I would even take up a collection to give the 'Poor Doggie a Bone'."

"You are a cruel man! Tom Bridges," laughed George. "Put me down for a donation!"

When the duty personnel fell in on the guard mounting parade, the Orderly Officer inspected them then gave them a reminder of their duties and the need to be more vigilant under the present circumstances. While the Orderly Officer was inside the guardroom signing the guard report George took over the parade.

"I am not going to repeat what you have already been told, I want to stress that it is serious, when you are on duty at the main gate if you have any doubts signal the guardroom and you will get help immediately. When you are on patrol, you *will* patrol none of this skulking in your favourite hiding place for a crafty fag, that is over. Why? because I will make it my business to have a snoop round anytime during the hours of darkness and if I found anyone of you NOT doing his duty he will not see the light of day for a very long time. Do I make myself clear?"

There was no response.

"I SAID DO I MAKE MYSELF CLEAR?" he shouted. "Are you struck dumb?"

They did not know whether to say yes they are clear or no they are not struck dumb.

"I will help you out. Do I make myself clear? Then he cupped one ear for the reply.

"Yes sir." They replied.

"If you act like that when you go out on patrol we will get swamped with bloody intruders! Have we got anyone on jankers? No? Then make sure none of you are on them tomorrow. To your Duties, Dis.s.s.Miss!"

"You can bet there will be no skulking or skiving tonight sir," said the Orderly Sergeant."

"You are right but make sure they see you having a wander around as well it will help to keep them on their toes. Right, I will be off now to get some dinner. Have a Nice Night," he said as he walked off chuckling to himself.

>>> <<<

Sergeant Franks, pace stick tucked under his arm was met at the entrance to the accommodation by the Corporals who were in charge of particular rooms.

"Are we all ready for this?" he asked.

"The recruits have got a sweat on wondering what is going to hit them," answered one of the Corporals.

"We shall start with room one, then proceed from there."

As he entered the room, the airman nearest the entrance to the room shouted. "NCO Present." Everyone came to attention.

Joe with a stern face looked down the length of the room. "DRESSING!" He snarled. "Get your toes in line with the end of your beds, Move!"

There was quite a lot of shuffling to comply with the order. Then he slowly moved down each line inspecting each bed space and its occupant pointing out the small adjustments needed to their dress. He approached a tall and well-built airman whose body language oozed out the fact that he was Cock of the Billet.

"Why are you standing on the left of your bed when everyone else is standing on the right?"

"I don't know Sergeant."

"Are you having trouble knowing your left from your right by any chance?"

"Sometimes Sergeant but I am taking lessons for it."

"The other airmen burst into uncontrolled laughter.

"Alright, quieten down then," reproved Joe.

"I see you have two floor pads peeping from behind your wardrobe what are they doing there?"

"I forgot to put them away Sergeant,"

"Are they your personal pads?"

"Yes Sergeant."

"Has everyone got personal pads in this room?"

"No Sergeant."

"Why not? If one airman has personal pads so should everyone else, don't you agree?"

"Yes Sergeant but there is not enough to go round."

"I see, you keep them permanently then?"

"Well I erm, er."

"I see; there always seems to be at least one of your kind in a flight. Seeing that you like the floor pads so much that you want them for yourself I suggest you mark each one of 'Your Pads' Left and Right then you will be sure of putting them on the correct feet."

He was interrupted by roars of laughter.

"Quiet," he yelled.

"And you can wipe that stupid grin off your face. I will inspect them to see that they have been done on my morning inspection tomorrow. Do you understand?"

"Yes Sergeant."

"Just make sure you do."

"He moved to the next man in line another big built lad. He could tell from his facial expression he was the pal of the previous airman. He stood in front of him and asked. "Are you French by any chance?"

"No Sergeant, I live in England."

There were a few suppressed titters from the room, which Joe ignored.

"You know, I was fooled for a minute because you wear your beret just like the French. Corporal accompany this Frenchman to the wall mirror at the end of the room and show him how it should be worn in the Royal Air Force."

That brought some uncontrolled laughter from the room.

"SILENCE!" he shouted. He concluded his inspection with. "Not bad!" He left the room humming the Marseillaise.

"I do not like bullies," he said when they got outside, "keep your eyes on those two."

He concluded the rest of his inspection. "Get them fell in and march them off" he ordered the Corporals.

All the sergeants reported back to the office after the inspections to report. The WRAF fared the worst not complying completely with what they had been ordered to do, consequently they had to go through the same routine that evening much to their dismay.

"Well done ladies, that is the best thing you could have done it is in their own time and they will not like that. You will see the difference from now on. Thank you, carry on."

>>> <<<

In the Mess bar that evening the three crackpots were discussing the daily events.

"Are you ready for Saturday morning Derwent?" asked Roy. "Got everything you need?" Are your passports up to date? What about currency?"

"I will change that at the airport."

"Don't go changing any at the hotels or you will lose out and do not use the phones in the hotel either it will cost you a bomb."

"If you have any currency left over I will buy it off you when you get back at the going rate of course." Bill said.

"Oh! So you are definitely going?" Smirked Roy. "I said you would never get out of this one. Have you fixed a date yet?"

"We have not even looked at the brochure together yet."

"What is there to look at, Barbara and I have told you all you need to know and when Derwent comes back he will run a replay through for you so what is the problem?"

"You know what women are like they have to see for themselves. What's betting after we see Derwent and Viv off I get holidays earache? You went half-board didn't you Roy?"

"Aye and it is worth it the meals are very good. Are you on half-board Derwent?"

"We are, I do not fancy having to go traipsing around looking for a decent restaurant each evening I want the lazy life style while I am there."

"Have you heard anything about a replacement for your ex-Sergeant Roy?"

"No and I am not pushing it either Corporal Graham is doing a great job, Eric Parkes did a good job training him to a good standard, I prefer him as opposed to another Sergeant "

"You may not have a say in the matter Roy," volunteered Derwent.

"Have you any idea when Jim Ball comes back from his resettlement course Roy?" asked Bill.

"Off hand no but I can let you know tomorrow and yes, we will have to dine him out because he gets his discharge soon after. We will have to get cracking organising that Bill, we don't want to be caught napping and we have to give him a memento from the Mess members, any suggestions anybody?"

"We can forget a clock or a tankard, they are definitely out," advised Bill.

"Those banjo style barometers are quite a nice thing, they gave one to a Sergeant at my last station, he was chuffed with it," added Derwent.

"Why don't we ask Tommy?" suggested Roy. "She will have seen countless presentations while she has been Mess Manager."

"There is one thing I know he would treasure but I would like your thoughts on it." Bill said.

“Go on then,” urged Roy, try it out on us!”

“An enlarged photograph in a really good frame of the BlueBelles Team with an inscribed name-plaque.”

“You have surpassed yourself there Mr Barrett, I must admit you do come up with some good ones now and again and in the circumstances you have hit the jack-pot,” admitted Roy.

“Thank you Roy, coming from you that is praise indeed.”

“I am sure we cannot better that,” exclaimed Derwent, “well thought of Bill. We will have to put the suggestion to the committee for approval though.”

“I will call a committee meeting as soon as possible then I can take the photograph that I have to a reliable photographer for him to make an enlargement, put it in a good frame and I suppose he will see to the inscribing of the name-plaque as well as fixing it. We need the meeting to organise the dining-out in any case, what do you say we call it for Monday?”

“Suits me,” said Roy.

“Suits me,” said Derwent

“What do you mean it suits you?” exclaimed Roy. “You will be in Portugal sunning yourself while we are sweating our socks off here!”

“So we are,” replied Derwent, “how could I forget that?”

“Because you are a plonker,” retaliated Roy. “Fill em’ up again Arry’ if you have time to get your nose out of that travel magazine?”

“It is a football magazine Roy and very informative.”

“What with you and your football/travel magazines and these two with their fishing magazine, where does that leave me?”

“On the sub’s bench,” laughed Harry’.

“Singing a ‘Line’ from South Pacific,” said Derwent.

“What are you talking about?” said an indignant Roy.

“Salmon Enchanted Evening!”

Roy being Roy just had to laugh along with everybody in the bar. “I suppose I asked for that.”

When the Mess committee convened Bill explained to them why he had called it.

“Most of you here know Flight Sergeant Jim Ball, who in about three weeks time is due to retire reaching the figure which most of us do not want to know albeit for different reasons. However, he is entitled to be dined-out and most of us or even all of us will agree he deserves one. We have to decide on two things, when do we have the dining-out and what do we give him as a parting gift?”

“Do you know which day he is due back?” asked Jock Webster.

“Roy will answer that,” said Bill.

"He is due to report back a week on Monday then the Monday after that is his last, so we have the time to get organised."

"Good," said Jock, then I propose we dine him out on the Friday before he leaves us."

"I will second that," said Viv.

Everyone was in favour.

"Now we come to the crunch, what do we present him with?" said Bill, "has anyone any ideas?"

There were various suggestions but none of them seemed appropriate.

"It is very difficult to give a person whose likes and dislikes are not known to us," voiced Mary Butcher. "The only solution I can think of is to ask his wife what she thinks would be appropriate then swear her to secrecy."

Murmurs of approval came from one or two of the team.

"Before I put that to a vote I would like to offer my idea. Jim was happiest when he was helping out with the build-up of the BlueBelles during Operation Smarty Pants; he thought they were out of this world. I have never told anyone this and even Jim does not know that I know. After the Victory I was told from a very reliable source he was seen with tears of pride and joy running down his face, he was a very, very, happy man. The reason I am telling you this is because it is a lead up to what my idea is. An enlargement of the photograph of the BlueBelles Team in a good frame and a nameplate or plaque whatever you want to call it, attached to the frame and inscribed with.....this is only a suggestion of course.

'Presented to Flight Sergeant James Ball by the Members of the Sergeants Mess RAF March for his Devotion to the WRAF BlueBelles Drill Team.' That inscription can be altered to whatever you think will be more appropriate. We will now take a little break before we come to any decision after a brew which Tommy is so kindly providing."

After the break Bill announced. "Now we have to decide on the ideas proffered, number one is Jim's wife and number two is the photograph. Please raise you hands for number one." None were raised.

"For the photograph?" All hands were raised.

"Then it is the photograph, I will make enquiries about that tomorrow, now what day shall we decide on for the dining-out dinner?

"The Friday before he leaves," suggested Mary Butcher, "like Jock said, I think that would be an ideal day for it."

"Has anyone got an alternate date from that?" Bill asked. "Good, I think it is the best date too. Incidentally it will be serving members only, the exception will be Mrs Ball naturally. There is something else I would like to put to a full meeting but I would like to test the water first before I do so by asking you your thoughts in advance. I would like this Mess to put on a dinner with all the trimmings for the Senior Citizens of March Village at

Christmas. We can give them a nice Christmas dinner, entertainment and a small food parcel to take home. If we hold it just prior to the Christmas break we could get volunteers from the young airmen and airwomen who I am sure would be delighted to come and fuss the old dears and mark my words the old dears would love it. Do you think it is worth proposing to all the Mess members?"

"I like it," voiced Jock Webster.

"Me too," said Mary.

"I think we are all in favour of that Bill," said another member.

"Thank you, I didn't want to fall flat on my face proposing that I realise it is giving you a lot of hard work but please contact me if at any time you want some extra hands. You are really doing a great job and I know all our members appreciate what you are doing. Thank you everybody if that is all we can stand down."

Bill thanked Tommy for the refreshments "They were very surprised to receive it and it was appreciated."

"Yes, they all thanked me as they left. We have a good committee there Bill. By the way, thank you for the travel brochure darling; when are we going to read it?"

CHAPTER 21

Their friends waved off Derwent and Viv to the Algarve. Tommy had asked them to bring back some local trip brochures because we will not be lazing around the hotel pool or in the sea for two whole weeks we want to see something of the local scenery."

"We will sort something out for you," said Viv, "we have made no plans, after the first week of lazing about we will probably be bored and want to do something a bit different."

"Remember you are going for a rest and to wind down," reminded Bill, "you can always take a return trip to enjoy yourselves."

"Don't be so miserable," chided Tommy, "You had better go with a different attitude to that when we go or you can go to Derwent's Tenerife, I *will* go to the Algarve."

"Well spoken Tommy," getting full support from Barbara and Viv.

"Go on, on your way," snorted Bill with pretence of disgust, "I have some shopping to do."

After the final kisses, hugs and hand shakes the holidaymakers left with "Enjoy Yourselves" ringing in their ears.

"Now let us get ourselves sorted out. Roy and I will go and find someone who will take on this photographic job while you two shopaholics go and have a good time. We will meet at the same restaurant we used before, you two will like it."

At the prearranged time the four met at the restaurant.

"I see you have no picture with you," said Tommy.

"Correct on the first count my dear we eventually found someone who will do the complete job and it will be ready in two weeks time."

"Oh that is great," exclaimed Tommy, that will mean another shopping trip, are you coming Barbara?"

"I am very tempted we do not get many chances like this on offer Tommy and you can stop pulling your face for a start Roy Shaw, do you realise that this time *you* can take *Me* shopping. Now give me a smile! I asked for a smile not a grimace, you know very well you are looking forward to it."

Roy attempted a smile.

"That is more like it, come here while I give you a kiss." She then grabbed his tie and drew his face to hers planting a big smacker on his lips.

"Stop it you are embarrassing me in public and me an officer in Her Majesty's Forces, what would she say if she heard about this?"

"She would say. "I wish *my* name was Barbara Page!"

"Bill, would you mind if Tommy drove this mad-woman back so that I could ride with you?"

"Look Roy, if you think I am going to put *my* head on the chopping block have another think, friendships can only be stretched so far."

"Right then, I will drive back on my own, you have room on your back seat for a passenger."

"Sorry Roy, the whole seat is taken up with Tommy's shopping."

"Okay, that's it, I surrender."

"Ooooo! I like the sound of that," cooed Barbara.

"Not that sort of surrender woman, I mean lost the argument surrender."

"Oh, how disappointing," she pouted.

Bill and Tommy were enjoying every minute of this exchange of endearments.

"Okay, how about burying the hatchet until we get home? Come on let us get on our way and you lead in front Roy where we can keep an eye on you."

"Suits me Bill, but you may have to pick up a hitchhiker on the way."

When they got in their respective cars, Tommy said. "Look there Bill at the lovebirds."

He saw them embracing and kissing before setting off. "That gives me an idea," he said, as he and Tommy did the same.

When they arrived at the camp gates they found security had been tightened up with extra personnel on duty.

"Looks like we may have had some intruders," said Bill.

When the two cars parked up in the Sergeants Mess car park Bill asked. "What are we doing this evening, Bingo? A quiet drink in the mess or the March Hare?"

Barbara said. "Bingo is out by the time we get in there they will be on interval. Personally I would like a quiet night in the Mess."

"So would I," agreed Tommy.

"What about you Roy," asked Bill?

"I have not won an argument all day I cannot see me winning one at this late stage so I will just go with the flow. A quiet night in the Mess!"

"Oooooo! You are so strong and masterful and I love the way determination oozes from you," sighed Barbara as she grabbed him and gave him a hug.

"If that is the affect the Algarve has on you," said Bill pretending to be surprised, "I think we had better change our plans to Tenerife."

"Oh, you coward Bill Barrett," exploded Tommy, why don't you take a leaf out of Roy's book and just give in gracefully?"

"I agree with everything you say Tommy," smirked Roy."

Bill grabbed Roy's arm. "Come on Best Friend," as he led him away, "I want to whisper a few niceties in your shell-like ear." Calling over his shoulder, "see you at Reception. 8.30."

When they entered the Mess bar the first thing that greeted them was.

"What do you think of the news?"

"What news? We have not seen any today we have just returned from Leeds." Bill answered.

"About that spy you caught Roy. It has been on the TV News it does not state where it happened and there are no names mentioned. It will be in the daily newspapers tomorrow you can bet; anyhow you will see it on the late news."

"You two ladies go and get a table, Roy and I will bring the drinks."

"Do you know anything about this news bulletin Arry'?" asked Roy.

"It was only a short one, it has not been confirmed yet but extra guards have been posted."

"We saw them when we came in we thought there had been more intruders. I suppose the extra guards are a precaution now there has been an announcement. The reporters will all be trying to get on the station hoping to get a scoop. What time is the news on tonight?" asked Bill. 9;15 he was told.

"We have time to have a drink first." He ordered for the four of them then he and Roy took them to the girls.

"The news is on in half an hour," Roy said to the girls. "Are you coming in to see it with us?"

"No, we will stay here; you can tell us all about it," said Tommy.

"Good Evening, here is the news. A breach of security has occurred at one our Military Establishments. It has been reported a man and a woman have been placed under arrest for an act of espionage. Two

servicemen have been credited with the discovery of the perpetrators. The Ministry of Defence has made no comment."

Bill and Roy reported back to the girls and told them what was in the report.

"Well you cannot expect the station to be named or we would be swamped with reporters and people who would just come to look at the station and have their photo's taken outside the gates. The local constabulary would need to come and protect our people on guard duty, that would be ironic," said Roy. "Mark my words, now it has got into the news the MOD will play it down but privately, Corporal Graham and SAC Barton will receive some reward."

As they were leaving they met Fred Fox and Chalky White the two ex barmen with their wives, they had been playing Bingo. The four ladies were introduced to each other but when it came to Bill and Roy they were introduced as 'the Crackpots we told you about, although one is missing'."

"Has he gone AWOL?" asked Chalky.

"He is sunning himself on the Algarve," answered Bill.

"How are you getting on with Appy Arry?" Asked Chalky. I heard there was a football scout watching him recently."

"That was no scout it was a Wolf Cub from the local Scout Troop!" laughed Roy.

. "Anyway it is good to see you both again and to meet your charming wives."

"We hope to see you again soon because we are dining-out Jim Ball, I think it is three weeks on Friday, anyway you will find out at the Mess meeting and make sure you are both there on both occasions. Shall we take bets on them coming Roy?"

"Oh no you don't." Fred and Chalky objected. "The next time we win a bet with you two sharks it will be our first. Come on let's go home these two are bad news." They all laughed as they made a quick exit.

CHAPTER 22

Roy picked up the handset of the ringing phone.

"Warrant Officer Shaw speaking. Oh hello Barbara, what can I do for you? What, the three of us, right now? Why? Yes I should have realised you cannot say anything Okay I will round up the lads and will be with you in two ticks." He spoke through the hatch. "Corporal Graham, SAC Barton get your headgear and come with me, chop, chop!"

When they came round he told them they had been summoned to the Wingco's office. "Don't ask because I do not know myself."

On entering Barbara's office she immediately buzzed the Wingco' to inform him WO Shaw and party were here. "Come on I will take you in." Knocking on the door she entered and announced them.

The three entered and saluted.

"Come in gentlemen, relax you are not on the proverbial carpet, far from it. I have been ordered to send you down to London for an interview with the Air Chief Marshal. You can guess the reason for it and he wants to meet you tomorrow!

You will leave here at 7:30am by staff car to RAF Yorkdale and at 9am flown to RAF Oxfordbury where a staff car will whisk you to your destination where you will be fed and watered. After the interview you will be driven back to Oxfordbury then flown to Yorkdale where our staff car will be waiting to return you back here. Have you got that Mr Shaw? Obviously you are in charge of your special party."

"Yes sir."

"Good, all that is left for me to say is. "Congratulations," as he shook each one by the hand. "By the way you will bump into our Station Commander there; he will be waiting for you. Good Luck!"

They saluted and made their exit.

"What do you think he wants us for?" asked the two lads.

"Probably a pat on the back for living up to the traditions of the Royal Air Force," Roy replied but secretly thinking that these two lads are going to get a commendation and I'll get a handshake and a "Well done Mr Shaw."

"We will straighten up and leave everything nice and neat not leaving any loose ends for others who may have to sort it out. Then when I am satisfied you two can knock off early to get your uniforms up to scratch. Take your small pack with necessities in case we have an overnight stop."

He called Corporal (w) Macken and informed her that she would be in charge of the orderly room for the next day. She was given her instructions to call on Flight Sergeant Webster for help if needed, he would be informed and would pop in now and again to see if everything was Okay. "Now I will leave you with Corporal Graham who will fill you in with anything that needs doing specifically tomorrow but do not keep him long he has a plane to catch. He will tell you all about it and I will be in my office if I am needed until it is time to shut up shop for the day."

At dinner Roy said. "Guess where I am going tomorrow Mr Barrett?"

"I have no idea Mr Shaw," was the reply "but you are dying to tell me because you are getting all excited."

"I am not getting excited at all!"

"Then keep your fingers still and stop tapping the floor with your feet?"

"You make me nervous when I try to talk seriously to you."

"Alright Roy, take a long drink of water then we will start from scratch. Good, now tell me where you are going tomorrow because I sense it is very important."

"It is Bill and do you know who has sent for me?"

"Here we go again Roy, take another drink."

"Your old pal the Air Chief Marshal."

"Well, I'll go to the foot of our stairs and he never told me. Are you sure they have not got the Warrant Officers mixed up?"

"Not this time Billy Boy it is the Spy Catcher he wants to interview. Andy Warhol was wrong I am getting a long extension to my fifteen minutes of fame."

"Come on then tell me about it."

"Myself and the two lads were summoned to the Wingco's office this afternoon. He told us we have to report to the ACM tomorrow to be interviewed. We fly from Yorkdale to Oxfordbury and back with a staff car thrown in."

"I am pleased for you old pal you deserve some recognition you and the two lads, I wish I could be present when you meet the ACM, you will like him Roy for he puts you properly at ease and does not talk down to you. I will look forward to tomorrow night to hear all about it, it will be an experience you will never forget and I hope we have something to celebrate."

"I will not be coming in the bar tonight Bill, I want to look to my uniform etc. must give a good impression as you well know, then I have to see Barbara."

The following morning the three of them were whisked away to Yorkdale where a Flight Lieutenant met them. "So you are the three VIPs', welcome to RAF Yorkdale." He took them into a lounge to wait for the call to board. "There are refreshments at the bar there, tea, coffee or whatever but no alcohol, against the rules. I will leave you to relax and will call you when it is time to board."

They thanked him and went for a coffee then sat at window seats watching the activity outside. They even tried reading the daily papers but none of them could concentrate on them. They were relieved when the officer came. "Righto chaps, let's go." He escorted them to the plane. "As soon as you get yourselves settled down you will be taking off. Good luck and congratulations."

They saluted and thanked him. Soon they were winging their way to Oxfordbury and for a time they were relaxed until they arrived there then the butterflies crept in and stayed with them until the interview was over. A staff car was waiting and after an hour or so they arrived at their final destination. At the security desk they went through the formalities then shown into a lounge and asked to wait there to be collected. Half an hour later an officer entered and introduced himself.

"I am Squadron Leader Sneddon the ACM's Aide-de-camp. So you are from RAF March?"

"Yes sir."

"Ah, RAF March we have fond memories of your station and some of its staff. Do any of you work with WO Barrett?"

"No sir," answered Roy we are all orderly room staff but WO Barrett and I are very good friends."

"We do keep getting reports of him and the tremendous impact he has on RAF March, he is held in very high esteem here. I will now put you in the picture of what is to happen. First you will be taken to the staff canteen for a meal then you will be returned here, I will come for you at 1:55 and escort you to the ACM. When the interview is over I will take you to another room where a photographer from the RAF News will take your photographs to be published in the next issue. Make sure you snap up a few copies for your families and fan clubs when it comes out."

That got a laugh and eased the tension.

"When the photo' call is completed you will be escorted back to your staff car then it will be 'Home James'. Come on then, I will take you for something to eat, I am sure you are ready for it."

At 1:55 on the dot the Squadron Leader arrived. "Enjoy your meal chaps?"

"We did sir, thank you."

He then led them to the ACM's office door, looked at his watch and at exactly 2pm he knocked on the door opened it and announced. "Warrant Officer Shaw, Corporal Graham and SAC Barton from RAF March sir."

The three marched in and saluted.

Standing behind the ACM was their Station Commander, Squadron Leader Sneddon joined him. "Stand easy gentlemen," said the ACM. He then came round to the front of his desk backed on to it then sat his backside on the front edge.

"Once again RAF March is in the news and again for very good reasons. I have sent for you because I want to see for myself the type of airmen who not only upheld the tradition of the RAF but also have set such a good example to us all. I would now like to hear from each of you the part you played in catching this scoundrel starting right at the beginning. Take your time and in your own words and without the military precision jargon."

Starting with SAC Barton they each gave a good account of how it developed, what action they took and the part each played with the S.I.B.

"Excellent, I have read your statements and the statements from the other personnel who played an active part. You two young airmen got quite a remarkable report from the officer in charge of the operation his praise for you was of the highest order. You Mr Shaw, it was through your intelligence in recognising the seriousness of the situation and your swift action in bringing it to the attention of authority saved what could have been a very serious blow to our National Security. Squadron Leader!" he called.

The Squadron Leader came forward carrying a tray covered by an Air Force Blue cloth. Immediately the three airmen sprang to attention.

"It is with great pleasure and a privilege to award each of you the British Empire Medal."

He approached Roy. He pinned on the medal shook his hand, "You deserve that Warrant Officer Shaw. B.E.M. congratulations."

He moved to Corporal Graham, pinned on the medal and said. "Congratulations Corporal not only do you deserve this medal you also deserve these." He then handed the astounded Corporal Sergeants chevrons. "With immediate effect you now hold the rank of Sergeant Graham. B.E.M.

He next moved to SAC Barton, pinned the medal on him and said. "Congratulations son, you have earned this medal and you have also earned these," as he handed him Corporals chevrons. "With immediate effect you now hold the rank of Corporal Barton. B.E.M."

Group Captain Wildeman and Squadron Leader Sneddon both came forward to shake their hands and congratulate them.

"Sir," said Roy addressing the ACM. "Normally when one gets a promotion he is posted from his unit. These two young men are part of my staff and I know they would like to remain so, is there a chance you would agree to that, please?"

The ACM looked at the two new NCOs. Is that true what your Warrant Officer has just said?"

"Yes sir."

"Why"

"Because RAF March is the best station in the RAF and at all levels it is a happy one sir."

"Well I have never heard anything like that in my whole career. What have you done to your RAF March, Group Captain? Apparently your troops are so happy there they do not want to leave."

"It stems from Operation Smarty Pants sir; we have obtained the best staff who care and weeded out all the bad apples which is now paying dividends."

"With the likes of these young men on your staff I am not surprised. Permission granted!"

Big grins and a "Thank you sir," came from all three.

"Go on, you are dismissed, go and have your photographs taken. Squadron Leader, take them away. By the way Mr Shaw have you been taking lessons from your friend Warrant Officer Barrett?"

"No sir but I am learning a lot by watching him and the manner in which he gets his results."

"You cannot do any better than that Mr Shaw."

"They saluted and as they were led away the Squadron Leader said. "Here are the boxes for your medals put them away after the photographer has finished with you. But first we will go into the lounge. Now take your personal possessions out of your tunic pockets then give the tunics to me, leave the chevrons in the pockets and now relax for half hour or so."

When he returned with the tunics, the chevrons and B.E.M. ribbons were sewn on.

Three very happy and proud airmen donned their tunics as fast as they could then they began admiring each other's decorations and shaking hands with each other.

"Come on," said a smiling Squadron Leader time to go and say 'Cheese.'

When that was over Roy asked if it was possible to use a phone. "I would like to contact our Sergeants Mess for them to arrange accommodation for Sergeant Graham sir he cannot very well go back into the barrack block now."

"I see your point Mr Shaw, come, I will take you to my office you can phone from there."

"Flight Sergeant Atkins, Warrant Officer Shaw speaking, will you please arrange for a room to be ready to accommodate a new member to the mess? Yes please he will need it tonight and for a long time. Yes you do know him, it is our ex Corporal Graham. Sorry I cannot go into any details but we will be celebrating tonight. Thank you, Bye. Thank you sir that is a problem solved for the lad."

They then returned to the lounge.

"It has been my pleasure to meet you all and I think you all have thoroughly deserved the recognition. When you see your friend Mr Barrett, will you give him my regards please and tell him that SIR still speaks of 'that crafty bugger' with some affection" He guided them to the staff car, shook hands and said. "Good luck and enjoy your celebrations."

They thanked him as they saluted.

At Oxfordbury they were ushered into the departure lounge. The ETD of the aircraft was in an hour's time. They were given a meal then various members of the staff came to congratulate them, they were treated as VIPs much to their amazement but delight. On the aircraft they were reminiscing on the day's events.

Sergeant Graham said. "I want to thank you sir from both of us for getting permission for us to stay at RAF March and coming from the ACM himself that was the icing on the cake."

"You don't think I was prepared to lose you two without a fight do you? Just think of the prestige to have three members of the staff with the B.E.M. that is something to be proud of."

"What happens when we arrive at March sir?" Asked Sergeant Graham.

"You Sergeant will come with me to be signed into the Mess. I phoned ahead asking for a room to be prepared for you, after one or two introductions I suggest you move out of your Barrack Block. Corporal Barton may volunteer to give you a hand because he can then move into your room. If anyone queries that move Corporal refer them to me. Now about your working uniforms and great coats which will have to be tailored, I will get the necessary permission in writing for the station tailor to act upon it. You cannot walk in and say I need these tailoring; we have to get written permission especially with it being a very special job. You see, it will be done in double quick time, top priority. When you have completed your move Sergeant if you feel like coming into the bar I will be there with WO Barrett, we would like to see you there and over a drink we can give you the gen on life in the Mess. I know you will feel strange for a little while until you get used to us but please come in we will really welcome you."

"Thank you sir I do appreciate all the help you are giving me, I will see how my move over progresses."

"I am sorry Corporal Barton I cannot invite you to the Mess even if it was for a drink, regulations you understand so you must celebrate with your friends without us."

"I understand sir, will it be alright for me to go into your living quarters helping with the move?"

"No problem there Corporal but I am afraid that is only as far as you will be allowed to go on this occasion. Here we are, seat belts unfastened, we have soon got here."

"The staff car was waiting and soon they were on their way back to camp the nearer they got the more nervous the lads became. When they passed through the security at the gates Roy asked the driver to drop the Corporal off at his accommodation and "Drop us at the Sergeants Mess please," said Roy.

"Before we go in the mess what is your Christian name?"

"Chris' sir,"

"When we are in the Mess if you call someone by their rank they will normally tell you to use their Christian name. You can now call me Roy because we are in private. In the office we are formal except, *I* can be informal but *you* cannot, unless we are alone in my office. I don't know why I am telling you this you have been an NCO long enough to know the score. Anything else you want to know Chris', before we go in?"

"I don't think so Roy; until I feel my feet I will stick to you like a shadow to learn the ropes."

"Good man, now we will meet Flight Sergeant Atkins, she is the Mess Manager and you will like her. Incidentally she is WO Barrett's lady friend."

They went to reception and saw that Jackie was on duty. "Jackie," said Roy, "this is Chris' Graham the newest addition to the Mess. Jackie is one of our civilian receptionists."

"I am very pleased to meet you Sergeant, and welcome to the Sergeants Mess."

"Thank you Jackie but please call me Chris' it is more friendly."

"If you will sign in Chris' I will call the Mess Manager she wants to see you."

Tommy came out, stretched out her arm and said. Congratulations on your promotion and welc….she stopped dead. "Oh my God, you both have got the B.E.M. come here Roy Shaw you lovely man, she then grabbed and kissed him, oh how wonderful for you both. Come here Chris'," she gave him a kiss too, "it is a pleasure to have you as a member. What a wonderful surprise, wait till Barbara and Bill see you they will get the shock of their lives."

"SAC Barton got the medal as well as promotion to Corporal." Roy informed her.

Jackie came forward and asked. "Am I allowed to kiss our two heroes?" she came forward and did just that.

Roy said. "Can Chris' have his key please because he has to move his gear over? Corporal Barton is going to help him."

Jackie gave him his key. "Come on Chris' I will show you where your room is."

Chris' held his hand out to Roy and said. "In case I do not get the chance to see you again until tomorrow, thank you for everything you have done for us today."

"Chris', Tommy called. "Come and tell me when you and Corporal Barton come over with your gear I will fix you both up with something to eat, you can have it in your room."

"Thank you Flight that will be lovely."

"Everyone in the Mess calls me Tommy, be sure you do as well, now be off with you."

"Here you are Chris' here is your new home," welcomed Jackie."

He opened the door and gazed around. "This is great; I am going to be very, very comfortable in here, thank you very much. Can I call you Jackie?"

"I would be offended if you did not," she replied. "Don't forget, let us know when you are back, there will be something to eat for you both."

In the meantime Tommy said. "Hang on here Roy I will go and bring Barbara."

She knocked on Barbara's door, when Barbara answered it Tommy said. "There is a message for you at reception."

"Oh, it will be from Roy."

When she saw Roy standing there she ran to him giving him a huge kiss and a hug. "I have been hoping you would be back today, it has been a long day for me waiting for you, has it been a good day for you?" Then she saw the medal ribbon on his chest, she let out a loud scream of happiness, grabbed hold of him again and literary smothered him with kisses. "Oh you wonderful man, I cannot wait for you to tell me all about it. Look at his medal ribbon Tommy isn't it wonderful? And it suits you my darling."

"Look, would you two like to go in my office? I will make you a brew and a sandwich Roy."

"I would love one please Tommy."

"Come round and you can have a good natter in private."

Roy told Barbara everything the responses he got were, "oohs, aahs and you didn't? Oh Roy it must have been a wonderful experience and he sounds like he is a very nice man."

"They all were nice and could not do enough for us it was the Aide-de camp who let me use his private phone so I could arrange a room for Chris'."

"I am right pleased that Chris' and Andrew got decorated as well for they are two lovely lads and were a big help to me when I worked in your orderly room. Look Roy, will you take me to see them before they have their meal?"

"Of course, we will wait here until he comes to tell Tommy they are back then we will nip down to see them and as soon as their meal arrives we will leave them to it."

When he arrived at reception he reported to Jackie that they were back.

"I will bring it down in about ten minutes," Jackie informed him.

When he had left, Roy and Barbara gave him a minute then followed on. Roy knocked on the door which was opened by Chris'.

"Chris'! I have brought a fan to see you both."

When Barbara showed herself his mouth opened in amazement. "I have come to congratulate you and Andrew."

"Please come in," he said beaming all over his face.

"Sorry I am not allowed in, regulations," she replied. "You will both have to step out here."

As they did so she gave them both a hug and a kiss as she congratulated them, it is simply wonderful and I am so pleased for you."

"Thank you" they both replied it is very kind of you."

"Hey up," said Roy, "here come your meals..." as Tommy and Jackie, each bearing a cloth-covered tray, approached.

"We will see you later," said Roy and Barbara as they made themselves scarce.

"Here you are boys, enjoy it. I am sure you are starving."

There were big thanks from the two lads and a couple of 'Wows' when they removed the cloths and saw what was on the trays.

"Welcome to the Hotel Splendide," Chris' toasted Andrew with a cup of tea. "You know something Andy, I think I am going to enjoy my stay at RAF March all the more now."

"Do you think the ACM will increase my promotion if I ask?" said an enviable Andrew.

"I doubt it there is not room for two Sergeants in that orderly room. I say aren't the staff going to get a shock when the three of us walk in tomorrow, be prepared for a bit of leg pulling."

"I have already had some when I walked into the billet. I will get some more when I move into your old room."

"It is tough at the top Andy' but you will soon get used to it."

"That was a cracking meal Chris', I did not expect that I thought I would not have been included, they certainly look after you here don't they? It is like being in a different world. Do you think I could stop for supper?"

"I'll supper you, get off with you and let me sort out my stall, I have to take these trays back as well." As he showed Andy off the premises he shook his hand and said. "We have had a great day together let us not forget it and remember we are still good pals."

"I won't forget." Then with a grin he said. "Goodnight Sarge'."

Chris' collected the contents of the two trays and wandered to reception. Nobody was there so he shouted "Hello! Anyone there?" Tommy came. "Here I will take those off you. Did you enjoy it?"

"Yes thank you, with all the excitement we did not realise how hungry we were."

"I guessed as much, you would have been starving by morning. Stay there, I will take this lot away then show you round the Mess."

In the dining room she explained the seating situation. "Those two top tables are for Warrant officers only, they are fondly known as the City Fathers that title goes way back when they used to sort out any problems before they went too far. Flight Sergeants and Sergeants can sit anywhere else they like. Meals are served there at the servery; you will see the meal times on the notice board plus everything else of importance. This is what we call the big room where meetings, dances etc. take place we have just reintroduced Bingo on a Saturday night. Actually it is only in the last few weeks that we have formed committees because the Mess has been run down for some time and Bill Barrett is getting the Mess members interested in it again, he is the Mess chairman. You are very fortunate coming to us at this time because in the next two weeks or so we will be dining-out Flight Sergeant Ball who as you know is leaving the service. All Mess members are expected to attend, everyone will be in uniform because it is a formal dinner in his honour and a farewell presentation and you Sergeant Graham with being the most junior by seniority in the Sergeants Mess will have the honour to propose the Loyal Toast. You will be instructed in what you have to do and say, it is very simple. A word of warning, beware of having plenty of drinks offered you, it is a sign of friendship and not something sinister like getting you legless because you are new but just be careful.

We have a television room and a billiard room and we are going to sort out a dartboard because we are trying to get some competitions going. No doubt Roy will chaperone you until you get used to us and you will find it a friendly Mess; we will do our best to help you to settle in. By the way at meal times, I realise with being new you will try to find a table to yourself, if someone asks you to "Come and sit here with us" do so because by doing that you will get to know more of the members. Well Chris', that concludes the tour, does that make you feel any better?"

"Thanks Tommy you have been great and so has everyone I have met so far, what a day I have had and it will stick in my memory always. I will go and sort myself out now, Roy said I could meet him in the bar later but I don't know if I will."

"Take my advice Chris, you go it is another step for you in becoming a Mess member, don't you worry they will look after you, go and enjoy it, they will be half expecting you. *They*, are Roy Shaw and Bill Barrett and you could not be in better hands."

"Thanks for everything Tommy I am feeling more at home now."

After he had sorted himself out he wandered into the bar and when Roy saw him he waved him in.

"I am glad you came because we were looking forward to you doing so. You know Bill Barrett well enough."

Bill shook his hand and said. "Congratulations Chris' on both counts your promotion and decoration and welcome to the Sergeants Mess."

"Thank you sir," he replied. I have been treated with nothing but kindness and help since I set foot in the place."

"Talking of feet, shall we start off on the right foot by you calling me Bill? You know the score about first names. Now it will be my pleasure to buy you your first drink in the Sergeants Mess, what are you drinking?"

"I will have a beer with you Bill."

"Arry. A beer please for our new Mess member.'"

Harry put the beer on the counter. He held out his hand. "Congratulations Chris' and welcome to the Mess and as it is your first drink in here it is on the house."

"Thank you Arry' and cheers everyone. He took a drink and remarked. "That is a good pint."

"Arry' here is the duty barman, he has it for one month then another Sergeant is detailed, it is only Sergeants who do this duty so you will be getting your turn when your name hits the top of the list. At the moment you are last on the list so it will be some time before we see you behind that bar." Roy informed him.

"Have you got yourself sorted out in your room?" asked Bill.

"Yes and Tommy has given me a guided tour of the mess and given me a lot of useful information. She also provided Corporal Barton and me with a right good meal; he helped me to move my gear over. It is like another world over here."

The others laughed at that.

Roy said. "I have been telling him what the ACM and his Aide said about him."

"That is true; how I read it they have you walking on water down there."

"Here, hold on Chris I did not say that we don't want to turn his head."

"Did you tell Bill that the Aide sent him his regards? And that the ACM still refers to him as that crafty bugger?"

"No, that slipped my mind."

"I think you and I Chris' should have a little private talk, then I will get the right tale of what happened and what was said. I think this man is holding out on me."

Harry intervened. "Don't pay much attention to these two Chris, there is a third WO who makes up the party and they have been christened the crackpots. At times you don't know if they are friends or enemies."

"I am not going to stand here and be insulted by a common barman," said a supposed indignant Roy, "I have a good mind to take my custom elsewhere."

"Where will you go?" asked Harry.

"Oh just fill em' up again and have one yourself while I think of somewhere."

"The banter that was passing to and fro' amused Chris no end. He was enjoying every minute of it.

CHAPTER 23

As Mess Chairman, Bill opened the meeting.

"Before I ask Sergeant Page to read the minutes from the last meeting I would like to introduce you to our Mess President Flight Lieutenant Cody, most of you already had that pleasure at the dining-in night, but not many of you know of the new member to the Mess. I will say that all of you have already had dealings with him in the past and will continue to do so in the future, please welcome Sergeant Chris' Graham of the orderly room." After the applause he added. "It is also my privilege and pleasure on behalf of all members of the Sergeants Mess to congratulate Warrant Officer Shaw *and* Sergeant Graham on being awarded the B.E.M."

As one, everyone stood up to applaud.

When the minutes had been read and accepted he began.

"I have here half a dozen chits asking to be excused from the meeting by various bodies which I intend to follow up and if any are not genuine that person will have some explaining to do to our President. Some of you do not realise this meeting is a duty as are any formal functions we hold. As from now anyone skiving from these meetings or formal functions without a legitimate excuse will find themselves facing the President, then for their sins voted onto one of the committees. Has anyone got any objections to that?

Silence prevailed.

"Then please pass that message on to the absentees you know."

"This meeting has been specifically called because we are to dine-out Flight Sergeant Jim Ball in fourteen days time after coming to the end of a long service career. Mrs Ball will be the only invited guest. It is customary to have a presentation to a departing colleague and the Mess committee after much deliberation agreed on what is thought to be the ideal present on condition the mess members accept it. You may or you may not know that the highlight of Jim's career was the famous victory by the BlueBelles over the other two services. Jim put his heart and soul into doing whatever he could to help them and on the day of the victory Jim was one of the proudest men in the RAF and he still is. The suggested item is an enlarged photograph of the BlueBelles team in a good frame; attached to it will be a plaque inscribed. 'Presented to Flight Sergeant James Ball by the Members of the Sergeant's Mess RAF March in recognition of his Devotion to the WRAF BlueBelles Drill Team.'

"Excuse me," interrupted Warrant Officer Johnson, "You have not told us what it is going to cost the Mess for this gift."

"If you had waited until I had finished describing the item WO Johnson you would have been told the cost but as you appear to be so impatient to know, here it is." He then told the cost.

"That ladies and gentlemen is what you have to decide but first we will have a few minutes break for you to discus it among yourselves." Bill spoke quietly to Wings. "I'll bet you a brew we will have an objection from that source first thing after the break."

"No way!" answered Wings, I have heard of your betting capabilities."

"Shall we proceed ladies and gentlemen?"

"Before we take a vote," said WO Johnson "I would like to say that I think the cost is much too high for just a Flight Sergeant."

"Does anyone else share that view?" asked Bill.

WO Chivers who was sat along side WO Johnson raised his hand and said. “I do.”

“Does anyone else share their views?”

There was no response.

Addressing the two WOs Bill said. “So you both think there should be a sliding scale from Warrant Officer down to Sergeant?”

“Indeed, rank has everything to do with it.”

This rank discrimination peeved Bill and he retorted.

“What has rank got to do with giving a retiring colleague a retirement present? The quality of the present represents the esteem by which a colleague is held in by his peers.”

That statement resulted in calls of “Hear! Hear!”

“If there are no more questions or objections I will carry on. First I need someone to propose it and someone to second it before it goes to the vote.”

“I will propose that,” said Warrant Officer George Miller in a loud voice.

“I will second it,” said Warrant Officer Harry Jackson in as loud a voice.

“Can I have a show of hands for the motion?” All but two voted for.

“Against the motion?” Two hands were raised.

“Motion carried by a majority.”

Applause greeted the announcement and the two WO.s rose to leave the room.

“Sit down gentlemen, the meeting is still in progress,” ordered the President.

“Anymore questions?” asked Bill.

“Yes Sergeant Fielding?”

“There has been talk of holding competitions of various games, when are they likely to start?”

“I will hand that over to Warrant Officer Butcher as head of the entertainments committee.”

“Tell me what games are you interested in Sergeant?” she asked.

“All of them, darts, snooker, and quizzes!”

“Have you put your name down for any of them?”

“No I haven’t.”

“There you are then, you have answered yourself.”

He sat down feeling rather embarrassed.

Mary continued. “There has been a notice pinned to our notice board for a little while now appertaining to these various games if you do not put your names down how do you expect the committee to organise any? We have been elected to help transform this Mess into one you will want to come to and we are doing our bit, now the ball is in your court.”

“Are there any more questions?” Bill asked.

“I would like to make a suggestion.” Voiced Mary. “If I can arrange a disco for say 9pm when we should have finished dining Jim out, what do the members say to your wives and female guests coming for a little entertainment until midnight?"

"What a good idea," said Bill, "show your hands if you are in agreement. Excellent, a very good majority want it."

"If you want a baby sitter please contact me in plenty of time, I cannot oblige you if you want one at the last minute," Mary warned them.

"There is another subject I would like to bring to your attention and approval," said Bill.

"A Christmas Dinner Party for the Senior Citizens of March village. It can be held prior to our Christmas break and I am sure we will get volunteers from the boys and girls to help out in looking after them. You can bet the old people will enjoy being fussed by our young people just as much as the youngsters will enjoy doing it. We can give them a nice meal and a token present and it will not break the bank. Some of you I hope will volunteer to use your own cars as a ferry service for them. That is the outline of the idea, if it is accepted our committee have said they will do all the arranging providing they can call on some of us for help. If you have any views or ideas I would like to hear them before it is put to a vote."

George Miller raised his hand. "I have been on many stations as have some of our older members where this has always been an annual event. Various types of entertainment have been provided but I always found that what went down best of all was a pianist who could play the old songs that the seniors knew and could sing along with and it usually finishing off with the popular carols."

"Thank you George, that is a sound idea which I am sure Mary and her committee can build on."

"Yes Flight Sergeant Chapel?"

"Would the committee consider putting a list on the notice board in plenty of time for us to pen our names to it and naming what we would like to volunteer for? Have we any hidden talents amongst us such as being a member of the Magic Circle." That brought laughs from everyone.

"It appears we have to vote on it ladies and gentlemen. Can we have someone to propose and someone to second it?" A flurry of hands was raised and two were chosen. "Now please raise your hands 'For' the proposition. Thank you very much that was unanimous," said the smiling Chairman."

Mary raised her hand. "I would just like to say to everyone. Please keep your eyes on the notice board, at this moment in time there will be plenty of information for you to read don't be the one to miss out."

"If that concludes the business ladies and gentlemen I will bring the meeting to a close."

"A very interesting meeting Mr Barrett I am glad I did not accept your bet, reputations like yours travel," said Wings "You nipped that rank discrimination in the bud very nicely but you may have lost two friends."

"I would not call them friends exactly sir they have had that attitude for such a long time they do not want to lose it."

"I will be off now Mr Barrett and I am looking forward very much to the dining-out evening."

"I will show you out sir, offered Bill.

He then returned to the room to talk over the events of the meeting.

"I will let you have the transcript when I have sorted the minutes out Bill."

"Okay Barbara and thanks."

"What do you think about that plonker?" asked Mary it makes you wonder how they get promoted."

"That is what we are up against Mary we can expect no help from the likes of that fellow."

"You are so right but they are always at the front of the queue when freebies are offered, hopefully his is an isolated case. Having said that what do you think of the two WO.s? They are the ones who are supposed to be respected by the lower ranks."

"Mary! Those are leaders of men."

"Leaders!" She said with a snort. "Follow me men I am right behind you more like it! But just watch yourself where they are concerned Bill, they will not take too kindly for the rebuke you gave them."

"I am aware of that Mary, there is a very thin line dividing us and they have only to cross it once!"

"Good man, I know full well you can take care of yourself. I have said it before and I will say it again, you and George Miller are like a couple of book ends and I am so proud of you both."

He bent forward and kissed her cheek. "Come on old girl don't go all sentimental on me. Now before you say it I know what it will be."

They said it together laughing. "Less of the old."

"I knew there was something I wanted to ask your advice on Mary. What are your thoughts on presenting Mrs.Ball with a bouquet of flowers?"

"I think that would be a very nice gesture Bill, I can get Sam to make up a nice one, have you anyone in mind to present it?"

"What about Sergeant (w) Roper?"

"That would be nice she will appreciate doing that I'm sure," said Mary. "Ask her Bill."

"Tommy approached them and said to Bill. "I have had a card from Viv, stop at reception on your way out and I will show it to you"

"Are they having a nice time?" asked Mary.

"They certainly are according to the card."

"I expect you two will be going next both of you could do with a good break; think about it Bill Barrett and stop pulling your face think of Tommy here I don't think I have seen her relaxed since I have been on the station. She needs a break even if you don't. Now get on with it and do as you are told for a change!"

"Yes Ma'am."

"See you later then."

"Bye Mary."

"She's nice," said Tommy.

"With a heart of gold," agreed Bill.

CHAPTER 24

Bill assembled his NCOs in his office. "When the new recruits arrive on Wednesday that is when we seriously commence the new training scheme. It will be the official change over, which means you do not stay as long in the ops' room but it will be a nice little break for you. Also as from Monday we can now stop the early morning barrack inspections, providing of course the recruits have learned their lesson and continue to toe the line. It is up to you Corporals to see they do so or we will start again at square one. Thank you all for your co-operation in that department, if any of you have anything you would like to bring up please feel free to do so. I would like to congratulate Sergeant Dixon and his team for the way they handled that special flight they were special all right; I thought the airmen were the most awkward individuals I have seen for many a year but their instructors persevered until they turned out a good little flight. It is a credit to the three of them as Drill Instructors. I am only singling them out because the rest of you appreciated what they were up against. Thank you all for the efforts you are putting in, you are a very good team that anyone would be proud of. Have a good weekend but don't forget or rather your wives won't let you forget that Saturday night is Bingo night, stop moaning and give them a treat besides helping the Sergeants Mess. Okay then, see you Saturday night and then 'BINGO' you could be winners!"

>>> <<<

"The usual Arry' and put one in for yourself," said Bill. "Oh here is Roy, one for him as well. Evening Roy owt' fresh at the sharp end?"

"Nothing of any importance Bill, thanks Arry' cheers Bill. One thing that is certain since young Chris' took over from Mata Hari, yes I know she was a woman spy but we are not splitting hairs are we? As I was saying before I was so rudely interrupted by Mr Brain of Britain here. The change in the orderly room is so noticeable now especially to me, there is a different atmosphere similar to when Barbara was in charge. Chris' is a good man and the staff respect him and young Barton has fitted nicely in the slot Chris' left. I am a very happy man with the staff I now have."

"I know the feeling," said Bill. What is it like in workshops with your lot Arry'?"

"It's alright, we get plenty of arguments over differences of opinions and it becomes a bit too personal at times for my liking. I just get on with what I have to do quietly until someone ruffles my feathers. We could do with someone like you Bill to sort out the bad apples, if I am honest I would like a posting which is a pity because this is a smashing little station and the family love it here."

"Come on Arry' don't get morbid, fill em' up and get yourself a drink it won't get you legless, if it does Bill and I will drag you into the cellar and take over till closing time."

"Then I suppose you will carry me home between you, knock on the door, push me in and shout. "Here's your Harry," then leg it back to the Mess before the wife catches you."

"Has somebody been telling tales about us Arry'?"

"Chalky was right, you are blooming crackpots."

"Are you coming to Leeds tomorrow Roy?"

"I doubt it unless Barbara changes her mind at the last minute, have you got any nearer to booking your holidays?"

"It is not a matter of where Roy it is when? Tommy has not come up with anything yet and I am not pushing her I think she waiting for a second opinion from Barbara before she commits herself."

"Have you been to Portugal Arry'?" asked Roy.

"Yes a couple of times."

"What did you think of it?"

"It seemed alright from what I saw of it."

"What do you mean from what you saw of it?"

"I went to Lisbon and Porto for the football, we got off the aircraft and straight to the stadiums, when it was over it was back to the airport and home."

"So all you saw was football matches?"

"We did have a few hours to have a quick look round Lisbon and the second time at Porto, they were both alright."

"Would you call yourself a seasoned traveller then Arry'?"

"Well I have been to one or two other venues on the continent."

"Only to watch football?"

"Yes, to watch football."

Roy looked at Bill who just raised his eyes.

"I am off now," said Bill, it is an early start in the morning and I must be fit enough to get round the shops before we go to the airport."

"Don't forget you have that photograph to collect," reminded Roy.

"I'll say goodnight Arry'," said Bill.

"Hang on I will come with you," said Roy. "Are you sure you can manage to get home under your own steam Arry'?"

"I will try my best," said Harry with a grin. "Good night."

"What are you doing when you come back from Leeds, are we all doing the same as we did when we got back have a quiet drink and a natter in the Quiet Room?"

"Well the girls will want a good chin wag to get all the gen from Derwent and Viv to find out what they have been up to, well you know what I mean. I think that is the best bet. Night Roy."

"Night Bill."

After an early breakfast the duo set off for Leeds and had a good look round the shops and stores. After a lunch they collected the two photographs, the original and the new one, congratulating the photographer on doing a marvellous job. "Jim will be over the moon when he receives this" said Bill.

When they arrived and parked their car at the airport and saw on the Arrivals Board they had an hour to wait they went for a drink then wandered round the airport until the arrivals board stated the aircraft had landed. After waiting for another thirty minutes Tommy began waving to Derwent and Viv as soon as they came in sight, Bill joined in when they were pointed out to him.

"Just look at their colour Tommy, it is plain to see they have had plenty of sun."

Hugs kisses and handshakes was the order of the day.

"Welcome home, my words but you both look very well, if you feel as good as you look then it has been worth while you going," Tommy enthused. "We have missed you haven't we Bill?"

"Indeed we have and it is great to have you back home again where we can keep our eyes on you both. Here, let me take the trolley Derwent." They went in front and the two girls needless to say were trailing behind chattering like a couple of magpies.

"Just listen to those two," observed Bill, "I bet they never stop for breath all the way home."

"Viv and I were talking on the way back about how we six got together and became so close friends and how we each made up couples straight after we met."

"It must be the March air, Derwent."

"What has the pub got to do with it Bill?"

"It has nothing to do with the pub. It is the air, A.I.R."

"Right!, now I get it, good one Bill. I am out of practice on the uptake aren't I?"

"Don't worry about it Roy and I will soon bring you down from cloud nine! Here we are load up and we will be off as soon as the girls stop to draw breath. Are you girls coming or staying?"

They looked at him then realised what they were doing then burst into a fit of giggles. "Sorry boys."

They all clambered aboard, the girls taking the back seats where they resumed chattering before they had got themselves seated.

"There they go," exclaimed Bill, nobody will shut them up, never mind we will have our little session and have I got news for you?" He told him the tale of Roy and his two lads receiving the award from the ACM.

"BLOODY BRILLIANT!" shouted Derwent startling the two girls with his outburst.

"What is going on there in front?" queried Tommy.

"I have just told him about Roy and his two lads Tommy."

"Oh yes Viv, I must tell you."

Viv was as enthusiastic as Derwent was. She clapped her hands together and said.

"That is absolutely wonderful, I am so pleased for Roy and the two boys of course wait till I see him he is going to get a great big juicy kiss."

"Now that is what I call a great home-coming surprise, said Tommy.

"If you two agree we will have a quiet night in the Mess as we did when Roy and Barbara came back."

"Suits us fine doesn't it Viv?"

"It certainly does, a nice quiet evening is what is needed after a long day."

"Then it is 8:30 at reception Okay? Will the pair of you be in for dinner?"

"I will," said Derwent."

"I do not feel like much to eat," exclaimed Viv.

"Tell you what we will do," said Tommy, "you and I will have a nice tasty sandwich in my office how does that appeal to you Viv?"

"That would suit me fine thanks Tommy that would be lovely we could then have a private chat without any rude interruptions."

When they met at reception Viv approached Roy and gave him a regal curtsey and a big juicy kiss. He took her hand and kissed it saying. "That is a sign of good breeding and a show of respect, please note that in future you peasants!" The remainder of the ladies then curtsied and the men bowed. "Take my arm Barbara we will lead the way." They entered the bar followed by their entourage who were curled up laughing.

"Go and get a table Sir and myself will bring the drinks."

"Evening Arry' greeted Roy, reading your travel magazine?"

"No, the football one Roy."

"Get the order Bill," he said in frustration.

Bill laughed and placed the order. When they carried them into the quiet room Roy said to Derwent. "Guess what Arry' was reading when we went to the bar?"

"The football magazine."

"Here's your drink tell us about your holiday then," the frustration flaring up again especially when Bill said that Roy had guessed it was the travel one.

To pacify him Derwent said. "Bill told us the wonderful news about you and your lads getting the awards we are proud of you Roy and you deserved it."

The conversation then went on about their holidays and comparing notes much to the delight of Tommy who was enjoying every minute of it. Finally she said. "We are definitely going there Bill Barrett."

"Whatever you say dear," much to the delight of the other four who cheered and gave him a round of applause.

"Now get on with it," said Roy gleefully, if you cannot afford the deposit we will have a whip round for you. Come on Bill let us go and get the drinks in."

"I'll go said Derwent."

"You stay where you are we don't want to overtax you, remember you have been travelling all day, we will see to it."

"I have to go Roy I want to see a man about a dog." When he returned to the bar to help Roy carry the drinks he saw him talking to Chris'. He grabbed hold of his hand giving it a warm shake. "Congratulations Chris' you thoroughly deserve your two awards. Come with us Viv would like to see you."

"It will only have to be a minute I am playing Bingo and it is due to restart."

When Viv saw who came in with Derwent and Roy she jumped up from her seat with a little squeal of delight then grabbed hold of Chris' giving him a hug and a kiss.

"Congratulations Chris'," she said, on your award and promotion and welcome to the Sergeants Mess."

"Thank you, everybody has been very kind and helpful welcoming me into the Mess especially Roy here he really has done a lot for me, I will never forget that. I am sorry but will you excuse me I am playing Bingo and I want to win some money to help me live in the manner I will now have to get accustomed to here in the Mess. I will see you folk again, bye for now."

CHAPTER 25

When Flight Sergeant Jim Ball reported to the orderly room he was very surprised to see Chris' in charge. "There certainly has been some changes while I have been away but congratulations on your promotion maybe we will get some decent service now but don't tell Roy that. What is the story behind the gong?"

"That is a long story Flight I will let the Warrant tell you about that, he told me to send you in to him when you arrived so he is expecting you and you will be in for another surprise."

"Thanks Chris'," then as he shook his hand, "congratulations on the award I am really pleased for you."

"Before you go I want to re-introduce someone to you, Corporal Barton!" he called.

Andrew came forward. "Welcome back Flight Sergeant."

Jim was amazed when he recognised him with his promotion and award.

"What has been going on here? What have I been missing? Come here Corporal let me congratulate you too on your promotion and award as he shook his hand. This *is* RAF March; tell me I am not dreaming all I need now is to walk into the WO.s office to see him wearing the VC. Then I will know I am having a nightmare."

Everyone in the office cracked out laughing.

Chris' then knocked on the hatch, opened it and asked. "Are you free to see Flight Sergeant Ball sir?"

"Of course," Jim heard him shout. "Come on round Jim!"

As soon as Jim walked through the door and saw Roy wearing his medal ribbon he could not believe his eyes. "What has been going on Roy? Before you tell me, congratulations."

"Sit yourself down Jim before you fall down." He then shouted through the hatch.

"Two teas please, I would give you summat' stronger for the condition you are in but you are on duty so you will have to make do with a good old honest brew.

"Welcome back Jim, it has seemed such a long time you have been away and we have missed you."

"I got the chance to do a couple of extra weeks so I took it and I am glad I did for I learnt quite a lot in that time."

"Your teas sir." said one of the airmen staff as he placed a tray on Roy's desk. Sergeant Graham wants to know has he to ring Sick Quarters and ask for a nurse to come and stand by in case the Flight Sergeant needs the 'kiss of life'?"

"Tell your Sergeant I would prefer a female nurse rather than one of you lot and in future not to be so bloody cheeky to his superior or I will see he gets moved to the top of the station duties list."

The lad left laughing.

A few minutes later Chris' put his face at the hatch. "Would you like a nice cream cake Flight Sergeant?"

“I’ll give you cream cake!” Turning to Roy he asked loud enough for Chris’ benefit, where on earth did you get staff like that, is that how you won your award, on sufferance? And *you* can shut that hatch after you have stopped grinning!”

“He is a great lad,” said Roy, he has made such a difference to that orderly room.”

“You are a very lucky man to have such a good staff but you deserve it. Now what have you got to tell me Roy?”

“Roy filled him in with the full story.

“Well done and you all thoroughly deserved everything you got, I did see the headlines on TV but had no idea what it was about or where it happened. It is apparently still under wraps because there has been no further mention of it. I was really gob smacked to see all the B.E.M.s before my eyes I thought for a minute they had come with the rations.”

“Did you know we have a new SWO?”

“Yes I did, the wife told me and Bill is full time training now. I understand the new chap is an old pal.”

”He is, George Miller is his name and he is a grand chap.”

”I have heard Bill talk about him they were at Chatworth together.”

“Anyway I will let Bill fill you in with the details when you see him.”

“Thanks for the brew and bringing me up to date, I had better start my arrival back on the station.”

>>> <<<

“I know I should not need to ask you Tommy but have you got everything organised for tomorrow?”

“Indeed I have Sir William, have you got the presentation organised?”

“Yes Ma’am I have, Viv will do the presentation which I think is appropriate being the leader of the BlueBelles, I think it is only fitting that she does the honours and Jim will be delighted with that and Margaret Roper will present the bouquet to Mrs.Ball. I will go now and see if Appy Arry’ is organised, I should think he will have no problems he has done this sort of thing before.”

“Are you organised for the dining-out night Arry’?”

“Of course Bill no problem.”

“What about the bar staff?”

“Tommy has got the stewards lined up for me who did the dining-in night they know what they are doing so everything should be tickety-boo as they say.”

“Well done Arry’ you are doing a great job.”

Bill knocked on Mary’s door and entered on command to see George Miller sat talking to her. They all greeted each other.

“What brings you here Mr Barrett got some good news for us?”

"No I just came to ask if you had been to see Sam?"

"I have and everything is organised."

"Have you owt' fresh George?"

"Only that I am looking forward to tomorrow night's do, things are quiet now after that little bit of excitement we have just had."

"I haven't seen you in the bar for some time what's up have you gone on the wagon or summat?"

"Nobody has upset me to such a state that I want to come in and murder a pint."

"You are having it too cushy here too much time on your hands, we will have to find something to occupy himself with won't we Mary?"

"Don't you dare drag me into this Bill Barrett; George is always there when I want him."

"Pardon e moi, I will leave you both to your little tete a' tete."

"George rebuked him with. "Watch your language in front of a lady."

"I will be off then and I will see you good people tomorrow. You know where to find me if you need anything at all Mary. Ta ra then."

>>> <<<

Harry and his staff were very busy serving drinks to the members prior to them going in to dinner. When Bill got the nod from Tommy that they should go into the dining room he called attention to the diners that they could take their drinks in with them. "One drink each please and no beer crates shoved under the table."

He then ushered the President and the guest of honour with his wife to their seats at the top table. Everyone else sat according to the seating plan which made sure there would be no confusion. Everything does not always work to a plan and such was the case when the odd one found himself sat in the wrong seat because he omitted to either read the seating plan or forgot where his seat was. Eventually everyone was sat where they should be after a few not very complimentary remarks and giggles.

Tommy waited until Sergeant Graham had proposed the Loyal Toast then signalled the waiters and waitresses to serve the food.

With the drinks in the bar prior to dining and the wines on the table it soon became rather a noisy meal. When everything had been cleared away Bill signalled to Tommy to bring in the Chef and the servers.

"Mr. President Sir, Ladies and gentlemen can I have your attention please. "I wish to thank our Chef for cooking us such an excellent meal, the proof was in the eating as was shown by all the clean plates returned to the kitchen and it is my pleasure to thank these young people for their expertise in serving the food and waiting on us like young professionals. Please join me in thanking them and the Chef in the customary way." Everyone rose to their feet to applaud.

After a few minutes to relax and have a drink Bill once more got to his feet.

"Ladies and Gentlemen, you all know why we are here. It is to pay tribute by dining-out a friend and colleague. Most of you know Jim, those of you who do not I would like to say you have missed out on the friendship of one of the most loyal, nicest and unassuming men it has been my pleasure to meet. Our friendship I am sad to say has been quite a short one up to present but I can assure you it is going to last a very long time. I will miss him and I know some of you will feel the same way. Service life for us all has to come to a close sometimes sooner than later and so it is with Jim, he will take memories of his service away with him but he will also leave us with us fond memories of him."

This brought a burst of applause from everyone.

Turning to face Jim he said. "Your fellow and lady members of RAF March Sergeants Mess would like to present you with something very close to your heart with their esteem and respect and who better to make the presentation than Flight Sergeant Viv Anderson, leader of the BlueBelles."

Viv came forward, hiding the face of the photograph until she came to Jim.

"From all the Mess members Jim, have a long and happy retirement, God Bless."

As she handed him the photograph she turned the face towards him.

"Oh my word!" he gasped. He placed it carefully on the table and held out his hand to Viv. "Thank you." He embraced her as he choked on the words. For a moment or two there was silence, a reflection on the emotion Jim was showing. Suddenly the applause began then everyone got to their feet to sing 'For he's a jolly good fellow.'

During the singing Sergeant (w) Roper presented Mrs Ball with a bouquet of flowers.

There were wet eyes from the ladies and some of the male members just mouthed the words not risking trying to sing. It took a few minutes for everyone to settle down again.

When Jim got to his feet to speak he was quite composed.

"Mr President Sir, Mr Chairman, Ladies and Gentlemen my friends. What an honour you have bestowed on me this evening, never in this world did I dream this could ever happen to me. I ask myself what have I done to deserve this? I am not royalty but just an ordinary bloke who likes people and it is here on this station I have made more friends than anywhere else during my service career. This is the best station I have ever served on. You younger members will look back during your service and agree after being posted from station to station during your career. If you will allow me to give you a little bit of advice on how to enjoy the service and what it can do for you is this: Liken it to a bank, *you* have to put something in to get something out. This presentation is the most wonderful thing you could have given me and I just choked up when I saw what it was. Of course the icing on the cake was having the honours done by The BlueBelles leader herself. Thank you my friends from the bottom of my heart for everything you have done to make this evening for my wife and myself the highlight of our career in the Royal Air Force. Thank you and God Bless You All."

Showing emotion after listening to Jim, the entire room erupted with applause, a sign of respect they held for him.

"Ladies and Gentlemen," announced Bill, after the prolonged applause had died down. "The photograph will be here on the table for anyone who would like to come and see it.

If you would please give us a few minutes grace to go and settle our honoured guests down it would be appreciated and please enjoy the rest of the evening along with your wives and friends"

When it came time for Wings to leave, Bill escorted him to the Mess entrance.

"He shook Bill's hand. "Thank you Mr Barrett for a truly wonderful evening and I must congratulate you on your ability to make so many people happy."

"It comes with practice sir and having the right frame of mind."

"Yes, I do realise that and I am learning Mr Barrett, I am learning, thank you. Good night."

CHAPTER 26

"Right then Mr William Barrett it is time you and I started talking holidays."

This conversation was taking place in Tommy's office, the only place in the Sergeants mess where they could talk in private without being disturbed, well nearly unless her staff came knocking for something or other but this was early evening and there was little fear of that happening.

"Okay then let us get on with it love, anything to make you happy."

"Don't be condescending with me Bill Barrett, we will go only if you really want to, if you don't we will kick the idea into touch it is as simple as that."

"Of course I want to go with you love, I have wanted to since the first time it was mentioned."

"You never showed it you horrible man."

"Well it started when Roy and Derwent began to lean on me to go, I had to give them a bit of the old macho stuff or they would have made me a member of the H.P.C."

"What on earth is the H.P.C?" Asked a puzzled Tommy.

"The Henpecked Club!"

She just curled up with laughter. "That is just typical of those two crackpots." She came and sat on his knee then putting her arms round him asked. "Are you really henpecked?"

"If I am," he replied, "I like it," then they kissed.

"I luv' you Bill Barrett!"

"I know," he answered.

Tommy jumped from his knee saying. "You are incorrigible *and* conceited to boot."

"Do you think you can change that when we are married?"

Tommy looked shocked from what she thought she was hearing. "Will you please repeat what you have just said," she asked in half a whisper.

"Jean Atkinson, will you marry me?"

She burst into tears then rushed into his arms. They held each other for a little while until Bill broke the silence. "Well?"

"Yes! I have been waiting for you to ask me that question since we first met."

"Sorry, I have just not had the time to get round to it with one thing and another."

She gave him a playful dig then asked. "Where do we go from here?"

"First things first, here are my thoughts. We keep it a secret for the time being and go ahead booking the holiday. In the meantime we must slip off to Leeds for an engagement ring which you will not be able to show off I'm afraid until we are good and ready to tell the world. Before we do go on holiday I want us to go and tell Nessie and John I want them to be first to know. When it eventually comes official we will need to get our heads together and plan the future. How long have you got left to serve before you can retire from the service with a pension?"

"I am eligible now dear."

"Great, that is in our favour there will be no hold ups where that is concerned, we don't want to have a long wait before we can get married because it will mean you leaving the service."

"Yes that makes sense but when the time comes it is going to be a wrench to leave, which is only natural after all these years. The good thing about it I will still be in touch for where ever you go so do I."

"Is there anything different or you want to add to what I have said?"

"At the moment no, maybe when it has sunk in I may think of something and then again I will probably go along with your way of thinking. Remember I have no family as such; we have never been in touch since I joined the service and I would like it to stay that way. When and how are we going to arrange that very special trip into Leeds, how about yesterday?" she said with a laugh and a kiss.

"Here is what we will do. Tomorrow I will ring the travel agent to ask for the earliest date he can book us into that hotel. If we can finalise it before Saturday then we will go to Leeds. How does that suit you?"

"Brilliant my love, I am going to be on pins from tomorrow hoping we can manage it."

"A word of warning pet, watch Eagle Eyed Jackie she can read you like a book and you can take it from me she will have her suspicions that something is brewing the moment she sees you. How are you going to get out of that?"

"To be honest Bill I don't think I can, she is so sharp. I will have to brazen it out the best I can and if I fail I shall have to take her into my confidence. We know she can be trusted and it will lift the pressure she will put me under by just looking at me."

"You are right, as soon as it becomes too much for you we will take her into our confidence"

The following day Bill rang the travel agent and explained what he wanted.

"I can book you into the hotel you want this coming Saturday unfortunately there are no seats available on the charter aircraft."

"Are there any other options?" Bill asked.

"Just one a scheduled flight I can get you on that but I am afraid there are only single seats available."

"Are there any double seats available in Business Class?"

"Oh yes, no problem there."

"That will do me. Can you hold it for me until tomorrow for confirmation please and what time is the ETD?"

"Yes I can hold it and the ETD is 10am."

"Thank you, I will try to get back to you today if I can. Yes, for two persons, thank you."

He went to reception and saw that Jackie was on duty.

"Good morning Bill, I presume you want Tommy?

"Good morning to you Jackie, how are you?"

"I feel fine thank you Bill, I will go and tell her you are here."

"She says she is busy at the moment but if you would care to go round she can spare you only a couple of minutes."

"That will be long enough thank you Jackie."

When he entered Tommy's office she held a finger to her lips.

"Just in case," she murmured.

He told her about the booking. "Can you get leave for Saturday? If so we will be going."

"I will go and see Mary shortly"

"As soon as possible please then I can confirm it. Have you had any any reactions yet from Jackie?"

"I am not sure, I have not had that look yet but I am feeling a little uneasy I feel it coming."

Speaking loudly Bill said. "Thanks for your help love. Roy wasn't sure that is why he asked me to ask you, he will be chuffed. Bye love," as he kissed her.

"Everything all right Bill?" asked Jackie.

"Yes, no problem, I said I would only be a couple of minutes," he looked at his watch. "Four minutes Jackie sorry about that. Be seeing you, got to see a man about a dog now."

"As she watched him leave she smiled and said to herself and pigs might fly"

Tommy had no problem getting Mary to initial her leave pass.

"That is what you both need badly," enthused Mary, "you see all it needed was somebody to give him a good kick up the backside to get him moving."

"Thanks to you Mary."

"Roy was delighted when she gave him the leave pass for him to get authorised.

"I will leave it to Bill to tell you abut it Roy he will be in shortly after he has seen Wings. I must get back it is hectic just now. See you Roy."

When his leave pass was authorised by Wings Bill took it to Roy.

"Tommy has just been in with hers, so you got fixed up alright I imagine?"

Bill told him the tale.

"You are travelling in style and it should be very comfortable."

"It was either that or we missed out for a time," explained Bill, what you might call a now or never situation."

"I could not see it being never Bill, Tommy would have been like a Rottweiler sinking her teeth into it and not letting go."

"I will leave you for now Roy to go and phone in my confirmation; I will see you at lunch."

There were no problems confirming. He gave the necessary information and "I will come to see you at lunchtime to settle up with you. When will I be able to collect my tickets?" he asked the travel agent.

"I will definitely have your tickets here tomorrow. I will have them sent to me by express delivery and I will have them by lunchtime tomorrow, sir."

"Can I use your phone Roy?"

"Help yourself do you want me to take a walk?"

"If you don't mind Roy, I will only be a couple of minutes."

He rang Tommy. Hello love, can we talk? Good, if you can you get tomorrow off we will go to Leeds."

"Just let anyone try to stop me," she said all excited.

"Calm down you know what will happen. Have you had any reaction yet?"

"Not exactly, I think the approach is 'softly, softly catchee monkey' but I can sense it is there if you know what I mean."

"I have a plan love, I will tell you later, bye for now, yes I do too, bye."

He looked through the hatch into the orderly room. "All clear sir" he called to Roy.

"Finished your business then?" asked Roy as he came in.

"I am sorry I had to turf you out like that Roy but it was very private. I have just realised how hard it is to have a private chat around here I know it is against the rules and regulations but who in authority does not do it?"

"I know how it is Bill believe me with the private conversations Barbara and I have. Shall we put it down to perks of the job?"

"By the way Roy I will be off camp tomorrow I have a personal errand to run, if I am not back for dinner I will see you in the bar."

"That is fine by me, you realise you will be questioned to what you have been up to and where you have been?"

"Roy that goes without saying, would you like a verbal or written report?"

"I think verbal will be better, I can then keep your glass replenished because I am sure you will have a lot to report."

"I cannot believe what I am hearing from you Roy you emphasise that YOU will be making sure my glass is never empty, have you come into some money and not told us about it and have you forgotten that our third partner in crime will be present. Are you keeping his glass permanently full also?"

"Oh my Gawd, what have I said? I could not have been thinking straight. Thanks for reminding me Bill."

"It was not being forgetful Roy you were concentrating so hard on trying to prise out of me what I am not going to tell you."

"You miserable cretin, that is after I let you use my phone." He then shouted through the hatch. "Cancel that brew!"

"Okay I will leave, I know when I am not wanted and I will not be in to lunch so do not come looking for me!"

"Too right you are and don't slam the door behind you."

He had an early lunch then set off to the travel agents. There were no problems so he paid up his dos and demands. "It will most likely be the afternoon when I can come to collect the tickets; I will make sure it is before you close."

"That will be no problem I do not close until six."

On his return to camp he went into the Mess and got a cup of tea then took it into the TV room to watch the news. He woke up from a doze and saw on looking round he was the only person left in the room and the TV had been switched off.

He went to his room to freshen up then went to see Wings.

He entered on command and saluted.

"Sit down Mr Barrett, what can I do for you?"

"I would like your permission for a day off tomorrow sir I have some business that needs attending to in Leeds. Everything is under control at the sharp end with Flight Sergeant Anderson in charge."

"I see no reason why not Mr Barrett I think you have earned it. I enjoyed that dining-out night, to be honest I am enjoying all the Mess functions, there is fun without being all stiff and starchy and you have a good laugh among yourselves. Your members have accepted me as their President and it is a good feeling when they come to me for a chat but losing none of their respect. I am happy here Mr Barrett, you and I understand each other and I hope I stay for a long time."

"I hope so too sir. Well I must be off and start cracking the whip, after I have had a brew of course."

"That is what I like about you Mr Barrett you have got your priorities right. I will have a brew shortly as well. It is Saturday you go on holiday isn't it? In case I do not see you before you go have a damned good one you deserve it"

Bill saluted. "Thank you sir."

"Viv, I am taking a day off tomorrow, I have squared it with Wings and you will be in charge here. Anything untoward get in touch with him."

"Are you doing anything special Bill? If you don't mind me asking"

"Apart from picking up our airline tickets I have some other business to attend to that is why I need the full day off."

"So you have booked, are you going to the same place on the Algarve?"

"That is where Tommy says we are going and I cannot argue with that after all you and Barbara have told her and we are leaving this Saturday."

"You both have made your mind up quick are you on the same flight as well?"

"No it was booked up we have had to go on a scheduled one there were no double seats even on that just singles so God knows where we would have been sitting so I booked business class, besides sitting together we will travel more comfortably too."

"You will enjoy it Bill I promise you, I could go again tomorrow."

"Sorry Viv you are needed here. Will you do me a favour please? Do not say anything to Derwent or Barbara, I will be seeing the lads tonight in the bar and I want to wind Roy up a bit."

"You men!" she laughed "what are you like? But as daft as you all are you have certainly changed that Sergeants Mess very much for the better."

"There is still a way to go before it really becomes the number one night spot for the married families but we are getting there. It looks like it is knocking off time, we will see if the gang has anything to report then we can shut up shop.

"Has anyone got anything to report?" he asked. Right then, tomorrow Flight Sergeant Anderson will be in charge in my absence."

"Are you going anywhere nice Sir?" someone asked.

"Not yet but I soon will. Who is on keys today?"

One of the Corporals said. "I am sir."

"Well do a good job on the security. Have a nice day tomorrow all of you. Come on Viv let us go for something to eat, then walked off whistling 'It's a Lovely Day Tomorrow'."

When Bill went into dinner he greeted Mary and his two compatriots.

"Anything new from either of you?" he asked.

"No." they answered. "Have you?"

"No afraid not."

"Hmm. It looks like we are going to have a very quiet meal that will make a change."

Mary finished her meal and as she was leaving she said to Bill. "If I don't see you before you leave I hope you and Tommy have a nice holiday and I hope she gets that costume she has had her eye on in Leeds."

"Roy slammed his knife and fork down on the table. "I knew it, I knew you were up to your bloody tricks again and what are *you* going to Leeds for, some new swimming trunks? You are up to something crafty Barrett and I will find out what it is you mark my words."

"Come off it Roy you don't think I would let Tommy go alone do you?"

"That sounds feasible but I still think there is more to it than that."

"Roy you are becoming suspicious of everything and everybody since that 'I Spy that Spy' episode. Would I hold back on my best friend?"

"That clinches it I have got you now, as soon as you made that statement you as good as admitted you were up to no good."

"Just forget it Roy and let us have our meal in peace as we intended to do in the first place."

"Roy laughed. "Until Mary let it out of the bag, you had not counted on that had you? You did not intend to mention it!"

"No Roy. Now that you found out my little secret can we get on with our meal?"

"I know you Bill Barrett I can read you like a book."

"Yes Roy."

"Stop being so condescending, it does not become you."

"Yes Roy but don't you mean condescending?"

"Oh I give up! You know I can't say condesceeding," said Roy in exasperation.

“Thank goodness for that,” exclaimed Derwent who had been just an onlooker, I thought you were never going to let it drop. You made your point every time you opened your mouth I thought you were going to put something else in it besides your foot. I am going now you have ruined my bloody meal.”

“See you in the bar tonight Derwent,” laughed Roy. He still takes us serious doesn’t he Bill?”

“Aye it is going to take him a long time to really know us but he is doing very well, he is a good friend.”

“You can say that again. By the way Barbara and I will do the airport run with you and Tommy. Remind me tonight to ask Derwent if he is coming.”

On the way out Bill saw Jill on reception. Will you see if Tommy is free Jill please?”

“You have to go round Bill.”

“Thanks Jill.”

A kiss and an embrace met him as she greeted him. “We will have an early breakfast and set off early,” said Bill, “because we have to pick the tickets up on our way back before he closes.”

“That is fine by me; now tell me about this plan of yours.”

“You wear your ring all through the holidays so that when you take it off you will have a white ring on your finger where the sun has not tanned. When we return try to keep your finger concealed until we go for the quiet drink in the Mess as we did with the other four and we will see how long it is before one of them notices it.”

“That will be fun,” said a delighted Tommy. “I would like to bet Barbara will be the first to notice it. Another thing my love, Nessie and John will not be the first to know.”

“I know, not unless I phone her up to tell her or, do you think we could manage to do a flying visit on the Sunday after the day we get back? Then promise to go for a weekend shortly after for a little celebration.”

“Let us wait until we return to see how we feel then we do not commit ourselves.”

“Yes, I think that will be best. Oh yes, Roy is ferrying us on the airport run. Okay love I will leave you for now I want to see the news on TV.” They kissed and embraced.

“You know,” said Tommy as she hugged him. “I think I will have a sleepless night thinking of tomorrow.”

On his way to the bar Roy met Bill coming out of his room. “Are you going where I am going Bill?”

“I certainly am and I am ready for a pint.”

“Come on then I will escort you to make sure you get there safely, besides it is your shout.”

“It isn’t!”

"It is you know."

They were still arguing about it as they went into the bar.

Derwent was already there. "Just listen to these two arguing 'Arry, they were at it at dinner and they are still at it. When are you two going to stop arguing?"

"When you get the drinks in," laughed Roy.

"Good one Roy," said Bill, patting Roy on the back.

"Get em' in 'Arry' and don't forget yourself while we have got them in a good mood. I do not know why you two fight like cat and dog one minute then the next minute act as if nothing had happened."

"That, Derwent, is called real friendship and it is about time you realised that. You have been a crackpot long enough," said Bill.

"Are you coming to see them off on Saturday?" asked Roy.

"I should think so Viv will jump at the chance of another shopping expedition in Leeds."

"What woman would turn a chance like that down? Barbara will be there like a shot."

CHAPTER 27

Bill and Tommy after an early breakfast drove off to Leeds. The nearer they got the more excited Tommy became.

"I will be glad when this particular shopping trip is over," complained Bill, "then perhaps you will get back to normal. At present you are a bundle of nerves, calm down."

"I am not nervous, just excited, it is all right for you but I have to wear it," she said giggling.

"If you don't want to wear one I can turn this car round and head back to camp!"

"Don't you even think of it Bill Barrett."

When they parked the car Bill asked. "Do you fancy a cup of coffee before we start?"

"I have a better idea than that," she replied smartly. "We will do what we came for first then have a cup of coffee!"

"Come on then, let us get it over with."

"You sound as if it was forced medicine."

"Sorry, I did not mean it to sound like that, what I meant was to get it over quickly before you become a nervous wreck."

"All I am nervous about is if I don't get one today, come love let us see what we can do," as she gave his hand a squeeze.

Of course being a woman she tried her best to get round every jewellery shop in Leeds. Eventually she made her decision but she had to look at every ring before she went back to the very first one that had caught her eye when they entered the shop.

"This is the one for me darling, can I have it please?"

"If that is your choice love how can I say no? Now you go and look over there at that display counter while I settle up."

When she had moved away he motioned to the salesperson to write down the price. When Bill saw the price he thought he was reading a telephone number. He looked at the salesperson who gave him a sympathetic smile but could not decide whether the return smile was a sign of capitulation. Out came the chequebook and Bill closed the deal. He called Tommy over and asked her if she wanted to wear it now.

"Yes please."

Bill then slipped it on her finger and gave her a token kiss. The salesman congratulated them and presented them with a small silver trinket box.

They left the shop arm in arm with her left arm linked in his right with the ring in full view with Tommy's eyes never leaving it.

"Are we going for a coffee or lunch?" Bill asked.

She did not answer. Bill looked at her to see her fully engrossed looking at her ring.

He twitched his arm to draw her attention. "I said, are we going for coffee or lunch?"

"Yes please darling," she replied.

"Yes please what?" He said grinning.

"What you just said."

"Shall we go to the restaurant we have been to before?"

"That will be nice," she replied talking to her ring.

"I give up," he said in frustration.

"Alright dear, we know it is a nice place and the food is good."

Bill was very relieved when the meal was over and they were back on the road. Gradually Tommy began to come round to reality much to Bill's relief.

When they arrived at the travel agents he told Tommy to stay in the car while he went to collect their airline tickets. They were there waiting his collection.

"Are you going to put your ring back in its box love? We are almost home now.

You can tell Jackie we have booked a holiday and did not tell her because we wanted to give her a surprise. That should stop her being suspicious and would lift the pressure off you. What do you think?"

"That should do the trick especially with us going on Saturday she will not have time to think of anything else. Well thought out my love."

"We are back in time for dinner and I will have to face the Inquisitors, you know what Roy is like when he gets his mind set on something he is like a terrier he never lets go. Here we are home sweet home, give me a kiss then we will go in."

After freshening up he made his way to the dining room. He gave a cheeky wave to the top table where Roy saw his entrance and continued watching his every move as he chose his meal.

"I am back gentlemen have you missed me?"

"Like a dog misses distemper," replied Roy, "you certainly took your time, been buying up Leeds?"

"Have you had a good day Bill," asked Derwent, "of course we missed you both at lunch and dinner I have had hardly a couple of words from this man, like being in a morgue."

"Bloody creep," answered Roy.

"It appears you are going to have two bad weeks with old misery guts here Derwent while I am away enjoying the sunshine drinking the odd pina colada by the pool wearing my new swimming trunks. Can you remember what Reginald Dixon's signature tune was? You know he played the organ in Blackpool Tower Ballroom."

"Oh I Do Like To Be beside The Seaside."

"That's the one it was a very catchy song."

"I will leave you with Joseph Locke's signature tune then, 'I Wish You All a Last Goodbye', smiled Roy as he made his departure whistling the song."

Jackie was on duty when Tommy returned to her office after freshening herself up and trying her ring on for size and appearance.

"Have you had a nice day Tommy?" Jackie asked.

"Very nice indeed," she replied. "Bill got his business sorted out all right."

"Anything else?"

"You are fishing; you think we have been up to something don't you?"

"Well haven't you? I can read you like a book Tommy Atkins you cannot fool me!"

"Alright you win clever clogs. We wanted it to be a surprise for you and now you have gone and spoiled it. We have booked a holiday to the Algarve and we have been to collect our airline tickets, we go on Saturday."

"Oh that is wonderful love I am so pleased for you both because you do need a break the way you have been working for such a long time. I knew there was something in the wind I could tell by just watching you. I am sorry I have spoiled your surprise but it is a nice one."

"What are you like? You watch over me like a mother hen. I like it though, come here while I give you a hug for being you!"

After dinner Jackie called Bill as he was passing reception. "Well done Bill you both really need a nice break. Tommy has just told me, you will send me a card won't you?"

"We were both supposed to tell you as a surprise but she has gone and let the cat out of the bag."

"Don't blame her Bill it was my fault for being a nosey old busy body, I am sorry."

"No problem Jackie and yes we will send you a card because we both love you."

"Come here you lovely man let me give you a kiss."

Tommy appeared on the scene as he was receiving his kiss.

"Get Off my man! So this is what happens when my back is turned, how many more Dolly Birds have you got hidden away you lady killer, I have a good mind to give you my airline ticket back."

"Good!" said Jackie quick as a flash, "I will use it!"

"You go and find another Toy Boy, this one is spoken for."

At the airport Bill and Tommy checked in then went to their friends to say their farewells.

Roy said to them. "Speaking for us all, I know we are being selfish but hurry back because we are going to miss you two. It is going to be a long two weeks wait for you coming home." He then shook Bill's hand and gave him a hug then a hug and a kiss for Tommy, the other three following suit with tears from the women and coughs from the men.

Bill and Tommy turned away quickly before the emotion got a grip, then made their way to the departure gate waving and blowing a kiss as they went through. When they were out of sight Tommy stopped him. "Just a minute, I want my hanky from my bag."

She not only produced the hanky but the ring as well and quickly put it on her finger giving Bill a big grin.

"You could not wait to do that he said giving her a quick peck."

Smiling, she said. "Well that is where it belongs!"

"You women never fail to amaze me."

A week or so later Viv, Barbara and Jackie received holiday cards.

Everyone in the Mess knew Jackie had received a card from Tommy and Bill, she was so excited she told everyone.

Barbara and Viv compared theirs. They showed them Roy and Derwent saying.

"She must have got a touch of the sun because everything she writes is 'Sparkling'."

"Well when you come to think about it," Derwent explained, the place *is* sparkling, the sea, the waterfront, the whole area, she must be really smitten by it."

"It is easily explained," added Roy. "They have never had a holiday together apart from the few days they had at Bill's sister's house after the BlueBelles victory, this holiday is so different for them they are enjoying ever minute of it and I wish they would hurry up and get back here it is so quiet."

"Don't be so selfish Roy Shaw," chastised Barbara, "we have had our holiday so let them enjoy and make the most of it while they can."

"Are we doing the same as we did when we got back, a quiet evening in the Mess?"

They all agreed on that.

Viv said, "Bill is going to be pleased to find Joe Franks behind the bar when he gets back."

"I had forgotten about that," Roy said. "His Staff are not excused bar duty they must take their turn like everyone else. Are you managing alright without him Viv?"

"Oh there is no problem there," she replied, "I'm coping but it is not the same without Bill, I think all the staff miss him as well."

"What do you think of Jackie? She is telling everyone she has had a card from Tommy, she absolutely idolisers her," Barbara laughed. "She is such a kind person though."

CHAPTER 28

As the aircraft was coming in to land Bill asked. "Are you ready to face the reception committee?"

"Yes, the ring has been returned to my handbag, have you got the receipt handy to show customs if they ask for it?"

"Yes dear I have. Well that little holiday is over with and it has been fabulous."

"When are we planning the next one?"

"I don't know, do you want to go again?"

"Couples usually do but it will need a lot more planning because there would be so much to take into consideration."

"What, for a holiday?"

"Of course it will be a special one."

"Why will it be special?"

"Wouldn't you class a honeymoon as special?"

"Ah! The penny has just dropped, you little Minx! Yes, I see your point it will have to be thought out very carefully indeed. Here we go and don't forget, keep that finger with the white ring well concealed until tonight."

They received a great welcome from Roy and Barbara. As usual the two men went ahead with the trolley with Roy pushing it and the two girls bringing up the rear chattering away like they had not seen each other for years.

"Come on you two." Shouted Roy stop lagging behind you will have plenty of time to natter when we are in the car."

Barbara said. "He has been a real pain since you have been away he has really missed Bill and waiting here for you he was like a cat on hot bricks. Where are they? Why are they taking so long? Do you think customs has got hold of them? Then when he saw you he changed, he was like a little lad."

"They are certainly fond of each other and I have never seen such close friends act with each other as they do." added Tommy.

"When you have finished would it be too much to ask if you would please climb in the back then I can get this man home quickly before he bores me to death with how many pina coladas he has drunk sunbathing by the pool."

"They were very good Roy and so refreshing, we really enjoyed them."

"I always said he was a bad influence on you Tommy."

"How have things been at the sharp end this last couple of weeks Roy?"

"Just fine, couldn't be better, the time has certainly passed quickly, I was only saying to Derwent yesterday we had better make the most of today for it will be a long time before we can have our meals in peace again. Guess what Billy Boy? Appy Arry' has finished his term of office we now have a new barman by the name of Joe, he is very good too and is very sociable, I don't know how it will affect him when you show your face."

"The only Joe I know is Joe Franks."

"Right first time, give the man a coconut."

"Well that is a turn up for the books, well done Joe he will have had plenty of experience doing bar work during his service, I am looking forward to seeing him behind the bar."

"Aren't you peeved about it?"

"No, why should I be? He has to take his turn with the rest of the Sergeants, my staff are not exempt."

"Have you had a nice time Tommy?" he asked changing the subject having lost that round to Bill.

"It was wonderful Roy we did not want to come home. I would have liked another week."

"There would be no fear of that Tommy it took a lot of arm twisting to get him on this holiday in the first place, no way would you have got a third week, you would have had more chance of getting a Royal Wedding Invitation."

"Here we are once again," said Bill as Roy pulled up at the camp gates. The sentry asked Roy for his I.D. When he saw Bill he waved them through, "I did not recognise you for a minute sir. Welcome back sir have you had a good holiday?"

Bill hardly had time to respond before Roy put his foot down and zoomed past the startled sentry. The two girls were helpless with laughter as Roy lost yet another round to Bill.

Roy jumped out of the car rushed round to the boot and hurriedly dragged out the luggage. "8:30 at reception and don't be late."

"Let me have the case Tommy I will give you a hand," said Barbara. "Are you alright Bill?" She said with a smile.

"Don't worry your pretty little head about me Barbara I can manage no problem."

"Hmm!" snorted Roy as he led the way into the Sergeants Mess.

"I hope you are in a better mood tonight Roy Shaw or you will be sitting on your own."

"There's nowt wrong with me."

"What's he like? Laughed Barbara.

They met at reception as planned and received a handshake and kisses from Derwent and Viv. "Good to have you back," they both said, "it has not seemed the same without having you two around."

They all went in Bill and the girls went to a table while Roy and Derwent went for the drinks.

"Your boss is back from his holiday, he will be in later to see you," said Roy.

When they returned to the table and all had got their drinks Roy said. "I would like to propose a toast to our happy little family and may it continue to be so and may the love and friendship we hold for each other never falter." They all drank to that then Barbara said. "That was lovely Roy, very touching and very true."

They began the exchange of holiday memories and stories. Suddenly, Barbara spotted the white ring on Tommy's finger she got hold of her hand and asked. "Now what is this all about Tommy Atkins?"

The others looked at the hand then Tommy, waiting for an explanation.

"Oh that, I bought a cheap ring you know from one of those little stalls selling knick knacks, I wanted us to look legitimate because I felt conspicuous. I am surprised you did not think of that when you were there."

"It did not bother us," both Barbara and Viv said,"

"Do you want to see the magic ring?"

"No, it does not matter but why go to all that bother of pretence it was nothing to be ashamed of."

Tommy then fished in her bag and slipped the ring on her finger below the level of the table as she brought it up where they could see it she said. "Bill said I had to do it properly."

"Oh my God," Barbara screamed. "You have done it. They have got engaged," she shouted. There was pandemonium, they all wanted to kiss and hug Tommy and Bill at once. Then the girls had to inspect the ring, they just sighed and drooled over it. While they were doing this, Roy and Derwent slipped away to the bar.

"Roy asked. "Do you happen to have a bottle of champagne in the fridge Joe?"

"If I remember rightly there were three when I took over and they all have the same labelling Roy." He then checked the price list. "They are a bit pricey Roy."

"Doesn't matter, give me one and six champagne glasses please Joe."

"Are you celebrating the wanderers return?"

"Yes, summat' like that. Can I settle up with you later Joe, I don't carry that amount of cash around with me."

"No problem Roy."

Roy carried the bottle and Derwent the glasses. "I will go halves with you Roy," said Derwent.

There were screams of delight when they returned to the table. Roy very quickly cracked the bottle open and filled the glasses.

"Here is another toast, my words two toasts in one evening coming from me that is unheard of but I would not miss this particular one for the world. I am a very happy man to see my best friend become engaged to the sweetest lady it is my honour to call my friend. I found out about you two remember on that infamous Sam Barnes' day when I finally squeezed the truth out of you Bill Barrett? I asked you a question there and then, does it still hold good?"

"It certainly does old friend, nothing has changed and it never will." Bill replied.

"The question I asked was. Can I be your Best Man? All I ask is that you give me plenty of time to prepare a speech. Friends, please raise you glasses to toast the couple we hold most dear to our hearts. Bill and Tommy."

The kissing and hugging began all over again, mixed with some tears of happiness.

Barbara said. "So that was what all that sparkling written on your cards was about, we thought you had got a taste of the sun."

"I could not resist the temptation of writing it she replied."

Holidays were soon forgotten, all talk was of the build up to the engagement and the future plans which included Barbara, Viv and Derwent.

"So was that the main reason you went to Leeds to buy the ring?" asked Roy.

Bill then told them about Tommy being in a trance when they came out of the jewellers and when she stopped to put the ring on her finger as soon as we got out of site of you at the departure lounge. They roared with laughter.

"You should have seen my mannequin act in my room the day I got the ring, it would have been ideal for a TV advert."

They finally called it a night and decided it was bedtime, they were the only ones left in the Mess. On the way out they stopped off at the bar to apologise to Joe for keeping him late. Bill shook his hand and greeted him.

"Nice to see you behind there Joe, you will be seeing us three quite a bit, but keep an open mind and thanks for this evening."

"Anytime you want to celebrate that is what I am here for."

Roy pulled Tommy forward. "You have met Bill's fiancée haven't you Joe?"

"Oh yes indeed, we have known each other for quite a while now."

"But that was before she became engaged to marry your boss!"

"What? Bill and Tommy have got engaged? Wait till I tell the wife she will be delighted, she has a soft spot for you Bill. Come here let me shake your hand in congratulations and can I kiss the future Mrs Barrett?"

Tommy blushed at that but she offered her cheek. "Thank you Joe you are the first person to call me that and I must say it sounds very nice."

"Your first drink is on me tomorrow Bill."

Roy and Derwent began coughing with their hands held to their mouths interrupting him.

"Have I said something wrong?" asked Joe.

"Yes!" said Roy and Derwent in unison. "We object to any favouritism in this bar if you don't mind," insisted Roy.

"Alright I will rephrase it. The first drinks are on me tomorrow gentlemen."

"That is very kind of you Joe, now isn't that a noble gesture Roy?"

"Yes very commendable Derwent."

"Come you crackpots lets us get you home to bed," said Barbara, to your own beds so don't get any ideas."

"Bloody spoilsports," grumbled Roy.

"Goodnight Joe. They all said as they departed laughing.

"There is no chance to go to Nessie's tomorrow after tonight's celebration," said Bill.

"Yes it is a bit late agreed Tommy what about next Sunday?"

"Yes, we can go then, I can phone her during the week but give me a reminder. About tomorrow morning, isn't Jackie on duty?"

"So she is I had forgotten about that with all the excitement tonight."

"Are you going to tell her or do you want me there?"

"I had better tell her first even if I did not wear my ring she would spot the white one in an instant. Then you know what would happen? She would stand at that desk all day in case she misses you. Come on, give me a kiss then I can get to my bed for my beauty sleep."

"No you don't, you will always be lovely as far as I am concerned."

"Get off to bed you old romantic."

Next morning at breakfast the three crackpots were discussing the previous evening.

"Here comes Mary," Roy informed them, "are you going to tell her Bill?"

"After she has eaten I will."

"It would be a shame to put her off her food laughed Roy."

"Perhaps that's why she sits by herself not wanting to mingle with us," ventured Derwent, "that would put anybody off their food!"

"You speak for yourself, she would enjoy my company retorted Roy"

"Good morning gentlemen," Mary greeted them. "You are very quiet. Is it hang-over morning?"

"Good morning Mary," they all replied. "The reason we are quiet, Mary, is seeing you, a vision of loveliness, enter, we could not believe our luck when you sat beside us," said Roy.

"Now why don't you come and join me Roy, and I will personally feed you with my fist! Why don't you two take him for a walk in the fresh air to clear his head, then I can have my meal in peace? Go on, hop it!"

"I will see him out Mary," volunteered Derwent. "Come on Roy, it would be safer if you came quietly…"

"You are not placing me under arrest are you Derwent?"

"Go on Roy," encouraged Mary, "you can always plead insanity. Are you not going with them Bill?"

"In a minute Mary, I want a quick word. After breakfast call at reception Tommy has something to show you."

"Will do Bill."

When Bill got to reception Jackie was waiting for him. She beckoned him to the counter and threw her arms round him; she could not speak for the moment she was so overcome.

"Patting her on the back to console her. "Come on Jackie it is not that bad is it and you do not have to feel sorry for me."

"She managed a little laugh. "Oh Bill it is so lovely, you are such a lovely couple and I do love you both."

"Well just pull yourself together because Mary Butcher will be coming to see Tommy anytime now, she is just finishing her breakfast. All I have told her is Tommy has something to show her."

"Here she is now, I will go and bring Tommy and I will prepare her."

"Jackie has just gone for Tommy, Mary."

"Bill tells me you have something to show me Tommy."

Tommy had her hands on the desk palms down. I am showing you Mary."

"I see nothing is this a leg pull?" She saw Jackie in the background holding up one hand and pointing to a finger on it. She then looked down and saw the ring. She gave a scream of delight, grabbed hold of Tommy and gave her a hug and a kiss then turned to Bill saying. "Come here and congratulations you dark horse," as she hugged and kissed him. "What can I say apart from you have really made my day? Congratulations to you both, you are well suited I could never have picked a better partner for you Bill you both deserve each other. Oh my goodness, just you wait until the word gets round and I will make sure it does too."

CHAPTER 29

Sunday evening the six of them decided to go to see Ann and Tim at the March Hare. When they entered they received a huge cheer from the locals.

"It is good to see you, where have you all been hiding? Has Captain Bligh been confining you to camp?"

The place was in an uproar for a few minutes until Ann came into the bar to see what the commotion was about. When she saw who was the cause of it she broke into a huge smile as she came from behind the bar and gave each one a hug and a kiss. "We have missed you all, where have you been?"

"It is that Captain Bligh, he confined them to camp," the locals informed Ann.

"We will have less of that from you lot or I will stop your tap."

She received some boo's in retaliation.

"Give them a round of drinks Tim, anything for piece and quiet."

"Thanks Captain," they shouted.

While the rest were being seated Bill went to the bar to order and Tim shook his hand. "It is good to see you all Bill, have you been busy? Oh, and thank you for your card, I must thank Roy and Derwent for theirs too. I hear you found a fifth columnist among your ranks, is that true?"

"I don't know if he was but they said he was a threat to the National Security."

"We had Tom Hardcastle in telling us what he knew he said one or two had received awards."

"That is true, three of them to be exact, they were awarded the B.E.M."

"That is really good. At the time Tom said he did not know who they were."

"Well we brought one of them with us for a treat."

"Who is that?" said Tim getting excited.

"Roy."

"ROY?" he shouted. He dropped what he was doing and made his way to Roy who was standing up in bewilderment hearing his name shouted. Tim grabbed his hand then embraced him. Every one of the locals looked dumbfounded wondering what Tim was up to. Tim turned to them and quietly said. "I am sorry about that but Roy here has just been awarded The B.E.M." Ann rushed to Roy giving him a kiss and an embrace and with tears of joy said. "Congratulations Roy you lovely man."

The locals wanting to get into the act came forward to congratulate him and shake his hand. When it had calmed down Roy raised his hand.

"Thank you very much that is very kind of you and I am touched by it and please will you do me the honour of having a drink on me?"

"Of course we will and drink to your health Roy thank you."

When everyone had been served with drinks and Tim came over to sit with them Roy told them the whole story. Suddenly they realised how quiet it was, the local people had been listening with rapt attention to every word Roy uttered.

"You are not very observant tonight Ann or you would get an even bigger surprise. We will not tell you but use your eyes," said Viv.

A very puzzled Ann was trying her best to unravel the puzzle and coming up with no answers. I cannot see anything at all you will have to tell me. wherever I look nothing rings a bell."

"You almost got it then Ann," said Barbara. Think what you just said it holds a hidden clue."

"What did I say I forgot?"

"Nothing RINGS a bell!" reminded Barbara, stressing Rings.

Tommy, Barbara and Viv put their left hands on the table palm down.

"Well Ding Dong," said Derwent in a poor imitation of Leslie Phillips the actor.

She looked at their hands and almost did a double take when she saw the ring.

She jumped to her feet with a scream startling everyone in the room. She grabbed hold of Tommy hugging and kissing her. "Oh you darling, what a wonderful surprise, congratulations. Where is that man of yours? Come here you lucky devil," she said as she smothered him with love. "They have got engaged Tim. Everybody, Bill and Tommy have got engaged."

There was uproar once again with the locals applauding and shouting their congratulations. "Come over here you two." They called.

They went over to receive the hand shakes, kisses and congratulations.

Bill then went to speak to Tim. Have you got any champagne in Tim? This calls for a celebration, our friends over there may be expecting a drink, lets give em' a surprise."

Ann came behind the bar to help sensing that something was going on. The bottles were opened quietly and the glasses filled below the level of the bar to stop any prying eyes. When the drinks were ready for serving Bill called Tommy over and each took a tray and carried them to the local people. They were gob smacked to each receive a glass of champagne. Ann told them to wait for the toast until everyone had a glass. Then she took centre stage.

"I will not call you Ladies and Gentlemen but Friends that sounds much nicer it is personal and that is what all of us here are, Friends! We have had two lovely surprises this evening from this small group who since they arrived here have won our friendship and respect right from the beginning and I can assure you they feel the very same about all of us. I will not say any more because I can see you all smacking your lips in anticipation of wetting them with champagne. Friends, please join me in toasting Bill and Tommy with our congratulations and may they have a long and happy life together."

Bill and Tommy thanked everyone and received a lot of cheers when they kissed.

There was a laugh from everyone when an elderly lady was heard to say. "Don't the bubbles tickle when they go up your nose?"

"Well this has certainly been a night to remember," said Tim, our seniors will be talking about this for a long time."

"Ann, the Christmas party for the seniors has been accepted and passed by the Sergeants Mess members." Bill told her.

"That is great," she replied aren't they going to enjoy it, thanks Bill on their behalf."

As they were leaving they all had to go through kissing and handshakes again, Tommy getting "Good Luck Love" from the elderly ladies. Bill got, "Good Luck Bill," from the men.

"What has happened to the Captain Bligh tag?" asked Bill.

"Not t'neet' Bill, only because tha's been a good lad."

Back at the Mess they all agreed it had been a good night out.

CHAPTER 30

Monday morning word was received that the Air Officer Commanding would be carrying out his annual inspection of RAF March on a date to be notified. This meant that the whole station would be involved and the responsibility for organising the annual clean up of the station fell on George Miller the Station Warrant Officer. It was his responsibility also for producing a parade and March Past of a high standard for the inspecting officer. This would mean many drill parades for all personnel until they reached a satisfactory standard and George's standards were very high in this respect. George got prior warning before it was published on Station Orders and immediately began his plan of campaign with Flight Sergeant Ian Roberts his right hand man.

"The first thing we will do Ian is to get all the Warrant Officers and SNCOs who head their sections to a meeting to tell them what I want and expect from them, that will be half the battle. Then the white tins of paint and brushes will have to come out and if it does not move it gets painted! You and I will pace out the parade ground and mark it out accordingly and I will ask Bill Barrett to loan me a sergeant to knock the permanent staff bods into shape, the AOC will expect a good display of drill from us and I will make sure he is not disappointed."

Ian answered the ringing phone. "SWOs office Flight Sergeant Roberts speaking, It is for you sir, Sergeant Page from the OC's office."

"Yes Sergeant, will do, thank you."

"Got to see the Wingco' it will be about the inspection."

"The Station Warrant Officer sir," Barbara announced.

"Good morning Mr Miller," he said in answer to the salute. "Please take a pew. I expect you will know why I have sent for you, we have to formulate a plan of action.

With your experience you are quite capable of ironing out any difficulties that are bound to arise, any serious ones you have only to come to me and we will rectify it between us. Apparently it has been a very long time since this station had an AOC's inspection, too long and the permanent staff will be lackadaisical in that respect and you can expect to be kicking a few backsides initially of all ranks I warrant. Mr Miller you have carte blanche to produce a display fit for the AOC that will be expected from RAF March. You are to parade two flights of airmen with rifles and one flight of airwomen. Have you any questions so far?"

"Just one sir, a flight of airwomen from the permanent staff, I think that may be a bit dodgy because most of them have key jobs which should not be neglected for the sake of a parade not counting the time taken up training. We have not enough airwomen otherwise to even form a flight sir."

"Then what would you suggest Mr Miller scrubbing the complete flight altogether?"

"Yes sir."

"Hmm! I agree with you it is a bit dodgy. Very well we will scrub it, if you hit any more snags come to see me immediately. Thank you Mr Miller."

All Senior NCOs who were in charge of the different sections of the station were summoned to a meeting in the Sergeants Mess presided over by the Station Warrant Officer.

"You all know why this meeting has been called and you all have experienced AOC's inspections and parades many times in your careers so you know what it is all about and what is expected from you. The Wingco' wants two flights of airmen with rifles and I need a list of names of airmen and SNCOs to form two flights with a frontage of twelve and bung a few extras in for reserves in case of dropouts and rejects. Apparently this station has not had an AOC's inspection since Adam were a lad, that means there is going to be a lot of hard work on somebody's part to knock them back into shape where arms and foot drill is concerned. I know you SNCOs should be capable of doing that but to save your embarrassment I will ask WO Barrett to provide a no nonsense disciplinarian to help us out. Do not dare suggest, "Well it is his job after all." Let me remind you, his job is to train recruits not retrain so called experienced permanent staff. You NCOs will support him and if you throw any wobblies you will find yourselves in front of the flights doing the instructing. The names you supply will be divided into two flights and are to be released by you when WO Barrett draws up a time scale for the training. I hope I have made myself clear, has anyone got a question?"

Warrant Officer Johnson from Workshops raised his hand.

"If all my staff are split up on both flights and have to report for training that would leave me with an empty section for God knows how long, how would you solve that?"

George could not believe what he was hearing from a Warrant Officer. "You have not listened to what I have said. Your men will be divided between two flights the drill instructor is not a superman he can drill only one flight at a time. I will repeat it to make sure you understand what I am saying. The names you all submit to me from each section will be divided in two, each half going in separate flights and you only lose one half of your staff at a time, my guess is they will be on different days. Are you all clear on that? You have all experienced many A.O.C.s parades so what is the problem?" One last thing before you leave. I want your lists of names on my desk by 09:00hrs the day after tomorrow, this training is going to take some time to reach a required standard and time is what we have not got a lot of. Instil into your staff the longer it takes to reach an acceptable standard the more training sessions they will have to endure and if need be in their own time. Your co-operation will be appreciated, thank you."

He then went to see Bill Barrett and as he walked through the door he was greeted by a cheer and "Welcome stranger what brings you over here old timer?" asked a puzzled Bill. "You must have something on your mind."

"No don't go Viv," said George. He then told about the meeting he had just left. That is why I am here to ask you for the loan of one of your drill instructors to make sure we can turn out a good parade."

"I have the very man you want George, at present he is duty barman in the Mess but I am sure he will be delighted to help out, he is of the old school and won't stand any nonsense from anyone whatever rank, if he is in charge then *he* is in charge. When we have finished the brew we will have a walk over to the Mess and have a word with him and try to sort out the times and days which would suit him. Come on then George, let us go and see Joe."

When they entered the bar they found Joe cleaning out the beer pipes.

"That is why you always get a good pint in here the pipes are looked after with TLC," said Bill.

"Good morning gentlemen what brings you in here so early in the day? I am sorry I cannot offer you a drink under the circumstances, anyway you would not have got one it is not opening time and I do not want to lose my license," he said with a laugh.

"It is you we have come to see," said Bill. "George has a very special job for you if you are willing to do it."

"Is it something to do with the meeting you had in here this morning?"

“It is,” said George then told him the tale.

“How is it going to affect my job in here?”

“You can put together a timetable which will be convenient to you and not interfere with this job and everyone will have to work to your timetable. What do you say to that?” asked Bill.

“That should be no problem, I will look forward to that challenge.”

“I will get the list of names from all the sections the day after tomorrow, as soon as I have sorted them out into flights I will let you have a copy then you decide when you want to start, that okay by you?”

“No problem,” replied Joe.

From there George went to see Roy Shaw.

“Hello George what can I do for you then?”

“I am a bit concerned as to whether I will have enough numbers from the permanent staff Corporals and below to form two flights.”

“You want me to supply you with a list of our full strength in that department.”

“I do because I have asked all heads of departments to submit a list of available bods to me. Incidentally I never saw you at that meeting Roy.”

“Sorry George I was tied up with the Wingco’ but I did detail Sergeant Graham to stand in for me. He did attend and right now he is drawing up a list of our staff for you.”

”Fair enough I just did not want you to miss out,” he said smiling.

“Just a sec’, George.” He shouted to the hatch for Sergeant Graham. “The Station Warrant Officer wants a full and complete list of all permanent staff of Corporals and airmen if it is at all possible can he have it yesterday?”

“Possibilities sir will be done immediately, miracles will take a tad longer!”

“Right Sergeant, the SWO says he will come back for it in an hour.”

“Then he is going to be disappointed sir, tell him not to blink.”

“George! As I keep telling Bill Barrett, this is the sharp end, the hub of the station, we do not hang about we get cracking and get the jobs done, we take pride in our efficiency.”

“Perhaps, so I tell you what I will do Roy, if those lists come through that hatch in shall we say ten minutes; I will put a Fiver towards your brew stakes. If you lose you do the same.”

Roy yelled through the hatch. “There is a five pound bet on you delivering in ten minutes, you would not want your poor old WO forced to cough up, would you?”

A unanimous shouted reply was. “YES”, followed by loud laughter.

“So much for having faith in human nature,” laughed George, it seems I have toppled you from the top of the popularity pole.”

Sergeant Graham called through the hatch. “Here are your lists gentlemen.”

"Roy with delight shouted. "We've won by four minutes."

George just could not believe what he had just heard. "Give me those lists," he said reaching out for them. "There must be a catch to this."

There were four sheets three with all the names George wanted and on the third sheet was printed. To Station Warrant Officer Miller from the Orderly Room Staff. All monies must be paid to Warrant Officer Shaw i/c The Sharp End.

"Well I'm blowed!" exclaimed George, never in this wide world did I expect your staff to come up trumps and that bet was a pleasure to lose. Bai gum Roy you have got a damned good staff and they are a credit to you. I will even say they are a credit to the station. Now I will have to get back and sort this headache out then see how the lists I get from the sections compare with it. You can bet somebody will try to pull a fast one."

"I will not give them much of a chance to get away with it, not with you and Ian on the job," remarked Roy.

"I'll be off now Roy thanks, I will just nip in and thank your staff." He went into the orderly room. "Thank you everybody you did a great job and if any of you fancy a change of environment I can accommodate you and yes, I have paid my debts." That statement brought a cheer from the staff.

"What do you make of these figures Ian? I want a frontage of twelve and to my reckoning from the list we have got from the sections we will be lucky to make one and a half flights never mind two. The list I got from Roy Shaw tells me I could make three flights. There is no chance of making a flight of airwomen they are too thin on the ground, so we can count them out."

"Can I suggest something George?"

"Go on."

"Inform the Wingco' what the situation is and suggest you have his permission to put the wind up the department heads by threatening to close all the sections down for training."

"I think you have got something there Ian, I will go and have a word with him maybe he can come up with a solution. Get Barbara Page on the phone and tell her I would like to see the Wingco'."

"She says you can go right away."

Barbara announced. "Warrant Officer Miller sir."

"Come in Mr Miller and let us sort out this problem."

"You know about it sir?"

"No but you would not be here to see me if you did not have a problem."

"George told him the situation. "I would like your permission to wield the big stick sir."

"What have you in mind Mr Miller?"

"To close every section down for training."

"That sounds a bit drastic, have you another solution."

That I call a meeting in the Sergeants Mess with you in attendance to lay down the law sir."

"I favour that solution for preference. Call a meeting for 14:00 hrs today and I will use *my* big stick."

"Thank you sir I will look forward to that with pleasure."

A Tannoy message was sent out to the effect that all Warrant Officers and SNCOs in charge of sections are to assemble in the Sergeants Mess at 14:00hrs to be addressed by the Officer Commanding, Wing Commander Pilling.

At 13:55 George met the OC at the entrance to the Mess to escort him in. "Good afternoon Mr Miller," he said as he returned the salute. "Are you expecting any fireworks at this meeting?"

"Only from you sir, I have had a sedative administered to the audience."

"I like it," laughed the OC. Are these the list of names you told me about? Good I will take those."

George barked. "Officer Commanding." Everyone got their feet in respect and remained standing until he was seated.

"Good afternoon gentlemen, I am sure you will have an idea why I have called this meeting."

He stopped when he heard someone talking loudly outside the door then it opened and two Warrant Officers entered laughing which stopped immediately when they saw the meeting and who was in the chair.

"Come in gentlemen, are you sure you have got the right time and day for this meeting? Sit yourselves down in seats as far from each other as is possible with the minimum of fuss and when I close this meeting you both will make your way to my office."

He then waved the sheets of paper in the air "This is the reason for this meeting.

These sheets here contain all the names of the permanent staff airmen and these sheets contain the lists you have proffered to form two flights for the parade, which is a damned insult to the AOC. We would be hard pressed to form a flight and half. This exercise has opened up your lackadaisical attitudes and gentlemen it stops here and now and I will make it my business to make sure it does. Here is a bit of advice, do some soul searching because if you are a bad apple in my barrel, Beware! You will, after this meeting make out fresh lists, The Station Warrant Officer wants a frontage of each flight to consist of twelve airmen, normally it would be a larger frontage but we are only a small station. According to this official list that target can easily be reached and as an added bonus you can provide six extra for reserves, as you should know we need to cover for eventualities. If you find you cannot make the target you will report to me and the reasons must be fool proof. Here is something you may wish to ponder over. If you have watched the Trooping of the Colour on Horse Guards Parade you should have noticed SNCOs dotted about in the ranks. Think about it.

If you have no questions I will close this meeting."

George brought the room to attention while he escorted the OC out.

"Thank you Mr Miller I enjoyed that."

"That will give them something to think about sir. There will be some panic buttons pressed."

"I don't think we will have any further trouble."

George saluted.

When the two Warrant Officers came out George said. "Well you two have made a pig's foot of it, what were you thinking of?"

"We were only in the TV room and obviously time caught up with us."

"It passed you by too, you were a right couple of plonkers, go and get your rollicking."

Barbara announced the two Warrant Officers. They entered and saluted.

"I shall not waste my breath asking for your excuse, what I am concerned is your lack of respect coupled with bad manners. You of your rank should be setting examples to your subordinates and from your attitudes I doubt if you get any respect from any of them. Would I lose my wager if I said that I think you two could be the main culprits for sending a shortened list to the Station Warrant Officer?"

"Yes sir you would," one of them replied.

"Then if I showed you the official list of the permanent staff and compare it to yours would that change your minds? By not answering my question I take it you agree with me. Pity, because it verifies your conduct and attitude. As Warrant Officers of long standing that is not acceptable and I will not accept it. Do you remember what I said at the meeting about bad apples in my barrel? Make sure it will not apply to you."

"Have you anything you would like to say that you disagree with?"

"With respect sir," said WO Johnson I think you are making a mountain out of a molehill."

"Do you think that too?" he asked WO Chivers.

"Yes sir I do and I think your assessment of us is unfair."

"Very well, would you like me to book you an appointment to see the Commanding Officer?"

"No sir," said Johnson.

He looked at the other.

"No sir," said Chivers.

"If that is your decision then get out of my office and act like Warrant Officers."

They saluted and left, two very chastened men with a flea in their respective ears.

When they exited the room Chivers said in a not very quiet voice. "Who does he think he is treating us like bloody erks? He is power crazy."

Johnson replied. "The man is a bloody idiot, officers! I've sh….he was interrupted by the voice of the OC ordering them back into his office.

"Apparently I don't appear to be the flavour of the month to you two and do you not think that even a lowly erk would have had the sense to close the door before shooting off his mouth? It was only because I went to close the door you had left open that I heard and witnessed your remarks."

"I do apologise sir," WO Jackson said meekly. "I was more angry with myself than you."

"What is your plea Chivers, insanity?"

"I admit it was an insane thing to say sir and I wish to apologise for my rashness."

"Do you both think I came out on the onion boat? If you had not been caught out you would have continued to bad-mouth me as long as we served on this station. You both have left me no alternative but to take disciplinary action against you.

Warrant Officer Johnson and you Warrant Officer Chivers I am charging you with gross insubordination to a senior officer namely myself." He administered the official warning and told them they would be notified when they would have to appear before the Commanding Officer.

"Is there any chance of you rescinding that decision sir?" asked WO Johnson.

"None whatsoever, you made my mind up for me when I heard you both bad mouth me. If you want to make any pleas then I advise you make them to the Commanding Officer. Now give me your service numbers and full names." After they did so he dismissed them.

They saluted then made sure they closed the office door behind them which brought a wry smile from the Wingco'. He made out the charge sheets and asked Barbara to type them out on the official forms.

Word spread like wildfire that the two Warrant Officers were on a fizzer causing glee especially from the ones who were under their command.

From the other Warrant Officers there was not a single word of sympathy, as one of them said. "Those two have been asking for it a long time."

George Miller finally got his full quota of bods for the parade. "These lists have proved very costly for those two idiots Ian, I am not surprised because they are nothing but trouble and they thought they were untouchable. I don't think they will be with us for much longer, the C.O will see to that he will not stand for their attitudes. I had better go to the Orderly Room and get a copy of the lists done for Joe Franks."

"Come on in George," welcomed Roy, business or pleasure?"

"Business Roy, will you run me a copy of these lists? I want one for Joe Franks."

"No problem. Sergeant Graham run a copy of these for your favourite SWO."

"The other thing is, I want you for escort when those two plonkers face the C.O."

"That will be a pleasure, I would like to see those two sods squirm they are almost as objectionable as Warrant Officer Sam Barnes. Our C.O when he was a Wingco' was responsible for him having to resign from the service and if I am any judge he will have those two posted away from here quick sharp."

"Here's hoping," said George. "Ah here comes my copy, thanks Chris', I will go and see Joe now."

When Joe read the list he said. "That is good, Number one flight will parade at 08:00 each Tuesday and Thursday mornings and Number two flight will parade at 08:00 each Wednesday and Friday mornings. If they are slow in coming to the standard required after the first week they will parade for extra drill in their own time namely at 18:00 for an hour. Can you have that circulated to the sections Sir?"

"It will be my pleasure Joe and I shall have great pleasure in watching you perform if you don't mind."

"Be my guest, they may perform better in front of an audience."

"I will be in the background Joe to lend a hand so give me a nod if you want me to show myself, I will not interfere but I will be there to support."

"Four eyes are better than two especially with the know it alls who will try to impress their mates. If you do spot anything you think needs checking, by all means show yourself."

CHAPTER 31

"Helen Fraser for you sir," said Ian Roberts handing the phone to George.

"Good morning Helen George Miller here."

"Good morning to you Mr Miller, the C.O. is taking those charges at 11:00hrs. He is taking them both together. I have informed the two Warrant officers to be outside the CO's office ten minutes before time."

"Thank you Helen I will be there with an escort."

He then rang Roy Shaw. "Roy, I will be escorting the escort to the CO's Office at 10:50, the charges are being read. Does that pun qualify me for the crackpots?"

"No chance George, I would have expected something better coming from you. Okay I will be ready I am looking forward to this."

"I am too replied George."

Both George and Roy were waiting when the two Warrant Officers arrived looking rather nervous. They greeted each other cordially. "I don't know what you two have been up to, to come up in front of the C.O. you must have been naughty."

"No comment," said Johnson, "You will find out soon enough."

"You know the drill by now or you should do," retaliated George but if you have forgotten I will refresh your memory."

"Don't bother snarled Johnson we are not your bloody little erks."

"Like it or not, you are going to get it and if you talk to me like that I will treat you like bloody little erks. Now fall in on your escort, remove your headgear then stand to attention. The C.O. is having you both in together. I will march you in, in quick time, you will get a right wheel then another right wheel and I will order you to mark time. Then you will be halted and given Left Turn to face the officer reading the charge. Do you understand that?"

There was no reply.

"I said do you understand that?"

Johnson snarled. "Get stuffed Miller!"

George put his face inches from Johnson's and calmly asked. "Do you like hospital food?"

"What sort of stupid question is that?"

"If you talk to me like that ever again I will make sure you will taste some."

At precisely 11:00 George got the word to proceed. The accused and escort followed his words of command to the letter.

"George then reported to the C.O. "Warrant Officers Johnson and Chivers, Sir."

The C.O. asked them to confirm their service numbers, ranks and full names. Then read out the charges. "Do you wish to question Wing Commander Pilling, Johnson?

"No sir."

"Chivers?"

"No sir."

"How do you plead, guilty or not guilty? Johnson?"

"Guilty sir"

"Chivers?"

"Guilty sir."

"You both have obviously recognised the seriousness of the offence you are charged with and there would have been only one way to go if you had pleaded not guilty and I do not think for one minute either of you would have relished a court-martial. Therefore I must ask you, do you accept my punishment?"

They both said they would.

"I then award each of you a severe reprimand. In my report to Command I shall request you both be posted from this station as quickly as possible. This station and its personnel do not deserve the likes of you and with immediate effect you will commence to hand over your responsibilities to your second in command until a replacement can be found. I can assure you it will be just a matter of days before we hear from command and I do not want you on this station longer than necessary.

March them out Mr Miller." Then with a parting shot. "Make sure the door is closed behind you!"

As George handed back their headgear Johnson snarled. "I suppose that verdict would please you."

"I suppose you are right, it could not have happened to two nicer blokes, you only shot yourselves in the foot. There was just one snag; you should have been kicked off the station straight away."

The pair of them left muttering. "It will be good to get off this ruddy station."

"Come on Roy I'll let you treat me to a brew."

"George, after laying into those two idiots like you did it will be my pleasure. I do not know how I kept my face straight."

"Sergeant Graham! Two teas with biscuits please we are celebrating."

Two days later the postings arrived for the two Warrant Officers that would take effect in seven days time.

>>> <<<

Joe Franks began his training of the permanent staff by having the flight form up outside one of the Barrack Blocks. He called the two Sergeants to him and told them he would not want them until he began rifle drill.

He then addressed the flight. "I shall drill you until you reach my acceptable standard and my advice is for you to put your backs into it if you do not want any drill sessions in your own time. I am not expecting that to occur because you are supposed to be trained airmen and each time you make a mess of it I will add a little bonus to give you the incentive to do it right."

He pointed to the tallest airman and said. "You will be right marker." He then ordered the flight to "Stand Easy." He then marched onto the parade ground and shouted. "Right Marker." The airman marched on to a designated spot facing Joe. "You made a mess of that didn't you? What should you have done?"

"I did nothing wrong Sergeant." The lad replied.

"You were stood easy weren't you?

"I did not come to attention Sergeant before marching on."

"Correct, only a highly trained airman would know that. Your bonus is to double round this parade ground twice then return to the flight and stand easy. MOVE YOURSELF!" He bellowed at the airman.

The lad doubled off to the accompaniment of catcalls from the rest of the flight. Joe waited while the lad had rejoined his flight then he marched over to them. He called the right marker to come and stand by him then addressed the rest. "Atten-Shun and what did the rest of you not do?"

Nobody answered.

"Well you have let me down, efficient and well trained airmen you are and you could not remember that you were STILL ON PARADE! And committed the cardinal sin of talking while you were on parade. Congratulations, you have been awarded a bonus. You will double round the parade ground three times then fall in on your marker here. You will then stand easy and when I call you on parade you will form up on your marker in two ranks and you had better do it right for I have a lot more bonuses to award. Now MOVE!"

As they were running past the SWO who was watching the proceedings bellowed at them. "STOP TALKING."

When the airmen had returned and Joe called for the right marker he asked him. Do you know what to do when ordered to size?"

"No Sergeant."

He told him and then shouted to the airmen, "March On!" The airmen came to attention and formed up on the marker. He explained what he wanted them to do then ordered. "In three ranks Size."

After the third attempt and a few circuits of the parade ground Joe was satisfied. "We will now proceed with some close order drill, hands up if anyone has a problem not knowing their left from their right." When no hands were raised he continued. "My words but the AOC will be pleased to know that and before we start remember if you do not do it right I will have you all out here this evening and I would not want you to feel embarrassed in front of the recruits who are only just learning drill. You can be sure they would be out here in force to see you give a polished display. It is now up to you." He then began to put them through their paces and to their credit they did very well.

George Miller listened to Joe's little pep talk and when he saw the result he smiled to himself. Well done Joe, Bill Barrett was right, you are a good instructor.

When Joe concluded the drill he said. "Well done, you have done really well so much so the next time you are with me you will be doing rifle drill. Dis…Miss!"

George met him walking off the parade ground. "I thought you would have been having a bit of a hard time with those lads Joe but you certainly hit the nerve spots when you mentioned about the recruits coming to watch them."

"That lot were not so bad I hope the other flight will have got the message, the word will get around and they will know what will be expected from them and the consequences if they do not perform."

"I will see you in the morning Joe; I am looking forward to that."

Number two flight came through with flying colours; Joe was very pleased with their performance. "The next time you are with me you will be doing rifle drill, make sure you put up as good a show as you have done today."

"The word has got around from the other flight Joe," said George Miller, "they put on quite a good performance. You are putting on a good show with them and it looks like we may have the makings of a decent parade for the A.O.C. although it will depend what they are like at arms drill, that will be interesting."

Joe marched number one flight to the armoury where they were issued with rifles. As they formed up Joe instructed them in the handling of the weapons and enforced that they do not in any circumstances point the weapon at another person, by doing so you commit a very serious and chargeable offence. If anyone does, his feet will not touch the ground all the way to a cell in the guardroom. Are you all clear on that?"

"Yes Sergeant."

"Then we will make doubly sure. Do you know what to do if I give the order 'Examine Arms'?"

He got a very unsure response.

"Then I will explain for the benefit of those who may think it is an inspection for the need of under-arm deodorant." That remark brought a fit of laughter from the ranks. He then explained the drill and when he thought they had grasped it he gave them the order, "Examine Arms."

"I am now going to look down the barrel of all the rifles, make sure your thumb is placed in front of the open bolt with the thumb nail facing the barrel so that it reflects the light, if it does it will mean there is nothing up the spout." He then began his inspection of the rifles. He stopped at one airman looked down the barrel of his rifle and commented. "You want to stop biting your nails it is a twilight zone inside the barrel. Do you know what that means?"

The airman replied. "No Sergeant."

"It means you have not got enough thumb nail to reflect the light."

When he inspected next airman's rifle he tut-tutted as he looked down the barrel. "Has anyone here had any dealing with dogs," he asked.

An airman replied. "Yes Sergeant, my father breeds dogs"

"Good lad closes the bolt on your rifle, ground it then come here."

The lad did as he was told then he was ordered to look down the barrel of the rifle the Sergeant was inspecting. He had a hard look then pulled away looking puzzled.

"Now tell me what you saw?" asked Joe.

"Just a lot of spots Sergeant," replied the still puzzled airman."

"What dog does it remind you of?"

"It doesn't Sergeant."

"Return to your place in the ranks, my wit is lost on you lot." Turning to the airman whose rifle was being inspected he said. "When you hand this rifle back into the armoury, tell whoever is in charge that Sergeant Franks says there is a Dalmatian stuck up the barrel."

Still there was silence in the ranks.

"Hands up those who can tell a Dalmatian from a Terrier?"

He pointed to one lad. "What is the difference?" he asked.

"The Terrier is a part time soldier, Sergeant."

It had to happen. The entire flight of airmen erupted in uncontrolled laughter including Joe and it was a few minutes before he could get them back to some sort of order.

"I just do not believe it," he said, shaking his head. He pointed to the dog breeder's son. "For goodness sake tell em' what the difference is."

"Its coat is covered in large black markings known as spots."

"That is what we saw inside the barrel of that rifle, Black Spots. Now do you understand the joke? Oh forget it, let us get back to sanity and do some rifle drill."

"Before we march off to the Parade Ground we will practice a little arms drill, we want to make a good impression, don't we?"

"Yes Sergeant."

"Very well, show me what you can do."

"That was good," he encouraged, "all it needs is a few minor adjustments and getting the timing right. Here, give me your rifle son and sit this one out," he said to an airman who showed promise with his drill. "Now, I will shout the orders and you follow me with the movements and timing."

After a few practice runs he was satisfied. We will now march to the Parade Ground and watch your dressing as you march if one of you is getting out of line just give him a whisper to get back in line, keep your left elbow tucked into your side and your forearm parallel with the ground." As they marched he gave individuals words of encouragement as he corrected them.

George Miller watched them march on and he was impressed.

Joe gave them a short rest then told them they would now march around the Parade Ground at the slope. After a few circuits with intermittent breaks he said. "We will call it a day now, you have done really well better than I expected. In our next session we will concentrate on the slow march, as you well know it needs more practice than quick time. Right then, let us return this weaponry to the armoury."

"Bai' Gum Joe but you are doing a grand job with those lads," said George.

"They are making it easy for me George, they have not entirely forgotten what they have been taught, they are just a bit rusty that's all."

The rest of the drill with both flights went very well.

"What we want now Joe is a full practice run with the officers and supernumeraries and hope they know what to do. In my experience I found them worse than the airmen."

"The difference George is giving orders as opposed to taking them. Between us we will take them by the hand and show them the way."

The AOC's parade was a success he congratulated the airmen for their smartness and their turn out which in turn pleased the Station Commander. Following the parade an inspection was carried out on the permanent staff's places of work. On his tour of inspection in the Station headquarters he asked to see the three who had been responsible for the capture of the security perpetrator. He congratulated them on their diligence and their award.

"After lunch I would like to run my eye over the recruit trainees," he informed the Station Commander.

"Would you like a word with the officers in charge of the training sir?"

"I would indeed then I can tell them what I want."

The CO asked Wing Commander Pilling to bring Flight Lieutenant Cody and WO Butcher.

"This is Flight Lieutenant Cody in charge of the airmen recruits and this is WO Butcher in charge of the WRAF recruits sir."

"Why have you got a non-commissioned officer in charge of the WRAF?"

"You will remember that incident with Flight Lieutenant (w) Adams sir, well WO Butcher had the qualifications and experience to be the ideal choice and it has proved to be if I may say so the right one."

"Hm! we will talk about that later. Flight Lieutenant Cody, at 14:00 I would like you to parade the entire training staff in review order on the Parade Ground. No dressing up, I want to see them in their working uniform that goes for everyone on the parade because this is an informal inspection. That goes for you too Warrant Officer Butcher. Now be off and get it organised."

"I don't know if I really approve of your W.O. holding that position."

"I did inform you at the time sir, besides there are not enough WRAF recruits to warrant a commissioned officer. We have one flight and just a handful in the specialised flight and Butcher in my opinion is worthy of the position, she is firm, fair and held in high respect not only with the airwomen but also with all ranks of the training staff. I am sure that if she was not up to the job Warrant Officer Barrett would soon let me know."

"Ah! Warrant Officer Barrett, I will have a word with him, I respect his judgement. Come on then let us see what chef is offering for lunch I am ready for something to eat."

At 13:50, every member of the training staff that included Joe Franks who was ordered to leave the barman's job to attend the parade were formed up in review order standing easy with Flight Lieutenant Cody in charge.

As the A.O.C. with his retinue arrived at the saluting base Wings called the parade to attention as he saluted. The party then walked onto the Parade Ground the A.O.C. leading.

"Right then Flight Lieutenant Cody I would like to do more of a walk-about than an inspection, I would like to be introduced to your training staff and also have a word with the recruits, lead the way starting with number one flight."

Wings ordered the parade to open order march, in readiness for an inspection, then flights two, three and four to stand at ease. Moving to number one flight Wings introduced "Warrant Officer Barrett."

Bill saluted. "Mr Barrett and I you can say are old friends Flight Lieutenant How are you Mr Barrett?" He asked shaking his hand and what do *you* think of this new system of having only one Recruit Training Establishment?

"Because we have been chosen to be that Establishment it is a privilege and an honour for the training staff. As for closing two down, with respect sir I think it was a big mistake, one would have been more acceptable."

"I am forced to agree with you Mr Barrett we did not have a champion to fight for us at the Ministry. Shall we carry on with the inspection gentleman? You tag along with us Mr Barrett in case your advice is needed."

"With respect sir I think you will find Flight Lieutenant Cody very knowledgeable in our training methods."

"Thank you Mr Barrett I will make my own judgements."

"This is Sergeant Dixon, said Wings, who is responsible for training the special flight, he was hand picked for the job and is proving his worth."

"How do you manage a mixed flight Sergeant?"

"With difficulty at times sir but with some old fashioned coaxing they soon fall into a rhythm."

He went down each rank stopping to ask questions here and there. How do you like being in a mixed flight? How do you think you are being taught, to a good standard?"

"It was strange at first sir but we soon got used to it and the instructors are very efficient."

Wings carried on introducing him to the staff by name at each flight. Joe Franks was introduced as the longest serving Sergeant Instructor.

"How long have you been instructing?" Joe was asked.

"For many years sir."

"Then why have you not got your crown?"

"Promotion from Sergeant is normally very slow in this trade and now with two training establishments having been given the chop promotion is just a dream sir."

"Explain yourself Sergeant," the A.O.C. snapped.

"With the closing down of the two stations, instructors of all ranks have been dispersed throughout the service, not as Drill Instructors but on General Duties and they are still holding their ranks, which means that we who are carrying out Drill Instructing have no chance of any promotion sir."

"Ah! I see what you are getting at now, you mean to say that we are over established with Drill Instructors who are not instructing but are blocking promotion prospects for the ones who are."

"Yes sir."

"You have a good point Sergeant, it is a problem I was unaware of, I will ask a few questions about that. Good man."

Wings then introduced him to Warrant Officer Butcher.

"Ah, Warrant Officer Butcher, you have been involved in the two BlueBelles teams much to your credit and gaining the B.E.M. for your services, I congratulate you on that score. You have now been given the position which is normally filled by a commissioned officer, why is that? You may speak frankly Warrant Officer."

"It was the Station Commanders decision sir."

"Of course but in your own words I want *you* to tell me why."

"Very well sir. Since I was posted to Training Command I have never had one WRAF officer who was qualified, experienced or with the ability to command and even show any interest. In fact, they were thrust into the sharp end without any experience and were only too willing to leave it to the SNCOs while they remained the figurehead. I have qualified in all those categories and carried them out over the years without holding a commission sir."

"Thank you, now show me round your flight."

"This is Flight Sergeant Anderson sir, she…

"Yes I know who she is. It is my pleasure to see you again Flight Sergeant," as he shook her by the hand. "After you raised the roof of the Millennium Dome, by God you did the RAF a great service that day and you were well toasted in the VIP lounge, you and all those who participated in that great victory. Congratulations on your B.E.M. it should have been a higher award."

"Thank you sir."

"I have seen enough now to know that these young people are being well trained by the best instructors and it shows.

Come on let us dismiss them for the rest of the day they have done us proud."

As the Station Commander escorted the AOC back to his car the AOC said. "You did the right thing putting WO Butcher in full charge of WRAF training. She is a very competent lady and I fully agree with what she said. The station in general was in good order I did not expect anything less. I was impressed with the permanent staff's display on the parade ground and the recruits and their instructors were well up to standard. You have certainly got an excellent team of instructors no doubt WO Barrett has something to do with that. He is a very remarkable man."

"He certainly is sir," replied the Station Commander.

The following day the Station Commander addressed the personnel over the station's Tannoy system.

> *"Attention please, this is the Station Commander speaking. I want to thank each and every one of you for your efforts in making the AOC's visit a success. Your places of work and the general cleanliness of the station plus the display the permanent staff performed on the parade ground really impressed him. The Training Staff and the recruits also came in for his praises. As a thank you he has given me permission to give you a free day which will be taken at your section commander's discretion... End of broadcast."*

CHAPTER 32

Everything was running smoothly at Royal Air Force Station March. Command was very pleased with the training schedules and the quality in the output of trained recruits. For the foreseeable future, it would remain the only Recruit Training Establishment.

The Sergeants Mess had become an attraction of entertainment for the members and their families. The entertainment committee headed by Warrant Officer Mary Butcher were promoting Mess functions to suit all tastes and never a week passed without some organised activity. Mary had even hinted the committee were thinking of volunteering for a second term of office. The Saturday night Bingo was a huge success increasing in its popularity to the extent that money prizes were well worth winning. The proceeds from raffles went towards buying extras for the Mess, the latest acquisition being a small fridge held in situ in the bar containing pies and tit-bits that members could buy with their drinks when feeling peckish. That turned out to be a good investment due to the increased numbers of members attending especially on a games evening.

The romances of Roy and Barbara, Derwent and Viv, was stronger then ever. There was even a whisper that there could be a budding romance in the offing between Mary Butcher and Sam Brown but nobody dare approach the subject with Mary.

Bill and Tommy with their big day in mind were trying to sort out their wedding plans and what would be the best option for them service wise. With Tommy having completed a pensionable engagement in the service they could comfortably set up home in Married Quarters and still remain a part of the service she loves. The other option of remaining in the service as a married couple could lead to the problem of living apart when duty prevails.

>>> <<<

Bill and Tommy were sat in her office discussing their pending marriage.

"It is going to take a heck of a lot of planning and organising dear," said Tommy.

"Wouldn't it be great if we could just nip off to the registry office then it would be over and done with in quick time?" replied Bill.

"No way, I want a church wedding," she insisted. We have too many friends who will look forward to dressing up in all their finery, not to mention the bride. So you can get that idea right out of your head."

"I said it would be great, not I would like it to be. It is our big day and I want you to make the most of it because you will not be having another one!"

She laughed. "Do you know what is going to be the hardest decision we will have to make?"

"Getting you to say I Will?"

"No silly, it will be who do we invite from the many friends we are so fortunate to have?"

"I see your point that is a difficult one, why not make a list and when we have run out of names we begin to whittle the list down until we reach our target figure whatever that will be. Choosing the wedding party will be no problem that picks itself, I know who I want and so do you. Then of course the main item on the agenda is choosing the date and the location. Tommy my love, we will have a few headaches before we are finished. There is a way out of course, as they say up here in the North. "Live o'er brush."

"I will hit you with the brush if you even contemplate that Bill Barrett, you have to uphold the tradition of making an honest women out of me, so get on with it! For a start I think we should think about where the ceremony will be then decide on the date, once we have done that we can start planning in earnest."

"Well there is no place like home," answered Bill.

"What do you mean?" Queried Tommy.

“The church in the village, it is a very old one and it is in a lovely setting, what could be better, most of our guests are going to be from around here.”

“There’s a thought and it sounds good to me but what about the reception do you think the local hotel could cater for us?”

“It depends how many bums will be on seats, we can make enquiries and we could always ask Ann Wilson for her advice.”

“Okay then love, we will leave it at that for the time being and concentrate on the guest list that will give us something to work on.”

“How do you feel about going to the village tomorrow afternoon, seeing Ann for information about the hotel and also with a view to hiring the village community centre for the evening or you could even ask Jackie about the community centre,” suggested Bill.

“Why not,” answered Tommy, “the more information we can get about what the village can offer the better. There is one more major point to consider or I should say two. Where are we staying for our wedding night? And where are we going for our honeymoon?”

“Now we do have a problem,” moaned Bill. Have you still got that Holiday Brochure or will we need a winter one?”

“We can look at the one we have got it may give us an inspiration and before you say anything we are definitely going abroad where we are sure of some sunshine.”

“That sounds very final as if you have already made up your mind.”

“It is! And I have!” was Tommy’s quick response. Now *you* decide on our wedding night!”

“I think we will…..

“Stay at the hotel,” she interrupted. “Bags already packed and Viv can collect my wedding regalia to take back to camp. Then we can go to the airport from there and you can rest assured our little family will drive us there to see us safely off.”

“How long have you had all this planned? You little minx.”

“If I left it to you I would still be in my pre-engagement stage. Keep nodding your head dear if you agree and shake it if you do not, I would appreciate more nods than shakes though. Come here you big softie let me give you a kiss and a cuddle, I would not exchange you for anybody.”

“Look, when are we going to take our little family into our confidence? You know they may come up with some ideas we have not thought of, besides they will need to know to make their own arrangements,” added Bill.

“Don’t tell me we are taking *them* with us on our honeymoon?” Said a startled Tommy, “if so I am filing for a divorce before we get married.”

Bill curled up with laughter and Tommy joined him after realising what she had said.

“Yes, I think we should take them into our confidence, when?”

"What about tonight in the Quiet Room over a very quiet pre-celebration drink?"

"That is fine by me," she responded. "Are you going to tell Roy and Derwent your supporters and me to tell Viv and Barbara my supporters?"

"Yes, we will do that for say about eight o' clock at reception?" You know love we are getting ourselves in a bit of a muddle, you have not decided yet whether you will be leaving the service as Flight Sergeant Atkins or Mrs Barrett."

"Oh heck, I haven't have I? That is something else I have to worry about, when is it all going to end?"

"When we are formally announced as man and wife," he said with a smile.

"Oh no it won't," she said giving him a kiss, "I will have *you* to worry about then!"

At dinner that evening Bill asked Roy and Derwent if they had no plans for tonight would they join himself and Tommy in the Quiet Room that evening meeting at reception about eight."

"Have you got an important announcement for us Billy Boy?" Roy asked.

"No, we are just asking for ideas. Tommy is asking Viv and Barbara to come along."

"It must be important if you are asking us for advice," spoke Derwent."

"I am not proud," smiled Bill, you are the only two I could think of from the top of my head."

"Another smart crack like that," retorted Roy," and you will be losing it."

"Well are you coming or not?" demanded Bill.

"Of course we are, we could do with a good laugh," tittered Roy. "By the way the replacements for Johnson and Chivers are due in a couple of days."

"Anybody we know?" asked Derwent."

"WO Mills for workshops and Sergeant Bell is replacing WO Chivers in education that post is now downgraded. Jock Webster will be pleased, Mills is a fellow Scot."

They met at the nominated time and as they made their way to the Quiet Room Bill said to Derwent. "Come on we will get the drinks while they find a table."

"This is my last week in here Bill," said Joe as he poured the drinks then I will be back with you on duty once more."

"Who is your replacement?" asked Derwent.

"I have no idea, whoever it is he will either come in to tell me at the weekend or he will wait until Monday for the hand over. If you want to know ask Ian Roberts he details the duty."

"Have you enjoyed it Joe?" Asked Bill.

"Yes, I have been busy and seen one or two functions and I have also been entertained with you daft sods. It is a good mess now, you have done a good job getting it organised into a place worth coming to in an evening. I'll tell you what, the entertainment committee are doing a cracking job and they will be a hard act to follow."

"Mary Butcher was telling me that the committee members are enjoying what they are doing so much and seeing the effects of their work, the majority are thinking of extending their time on the committee if the members want to vote them back on."

"There will be no fear of that I can assure you," answered Joe, "I doubt if you will get any volunteers unless you call in the 'Press Gangs'."

When they all had settled down with their drinks, Bill and Tommy explained why they had called for a meeting.

"We are hoping you can come up with some ideas."

"You do realise," pointed out Bill, "you four will have to go through this when it comes round to your turn, so you may as well get some practice in now. The only advantage we may have is we will probably have less family to consider than you."

"You are hoping to name the day this year are you?" Asked Viv.

"Oh yes," emphasised Tommy, the sooner the better, I do not want to give him the chance to change his mind," she said with a giggle."

"Tommy Atkins! That is an awful thing to say," said Barbara with indignation, "but I agree with you!" which brought loud laughter from everyone.

The roles of the four friends were sorted out to everyone's delight. Transport from the hotel to the airport would be arranged at a later date.

"Now what is the dress going to be?" asked Roy. "I propose we rule out uniforms, which leaves us with Morning Suits or Lounge suits."

The girls in unison said "Morning Suits."

The men voted for lounge Suits.

"We have a stalemate," said Derwent, "because we men will be wearing them we should have the final say."

"Hear hear," agreed Roy.

"You have just had your final say," said Barbara. "It is regarded as the bride's day and you want it to be the happiest for her, don't you? It is no good you looking at each other for some kind of help. Do you or don't you want it to be Tommy's happiest day, don't you think she deserves that?"

"Putting it like that love," whimpered Roy, "of course we do and we will make sure it is, In Our Lounge Suits!!"

"Roy Shaw you are incorrigible, you are grounded, no wedding for you!"

"Sorry to disappoint you love but my presence is required to support the groom and those are his wishes."

"Then the groom will be grounded! Are you with me girls?"

“We certainly are.” They both replied.”

Bill was having a quiet laugh to himself, when he winked at Tommy she smiled and winked back enjoying it as much as Bill.

Roy still sticking to his guns retorted. “You cannot ground the groom it is not your wedding!”

“And it won’t be *Your* wedding if you insist on wearing lounge suits at this one. So think about it Bachelor Boy!”

Viv was crying with laughter, Derwent was laughing his head off. Tommy was clapping her hands in glee while Bill was shaking his head in disbelief.

Bill finally got their attention and said. We will now settle this once and for all. I will nominate Roy to make the decision. Roy! Morning Suits or Lounge Suits?”

There was a long pause. Roy looked round at all the faces, four were smiling and one was glaring. “Ladies and gentlemen, I do not know what all the fuss was about because it is the easiest of decisions to make.” Another long pause as he searched the faces, no change there. “Morning Suits of course!”

Barbara gave a scream of delight. “Come here you loveable fool,” as she grabbed him and gave him a kiss. “Isn’t he just wonderful?” she asked of the others.

“Come on Derwent,” said Bill, “shall we go and get the drinks in? I think we need one after that.”

The rest of the evening they just chatted about things in general. After deciding a word with Ann Wilson at the March Hare would be beneficial to get any information about the local hotel and the village community hall. Bill and Tommy would go the next day to see Ann.

“But we are still going to see her on Saturday evening,” Tommy added. “She probably will have some answers by then.”

The pub was closed by the time they got there but a press on the doorbell soon got an answer. Tim got a surprise when he opened the door to Bill and Tommy.

“Come on in,” he greeted them with a kiss and a handshake. “We have visitors Ann,” he shouted.

She was delighted when she saw who it was giving them both a welcoming kiss

“What brings you here in an afternoon? It must be something important. Come, sit down and I will make us a brew.”

“See,” said Bill, “it never leaves us I will make a brew, not a cup of tea but a brew.

“Old habits never die Bill,” replied Ann, “you are getting mugs have no fear.”

When they all had settled down Ann asked. “Why this visit?”

Tommy explained about everything and said. "We are hoping you can help us out with the information we need."

"What I will do," said Ann, "is see the committee of the village hall and sound them out. You will be coming Saturday night won't you with the rest of your little family?"

"Indeed we are intending to do so," replied Tommy.

"Good, I should have something for you then."

"The hotel, it is a good one with a very good reputation for cleanliness, food and excellent service. I do not know the amount of people they can cater for, we will have to go and ask them, and I suggest we do it this afternoon, oh yes I am coming with you to introduce you, the owner and his wife are good friends of ours."

"We have heard all about your exploits from Ann here and we followed your progress with interest, even to joining the celebrations at the March Hare on your famous victory," said the hotel owner.

Tommy explained about the forthcoming wedding and the liking for the reception to be here providing you can accommodate us with all the arrangements. At the moment we are only at the drawing board stage and at a guess we would need catering for say, fifty guests. We would need a room on the wedding night but I do not know how many rooms would be needed for guests who would need to stay overnight, that of course we would find out in due course. The date of the wedding has not been chosen yet but you will understand we are forward planning at this stage gathering all the information we need, then and only then when we are satisfied will we do the necessary bookings."

"I will tell you what we can offer you." He went into great detail and assured them he could easily cater for double the amount mentioned. "I have ten guest rooms so that should be no problem. It then depends when your big day is and the number of other guests who may be staying here. I will now give you a guided tour of the hotel taking in the kitchen, the reception room and the bedrooms and of course, the bar. We do keep a good wine cellar too. I think we can provide everything you will need."

Bill and Tommy were very impressed with everything and told the proprietor so.

"Thank you very much this has been a big step forward, now we can begin in earnest in setting our stall out."

"I will look forward to hearing from you in the near future, here is our hotel brochure containing the tariff which I hope will help you to choose us."

Back at the March Hare they all agreed they were impressed with what they had been told and saw.

"I am all for," it said Tommy, it is on our doorstep and has everything we want, I think we would be foolish to go elsewhere."

"That settles it," said Bill, "we will go for it, hopefully we can get the same result with the village hall but what do we do for caterers Ann and a dance band or a disc jockey? Most of the villagers will be there and we cannot disappoint the elders."

"Don't worry," said Ann putting them at ease, "just leave it with me I have some good contacts, I could have some good news for you on Saturday. Is there anything else to see to?"

"The church, responded Tommy, we must not forget the most important item."

"There will be no need to rush to see the vicar. As you can imagine with this being a small community he does not perform many marriage ceremonies," volunteered Ann.

"We must get back now," said Tommy, "thanks very much for your help Ann, we can now start on the guest list, we will let you know in plenty of time for you to arrange a stand-in for the March Hare."

"Yes, we will go back and stand in front of the inquisitors to report every minute detail especially for Roy the Ferret." Bill then told them about the incident choosing the dress for the men.

Ann and Tim had a right good laugh about that.

"I wish we had been there to witness that said Tim, he is some character make no mistake."

"But he is a good friend," said Bill."

"You would think they were bitter enemies never mind friends when you hear them tearing into each other. I have never met a friendship like it," laughed Tommy.

"Anyway, we will be off and see you both on Saturday."

"Just one minute," said Ann. "We have a major problem and have been carried away with the euphoria of this wedding but one of the main characters is missing. Has anyone any idea who that person is?"

They all looked puzzled but none could come up with the answer.

"Put us out of our misery Ann," pleaded Tommy.

"Who is going to give you away Tommy?"

"Oh my God!" screamed Tommy. "How on earth could we have forgotten that?"

"That is a problem alright," said Bill. "What are we going to do about it love?"

"I just do not know. Do you know if a woman can carry out that duty, Ann?"

"I know someone who will know. She then phoned the vicar who assured her there was no law forbidding it. She told Tommy then asked. "Have you got someone in mind?"

"Yes, Jackie!"

"I will definitely agree to that," said a very pleased Bill, "she will fit the part perfectly for she is like a mother to you."

"I like it too," said Ann. "She is a lovely person and is well thought of here in the village."

"Thanks again for everything Ann you are truly a real good friend. We must be off now but we will see you on Saturday."

CHAPTER 33

"Station Warrant Officer's Office, Flight Sergeant Roberts speaking. Hello sir, no the SWO is not in just now can I give him a message? Yes I will tell him."

As George walked into his office Ian said. "Roy Shaw would like to see you when you have the time."

"Did he say why?"

"No."

"Right then I had better go and see what he wants."

"Come in" was the answer to his knock on Roy's office door.

"Good morning George, just the man I want to see. Are you ready for a brew?"

"Aye go on then if you are twisting my arm."

"That will be the day when I have to do that for you to accept a brew. Two teas please," he shouted through the hatch and make one a Sergeant Major brew for your favourite SWO."

"Our pleasure sir," was the reply.

George smiled. "It is good to see you have them well trained. Now what is it you wanted to see me about Roy?"

"I have just received a signal that your Corporal Brown has been promoted on posting to Cyprus."

"That is good news, I am pleased for him and he will enjoy Cyprus, I can put a good word in for him with some of my associates who are still out there. I hope I get a good one to replace him because I have nobody on my staff who qualifies for any promotion."

"You will soon find out because Brown's replacement is due to report here on Monday from RAF Camberly. Apparently his section has just finished handing over to 'Care and Maintenance' hence the quick posting. That has worked out very well for you because Brown will have plenty of time to teach him the ropes."

"What's his name Roy?"

"That was a very good guess George," replied Roy laughing. "Actually his name happens to be Roy. Corporal Roy Hermett ex National Service with eight years service."

"Is he English? With a name like that it sounds German."

"He is English alright and according to his records he is a bit of a footballer, ex Lancashire schoolboy goalkeeper, wait till Harry Gordon gets to know of him he will be after signing him on for the village football team."

"Well he sounds promising," said George, "I hope he is as good at his job,"

"We will just have to wait and see," replied Roy. "Now I will have to call Corporal Brown in to tell him the good news."

"When does his promotion take effect?" asked George.

"Tomorrow"

"Shall I send him to you first thing in the morning Roy? Then you can send him back to me after you have briefed him? I will take him to clothing stores for his chevrons then to the tailors to get a quick job done and tomorrow night I hope you will join me in the Mess Bar to introduce him to the Sergeants Mess, will you let the other two crackpots know?"

"You can count on us George," said Roy with a laugh.

When George returned to his office he rang Workshops and asked to speak to Sergeant Gordon.

"Sergeant Gordon speaking."

"This is the SWO, I am hoping you can give me a bit of information concerning a Corporal Hermett he has a reputation of being a football player, have you ever heard of him?"

"Not Hermit the goalie, he was known as Hermit because of his name but he was far from being one. If he is the one I think you mean we both played in the same station team, he was a pretty good keeper too. He had a trial with the RAF Team but they said he was not tall enough. That was a few years go, he was not a Corporal then. Why the interest in him sir?"

"He will be joining my staff on Monday. He is posted here from RAF Camberly."

"That is great news sir I will be looking forward to seeing Hermit again, now that has made my day, thank you."

"Well I have made one Sergeant very happy Ian."

"How come?"

"Corporal Brown's replacement is a footballing colleague of Harry Gordon. Harry will have him in the village team in no time at all providing he still plays of course. Ring Corporal Brown and tell him to report here at 09:00 tomorrow Ian."

Corporal Brown arrived on the dot and was immediately sent to the orderly room. "Corporal Brown here sir," said Sergeant Graham.

"Send him round Sergeant "

"You wanted to see me sir?"

"Yes Corporal would you mind reading this," giving him the document announcing his promotion.

"Oh, that is great and it is certainly a surprise, I never expected to be getting that yet."

"Congratulations Sergeant Brown I will see you in the Mess Bar this evening, now go and report back to the SWO."

He knocked and entered on command and was greeted with a handshake and "Congratulations Sergeant Brown," from both George and Ian."

"Come on er', what is your name?" asked George.

"Ken."

"Come on then Ken, let us go to the clothing stores and get you fixed up with some chevrons then to the tailors to get them sewn on, we can't have you traipsing round the station impersonating a Corporal. This evening you will attend a celebration drink with a few friends in the Mess Bar. Have no fear we are not going to get you legless it is just a welcome to the Sergeants Mess Sergeant Brown. Were you told about your replacement coming on Monday?"

"Yes sir Hermit happens to be an old pal of mine."

"It could not be better for you showing him the ropes. I understand he is a bit of a footballer."

"He is or was pretty good, I do not know if he stills play, pity we have no team here he would have walked into it."

"I think Sergeant Gordon has his sights set on him joining the village team."

After getting him fixed up with chevrons he took him to the tailor. George told him.

"Off you go and bring the rest of your uniforms to the tailor; your wife is in for a nice surprise. Then go and give your lads a shock and I will see you tonight."

"Thank you sir."

The new Sergeant's introduction to the Sergeants Mess went down very well. Apart from the crackpots, George Miller and Ian Roberts and a few more SNCOs came to join in wishing him well. George kept a watchful eye on him to make sure too much drink was not forced upon him. He also promised to give him the gen on his Cyprus posting. Bill and Roy emphasised while he was still on the station he must bring his wife to any functions especially the Saturday night Bingo.

Saturday night saw the family of six at the March Hare and getting a good welcome from the locals. "Good to see you all again," welcomed Tim as he served Bill.

"You had better give them drinks too," said Bill, I see there are suddenly a few empty glasses on their table do you think they are telling us something Tim?"

"Aye," he replied, "they don't miss a trick."

"Come on you lot, come and get your refills I am not a waiter," shouted Bill.

"Well come and push my wheel chair" and "How can I when I am on crutches?" were the replies he got.

He gave Tim a wink. "Tough!" he replied to them. "I have got mine," as he held his glass up to them in salute.

That caused a mighty uproar. "Ban him landlord!" and "Get rid of Captain Bligh."

Bill returned to his party who he saw were in hysterics.

"You certainly know how to stir up the natives," said Roy. "Do you think I should go and make peace with them?"

"It will cost you drinks all round as a peace offering if you do," laughed Derwent.

When Ann came in from the living quarters a voice from one of the locals muttered "Hey-up, here comes trouble."

"Yes and I will give you trouble if my friends decide to leave because of you lot."

"Captain Bligh started it, he expected us poor old folk to try and hobble to the bar and carry our drinks back to the table."

"I notice you don't have any difficulty hobbling to the bar when you come in to order your first drinks."

"Ah! But we are fresher then, you will find out as you grow older that you can't keep up the pace."

"You can keep up the pace with the best of them when you have a drink in your hands."

"That is only being sociable, landlady."

"I give up, you are incorrigible"

She came to the table and greeted everyone with a kiss. You certainly liven this place up Bill as soon as you walk in."

"They are a grand crowd, the salt of the earth, I enjoy every minute with them," he replied.

"Okay," said Ann, "let us get down to business. The Village Hall is yours when you want it. We have a music man who runs a disco, he is not a Whiz Kid but a very sensible man and he would be delighted to play the type of music you want."

"What about catering?" Tommy asked.

"The local Baker and Confectioner will supply all your needs from food to hot and cold drinks. The Village Hall committee do stipulate no alcohol whatsoever and the jollifications to stop at midnight."

"That is fair enough," offered Bill, all that remains is to name the day, count the guests and then we can go ahead with the bookings."

On leaving they thanked Ann who said she would be in touch if there were any further developments. The locals wished them all Goodnight and hoped to see them next Saturday.

"Right Bill Barrett, tomorrow we start to sort our guest list out in earnest."

"If you say so dear," he replied acting meekly.

"I do! Now give me a kiss and then away you go off to bed."

"Will you come into my office please Jackie?"

When Jackie sat down Tommy brought her chair to face her and held both of Jackie's hands. "You are like a mother to me Jackie and I love you for it. All the planning for the wedding is far from being complete especially where I am concerned and I want you to complete it for me."

"But how can I do that love? You know I will do anything for you because to me you are the daughter I never had."

"That is the point Jackie; I want you to be my mother at the ceremony. Please Mum, will you give me away?"

"Jackie burst into tears and threw her arms round Tommy. It was quite some time before she could compose herself.

"Of course my dear, thank you for making me the happiest woman in the world."

CHAPTER 34

"Are you still playing football Corporal? Roy asked Corporal Hermett who had reported to the orderly room to get his arrival chit.

"Not as much as I would like sir."

"Do you remember Sergeant Gordon who I understand used to play in the same station team as yourself?"

"Indeed I do, is he stationed here?"

"He is and looking forward to seeing you again and I think to get you signed on for the village team."

"That will suit me fine sir, it will be grand to see him again it has been a long time."

"Here is your chit and welcome to RAF March I am sure you will find it a very good posting."

When he reported to the SWO's office, he was greeted with. "So you are Hermit the goalie? Don't look so puzzled lad when we got news of your coming wheels were set in motion and who rolled with them? Sergeant Gordon and Sergeant Brown who you knew as Corporal Brown and who you are replacing. How do you fancy the bedding store job?"

"I do sir I have had plenty of experience doing that."

"Good, I expect you to show a good example to your staff, you will be smart at all times and if I find you or your staff not keeping to my standards you will wonder what hit you. Do I make myself clear Corporal?"

"Perfectly sir, there will be no problems where that is concerned."

"Come with me and I will introduce you to your new staff and meet your old friend."

He knocked on the Bedding Store door and almost immediately an airman opened it.

"Must have been expecting us," he said. "Is Sergeant Brown at home?"

"No sir," was the reply, "he is in here."

Both the SWO and the Corporal grinned, "For your sins Corporal you are going to inherit a very smart staff and I wish you the Best of British!"

"Sergeant Brown, here is your old mucker Corporal Hermett to take over from you, I will leave you to it." As he was leaving he glanced up to the top of the blanket racks then asked one of the airmen. "Where is the bed Jones?"

"What bed sir?" asked Jones.

"Good man, well done. Carry on." He left smiling and thinking, they are learning.

>>> <<<

After making individual guest lists Bill and Tommy read both lists then began to compare notes. "We have not got many when we have sorted out the ones we have doubled up on," said Bill.

"We haven't have we?" replied a very surprised Tommy. "That is the basic list, we can always add to it later if need be. Now what about the date? And when am I leaving the service, before the wedding or after? If I leave before I shall need somewhere to stay temporarily, I am sure I can arrange that with no problem. On the other hand I could go through the channels to find out if I could carry on here and live in Married Quarters?"

"I like that idea," Bill enthused if you don't ask you won't know and I suggest you get on with it right away, ring Barbara for an appointment with the Wingco'."

"Barbara, it is me Tommy, can you get me an appointment with the Wing Commander please? Yes please, the sooner the better. Oh that will be lovely, see you shortly Barbara, thanks. If I go now Bill he will see me as soon as he can."

"I want to ask him if I can stay on in the service after my wedding Barbara. He will want to take it to a higher authority I'm sure but he may have views on the subject."

"Won't it be wonderful if you can?" said Barbara sounding very excited at the thought. The buzzer sounded. "Right away sir. Come on Tommy in you go and the very best of luck. Flight Sergeant Atkins sir," she announced.

Tommy saluted and was told to take a seat. "This is an unexpected pleasure Flight Sergeant, what can I do for you?"

Tommy told him her story.

"Can I ask who the lucky man is?"

"Warrant Officer Barrett sir"

"Well I'm blessed, I am delighted for you, I am delighted for the pair of you. It is not unusual for a married couple to serve on the same station. I cannot give you a positive answer because it has to run it's course through the channels, but I promise you this, I will do all I can to bring it about for you both. When the hierarchy get to hear of this you can rest assured they will certainly look at it very favourably. Your WO Barrett is well respected in very high places and not being over confident I think you are on a winner there. I am going to look forward to the outcome with interest and I will contact you immediately we get a result. You can tell your future husband from me that he is a very lucky man."

"Thank you sir," she then saluted and took her leave.

The Wingco' smiled as he heard the squeals of delight coming from his PA's office.

Bill gave a wry smile when Tommy briefed him. "There is a very good chance for us yet it will give us time to get used to married life before you may have to call it a day if a posting comes through for you."

"I wonder when we will hear something?" asked Tommy.

"Just as long as it takes," was the reply. "Now let us start thinking of a date and getting a brochure for the honeymoon. Have you got any thoughts on that?"

"A Caribbean Cruise and before you blow your top, remember it is our honeymoon and what better way to relax and enjoy each other. So if you can nip off tomorrow to the travel agent for a brochure and ask him what he can recommend, who knows he may even come up with a snippet."

At dinner Roy said. "It looks like Tommy could be staying with us for some time when you get married."

"What am I missing?" asked Derwent.

Roy told him what he had heard from Barbara.

"That will be great it will mean our little family will still be together enthused Derwent."

"When they go into quarters just think of the home cooked dinners we will be invited to with Bill playing mine host. What's up Bill? You have gone quiet all at once not like you to be stuck for something to say."

"I was just thinking if we are we doing the right thing and would it be better for our peace of mind to get away from here and enjoy a nice quiet, peaceful and homely married life as opposed to living here in Married Quarters with the door constantly locked. I will have a word with Tommy about that, I cannot see her objecting."

Roy turned to Derwent. “Ignore him he is attention seeking, wait till I tell Tommy about his little Darby and Joan story, I just hope I can be there when he comes to grief.”

“Roy! Roy! I do not make snap decisions. Tommy and I will have plenty of time to discuss it on our Caribbean cruise.”

”You are winding me up again and I am not going to bite, my contact will tell me where you really are going.”

“Even Barbara does not know yet and neither does Viv. You two are the first to be told so be thankful you are being taken into our confidence. That is worth a “Thank you Bill,” isn’t it?” or even, “I will treat you to a drink tonight on that Bill.”

“I am going I need an indigestion tablet after listening to that.”

As he was passing reception on his way to his room Tommy called.

”Hello Roy, where are the other two reprobates?”

“Derwent is still in there getting earache from your finance’.”

“Don’t you mean fiancé Roy?”

“Of course but I can’t say fiancé.”

Tommy laughed. “You are funny Roy.”

“Tell me then what has Bill been up to?”

“Some cock and bull story about you going on a Caribbean cruise.”

“No cock and bull story Roy that is where we are spending our honeymoon.”

“Then he was not winding me up, looks like I need to agolopise besides buying him a drink.”

“You mean apologise Roy.”

“Yes, but I can’t say apologise.”

“Anyway,” continued Tommy, you are the first to know I have not even told Barbara and Viv yet, so I will let you do the honours.” On saying that she gave him a kiss and he went off smiling.

>>> <<<

“There you are Hermit,” said Sergeant Brown, I can now hand over to you officially, you knew the ropes after doing the same job as long as you have and there was no problem. I am on embarkation leave for a fortnight starting next week then I will be back for about another week or so before I am off to sunny Cyprus. The SWO reckons I will get a married quarter pretty soon he has been in touch with one or two of his old pals who owe him favours so I think I will be alright. Have you seen Harry Gordon yet?”

“I have and he has arranged for me to have a trial with the village team.”

“You will have no trouble getting in that team, actually it is a pretty decent one and a good set of lads, they will make you welcome.”

>>> <<<

"So Tim here is the new barman, Joe." Said Bill.

"He is and he has taken over, I decided to stay with him today just to make sure he has got the hang of it. It is a long time since he did this duty consequently he is a bit rusty. Also I need to put him in the picture of what he will be up against when you three crackpots start your antics."

"Don't you worry we will look after you Tim," spoke up Roy. "Now will you replenish our glasses please, and take one for yourself and Joe who can now as the ex-barman take a drink in comfort and enjoyment. William your very good health and with it my agolopy – I know, don't say it, you know I can't say apology!"

"What did I tell you Tim?" said Joe, "you will not find any bigger crackpots than these three anywhere and you are going to suffer a month of them. They will not go away because they are your best customers."

"You are peeved," said Derwent "because you have been refused permission to extend your duty for another month."

"Not likely," replied Joe, let me get back to instructing and sanity."

"Then why are you hanging on as long as you can?" interrupted Roy, "you do not want to leave us do you?"

"I am staying as I said previously just making sure that Tim is happy with the take-over."

As one the three crackpots pretended to stick a finger down their throats.

"I told you," said Joe choking with laughter, "this lot will drive you bloody crackers before your duty finishes."

"Come on Tim," said Bill, "fill em' up and one for yourself and give Joe one, I think he deserves one for the sufferance he has had to put up with us."

CHAPTER 35

"Sergeants Mess, Flight Sergeant Atkins. Oh hello Barbara. Yes of course right away, thanks. Jackie! I am off to see the O.C. if anyone wants me."

"Good luck love," said Jackie as she crossed her fingers.

"Hi Barbara, have you got your fingers crossed, everyone else has?"

"And everything else Tommy, oh I do hope it is good news. Sir, I have

Flight Sergeant Atkins here. You can go in and please come out with good news Tommy.

"Come and take a seat," the O.C. said in response to the salute. I know you have been waiting impatiently for the word to come through and it has finally arrived and I might add from the highest authority and you can guess who that person is. I am pleased to tell you that your application has been accepted. You will still hold the position as Sergeants Mess manager until such time you decide to retire from the service or you are posted to another station, which between you and me is very unlikely because of the esteem in which WO Barrett is held at top level. I suppose it will now be full steam ahead to rubber stamp the arrangements for your wedding. I am very pleased for you both and if you do not mind, I will leave my congratulations until later. So off you go and make my PA's day with the good news."

Tommy saluted and thanked him.

The Wingco' gave a laugh on hearing this time not squeals of delight but screams of delight coming from his PA's office.

"This calls for a little celebration," said Barbara, "shall we have one tonight I know the boys will not refuse?"

"Good idea," replied Tommy, "we may be able to do some forward planning. I will go and tell Bill and Jackie the news she will be over the moon when I tell her."

That evening in the Quiet Room when they had got over the excitement it was decided that they would drive to Leeds to get fixed up with the wedding dress and dresses for Viv, Barbara and an outfit for Jackie and also the men to get fitted for their morning suits. The date for the big day was also chosen, all that remained was to confirm it with the church, the hotel, the caterers, the village hall committee and the travel agent had to be contacted to get a date that will be compatible with the wedding date.

"I suggest, Viv, that you and I go to the village tomorrow and try to tie all the loose ends together; there will be no problem getting the day off."

"When are we going to Leeds?" asked Viv.

"I suppose that will depend on when we can book an appointment with a gown shop, I shall have to do some phoning for that but a Saturday is the best day for all of us. You will have to do some phoning too Mr Barrett to book an appointment with your gents outfitters. I don't think you can go far wrong with Moss Bros' suggested Tommy, what do you think Bill?"

"What ever you say dear," answered Bill.

That brought a bout of laughter from everyone and the remark from Derwent, "Three cheers for the HPC!"

"What on earth is the HPC when it is at home?" asked Barbara.

"Tommy enlightened her. "The Hen Pecked Club."

"Serves him right," said a delighted Roy above the laughter. "If he can't stand a joke he shouldn't have joined."

>>> <<<

The SWO, George Miller tried the door to the bedding room store only to find it locked. He knocked which was answered almost immediately by one of the airmen.

"Have you settled in alright Corporal? Where is Sergeant Brown?"

"On embarkation leave sir."

"Oh yes, so you are now the full time boss, let me know if you get any problems. Do you three attend the morning work parade?"

"Yes sir, we all do."

"Good, I see you are all keeping yourselves smart, clean and tidy. By the way did you get signed on for the village team?"

"Not as yet sir, I have handed in my application to the orderly room for permission to play for them and it has to be approved by the CO."

"Do you do any training?"

"I go to the gym most nights and train with Sergeant Gordon and a couple of mornings a week we do a bit of road running together."

"I don't suppose these two lads go training with you." He said looking at the two lads.

"No fear sir," they replied.

"Then the only training you do is Egyptian PT."

"What's that sir?" they queried.

"Doing nothing but just lying on your 'pit'!"

"Good to see you have everything ship shape Corporal keep up the good work and if anytime you run short of reading material let me know and I will see what I can do for you." He then left them having a good laugh.

As he was making his way back to SHQ he saw Bill and Tommy driving in the direction of the station's entrance, so he flagged them down. "I want a word with you two, is there any truth in this rumour I have been hearing about wedding bells?"

"George we are in a hurry just now because we have to see the vicar at the village church to book our wedding ceremony. So if you will excuse us and can wait a little longer I will put you in the picture when we return."

"Well I'll go to the foot of our stairs," he said in astonishment, "then it is true, you are a couple of dark horses, wait till I tell the wife."

"We wanted to get everything finalised before we broke the news but it appears we have a security leak, anyway we will see you in a bit and keep it to yourself. Ta ra." He then drove off.

The first stop was to see Ann and Tim who were delighted with the news that Tommy could stay in the service at March. "Would you like me to come with you?" Ann asked, "the vicar and I are good friends and it might help."

"Yes please," Tommy replied.

The vicar was very obliging and booked them for the day they wanted. The hotelier was also very pleased to see them and he guaranteed everything they asked for.

"We will finalise the number of guests as quickly as possible," they assured him. The same applied with the caterers.

"I will make the arrangements with the Village Hall Committee," said Ann as soon as I can get in touch with the chairman."

"We have now to go to the travel agent and hope the arrangements run as smoothly with him. Thanks Ann, we do appreciate everything you are doing for us you are a very good friend. We are going to Leeds on Saturday hoping to get fixed up with dresses and suits."

"Come back to the pub with me and I will give you the address of a wedding gown outfitter, the owner is also a good friend of mine."

"Oh lovely," said Tommy, with a squeal of delight."

"Here you are and here are the directions Bill, it is easy enough to find, I will telephone her to tell her you are coming."

At the travel agents everything slotted in, they got what they wanted and left a very happy couple. After parking the car, Bill went to see George and filled him in with all the events up to the present time.

"You will be going to see Mary," said George, "she will never forgive you if you don't tell her in advance."

"Then I had better go and see her now before she hears any rumours."

Mary welcomed him. "It is always nice to see you Bill even if it is only briefly, how is Tommy?"

"That is what I have come to see you about Mary."

"No bad news I hope."

"On the contrary, we are getting married!" He then told her everything.

"That is the best news I have heard since your engagement Bill, I am really happy for you both."

"I would like to ask you something Mary. On your invitation card, do you want to go as a single or as a couple with Sam? Come on Mary do not go all bashful on me I know you like each other and that you have had one or two little outings together. I have never said anything to anybody not even to Tommy knowing that when you were ready you would tell me."

"How on earth did you find that out Bill, we have been so discreet too?"

"That does not matter, only three people know, you, Sam and me. Now back to the invitations, if you want my advice I suggest you go as a couple because you will only pair up when you get there and that is when it will come to light."

"I think you are right Bill, everyone will know sooner or later, yes! We will go as a couple. Thanks Bill."

"I will have to tell Tommy because of the invitation but rest assured old girl that is as far as it will go, let everyone find out for themselves."

"I keep telling you Bill Barrett. Less of the old girl! Come here you lovely man let me give you a kiss for being such a good friend."

At dinner, Bill told Roy and Derwent about the day's events. "Everything is now organised and we all go to Leeds on Saturday to get measured for our finery and Saturday night we go to the March Hare to celebrate a successful day and tie up any loose ends with Ann."

"Sounds good to me," said Roy.

"I am really looking forward to that added Derwent."

Tommy spoke to Viv and Barbara as they were going in to dinner and told them the arrangements for Saturday.

After breakfast on the Saturday they set off in two cars. After parking them they agreed they would meet up at the restaurant they had used before from one o' clock onwards not knowing how long the process of choosing dresses and being measured up would take. They found the shops easily enough by following the directions Ann gave them. The girls received a right royal welcome and received special treatment because of Ann's friendship with the owner of the gown shop. After a welcoming drink of coffee they were introduced to the many fashion books of gowns and accessories. They had pre-decided on simplicity so were able to choose their gowns with the minimum of fuss while Jackie chose a very nice suit. They would have to return the following Saturday for a fitting.

There was no trouble fixing the men up, arrangements were made as to when they could collect the suits and when they had to be returned.

At the prescribed time they all met for lunch exchanging stories of the morning.

Tommy said to Bill. "We must get some invitation cards while we are here then we can distribute them, giving the guests plenty of time to make any arrangements."

"Good thinking," replied Bill, do you four want to do a bit of shopping? Jackie can come with us and then we will meet up at the car park. Remember, we have shoes and socks to buy; you women also have shoes to get so you may as well have a look round while you are here. "Won't you two ladies need to get matching shoes if you are going to wear similar coloured dresses?"

"That is already taken care of, informed Tommy, "all we girls need is a nice big cheque from you to pay for our outfits! Do you hear that chaps? Make a note of that for when it comes your turn to get married."

"You know," said Roy, "I have got an inclination for a Gretna Green job when it comes to my turn. How about you Derwent?"

"I have got two options, a hot air balloon but that could be a bit dicey on account of the weather. The one I really fancy is Las Vegas!"

"Now why did I not think of that one?" said Roy, "we could even make it a double wedding."

"Don't even think of it lover-boy, the only time your tootsies leave England's shores is on our honeymoon and I do not want bagpipes playing at my wedding either! What about you Viv?"

"I would like to honeymoon abroad but only after an English Church Wedding and my choice would be The Seychelles."

"Why are you gulping Derwent have you swallowed your tongue?"

"I have Barbara that is why I am speechless."

"Has 'Jock' Shaw nothing to say?" asked Barbara.

"No I have not, I am resigned to the fact that we will be tying the knot in your home town and that will serve as a honeymoon as well."

"Where is that Barbara?" asked Viv.
"Christchurch."
"What in Devon?"
"No, New Zealand!"
"She is one of the 'All Blacks' piped up Roy laughing.
"I am NOT!" retorted Barbara. "I am English. We emigrated when I was in my early teens then I came back here to study at university. After I graduated I got a decent job in London but after a while I decided it was not for me so I enlisted in the WRAF and have enjoyed every minute of it."
"Don't you ever go home to see your parents? Viv asked.
"My mother died some years ago and my father re-married. My stepmother and I do not see eye to eye so I keep away and my father does not keep in touch any more. England is my permanent home now and you are my family."
"Then you will not be getting married in New Zealand then?" asked Viv.
"No it will probably be in Roy's home town… if he behaves himself."
"Thank God for England," exclaimed Roy as he gave her a kiss "and our little family."
"And so we are Barbara," said Tommy, as each one of them in turn kissed and embraced her.

CHAPTER 36

Sam Brown was thrilled to bits with his invitation. He asked Mary if she thought it would be in order for him to provide all the flowers for the wedding including decorating the church for a wedding present. "They will be made up properly and Tommy can come to see me to choose what she wants."
"I think that is a lovely idea Sam but how are you going to arrange them?"
"I will ask the Ladies Flower Arranging Society to do the honours and believe me Mary they are very good and they will be thrilled to bits with the chance to show their talents."
"I will have a word with Tommy and tell her."
When Tommy heard what Mary had to say she responded. "What a wonderful gesture from Sam please tell him it is the nicest present he could give me."
"Well have you the time to come now and do your choosing? The sooner the better then Sam can give the flowers plenty of TLC in preparation."
"I will hand over to Jackie to tell her where she can get in touch with me if needed."
"Can I come with you?" asked Mary or do you want your choice to be a secret."
"By all means come with me you will be a big help."

Sam was delighted to see the two of them. "I promise you will not be disappointed with the flowers and I can also guarantee the bouquets etc will be first class and thank you and Bill for the invitation I will treasure it. Right, come on then let us go and choose your flowers."

>>> <<<

The four dresses went to Jackie's house where Tommy would stay overnight. Viv and Barbara would stay overnight at the March Hare and would dress at Jackie's' from there the taxi would convey them to church. Bill, Roy and Derwent would dress in their rooms in the Sergeants Mess and Derwent, as groomsman, would commence his duties from there.

Bill took the three girls to the March Hare to drop off Viv's and Barbara's overnight necessities then took them to Jackie's house. "Tommy and I are going to see if my sister and her husband have settled in at the hotel and to leave our holiday luggage with them. I will bring Tommy back then go for a drink with Roy and Derwent back at camp and go through the itinerary to avoid any slip-ups."

After spending an hour at the hotel, they returned to Jackie's house. "You girls have a good natter and I will see you all tomorrow and don't be late. Goodnight Mum," he said to Jackie. She came over to him, gave him a kiss and with a smile said. "Goodnight son."

Roy and Derwent were already in the bar along with his training staff and other well-wishers. When it began to get a little rowdy, the three crackpots excused themselves and left to go over the details for the last time before finally turning-in for the night.

At breakfast, they ran through Derwent's plan of action again until they were satisfied there would be no slip-ups on his part. "The wedding car will be here on the dot at the specified time and that is when my duties commence, so you two had better not be late or I will be off and you can make your own way to church!"

"Viv would be so proud of you Derwent if she could only hear how masterful you are," said Roy.

"Don't you soft soap me," retaliated Derwent, "you are not getting to sit beside the driver, you are going in the back with the groom and God help him. Sorry to lumber you with him Bill especially on your wedding day but you know the rules, protocol and all that."

"I understand Derwent; we all have a cross to bear!"

Roy answered back. "Don't you patronise me Bill Barrett, just you remember I have a speech to make, I would think about that if I was you!"

"Come on let us get ready or the car will be here before we know it," insisted Bill.

Viv and Barbara had reported to Jackie's house. "Have you had breakfast?" Jackie asked.

"Yes, Ann cooked us a lovely one, a good old fashioned English breakfast and it was good. Ann insisted we have a nightcap to enable us to have a good night's sleep and it certainly worked. Ooh! Those feather mattresses they were out of this world, I think I fell asleep as soon as my head touched the pillow," exclaimed Barbara.

"That is exactly what happened to me," said Viv, it was luxury."

"Feather beds were not exclusive to you," retorted Tommy, "unfortunately I was awake for ages, my brain was too active but I did enjoy a good home made breakfast. I could do to engage Mum as my housekeeper when we get back on duty, she could come and cook my meals anytime."

"Right then, come on you girls it is time we were all putting on our finery," said Jackie.

Derwent did a great job collecting all the guests and got quite a shock to see an Outside Broadcast Yorkshire TV Van pull up outside the church. Unbeknown to anyone Ann had rung Yorkshire TV and told them the whole story of the BlueBelles and the forthcoming wedding. She also got word to the old and new BlueBelles informing them of the wedding, the response was beyond all expectations.

When Bill and Roy came from the vestry they could not believe their eyes and entered to applause and a shout of. "Your BlueBelles are here Sir!"

Bill gazed around to a packed church he gave a big smile, waved and said. "Thank You."

"That was really something," said Roy, "the church is jam packed, do you think they have come to see the 'Best Man?"

"Now you come to mention it Roy, I wondered why I saw so many senior citizens, I can understand the BlueBelles coming to see me but it looks like you have got yourself a fan club, Old Boy!"

"Remember my speech Billy Boy, don't push your luck."

"Be prepared for a big surprise at the church ladies." Derwent said chuckling.

"What do you mean?" asked Tommy "and why are you laughing?"

"Just you wait and see."

When they arrived at the church they could not believe what they saw. TV cameras, press reporters with cameras and villagers with cameras who could not get inside the church." Where have all these people come from and why?" asked a bewildered Tommy

"Wait till you get inside," said Derwent, "this church has never seen anything like it."

The vicar was at the entrance to greet them. "Welcome ladies, my words you have certainly put this village and church on the map. Bless you and thank you. Are you ready to meet the throng?" he said with a smile, "I'm afraid it is standing room only."

When the bridal party entered, they did so to the Wedding March accompanied by applause, something that had never happened before in that church. The vicar entered into the spirit of it by leading the party with a huge smile on his face while the bride and her attendants did well to suppress the emotion they were feeling.

Bill turned to face Tommy as she approached him, both faces lit by lovely smiles to each other.

"Before I commence with the marriage ceremony," announced the vicar. "I would like to thank each one of you here for coming. Yes, you have come to witness and celebrate this couple's marriage to each other but you have also helped to draw the media to our lovely village and church. Watch Yorkshire TV this evening you never know you may even be featured." This brought a burst of laughter from the congregation. "We have also been honoured with some ladies who have come from far and wide to attend this service because it means so much to them and *they* mean so much to this village of March. Ladies and Gentlemen, I bid welcome to the famous BlueBelles!"

It was Jackie's proudest moment when she responded to the question, "Who gives this woman to this man?"

In a firm voice she answered. "I Do."

After the signing of the register, the congregation applauded them all the way up the aisle to the church entrance where they were greeted with cheers and flashing cameras from all angles.

Then came the official family photographs and a group photograph with all the BlueBelles. This one Ann was determined would join the other two gracing the bar in the March Hare. Ann and Viv introduced Tommy to the old and new BlueBelles with Bill trying to remember names but giving it up as a bad job. "Come here Bill I don't suppose you remember this lady," said Ann, "but you should do by reputation."

"I am sorry but I just do not know, the only one that sticks in my mind is the Knock-Out Kid."

"Right first time," said Ann.

Bill said. "Well I'll be blowed, you are a mature woman now, do you mind if a newly married man gives you a kiss for old time's sake?"

"You would make my day sir and the other girls jealous. I too am married and to the lad I thumped and we have a baby daughter we have christened Bluebell."

"Mrs Barrett" Bill shouted. When there was no reaction, he shouted "Tommy." This time she acknowledged and wondered why everyone burst into laughter. When she came over, Bill said. "Do you remember me telling you about the BlueBelle Knock-Out Kid? Well let me introduce you to her, she is now married and has a baby daughter called Bluebell."

"Oh how lovely and thank you for coming, said Tommy, "not only has it helped to make Bill's day but mine also and it is such a pleasure to meet you all in the flesh as opposed to photographs."

After having a very long session with everyone, they said thank you and goodbye then strolled escorted by their guests to the hotel, which was nearby, getting calls of "Good Luck" from passing villagers.

Following the meal was speech time. Roy being the 'Best Man' was to start the ball rolling in true tradition.

"Ladies and Gentlemen, I should start by thanking you all for attending this very special occasion when we should be the ones thanking Mr and Mrs Barrett for inviting us. On the other hand, what kind of a wedding would it have been without us the cream of society but whichever way you look at it you will agree it was a lovely occasion. If you do not agree you should have told us before you sat down to the meal then you could have been escorted to the bus stop just down the road. If anyone is thinking of leaving now please do so quietly, it will mean I can shorten my speech with not having as many people to talk to. One of my many duties and I stress, many duties, you have no idea the amount I was lumbered with. I suddenly I had a name change, I was Christened Roy but now I am called 'Will'. Will you do this? Will you do that? Will you bring? My favourite one is, "Will you say a few kind words about us please?" I did not need to be asked that Bill and Jean because they are the most well loved couple not only to their relations and close friends but also to everyone who has been fortunate enough to have met them. The only way I can express my personal feelings, it may sound a bit soppy coming from a man but who cares. Bill and Tommy, I love you to bits.

Thank you Ladies and Gentlemen for not leaving before the end of my speech."

That light-hearted speech brought tremendous applause from the guests and Tommy called him to her to give him a kiss and a thank you.

When the glasses had been replenished and ready for the toast, Roy got to his feet to announce. "Ladies and Gentlemen will you please be upstanding to toast the Bride and Groom, may they have many years of happiness together."

When everyone had sat down, he said. "This is another of my duties. Will you read the cards please?" Honestly folk you will be amazed at the number of Congratulatory Cards we have received. To say we have received a sack full would be an understatement, that itself proves the popularity of this lovely couple. Unfortunately I have not the time to read them all so please do not be disappointed if yours is not read out. Instead, I have picked one out at random which should cover all and here it is. To Bill and Jean, with Tommy in brackets. Congratulations blah, blah, blah. From Roy and Barbara. Well would you believe it?" he said among the roars of laughter.

"For the benefit of the guests who do not know who Roy and Barbara are, will someone tell them? I dare not."

After the laughter had died down, he read quite a few out. "I am sorry folk I cannot read them all out there are too many."

Again, he got thunderous applause.

When it had quietened down Bill got to his feet.

"That is a hard act to follow." He looked at Roy who smiled and gave him a wink of encouragement.

"Ladies and Gentlemen, I will not go into the nitty-gritty of how Tommy, I mean Jean, it is going to be very difficult to break the habit of calling you Tommy, love." In a stage whisper which all could hear she said. "Then don't!"

Amid the laughter that followed, Roy was heard to say. "Remember the HPC Bill."

Bill refused to take the bait but carried on. "Of how Tommy and I met, it is suffice to say the BlueBelles take credit for that and we will be forever grateful to them. However, while I am on the BlueBelle theme I want to pay tribute to a lady who without her help in arranging the wedding we would still be running around in circles." As he was speaking a member of the hotel's staff was in the background holding a magnificent bouquet of flowers ready to present them when she got the nod from Bill. "Mrs. Ann Wilson, will you please accept this token of our thanks, love and friendship. The bouquet was presented to Ann who with an emotional smile mouthed "Thank You."

Bill continued. "You all may have been surprised to see a lady giving the bride to me at the ceremony. That lady is Tommy's adopted Mum who has mothered Tommy for a very long time and she graciously accepted the responsibility of giving Tommy away and because I was the chosen one to be given Tommy it has now made her my adoptive Mum-in-law and I like it. To the two lovely young women who were the bride's supporters, thank you, we are so proud of you as I am sure Roy and Derwent your fiancées must be. Mum, Viv, Barbara, please accept these gifts as a memento of this wonderful day and the parts you played in it so beautifully." He then handed each a wrapped gift. Tommy and I thank you so much for your presents, your cards and for being here; you have helped to make it a very memorable day for two very happy people. I would also thank and pay tribute to the Ladies Flower Arranging Society for the wonderful display in the church. For you who are unable to stay for this evening's celebration we would like to wish you a very safe journey home."

That evening in the Village Hall there was barely room for dancing there being so many villagers joining in the celebrations. Many of them wanting their photographs taken with the bride and groom especially the regulars from the March Hare who demanded a group photograph with 'Captain

Bligh' and his bride. After a while, the bridal party left deciding to change out of their formal clothes to go and have a quiet drink in the March Hare to relax. Bill's sister Nessie and husband John who were staying another night at the hotel went with them and spent a couple of hours chatting about the days events besides getting to know Bill and Tommy's personal friends more intimately. Before the party broke up, they went through the itinerary for the following morning. Roy, Barbara, Derwent and Viv, would collect Bill's suit to return it with theirs while Viv would collect Tommy's dress etc and take it back to camp. The four of them were going to the airport to wave the honeymooners off on condition they did not broadcast it that Bill and Tommy were honeymooners.

"I want your solemn promise on that score insisted Bill."

"I am sorry I cannot come to the airport as much as I would like," apologised Jackie, "because I am on duty in the morning but I will see you off from the hotel. Thank you for giving me the most wonderful day."

It was hustle and bustle at the hotel the following morning, voices coming from all directions asking Bill and Tommy. "Have you got this, have you got that?"

"Calm down everybody," called out Bill. "Before we retired last night we checked and double-checked that we had everything we need and what we want to take. My suit is boxed and so are Tommy's dress, bits, and pieces. All you have to do is return my suit along with yours this morning after you see us off. There are also some wedding presents to take back to camp if you would be so kind and that covers everything. Now is everyone happy?"

"No! said Roy. "We all want to come with you the Sergeants Mess is going to be dead without you two"

"I'll tell you what we will do," said Tommy. "At each port of call we will send you a postcard, albeit we will arrive back home before you get the cards, telling you what we have been up to." Then realising what she had said after seeing the grins on the four faces she continued. "Up to a point of course, you don't expect us to tell you everything."

"Right gang, shall we make a move?" asked Bill, "I want a word with the manager before we leave."

"Downstairs Bill's sister and her husband were waiting plus Jackie and also Ann and Tim. Bill and Tommy went to see the manager to thank him for everything and to put Nessie's account on his bill.

They said their goodbyes to everyone leaving Jackie dabbing her eyes. They climbed into Roy's car and away they went waving to a few of the villagers as they did so.

After quick farewells and a reminder to Roy to have a married quarter ready for their return, they made their way to the departure gate turning to wave as they set off on their honeymoon.

CHAPTER 37

The aircraft carrying the returning honeymooners touched down at Leeds & Bradford airport.

"Well Mrs Barrett, here we are back home once more and I expect to see Roy and Barbara there to meet us and just bursting with questions."

"If he is in the same state he was when we returned from the Algarve full of nervous excitement like Barbara said he was, then I imagine he will be like a cat on hot bricks. It will be lovely to see them again don't you think so Mr Barrett?"

"Yes, I wonder if he has sorted a Married Quarter out for us."

"Knowing Roy, he is sure to have a surprise up his sleeve but we will just have to wait and see. Here we go then, let us go and meet our welcoming party, I don't know about Roy being excited, I feel just the same way now."

"You are not alone." replied Bill, "it must be catching."

As they emerged from the customs exit, they could not miss but see not only Roy and Barbara but also Derwent and Viv waving madly then making a mad dash to hug and kiss them both with tears of joy flowing from the three women as they did so. Derwent grabbed the trolley; Roy grabbed Bill while Viv and Barbara linked up with Tommy.

"Listen to that chatter," remarked Roy "Isn't grand to hear them at it again?"

Bill gave Roy a puzzled look and said. "You have certainly changed your tune since I have been away. What has happened to the 'I hate chattering women' syndrome?"

"Don't worry about it Bill, it is only because this is a special occasion."

"Thank goodness for that, I thought you may have turned over a new leaf and I could not have come to terms with that. Hello! has somebody splashed out on a fresh car?" he asked as Derwent went to open the boot of a car Bill had not seen before.

"It belongs to Fred Fox, when he knew the four of us wanted to come and meet you but had to use two cars he offered the loan of his," explained Derwent.

When everyone had settled themselves down, they set off.

"Are you glad to be back?" asked Roy.

"No and Yes," answered Bill

"What sort of an answer is that," asked Roy, no and yes?"

"No, because we were having such a great time and would have liked to have stretched the cruise a bit longer and yes, because we thought you would not cope with us being away from the bosom of our little family much longer."

"Pshaw!" snorted Roy. "When Derwent asked if I was coming to meet you I asked, what already? They have only been away a week. I was very surprised when he said it is three weeks, it is amazing how time flies."

"Roy Shaw!" interrupted Barbara, "you are up to your old tricks again telling Porky Pies. Now tell the truth and shame the devil."

"Did you have a nice time Tommy?" said Roy ignoring Barbara amid the laughter.

"It was wonderful just lazing on those special deck chairs cruise ships have."

"Now do not go and spoil it by saying and relaxing with pina coladas."

"Oh no, sometimes we had a sunset cooler which was very refreshing."

Roy once again feeling deflated changed the subject once more. "What are we doing tonight Derwent going to the March Hare?"

"What we said we were doing, the usual chat in the Quiet Room to catch up on the honeymoon news and our news," said Derwent looking at Bill and grinning.

"You can slope off to the March Hare if you want Roy Shaw but you will go alone, we girls have a lot to catch up on," Barbara said defiantly.

"Ah well, I suppose I will have to suffer with earache all night unless I go for a game of Bingo."

"Then I will Bingo you, old misery guts."

On arrival at March, the guard on the gate saw who the occupants were and said. "Welcome back sir and you Mrs Barrett."

"Get moving Derwent, are you stopping here all day?" Snapped Roy.

Instead of driving to the Sergeants Mess, Derwent drove into the Married Quarters and pulled up outside one. Roy jumped out of the car and held the door open for the girls to get out. "Here you are Bill, you are home," he said as he handed him the key to the house. Come on carry your bride over the threshold."

Bill shook his hand. "Thanks Roy." Tommy gave him a kiss and said. "Thank you, you lovely man."

Bill and Tommy walked hand in hand to the door. Bill unlocked it then gathered Tommy up into his arms and carried her inside kissing her as he did so. The rest followed them in carrying the luggage.

There were vases of flowers and welcome home cards displayed all round the room.

"We have more flowers in here than Sam Brown has in his greenhouse," said an amazed Bill, "his greenhouse must be nigh on empty."

Tommy was speechless with emotion.

"It is too early in the day for celebration drinks," pointed out Viv, come on Barbara help me make a brew for everyone."

"You will find said Roy we have done some shopping for you there is food in the fridge to see you over the weekend, you will not need to embarrass us now at the Mess with begging bowls. What I suggest you do after the brew is go to bed, you will need some sleep after your all night flight and we want you fresh for this evening. We also took the liberty of bringing your clean nightwear over, anything else you may need you will probably have in your luggage. I have made a 'Do Not Disturb' sign to put in your window because a pound to a pinch of ….' Somebody will want to come to see you and that should be a deterrent for them to leave you in peace."

"Thanks old friend you have really thought of everything."

"I cannot take credit for everything Bill, you will be surprised at the amount of helpful suggestions we have had from the married families."

As they all sat, having their brew Bill and Tommy were told of the various people who had helped in some way to make their homecoming a sincere welcoming one.

"How can we thank all these lovely people," asked Tommy.

"You already have done so," said Roy, "with both of you being just who you are and that is the esteem you are held in. Are we ready then gang? Let us be away and leave these to get their beauty sleep, although Tommy does not need that. By the way keep your noise level down when you are having an argument your next door neighbour might object."

"Who is it Roy?"

Roy put a finger to his lips and whispered. "It is the Station Warrant Officer."

"Good old George," said a delighted Bill, it could not be better. Thanks for that Roy."

They all kissed and the men shook hands. "See you at the same place at the same time tonight," said Viv, and we are certainly looking forward to it." They then left quietly.

After they left, Tommy said. "Aren't we lucky to have such good friends?"

At lunchtime in the Sergeants Mess, there were many enquiries of Bill and Tommy, not least Jill the receptionist and Mary Butcher.

They were all informed that the newly weds were sleeping off their all night flight and trying to avert any jet lag.

In the middle of the afternoon, Bill and Tommy now refreshed and feeling better after a very sound sleep went to the Mess to collect all their possessions and to vacate their rooms. Tommy had a quick word with Jill who was delighted to see her. She then went quietly to her room but not quiet enough for Viv to hear her and came to offer help. With the aid of two suitcases loaned from Viv, they completed the loading up of Tommy's car. "Would you like me to help you unpack?" asked Viv.

"No thanks Viv, thank you ever so much but I will go and see if my better half has packed up, we can then manage alright between us." She gave Viv a kiss. "Thanks again, we will see you later, as soon as I have unpacked I will return your cases."

Bill opened his door in answer to a knock. "Have you nearly finished love?"

"Just about, I have a couple of things to put in the holdall and a quick check of the drawers. That's it now let us go 'home' he said with a big smile."

As they began unpacking both cars, they heard a voice bark. "I hope you are going to be good neighbours, Betty! The Barretts are back."

George Miller the Station Warrant Officer a very close friend came forward with hand outstretched while his wife came to Tommy with arms open wide to greet and kiss her. "Welcome back, the station has not been the same without you two."

They stayed a little while chatting about the wedding and the honeymoon. "I thought you would be back today, said George, your two crackpots were here with their lady friends at an unearthly hour taking stuff inside, they even gave me a wave and thumbs up when they saw me at the bedroom window. I said to Betty, Bill and Tommy must be on their way home. Anyway, I will see you later then we can swap stories, do you want a lift in with your gear?"

"No thanks George I have to train my wife to do jobs around the house, I don't want you spoiling her. Are you the boss in your house George?"

"Only when he is in by himself as you will soon learn Bill," added Betty with a laugh.

"Come on Bill Barrett," shouted Tommy, we have work to do; you have not the time for gossiping with the neighbours all day!"

"That's my girl," said Betty with a cheer, "I like it."

George just looked at Bill and shrugged his shoulders as if in sympathy.

At 8pm the family met up and were given a nice reception from the Bingo players as they made their way to the Quiet Room while Roy and Derwent went to order the drinks from the bar. When they had settled down Roy made one of his famous toasts. "Once again our little family is reunited it has been a long three weeks without you. Promise us that the next time you decide to go on honeymoon it will only be for a short weekend." Holding up his glass he proposed, "here's to our lovely little family, may it ever remain to be so."

Bill and Tommy then took the stage to give their account of the honeymoon cruise and the highlights.

Barbara told of the delight each time the postcards arrived and how Jackie told everyone each time she received one and how Roy wanted to read every ones card.

Derwent said, "Things have been quiet with nothing exciting happening. "Tim hands over duty barman on Monday to that plonker from the Armoury, you know the guy who complained about the games evenings but had not put his name down. What is he called Roy?"

"Herbert Fielding, I think we will have problems with that lad I think he is a bit of a thicky."

So the evening passed away very nicely and it was time to leave the Mess. Bill and Tommy said goodnight at reception. "It feels strange leaving the mess at night to go home they said."

"But it is brilliant now to be able to go down a snore free corridor and get a good nights sleep," said Roy with a chuckle.

Sunday was a busy day for the newlyweds setting their house in order. After breakfast Bill phoned his sister and had a long chat with her. Once they had it more or less to their liking they concentrated on shopping to fill their larder. Most things they could purchase from the NAAFI grocery shop and fresh vegetables from Sam Brown at the station market garden, their main shopping could be done in the village. Breakfast and dinner they would eat at home and pay for lunches at the Sergeants Mess. "I have just had a thought, said Tommy, why don't we ask Sam if he can get somebody to supply us with eggs as we need them and other things such as fresh chickens and perhaps a flitch of bacon, he could get them from the villagers. It would be worth having a chat with him to see what he could get us, young James Bond could deliver it to me with the vegetables."

"Good thinking love, I will find time to go and have a word with him tomorrow.

CHAPTER 38

Monday morning they reported back for duty. Tommy got a lovely welcome back from Jackie who had been on pins all weekend impatient for Monday morning to come around quickly. "I am sorry we could not come and see you at the weekend Jackie." She then told her about the Married Quarter and how busy they were getting it sorted out.

"Never mind love you are here now and that is all I want."

Bill was facing a barrage of questions about the cruise and the homecoming that showed they were all genuinely pleased to see him back.

"Have you had any problems at all Viv?" he asked.

"No, everyone has been on their good behaviour and the special flight is a very good one, they have mixed very well and are enjoying their training. Bob Dixon still cannot believe the difference between them and the previous flight. He thinks somebody up there was giving him a good testing with that first lot."

"Do you mind holding the fort Viv? I want to see Sam Brown. He then told her the reason."

"That was good thinking on Tommy's part it is the sign of a good housewife. No problem Bill, take your time everything is under control here."

"SAM!" he shouted when he could not see him. "Where are you?"

"Here I am," he said as he came out of the potting shed wiping his hand. "Hello Bill," he said as they shook hands. "It is grand to see you back with us again, how is Tommy?"

"She is fine Sam that is why I am here. She has started to make her mark as a good housewife by sending me to see if you can do something for us."

"Look, let us go and have a brew then we can discus whatever she wants me to do."

"Not wants Sam, it is can you?"

"Like old times sitting here with a brew Bill. Now what is her problem?"

Bill told him about the move into the Married Quarter and being concerned over the main food items. "She knows she can purchase fresh veg' from you but she hopes with your contacts you could perhaps supply us with fresh eggs ham and bacon, things like that. We know it is asking a lot of you but she got this idea in her head and asked me to come and see you and what you thought about it."

"Bill, I take my hat off to her, you are a very lucky man she has the makings of a first class house wife. I see her logic regarding the fresh food you will not find many women with those qualities. Yes, I have some very good contacts in the village and around the district. I cannot see any problems but you will have to give me a few days to see my contacts and to get organised. Leave it with me Bill and tell Tommy not to worry I will look after you both."

"Thanks Sam, you are a good friend and we do appreciate what you are doing for us. Tommy will be delighted when I tell her. How is Mary? I have not had time to see her yet."

"She is fine Bill, still cannot stop talking about the wedding, we had a great day. I will let you know when I have some information for you Bill."

"Thanks Sam for the brew and everything else. By the way, your greenhouse must be empty with all the flowers you provided to welcome us home, they are a treat, Tommy was quite overcome when she saw them."

On his return to his office, he told Viv what had transpired with Sam. "I am going for a walk to have a look at the trainees Viv, do you want to come along?"

"Yes, it will get me out in the fresh air for a little while it is pretty quiet in the ops' room."

As they were doing a tour of the flights Corporal Pryce from the ops' room approached and said. "There was a telephone call from OC Training sir, asking you to report to his office."

“Thanks Corporal I had better go and see what Wings wants with me Viv, I hope it is not anything sinister. You carry on and let them see you are interested in them.”

“Come in” was the answer to his knock on Wings’ door. He entered and saluted.

“You wanted to see me sir?”

“Indeed I do Mr Barrett. He then got up from his chair and held out his hand.

“Congratulations on your marriage. It was a very nice service.”

“You were there asked Bill in amazement?”

“Oh yes, I sneaked in quietly and sat at the rear, fortunately nobody recognised me and I might tell you I was very lucky to get a seat. I have never seen a service like it, the whole congregation joined in, including me. I must say you certainly made a very handsome couple. The reason I sent for you is because I want you to take command of training in my absence. I have to report to Command and will probably be there a few days. I shall be leaving after lunch so you will be in charge as from, shall we say, as from now?” he said with a grin.

“No problem sir there will be no changes when you return.”

Wings paused looking very thoughtful. Then he said in an undertone. “I hope not Mr Barrett.” On seeing the puzzled look on Bill’s face he quickly changed the subject. “Tell me about your cruise Mr Barrett, I have never been on one but always fancied it but I have never found the time to do anything about it.”

Bill filled him in with what it entailed and what went on. “It depends on what you wanted from the cruise, Tommy and I just wanted each others company as of course newlyweds do and being more mature we wanted rest and relaxation as opposed to a having a real good time as the younger end wanted and believe me they made sure they did have a good time.”

“That is more in my line Mr Barrett I am going to have to put my thinking cap on and give it some thought.”

“Have you got a girl friend?” asked Bill.

“Well, sort of, we have been seeing each other for quite some time and we enjoy each others company but we have not thought of anything serious. In reality, we are just a couple of pals you might say but who knows? Well, I must do some tidying up then go and pack a case, so I will leave you to it Mr Barrett.”

“Whatever is waiting for you at Command sir, I wish you the Best of Luck.” He then saluted and made his exit.

As he walked back to his office, he mused over what Wings had said and how he said it. “I hope not Mr Barrett.”

"I think there is something going on Viv that involves Wings and I am feeling a bit concerned about it." He then told her the gist of the conversation.

"I can understand you being concerned because it is so out of character, it sounds as if he is concerned about having to report to Command. Oh Bill, I do hope we are not going to lose him already that will be a real blow to all his training staff and I am sure he will feel gutted."

"That is the way the service works Viv. I would not be surprised if Command has recognised his potential and want to move him to some station that needs an officer with his qualities. If that is so it will mean he is in contention for promotion and I wish him well, then we have to start all over again training up someone else unless he objects to accepting it from us." He then banged his fist on his desk in frustration. "We will never get another Wings!"

"Bill," said Viv quietly. "Don't you think you are jumping the gun? It will probably have got nothing at all to do with that. You have a bee in your bonnet and are thinking the worst because we have come to like to him and the thought of losing him, rankles. I will get you a brew, it will help to calm you down, then take yourself off and go and have a word with Roy."

>>> <<<

At 11pm that night there came the sound of screaming from Room 1 of the WRAF's accommodation. The duty WRAF corporal who had just got into bed jumped out immediately and rushed to switch on the lights of the dormitory. The room door was open and four airmen came rushing out, knocked the corporal aside, and ran off. She quickly recovered and entered the room to find many beds turned over. Some of the girls were in tears and two of them were in pain each holding an arm, crying. "My arm is broken." The Corporal phoned the Station Sick Quarters and reported there were casualties. She then rang the guardroom and explained what had happened, the guard commander in turn got in touch with the Orderly Sergeant who reported the incident to the Orderly Officer. After a few minutes the Medical Officer and a medical orderly arrived and examined the casualties. Two girls were diagnosed with a broken arm and were immediately transported to the local hospital casualty department for treatment and four others were taken to the SSQ with bruises and shock. When the cavalry arrived consisting of The Orderly Officer, Warrant Officer Mary Butcher and the Orderly Sergeant. The Duty WRAF Corporal told what action she took on first hearing the screams.

"Did you recognise the intruders?" she was asked.by the orderly Officer.
"Yes sir, they are all from the senior flight."

"Do you know them by name?"

"No sir but I did recognise them."

"Sergeant," said the Orderly Officer go and turn the senior flight out on parade fully dressed. Can I leave you to counsel these girls Warrant Officer Butcher while I take the Corporal to identify the airmen? Then to arrange a cell warming party."

"Yes of course sir although I would prefer to play host to that particular party."

"Sorry Warrant, I would prefer them to be in cells as opposed to the comfort of a hospital bed," he said laughing.

The Orderly Sergeant went to the airmen's accommodation and woke up the Corporal in charge of Room 1. "Which room is the senior flight in Corporal?"

"This one and Room 2 Sergeant."

"Good, slip your uniform on then come with me." He then woke up the Corporal in charge of Room 2. Get your uniform on and come with me quickly."

When the two Corporals joined the Sergeant he ordered them to get the occupants out of bed and to fall in fully dressed outside then stay in the room until everyone has vacated it. Check the bogs and any unlocked wardrobes, he then switched on all the room lights as the Corporals entered the room shouting to get them awake. When they formed up on parade the Sergeant ordered the Corporals to do a name check.

"Number 1 flight." "One airman missing by the name of Kelly," Sergeant

"Number 2 flight." "All present and correct Sergeant "

"Did you check the toilets Corporal? "Yes Sergeant Then you two Corporals go and check the rest of the building and it's occupants."

He reported to the Orderly Officer, "AC Kelly is absent otherwise all present and correct sir."

The Orderly Officer explained to the WRAF Corporal what he wanted her to do. As you identify the airmen just point to them but say nothing. Are you ready Corporal?"

"Yes sir."

They began the slow walk down the ranks studying the faces intently. She identified three airmen in Number one flight, each one was ordered to take one pace forward. In Number 2 flight she could not identify anyone.

The Corporals rejoined the parade reporting they could not find the missing airman.

"Is Kelly the fourth member of your little party?" the Orderly officer asked the three airmen.

"Yes sir, and he has done a bunk."

"How long ago?"

"An hour sir."

"Sergeant, dismiss the parade but take these three back in the billet to collect their small packs then march them to the guardroom."

"Sir!"

When they arrived at the guardroom the Officer addressed them.

"I am placing each one of you under close arrest and the charges will be read out to you tomorrow." He then entered all the details in the diary, including Kelly absconding. The Corporal guard commander signed for the three airmen. The Orderly Officer and the Orderly Sergeant left and went to the WRAF accommodation to see how WO Butcher was coping but the place was in darkness. "She must have got them settled down Sergeant. Let us hope that we can settle down for the night now. Goodnight Sergeant."

"Goodnight sir."

At 5am the following morning when the duty cook came to draw the keys for the airmen's mess he was informed three airmen under close arrest would be coming for early breakfast at 6:15. At 6am, they were brought from their cells for their ablutions.

"You had better be quick about it your breakfast starts at 6:15." At 6:10, they were being marched to breakfast with an escort.

When Flight Sergeant Bridges entered the guardroom to take over little did he know he had three cells occupied. "What has been going on then?" he asked the guard commander. When he was told the tale, he said. "Then I had better check them to see if they are still alive and kicking before I sign for them. "Open the cell doors and get them out here," he ordered. They shuffled out wearing shoes which had the laces removed. "Who have been naughty boys? I said. Who have been naughty boys?"

"We have Flight Sergeant."

"Hmm, you look well fed, have you got any complaints of the treatment you have received while you have occupied the suites of Hotel Splendide?"

"No Flight Sergeant."

"Good, then you will be in *my* care for a little while as soon as I have signed for you. Lock em up!"

When the phone rang, he answered it. "Guardroom, Flight Sergeant Bridges speaking… Oh hello George, outside your office at 09:45, will do. Aye, we will talk about it later…. Get them out here," he ordered his Corporals. "Give them their belts, ties and shoe laces. You are to appear in front of Wing Commander Pilling at 10:00 and you will report to the Station Warrant Officer at 09:45. One of you two Corporals will be on escort duty. Come on now tidy yourselves up and try to look as if you belong to the RAF, but not for long I reckon. Okay Corporal, fall them in outside and march them off."

The Corporal knocked on the door of the SWO and reported in. George came out looked at the airmen. He then explained the procedure to them "And I want it done smartly." He marched them to the office of the O.C. and waited outside until he got the all clear to enter.

They marched in smartly and were brought to a halt facing the O.C. He read out their numbers, ranks and names and asked them to confirm them.

"I have here a list of three offences you are charged with. One… breaking in and breaking out of an Out of Bounds area namely the WRAF accommodation. How do you plead, guilty or not guilty?"

All three pleaded Guilty.

"Two… Causing injury to six members of the WRAF by overturning the beds in which they were sleeping, two of whom received broken arms. How do you plead, guilty or not guilty?"

All three pleaded guilty.

"Three… Assaulting the WRAF Duty Corporal to make good your escape. How do you plead, guilty or not guilty?"

All three pleaded not guilty.

"Would you like me to call Corporal Banks as witness?"

"Yes sir."

"Bring in Corporal Banks, Mr Miller… "You are…" he then read out her number, rank and name and asked her to confirm it. "You were on duty in your accommodation the night the offence took place?"

"Yes sir."

"You were physically assaulted by the perpetrators as they made their escape?"

"Only one of them used violence sir, the others fled as I was knocked to the floor."

He told the three airmen to face the Corporal.

"Is that person one of these three Corporal?"

"No sir, it was Aircraftsman Kelly."

"Thank you, march her out Mr Miller."

"Well, that information has cleared you of that charge. You have now to answer to the other two. I now remand you for the Commanding Officer. Until you are called upon to answer your charges you will remain under close arrest. March them out Mr Miller."

George marched them to his office. "They are all yours Corporal," he said to the escort, "take 'em away…"

CHAPTER 39

When Bill arrived at his office Viv greeted him with the events of the previous night.

"We are now minus four airmen, three in custody and one who has absconded. Six airwomen, two in Sick Quarters each with a broken arm and four excused duties suffering from shock and bruises."

Bill got on the phone to Sam Brown. "Market Garden SAC Bond speaking, can I help you?"

"Ah! SAC Bond, WO Barrett here, is Sam there?"

"No sir he is on an errand, can I help you?"

"You certainly can young man. I would like you to make me up two bunches of flowers as soon as possible. You heard of the fracas last night well the flowers are for the two airwomen in Sick Quarters, so I would like them to be a bit special. Call me when they are ready and I will send someone to collect them."

"I would bring them myself sir but with Sam being away I am in charge here until he returns."

"Have you got a couple of cards Viv we can put with the flowers, With Best Wishes for a speedy recovery from The Training Staff. Will that be alright?"

"Of course it will you big softie."

"WO Barrett speaking, thank you Bond I will send someone now to collect them, I will settle up with Sam when I see him. Come on Viv, we will collect the flowers and take them round to SSQ. Have you got the cards?"

SAC Bond was surprised to them. "I thought we could pick them up and then carry on to SSQ," said Bill.

When the lad brought the flowers, Viv said, "Oh how lovely, you certainly know your flowers James and how to present them, they are a credit to you, thank you so very much."

"If these don't cheer the patients up I don't know what will," added Bill, "thank you."

When they entered SSQ an orderly asked them to wait, then went off and returned with the Sergeant Medic. Bill asked. "Can we have a couple of minutes with the two casualties from last night please?"

"It will only have to be a couple of minutes sir because the girls at present are under sedation and if they are not asleep they will be very drowsy. Come with me and I will just pop in to see if it will be alright." When he returned he said "you are in luck, they are half awake, but please sir, just a couple of minutes."

"We have brought these from the training staff with their best wishes. The girl's faces lit up to receive flowers especially from the heads of training. "Thank you so very much sir and Flight Sergeant, they are beautiful."

"We have to leave because we were only allowed two minutes with you. Both he and Viv then bent and kissed each one on the cheek saying. "Be good patients and we will look forward to seeing you back with us very soon." At the door, they turned to give them a wave and the girls replied by blowing kisses. They thanked the Sergeant and his staff before leaving.

The Sergeant told his staff. "There goes the finest Warrant Officer you will ever meet he is a gentleman in every sense of the word."

As they walked back to the office, Bill remarked. "I wonder how Wings is getting on and will he bring us good or bad news?"

"Stop it Bill you are getting morose, whatever happens to Wings there is nothing we can do about it."

"You are right Viv, that is service life and I should know better, sorry. I did think of going to see how those lads are even though they deserve whatever punishment is meted out to them. If I did go I could not sympathise with them it would be like rubbing it in, best to leave well alone."

"What do you think of Kelly and him doing a runner?" asked Viv.

"Now that lad deserves the book thrown at him, I think he was the ringleader, a definite candidate for the Glass House. You know Viv; I am going to have a friendly little chat with our RAF Corporals. If they had done their supervisory job right they would instinctively have known the airmen who needed to be watched. As NCOs, it is imperative they read the characters of the airmen under their command. Incidents like what has just happened can either be avoided or nipped in the bud if found in time."

"I agree with you Bill, there is more to being an NCO than in their case being a Training Instructor."

"After training today I want all Corporals that includes the WRAF in the office."

"I have brought you NCOs in here to have a little heart to heart talk with you. The result of last night's incident and could it have been avoided? I say there was a possibility it could have been. You all know only too well there is always someone who is a dominant character who will tend to take charge, and preen himself as 'Cock of the Billet'. We have seen it happen all too often. It is your job to pick these people out and to keep a watchful eye on them for they have the tendencies to become bullies. Being an NCO does not mean because you qualify in your particular trade for promotion that it is the end of the story. That is only half of it. Does anyone know what the other half is?"

There was silence for a minute or so, then Corporal Harper stated, "Discipline sir."

"Exactly, Discipline. What would happen if all NCO tradesmen said. "That is not my job, discipline has nothing to do with me I am a tradesman? As instructors, your job is the nearest thing to being disciplinarians but the icing on the cake is knowing how to carry it out. Think about it, your responsibilities are also in the barrack room. As from now you will pay more attention to what goes on in the dormitories. Remember, you will always find one who thinks he is God's Gift. Have you any questions?"

"Yes sir. If I find such a person what action do I take, come running to you saying Joe Soap is acting up?"

"No, you use your NCO qualities, take him on one side and tell him you are not satisfied with his behaviour and if he does not kerb it you will march him to my office.

Do not jump in with two feet, make sure he understands that while you are in charge of him he toes your line, or else. Does that answer your question and is everyone clear on what I have just said?

"Yes sir."

"Excuse me sir. Carrying out the basics in dealing with these misfits does that mean we have to wet nurse the rest?"

"Corporal Latham before I answer your question will you tell me what you think your duties and responsibilities as a junior NCO are."

"You are putting me on the spot sir."

"No corporal, all I want is an honest answer and I will give you my honest answer."

"My trade is Recruit Training Instructor which incorporates discipline on the Parade ground. Off parade I am in charge of airmen in accommodation. There I enforce discipline by ensuring they carry out the duties laid down in the Barrack Room Rules and I make sure they do. Their personal lives mean nothing to me, if it did it would be like having a mill stone round my neck."

"Thank you Corporal Tell me, how long have you been an NCO?"

"Two years sir."

"I think you are a good Training Instructor but that is as far as it goes. I find that after two years as an NCO you are still lacking in the discipline department, which was proven when we had to enforce daily billet inspections because you Corporals were not doing your job. Not interested in their personal lives? What do you tell them if they come to you with a problem? See the Warrant Officer in the morning I am not your nursemaid. This is not directed solely at you Corporal Latham; you had the courage to say what the others were thinking, what I am saying is, spend a little time to get to know your charges it will give them confidence in you and respect. I have a favourite saying, treat them right and they will respond. Right, off you go and thanks for your time.

"What do you think Viv?"

The old, old story, they want the promotion but none of the responsibilities that go with it. I feel sorry for Corporal Harper and Corporal (w) James, without doubt they are the two best junior NCOs we have and they would feel they were being tarred with the same brush as the rest."

"When we get a chance we will have a little word with them."

>>> <<<

At the end of the day, Bill went to the mess to collect Tommy. Jackie greeted him with. "Hello Bill I don't think you will have to wait long,

Tommy was clearing her desk a few minutes ago. Are you settling down and getting used to living in married quarters?"

"We certainly are Jackie, I think the hardest part as yet is getting into some kind of routine but it will come. Ah, here she is."

"We will see you tomorrow Jackie," said Tommy.

"Goodnight Mum," said Bill giving her a kiss.

"Goodnight son," smiled Jackie.

On their way out Tommy said. "Why don't you see Roy and Derwent before we leave and tell them you will see them in the bar tonight? I will go and see Viv and Barbara and invite them over to the house for a girlie night."

"Good idea, I will see you back here in a couple of minutes."

When they got home they found they had some mail. "Are we dining first love before we open the mail in case there will be something there to make us lose our appetite?" laughed Bill.

"We will eat first and take a chance on not getting indigestion," Replied Tommy.

"We should be hearing from Sam soon then we can do some real shopping and I can serve up some gourmet food a-la- Madame Barrett."

"I am looking forward to that ma Cherie," giving her a kiss.

"Oooh! Our wedding photo proofs are ready for collection," cooed Tommy, "we will go for them Saturday morning and perhaps a little peek at the shops?"

"Shall we go to the March Hare on Saturday to show Ann the photos'? Then invite our family over Sunday evening for them to choose theirs?"

"Why not," said an enthusiastic Tommy that will get the ball rolling."

"I have got a letter from Nessie she wants us to find time to go for a weekend to hear all about the cruise. I tell you what, how about going when we have chosen the photos' we want for our album? Take that with us they can then choose what they want."

"You do realise that will mean a wait of about four weeks, we have to choose our album the gang will want to chose theirs plus Jackie and anyone else who wants some. The photographer cannot do all that overnight. I suggest you tell Nessie what we intend to do and explain the situation to her, she will understand."

"Yes, you are right; I will ring her in a bit. Now then, let me see what we have here. Aye, I thought they would be coming anytime. The bills my love, It is a good job we ate first. They are all here except the photographer's, it looks like I am going to ask Sam if he can find me a part time job in the village or go farm labouring."

"Cheer up love," said Tommy as she came over to give him a kiss and a cuddle "At least you got a good bargain with me."

"Of course I did. What I will do is take an hour or two off in the morning and pay them. Everyone was so helpful and accommodating I do not think it fair to keep them waiting for their money. I am satisfied, you are satisfied and they will be satisfied when I do. What time are the girls coming?"

"Eight, so there is no rush for you to be off to see those other two crackpots."

"Well look who has turned up at last, the president of the HPC" exclaimed Roy as Bill walked in the bar.

"Been let off the leash have you? Give him a pint Bert," he said addressing the new barman Herbert Fielding.

"As a matter of fact I came over here to let my wife entertain your lady friends who I expect will welcome having a civilised conversation with someone who is not non compos mentis."

"I am glad you came over Bill," Roy replied, "are we going to the March Hare on Saturday? We always have a good night there."

"I should think so, Ann and Tim will think we have forsaken them and they will want all the news of what has happened since the wedding. We are off to Leeds Saturday morning though to pick up the wedding photo proofs. Tommy is quite excited about it and I think we will be taking it with us to show Ann to see what they want to order. No doubt you will be invited Sunday evening to choose yours."

"I will be looking forward to that said Derwent; it should be a good album the photographer certainly took a lot."

"By the way did you realise that Wings came to the wedding, he sat himself at the back of the church to be inconspicuous, he said he really enjoyed it and even joined in with the congregation, he thought it was great. He is at Command at present and I have a gut feeling there is more to it than meets the eye."

"I can't help you out there, that is the first time I have heard about it," said Roy.

"What I do know is that Kelly has been re-arrested in Liverpool and is on his way back."

"That's him for Colchester, I reckon he will get a good spell in there," added Derwent.

"Well gents," said Roy, "I am off to bed."

"Hang on while we sup up and we will walk you home," said Bill."

When they had left the bar Bill asked. "What is Herbie like as a barman? He does not appear to be interested in what is going on this side of the bar."

"He does not have much idea in the job or what goes on around him," said Derwent. "I hope we do not have a big function during his stint as barman, he will never cope."

"He will," stated Roy, he will be made to pull his finger out or he will get leaned on."

"Goodnight chaps," said Bill, "see you tomorrow."
"Night Bill."

CHAPTER 40

"Flight Sergeant Anderson speaking, it is for you Bill, Sam Brown."

"Hello Sam how are you and what can I do for you? Right! It is what you can do for me," he said laughing. "Yes, I will be over to see you shortly and thanks Sam. He has some news for me regarding the fresh produce from the village I told you about Viv. I will pop over and see him then I will carry on and tell Tommy. You can spare me for a little while can't you?"

"Away with you, you daft bat," she laughed.

"Where are you Sam?" Bill shouted when he could not see Sam around.

"I am here in the office," was the reply.

Bill entered Sam's shed cum office, he found it just as neat and tidy as always.

"I will put a brew on then we can get down to business," said Sam. How are you both liking married quarters?"

"It is taking a bit of getting used to. It is all new to Tommy but she is coping really well and I am finding out what a good housewife she is. I know I am a very lucky man to have found her."

"Aye and I know for a fact she echoes those very same sentiments regarding you. Now here is what I have got for you. I have been in touch with my contacts and they all will supply you with whatever you want at anytime providing it is the right season for it. Having said that there should be very little problems there, you will get your supplies straight from the farms."

"Sam, that is great, the problem now is deliveries, how and when?"

"No problem, give me a week's notice for your meat orders, eggs are no problem, I can get you those as you want them. If at any time you find you are running short I can always come up with something. Delivering is no problem either, the suppliers will deliver to me early in a morning and you will receive it fresh that same morning. I would suggest you make your order out for a Friday delivery then you have the weekend to sort out your menus."

"Good thinking Sam I am sure Tommy will agree with that. You can tell your suppliers they will be paid in cash on the day of delivery so make sure you bring the bill with you Sam."

"You have a good name and are well respected around these parts Bill. I tell you, these friends of mine would not give a service like that to anybody."

"Thanks Sam, you are good friend to Tommy and me. Her little face will really light up when I go and tell her and that is where I am off to now." He shook Sam's hand. You are a good man Sam Brown and it is a privilege to have you for a friend."

When he told Tommy the news she was delighted. "Sam has thought of everything hasn't he? I don't think I would have thought about putting in an order for a Friday but when you think about it, it does make sense. I must go and thank him personally for he is really putting himself out by looking after us. I will have to start making my shopping list out now and planning our future menus. When we have settled down a bit we must invite him and Mary to dinner, I know our little family are looking forward to a dinner invite."

"Well when you make out your order, do so with a mind to inviting the family because you know what Roy is like he will keep plugging away until he is invited."

"That settles it, we will have them a week on Sunday. I will make out the list for Sam and you can give it him tomorrow."

>>> <<<

"Telephone for you sir," said Ian Roberts the SWO's right hand man.

"Ah! Good morning to you Helen, yes, I certainly will 11:00hrs.I will be there at 10:50 thanks Helen. The CO is taking the charges this morning Ian, get me Tom Bridges. Tom, George Miller here, the CO is taking the charges at 11:00, can I have them in their best uniforms with an escort by 10:45? Thanks Tom, now get me Mary Butcher Ian.

Mary, George here, the CO is taking the charges this morning can I have your WRAF Corporal Banks as a witness to be at my office by 10:45? Thanks Mary."

At 11:00hrs precise, the three airmen were standing facing the Commanding Officer.

After going through the procedure he asked each airman in turn how they pleaded to each of the charges?

"Guilty sir," the three answered.

"You will now realise just how serious your stupid behaviour was. My report tells me you were led on by a fourth airman who absconded but has now been re-arrested and is on his way back here to receive his punishment. That is no excuse for your behaviour which made it more serious because of the injuries you caused to six members of the WRAF. Two of whom suffered broken limbs, that sort of conduct has no place in the RAF; therefore I am sentencing the three of you to 28 days detention to be carried out at Colchester Detention Centre. On completion of your sentence you will be discharged from the Royal Air Force. Is that understood?"

"Yes sir," all three answered.

"March them out Mr Miller."

He marched them back to his office. "Before you are marched off I have a little bit of advice you should heed. It is not going to be easy for you at Cochester but keep out of trouble keep your noses clean and always try your best, why? You will get remission from your sentence for good behaviour. March them away Corporal. You were not needed after all Corporal Banks that is because they pleaded guilty. Tell the girls who were involved not to feel sorry for them, they got what they deserved. Now go and report to WO Butcher."

"Twenty eight days in Colchester Ian and a discharge."

"They are better off than what Kelly will be when he faces the CO."

>>> <<<

Saturday morning saw Bill and Tommy at the photographers in Leeds. He went through the album with them explaining the reason he took some of the shots. "We were fortunate having such a lovely setting and the weather did it best for us."

"They are lovely," enthused Tommy as she drooled over each photograph, aren't they just wonderful Bill? And these are just the proofs. Thank you so much you have really done us proud, when we show these to the family and friends I can see you getting a big order."

"That is nice to hear Mrs Barrett; we pride ourselves on the quality of our products that is why we are at the top of our profession."

"It will be a little while before we can get back to you with the order, would you like me to place a deposit?" asked Bill.

"That is not necessary," was the reply.

"Look, I feel I should and I will feel easier by doing so."

"It is entirely up to you Mr Barrett thank you."

After a cheque was made out for a substantial sum, they thanked him, shook hands then left for lunch at the restaurant they frequent when in Leeds.

Tommy could not stop talking about the album all the way back to camp and as soon as they arrived home the album was opened and she just drooled over it.

At 8pm they heard the tooting of a car horn. "That will be Roy and Co.'," Said Bill.

"Come on before the neighbours start to complain."

At the March Hare they were greeted by the locals with. "You took your time in coming to see us, where have you been?"

"We have only been back a few days," replied Bill, "give us chance!"

"No, not you, the other four, did they not have permission or summat?"

"Alright," spoke up Roy,"you have made your point, fill their glasses landlord please."

The locals began with audible whispers to each other. “He is a proper gentleman. “The first time I set my eyes on him I could tell he was of good breeding.” “He is not tight with his money.” “He respects us old folk.”

“Alright you lot,” said Ann as she came into the bar, “any more of it and I will have to provide buckets for my other guests to be sick in.”

“That’s the difference between us landlady, we do know a gentleman when we see one.”

“All you see coming through that door is free pints of ale. Now cut it out or I will ban the lot of you.”

“Then you will lose all our custom.”

“What custom? If nobody comes in who is a soft touch you will sit there all night with one drink.”

They began talking between themselves in audible whispers. “She has heart of stone.” “She welcomes us with open arms when nobody else comes in.” “Aye and she is quick to take our hard earned money.”

“I give up, you lot are incorrigible.”

“You are out of order swearing at us landlady, if we came out with that sort of language you would throw us out.”

“Yes, shame on you,” was the cry from the group.

During this exchange the party were laughing their heads off.

“I don’t know what we are going to do with that lot,” said Ann. “They are as quiet as mice when you are not here, they miss you all and constantly ask after you. Now let us talk wedding and cruising I have been dying to know all about it.”

When the wedding album was produced there were screams of excitement at each photograph accompanied by ooohs and ahhhs.

“Will you have time to make a selection Ann?”

“I could not possibly do it tonight Tommy.”

“Bill interrupted. “If we leave it with you overnight I can collect it late tomorrow morning because tomorrow evening we have these four coming to select theirs. How will that suit you?”

“That would be fine Bill. Then I would not have to choose in haste.”

Derwent went to the bar to order the drinks. “Fill their glasses up Tim please, they have stayed quiet long enough to have earned one.”

Viv asked Ann. “Do you know if anyone saw the TV News on the wedding day?”

“Oh yes, it was very good, I was given to understand it gave a good account of the wedding and the interview with Bill. The day after, the village got quite a number of visitors and the vicar was delighted that so many had come to visit his church.”

Before they left the March Hare Bill gave Tim money to treat the locals. “After we have gone.”

"Your party spoil those rascals each time you come in, no wonder they look forward to you coming."

"They are worth it Tim and we like treating them, they do not get many treats at their time of life. We must be off now and I will see you sometime in the morning. Goodnight Tim."

"Goodnight Bill and thanks."

Back at camp, Barbara asked. "What time shall we come tomorrow night?"

"Come when you are ready," replied Tommy.

CHAPTER 41

"It is Helen Fraser for you Bill."

"Hello Helen and good morning to you, what can I do for you?"

"You can be at my office at 10:30hrs. The CO wants to see you."

"Your word is my command and I hope it is good news, thanks Helen."

"I wonder what it is this time Viv."

"I am as curious as you but as soon as you walk through that door I will know if it is good or bad news."

On the dot, Bill reported to Helen Fraser's office. She greeted him with a smile.

"So we meet again Mr Barrett."

"Why are you so chirpy Ms Fraser? I find it unsettling, there is something in store for me and you are making me nervous."

"On the contrary Bill I am just being pleasant because I am always pleased to see you."

"That is whitewash, you are covering up something, come on Helen open up."

"You know very well Bill I cannot divulge anything, just go in there with an open mind. She pressed the inter-com buzzer. Warrant Officer Barrett has arrived sir."

"Show him in Helen."

"Come on Bill." She knocked on the door opened it and announced. "Warrant Officer Barrett sir."

Bill saluted.

"Come and sit down Mr Barrett. How are things at the sharp end? Have you got any problems or snags you want to get off your chest?"

"No sir everything is fine or was fine up to my being summoned here and my gut feeling tells me you are going to spring a big surprise on me." The CO roared with laughter. "Mr Barrett, you never fail to astound me, he has to be a good one to get the better of you. As a matter of fact you have hit the nail right on the head. Yes I do have a surprise for you and I am looking forward to your reactions to what will initially come as a shock. It stems from Flight Lieutenant Cody being summoned to command where he went through a very intensive gruelling. From sources which I will not disclose I was given to understand you were very much concerned for him. Your concern was fully justified and I have to tell you that Flight Lieutenant Cody has been replaced by a Squadron Leader." He saw the look of dismay on Bill's face. "Well Mr Barrett?"

"Just our bloody luck sir, I will not apologise for swearing because that news is enough to make a parson swear. That young officer has the makings to become a high ranker, mark my words sir he has the ability to get to the top pretty quick. He is the finest young officer I have ever served with and he will be sorely missed here."

"Yes, I know you have bonded well and he certainly owes you a debt of gratitude for all you have done for him. Anyway, I want to introduce you to the Squadron Leader who is taking over from Flight Lieutenant Cody. I think you will take to him." He buzzed Helen. "Send the Squadron Leader in please Helen."

A knock on the door was answered by "Come in. Warrant Officer Barrett, meet your new boss, Squadron Leader Cody."

Bill could not believe his eyes, then he matched Wings' grin with his. They met in the middle of the room grinning as they shook hands, then Bill's emotion got the better of him. "Come here you crafty bugger!" They embraced like brothers as the CO, smiling, looked on.

"Congratulations sir, I knew you would make it sooner than later."

"Thanks to you Mr Barrett, you made it happen and I will always be grateful."

"Not only is he your OC, Mr Barrett, but also to the rest of the station. He has replaced Squadron Leader James, who you know was medically discharged and now Squadron Leader Cody becomes Wing Commander Pilling's second in command."

"Excuse me asking sir, but what will we do for a Sergeants Mess President now?"

"You have a point there Mr Barrett; we will have to see what we can come up with."

Wings interrupted. "Would regulations permit me to stay on as President sir? I would like to continue."

"I can see no reason why you cannot continue, if that is what you want you have my permission."

He got a grin and a "Thank you sir," from them both.

"One more thing before you go Mr Barrett, I have something that will also be of interest to you. Command has decided that our WRAF personnel need a commissioned officer in charge of them. It is no reflection on WO Butcher she remains in charge of the recruit training. We shall have one posted in very shortly. You can now go and spread the good news to your staff."

"That will be a great pleasure sir. He saluted then left.

As he reached the door he turned as the CO called. "A happy ending Mr Barrett, eh?"

"Very happy sir." He answered with a big smile.

"They broke the mould after they made him Bill," using the nickname Wings is known by in the Officers Mess.

"I could not agree more sir."

"I suggest you now pay a visit to the Station Warrant Officer and take him with you on your visits to Admin' Wing and Tech' Wing. Incidentally, you will need a larger office now, if I remember yours is quite small, furthermore you are going to need a PA and believe me you will need one. It looks like we shall have to import one because I do not think we have one here with the qualifications."

"There is a WRAF Corporal In the orderly room sir perhaps if we were to ask WO Shaw's opinion of her, I know he would not like to lose her but needs must."

"I tell you what we will do Bill, get yourself sorted out with a larger office first then have a word with WO Shaw. Get his views and if you like them have Helen Fraser interview her for suitability."

"I will get on with it right away sir." He saluted and turned as the CO said. "Bill, WO Butcher has a grand big office."

"Yes I know sir I already had that in mind."

He made his way to Mary's office and entered on command from his knock.

Mary stared when he entered, got to her feet and said. "Well bless my soul, what a lovely surprise, congratulations sir."

"Thank you Warrant it has caused a few surprises already including our good friend WO Barrett."

"Knowing Bill he will be so proud of you."

"Ms Butcher, this is not altogether a social call; my role now is being second in command to the Wingco'. I also am now OC of Admin Wing, Tech Wing and still Recruit Training. Becoming higher in status adds more responsibilities I shall need….

Mary interrupted. "A much larger office, which is understandable. Can I suggest we swap offices, this is much too big for me and it will be ideal for you?"

Realising Mary was way ahead of him he played along with it. "That is a good idea and it would suit my purpose ideally because I am going to need a PA and I shall need room for whoever it will be."

"Can I make a suggestion sir?"

"Please do because I am going to need a lot of help to settle down; I have still not come to terms with this jump up in rank. Remember Ms Butcher you are still WO i/c the WRAF therefore my door will always be open to you. Sorry I digressed but you were going to suggest?"

"That you interview Corporal (w) Macken she works in the orderly room, I find her a very bright girl and from what I have heard she is very good at her job."

"Thank you that does sound promising although I doubt if WO Shaw will relish having to lose her."

"He will have to come to terms with it, after all, you do outrank him." They both laughed.

"Now when do you suggest we do the flitting sir? because it will not take me long to get organised. If you can see the SWO and get a couple of his lads to move all your gear over, there is plenty of room to put it in here while we sort it out. Once your office is clear they can take my things over then return here to help you move things around as you want it. Once that is done you can interview that girl tomorrow."

"Ms Butcher, I take my hat off to you for the way you have organised me and it is appreciated."

"Right then, off you go sir and get those lads organised then we will start in earnest after lunch."

"Yes Ma'am," he acknowledged making them both break out laughing.

On returning to his office Bill put on a very serious face for Viv's benefit.

"Oh, Oh, I smell trouble," was her first words. "Just tell me the worst then we will see if there is anything we can do to get it changed. Or, failing that come to terms with it."

"Sit down Viv, this is very serious. Remember you played pop with me because of that gut feeling I had concerning Wings? Well it has proven me right yet again."

"Oh no, we are not going to lose him are we Bill?"

"I am afraid so. He has been replaced by a Squadron Leader."

"That is a bit drastic isn't it? We don't merit a Squadron Leader."

"Command seems to think so, because they have taken the trouble to promote one to fill the post and to be the Wingco's second in command. He is now our OC Admin Wing and Tech Wing."

"I suppose we will see very little of him."

"Not as much as we used to."

Viv thought a minute. "What do you mean, 'not as much as we used to'?"

"Because the new Squadron Leader happens to be our Squadron Leader Cody."

She gave a loud scream. "Bill, you are not winding me up are you?"

"Now would I do that to you, Viv?"

"Yes you would, and so would those other two crackpots."

He then told her the tale of how the news was sprung on him by the Commandant.

"Viv, I was gobsmacked when he entered the room. We just looked at each other and started grinning, then we just hugged each other. I will never forget that."

"You both hugged in front of the CO, what was his reaction?"

"He had a grin as big as ours."

"When are you going to tell the staff?"

"When they finish training. He also asked the CO for permission to carry on as our Sergeant Mess President and got it."

Wings rang the orderly room and asked for WO Shaw.

"WO Shaw speaking…"

"Squadron Leader Cody here. Mr Shaw could you spare me a few minutes of your time please, I am now in WO Butcher's ex office."

"Come in," he called in answer to the knock on his door. "Sit yourself down Mr Shaw."

"Congratulations on your promotion sir." Wings thanked him and they shook hands.

"I know someone who is probably as happy as you are with your promotion sir."

"Indeed he is, Mr Shaw, and I owe him a deep debt of gratitude."

"In your position at the sharp end, as you are so proud to call it, and with some justification, I might add, you will also know what my role now is on the station and the step up in rank has given me a lot more responsibility as you can appreciate. However, to cut a long story short I need a PA and your Corporal (w) Macken has been highly recommended for the post. I have asked you here for your thoughts on the matter but before you give me them I would like to tell you this. If you think that she is up to the job, she will spend a little time with Helen Fraser who will assess her. If she gets through that she will then spend a little time with Sergeant (w)Page to be shown the ropes. The bonus for your Corporal will be a quick promotion as soon as she has proved to be satisfactory. That bit of information is just between you and me. For your replacement I will contact Records for a highly qualified Corporal. You may ask yourself then why doesn't he get one himself from records instead of taking my Corporal? I want to do right by you and your Corporal by giving her the chance of promotion pretty soon. How long has she been a Corporal?"

"Off hand about six years sir and I think she will be due a posting quite soon."

"Do you want time to think of it Mr Shaw?"

"No sir, I will do right by the girl, an opportunity like this does not arise every day and I am sure working for you will prolong her stay at RAF

March because I know she loves it here. Can I go and get her thoughts on it now sir."

"By all means Mr Shaw, let us get the ball rolling. If she is interested send her in to me, if not just give me a bell."

"Thank you sir, for giving her the chance to better herself."

Back in his office he called through the hatch. "Corporal Macken, to my office please."

When she came in Roy told her to sit herself down. "What I am about to tell you is strictly confidential for the time being." He excused himself and closed the hatch.

"Don't want any eaves droppers."

"Then we had better lower our voices sir, they can hear quite clearly when they put an ear to the shutter."

"You would not be giving any orderly room secrets away would you Marion? I am only teasing; I know most of the tricks that go on in there." He then explained to her about the PA job. "It will improve your chances of promotion and you must remember you should be due for a posting soon. You could go with a promotion but who is to say you will and I know you like it here at March."

"But I enjoy working for you sir."

"Marion, you know what the service is like; I cannot keep you for ever."

"What do you suggest I do sir?"

"You are the only one to make that decision but if you want my honest opinion, take it while you have the chance you may never get the opportunity to work for such a nice gentleman again and it can only be good for you. Does it appeal to you?

"Yes sir."

"Then go and knock on his door now."

"Come in," Wings said. Do sit down Corporal and thank you for coming which means you are interested in the PA post. That is good, have you any objections to having a brief interview with the CO's PA to assess your qualifications."

"No sir I would welcome that."

"Good, then would you mind waiting outside while I put Helen in the picture and find out when it is convenient for her to see you? Helen, Squadron Leader Cody here. Has the CO told you about me having a PA? He has, excellent. I have Corporal (w) Macken from the orderly room here could you please have a little chat with her to see if you think she could fill the bill. That's great Helen, thank you when can you see her? Right away? That is better still I will send her at once."

He went to the door and said. "Will you make your way to Helen's office she will have a chat with you now and do not feel nervous for she is a lovely lady?"

He then rang Barbara Page and told her what was happening. "If Helen gives her the okay could you find time to put her in the picture of what being a PA is all about please and if so when can she report.?

"When she gets clearance from WO Shaw sir and when she will be free."

"Thank you very much, everyone is being very helpful."

"Squadron Leader Cody speaking… hello Helen, what is your verdict?

"She has passed my test with flying colours. She is bright with a good head on her shoulders and she knows her job. She has a nice disposition and I think you both will get on very well with each other. Congratulations sir, you have got the makings of a very good PA."

"Thank you very much Helen I do appreciate your help."

"WO Shaw, Squadron Leader Cody. We have cracked it; Corporal Macken has passed with flying colours. Can you see to the necessary by seeing she clears her desk and is cleared by you then will you contact Sergeant Page to say she is free to report to her? Thank you for your help and support Warrant. I will now get in touch with the CO to ensure you get a good replacement."

He got an interview with the CO and put him in the picture concerning his PA.

"Could I ask you sir if you can use your influence with records to ensure WO Shaw gets a first class replacement for losing his Corporal Macken?"

"I think he deserves one, you know Eric robbed him of Sergeant Page and in return he got a really bad apple. Now you are robbing him of his Corporal (w). Leave it to me Bill we owe WO Shaw one, he will have his replacement in a few days. By the way have you sorted an office out yet?"

"Indeed I have sir, WO Butcher actually volunteered for the exchange and with foresight she saw the complications."

"You are a very lucky man Bill, you have got the support of some very important people and they are showing it. You must give me a few tips on how to increase my popularity."

"You do not need any sir; the rank and file have you walking on water and with good cause."

"That is where you are wrong Bill. There is only one man on this station who walks on water and even I with all this fancy braid take my hat off to him. Just remember, you have a good friend there."

"That is something I will never forget sir." As he got to the door he turned when he heard "Bill…. Well done."

CHAPTER 42

"All the staff are assembled in the ops' room Bill."

"Thanks Viv.

"I have brought you here because of some breaking news which concerns us all. Which do you want first, the good news or the bad news?"

“The bad news.”

“We have lost Flight Lieutenant Cody.”

“Whose stupid bloody idea is that? It could only come from those idiots at Command who do nothing all day but sit on their brains”

“What brains?”

“The best officer we have ever had, somebody is completely out of touch with reality.”

“Calm down please, it was a blow to me when the CO told me, I just could not believe it when he told me he was being replaced by a newly promoted Squadron Leader. That really floored me.”

More groans from the staff. “What do we want with a Squadron Leader another passenger to carry, another glory boy at our expense.”

Bill continued. “Then came that awesome knock on the door. “Mr Barrett, meet your new boss,” said the CO … and in walked Squadron Leader Cody.

There was a pause, then, when the staff realised what Bill had said, there were cheers, laughter and applause. When it had quietened down Sergeant Joe Franks said.

“Don’t ever put us through that again Bill Barrett, you are evil.”

“There is something else which concerns you SNCOs, Wings has got permission from the CO to carry on as Sergeants Mess President.”

“Three cheers for the CO,” someone suggested.

“Away you go now and enjoy your dinners.”

“Joe Franks was right about you Bill, you were an evil so and so,” Viv said, laughing.

>>> <<<

Wings answered his ringing phone. “Squadron Leader Cody speaking.”

“Bill, Wingco’ Pilling here will you come round to my office please?”

“Wilco Wingo,” he said, laughing.

There was a loud laugh from the other end of the phone. “That’s funny Bill, ‘Wilco Wingco’ – I like it.”

>>> <<<

“Go straight in sir,” said Barbara.

“Any news from Corporal Macken Barbara?”

“Yes sir, she comes to me tomorrow. There will be no problems I can assure you, I have worked with her and know her capabilities, she has the makings to be a good PA and I can tell you now, you both will be compatible.”

“Thank you Barbara that is really good to know.” Then he leaned forward and said in a more confidential tone. “I will take good care of her.”

"Come in Bill and take a pew. "You have heard about the fracas in the WRAF accommodation."

"Yes sir and the main culprit has scarpered."

"He has just been returned and is languishing under close arrest in the guardroom. I have sent for him to officially keep him under close arrest and refer him to the CO. I sent for you to stay with me to learn the proceedings and no doubt the CO will want you to continue with your education when he takes the charge."

There was a knock on the door and the Station Warrant Officer entered on command. He saluted, "I have the prisoner, escort and witness outside sir.

"Everything is ready Mr Miller, wheel him in."

"The prisoner with a police escort was marched in smartly under the sharp commands of the SWO.

"Aircraftsman Kelly, sir."

The Wingo' commenced. "You are," then read out his service number rank and name."

"Yes sir."

"You are charged on four counts… One… Breaking in and Breaking out of an Out of Bounds area, namely the WRAF accommodation. How do you plead?"

"Guilty sir"

"Two. By tipping six members of the WRAF out of their beds causing two of them to suffer a broken arm and the remaining four cuts and bruises. How do you plead?"

"I did not tip all six out of bed sir there were three others with me."

"Of course and they have been dealt with, but you were a member of that foursome who assaulted those girls."

"We did not assault them sir, we never laid a finger on them we just tipped them out of bed."

"Kelly, you have placed assault in the wrong context. You are not being charged with indecent assault but bodily harm assault. Are you now clear on that?"

"Oh yes sir, sorry."

"Then how do you plead?"

"Guilty sir"

"Three. Assaulting the Duty WRAF Corporal Banks to make good your escape. How do you plead?"

"Guilty sir"

"Four. Absconding from the confines of RAF March to avoid arrest and being absent without leave for ten days. How do you plead?"

"Guilty sir"

“I now refer you to the Station Commander to answer to all charges. Until you are called upon to do so you will remain under close arrest in the guardroom of RAF March. March him out Mr Miller.”

“What do you think of it so far Bill? Without any Morecambe and Wise replies.”

“I am learning sir, it was straight forward though and he did not try to come the barrack room lawyer lark.”

“That is when it does get a bit difficult when the accused tries that on but they cannot beat QRRs. I advise you to study that book in your spare time, it is complicating but you can always find what you are looking for in it.”

“I will bear that in mind sir.”

>>> <<<

“Eric, will you come round to my office please?”

“Yes sir I am on my way.”

“We have at last got confirmation. Sergeant Page has got her crown she is now officially Flight Sergeant Page. I’ll bet that will please her.”

“It will indeed sir, she has earned it and it is well deserved. I do not know how I would manage without her.”

“What would any of us do without our PA.s Eric, they are the salts of the earth. Will you send her in please; it is going to be a pleasure to tell her.”

He returned to his office then popped his head round their connecting door and said. “Barbara the CO wants a word with you.”

She became all flustered wondering why he had sent for her.

“Calm down Barbara you are not on the carpet although it could be a red one.”

She looked at him quizzically.

“Go on; be off with you, you cannot keep the Station Commander waiting.” You nearly said the wrong thing then Eric, he said to himself, phew!

“I have been summoned to the CO Helen; goodness knows why my heart is pounding like mad.”

“Sit down for a minute and compose yourself, it is not anything sinister he wants you for.” She then buzzed the CO. “Sergeant Page is here sir.”

“Bring her in Helen.”

“Come in and sit yourself down Sergeant. Tell me, how do you like working for Wing Commander Pilling?”

“Very much sir, he is so considerate and kind, he is in my eyes a perfect gentleman. You are not thinking of relieving me of that post are you sir?” She said showing some consternation.

“No, no, whatever gave you that idea?”

“It is the first time I have ever been summoned to your office sir and my brain was way ahead of me.”

"Nothing like that at all Sergeant, I would not risk losing the Wing Commander's friendship by doing that. No, I have more pleasant news for you. He decided that you deserved some reward for the way you are managing him. Between you and me he claims you are the perfect PA."

She blushed at the compliment. "I just do not know what to say sir."

"What is there to say Flight Sergeant?"

She looked at him not believing what he had said and it did not sink in until the CO rose from his chair to shake her hand in congratulations and present her with the badges of rank.

"Thank you very much sir, I feel overwhelmed."

"Don't thank me Flight Sergeant thank the Wing Commander."

On the way out she stopped by Helen to tell her the news.

"Congratulations Barbara, you have deserved the promotion, Wait till Roy sees those crowns he will be like a dog with two tails."

When she reported back to her office she went straight in to see the Wingco'.

"Thank you so much sir for recommending me for promotion. I thought from how the conversation was going with the CO that I was about to lose my job. What a wonderful surprise I got instead, I am ever so grateful to you sir."

"It is what I thought you deserved Barbara."

"Would you please do me the honour of fixing the crowns to my sleeves sir?"

"It is my pleasure. He then pinned the crowns above the three chevrons.

Congratulations Flight Sergeant Page." he then shook her hand.

"Thank you so much sir."

"Now go and give your boy friend a great big surprise."

When she walked into Roy's office he could not believe his eyes. "Well aren't you going to say something?" she asked.

He jumped up from his chair and came to her with arms outstretched and gave her an almighty hug.

"Steady on grappler we are not in a wrestling match."

"Sorry love you took me completely by surprise, congratulations at last you have got what you really deserve and I am so proud of you. Come and sit down and tell me all about it because I have not received the notification yet. Before that, come on round to the orderly room I want to show you off and they will be really chuffed to see you."

Roy entered and addressed the staff. "Pay attention everybody… I want you to meet our new Flight Sergeant."

When Barbara appeared they rushed forward to congratulate her with applause and cheers. "Are you to be WO Shaw's replacement?" they asked.

"Get back to work you mutinous rebels before I march the lot of you to the guardroom." He left to an accompaniment of boos.

"There will be a few very surprised people very soon when I pass the message before it comes out on Station Orders. I can't wait to hear our family's reactions."

"I must leave you Roy and get back to Wingco' I do not want to stay away too long."

"They kissed, see you tonight love,"

As soon as she left, Roy was on the phone to Bill. He was delighted. "How about us having a little celebration in the Quiet Room tonight Roy? We will meet at the same spot at the usual time. I will tell Viv who will tell Derwent the good news and I will phone Tommy. Is that alright with you?"

Viv clapped her hands with joy. "I can't wait to tell Derwent!" Bill got the same reaction from Tommy. "Oh yes, we are celebrating alright," she said bubbling with excitement and we must remember to invite them for dinner on Sunday too. Now listen carefully, stand Viv down earlier today because Barbara may feel she would like Viv's support when going into dinner."

"Yes Ma'am, I will do that."

"Don't you be facetious with me Bill Barrett, it does not become you!"

>>> <<<

"It is for you sir," said Ian handing the phone to George mouthing, "The Wingco'."

"Station Warrant Officer speaking, yes sir, 11:00 hrs Friday, very good sir."

"Kelly up for t' jump Friday morning Ian. Phone Tom Bridges tell him I would like Kelly outside my office at 10:45 sharp."

CHAPTER 43

Roy phoned Mary Butcher. "Some news for you Mary, you are getting a WRAF boss, she is due in on Monday. Her name is Flight Lieutenant Simone Stuart-Nightingale.

"Oh no not her. I don't believe it. Heaven spare us from Flossy. Bang goes the peace and tranquillity of RAF March. Where the dickens has she been dug up from?"

"Why?" asked Roy, "is she a little treasure?"

"Treasure! 'Denis the Menace' is an angel compared to her. You will never guess who her heroine is Roy."

"With a name like Nightingale it must be Florence."

"No way, it is Flight Lieutenant Stuart-Nightingale."

"Looks like you have drawn the short straw Mary. Would you like an application form to volunteer for an overseas posting?"

"Roy, I could not desert my girls in their hour of need. You can bet it will be gloves off between the pair of us because she hates my guts."

"It sounds like you are old friends Mary. Am I the bearer of bad news?"

"Not your fault Roy but I would like to know who has offloaded her on to us, thanks for the prior warning."

She then rang Viv asking her to come to her office. When she arrived Mary told her. "Sit down Viv I have some disturbing news for you." She then told her all she knew about Flossy. "Be sure to tell your staff because she will go through the accommodations like a Ferret. Believe me Viv she will tear those barrack rooms to pieces, she misses nothing, she will find something wrong that is not there. We had an RAF officer with the same tendencies at RAF Chatworth and he finished up with a medical discharge but the mayhem he caused was unbelievable."

"Thanks Mary I will be on my guard and I will tell my staff to do likewise. I see you have swapped offices with Wings."

"Well he will need something bigger than this for his status and he is getting Corporal (w) Macken from the orderly room to be his PA?"

When Viv reported back to the office she told Bill what Mary had said, He in turn told her about Chambers-Jones. "If she is as bad as what Mary says it will not be good for our female staff. A woman like that has no place on this station, if she has such a reputation who has sanctioned her posting to here? This station is a Flagship and nobody and I mean nobody, is going to turn it into a bloody banana boat."

>>> <<<

Wings knocked on Roy's door and entered. "Please remain seated Mr Shaw," he pointed to a chair, "may I?"

"Please do sir, can I offer you a brew?"

"I could murder one Mr Shaw."

"Two teas and biscuits," he shouted through the hatch. "What can I do for you sir?"

"There is a room next to mine which I never see being used?"

"That was the old duplicating room but is only used to store junk now."

"Sounds promising, who holds the keys to it?"

"I do sir."

"Will you open it up for me to have a nosey?"

"Certainly let us go and have a shufti we can have our brew when we come back and discuss it then because I know why you want it.

"Yes, it is pretty obvious Mr Shaw."

Roy opened it up and as he previously said, it was full of junk.

"It is quite roomy," said Wings, do you think it will do?"

"With a connecting door it will be perfect. You will need to contact Tom Hardcastle."

"Who is he?"

"The MOD manager and you will find him very helpful. You will also need the advice of Flight Sergeant Page to tell you what your PA will need regarding equipment and furniture."

"Can we get them here together Mr Shaw?"

"Let us go and have that brew and I will get in touch with both."

He rang MOD. "Tom, Roy Shaw orderly room, can you spare a little time to come across to SHQ, Squadron Leader Cody wants your advice on one of our rooms.? You will be here in half an hour? Thanks Tom. Now for Flight Sergeant Page. Barbara, I have Squadron Leader Cody here and he would like your advice on the equipment etc his PA will need, can you come here in half an hour please? You can? Brilliant. Yes, Corporal Macken will have to stay in the orderly room for a little while, thanks. That is sorted out sir; the only thing that worries me is if Tom would be allowed to make a connecting door."

"Then perhaps he could make a hatch like you have Mr Shaw, maybe that would be more practical."

"Here comes the Flt. Sergeant "

"May I congratulate you on your promotion Flight Sergeant Page," he said shaking her hand."

"And congratulation on yours too sir."

"Come on over to the room, Tom will see us as he arrives. Here he comes now."

Roy then did the introductions. He then put Tom into the picture to the reason they had sent for him.

Tom looked around. "It is a good room and will be when it has had its spring clean. I am sorry but I would not be allowed to make a connecting door, but I could fit you the next best thing sir, a small hatch."

"Then that would be ideal Mr Hardcastle," said Wings. "When could you arrange that?"

"When you get this place cleaned up sir just let me know. Give me a list of the office fittings you want and what I have not got I will put in a demand for them."

"What about a telephone and intercom Mr Hardcastle?" Barbara asked. "They are essentials."

"I see no reason why this room cannot be turned into a nice office fitted with all your requirements. My advice is, the sooner you get this place clean, the sooner I can start to convert it."

Wings shook his hand. "Thank you very much indeed Mr Hardcastle for your co-operation. Mr Shaw, I would like you to hold Corporal Macken until I have an office fit for her to work in. I presume you are satisfied with her qualifications, Flight?"

"Indeed I am sir, she has got the makings of a darned good PA and I might add, you are very lucky. If you don't mind me giving you a word of advice on how to get the best out of your PA, she needs to have full control of your office to carry out her PA duties properly; otherwise you may just as well just have a clerk. I will also need your signature on a demand note to stores for some essentials she will need and I will take her personally to stores to make sure she gets the right equipment."

"Thank you Flight that is good advice. Incidentally would you be so kind as to make a list of office furniture we will need for the office? I will now go and have a word with Mr Miller about cleaning this place up."

It took a full day for four of George Miller's staff to get that room cleared and squeaky cleaned. Wings contacted Tom Hardcastle to inform him the room was ready for his workmen to move in.

>>> <<<

At 10:45 on Friday morning the prisoner and escort were stood outside George's office. "You know the drill by now Kelly and I want you to be at your smartest. He then marched them to the Commandant's Office and waited until he got permission to march him in to face the Commandant. Wing Commander Pilling and Squadron Leader Cody were stood in the background watching the proceedings.

Kelly confirmed his number, rank and name when he was asked.

The four charges were read out to him. "At your previous hearing you pleaded guilty to all charges. Do you wish to change your plea on any of them?"

"No sir," was the reply.

"Then I will ask you again. Do you plead guilty or not guilty to all four charges made against you?"

"Guilty sir."

"As Station Commander of RAF March I sentence you to 56 days detention to be served at Colchester Detention Centre. On completion of your sentence you will be discharged from the Royal Air Force. Is that understood?"

"Yes sir."

"March him out Mr Miller."

"That Bill was an easy one," said the CO talking to Wings. During your service you will come across the odd nasty one especially at a court-martial. I don't know about you two but I am ready for lunch."

Outside his office George said. "A bit of advice lad, keep your nose clean, and do as you are told and if you behave yourself you will earn some remission. That is worth its weight in gold in the Glass House. March him away Corporal."

"How did he get on George?" asked Ian.

"56 days and discharged."

>>> <<<

Friday afternoon Tom Hardcastle took Wings on an inspection of the finished office.

"There you are sir all done up and dusted."

"You have done a great job there Tom; I hope you don't mind the familiarity."

"Not at all sir I think it is friendly."

"When we are alone Tom please call me Wings. The training staff is not aware that I know that it is what they call me and I rather like it"

"I must say it is appropriate and still respectful, it could have been something a lot worse."

They both had a laugh about that.

"Yes Tom, you have certainly transformed that junk room and it has got everything she will need even to priority one, a kettle. I like my brews Tom and I also like that hatch, it is a better one than WO Shaw's, I can visualise his eyes turning green with envy when he sees that. He has got a nameplate ready to fix on the door. I think we will have an opening ceremony on Monday morning for Corporal Macken and hand over the office door key to her. Well thanks again Tom you have done us proud and it is appreciated. By the way have you a flower vase amongst your stock that is going begging that nobody wants?"

Tom laughed. "I will see what I can do for you Wings."

Wings then paid a visit to Roy to tell him the office was ready for occupation and about the opening ceremony.

>>> <<<

Sam Brown got in touch with Bill to tell him he had got Tommy's order. "Have I to send it to Tommy with young James?"

"That would be a good idea Sam then I will make my way there to take it over to the house. Send the bill with young Bond and do you want me to pay him or me come and pay you?"

"If you have another order ready you could bring that over as well then I can check your order at the same time."

That was settled and every one was happy. Tommy was thrilled to bits with the quality of everything. She had a word with chef asking his advice on the menu she was serving for her guests. Although she was quite a good cook in her own rights she was never afraid of asking advice. Chef put her right on one or two points.

>>> <<<

At lunch Roy asked. "What is the programme for tomorrow night? Have you two got any ideas?"

"I suppose it will be what the girls want to do and we just go along with them to keep the peace." offered Derwent. "It will be either Bingo or the Quiet Room.I have a feeling they will not want to go to the March Hare this week."

"Well I don't fancy playing Bingo," said Bill.

"Then it looks like being the Quiet Room," added Roy, "that is our choice but will it be theirs?"

"I will just go over and ask Viv and Barbara what they want to do," volunteered Derwent. When he returned he said, "The Quiet Room, I expect Tommy will go along with their decision, do you think she will Bill?"

"I think so."

"I am getting my replacement for Corporal Macken on Monday along with Flossy as Mary calls her. The Corporal is coming from Records Office so she should know her stuff. As for Flossy, from what Mary says we can expect a female Tornado to hit the Waffery."

"What I cannot understand," said Bill, is why Command sent her here; they must know of her reputation. I don't think the AOC knows anything about it and it is the same idiots who thought up the last brainwave who are trying to put a spoke in our wheel for showing them up for being the idiots they obviously are. She will get a fair run from me but if she upset the girls then the gloves are off, nobody is going to bring down the reputation of this station and get away with it, I will see to that."

"Watch this space Derwent from Monday because somebody's feathers are going to get ruffled."

Saturday night in the Quiet Room the main topic was the happenings of the week, ranging from the promotions to the effect Flossy was likely to have on the WRAF.

"I think," said Barbara, "If this Flossy person is as bad as her reputation then I think Wings will clip *her* wings; he is one who will not stand by and see her ride roughshod over us airwomen."

"I agree," said Bill he is the type to put a stop to any shenanigans if he thinks it is out of order."

"I have just had a thought," said Roy. "As Flossy seems so popular shall we have a little wager as to how long she will reign at RAF March and I will start the ball rolling with four weeks."

"Three weeks," offered Derwent.

"One week," said Bill.

"That is a short spell she is going to have Bill," said a surprised Roy.

"It is my gut feeling Roy, it never lets me down."

"Are you all coming to dinner tomorrow?" Asked Tommy. "Are there any abstentions?"

"I will definitely be there," said Roy holding up his hand, the others followed his example with a laugh.

Tommy said. "You can put your hands down I am not counting numbers for school dinners."

"Just come when you are ready, I may need an extra pair of hands to do the spud bashing and please do not bring any bottles everything has been catered for."

CHAPTER 44

Monday 09:00hrs. Corporal (w) Alice Springs presented herself at the orderly room. She introduced herself to the clerk on the counter. "I am Corporal Springs and I have been posted here."

The SAC's face widened into a big smile and a titter was heard.

"Have I said something to amuse you airman? If not wipe that stupid grin off your face."

Sergeant Graham got to his feet and approached the counter. "Is there a problem Corporal?"

"I would not call it a problem Sergeant, just a show of ignorance and disrespect. I am aware you have my documentation and if I am right my full name is causing some amusement."

"I can only apologise for the lack of respect shown Corporal. I can assure you there will be no re-occurrence in future from any of my staff. Actually, we have been looking forward to you coming. Our WO has informed us you are, besides being highly skilled, a person of high integrity and I would like to welcome you on behalf of the orderly room staff. Come on, come and welcome our new Corporal."

They each shook her hand in welcome and the duty clerk apologised as did the one who tittered. That welcome brought a smile back to her face.

"When you have finished officially arriving on the station you will report to WO Shaw, he is our boss and he is one of the best. At present he is at an official ceremony across the corridor. Corporal Macken who you are replacing has just been appointed PA to our Squadron Leader and she is being handed the key to an office which has been customised for her."

"Oh that sounds nice and how unusual."

"That Corporal Spring is an example of how we treat our staff. Come on we will stand at the door and watch the ceremony.

Across the door was stretched a ribbon. Waiting there was Wings and Barbara. Roy Shaw brought Marion from his office. Wings handed her a pair of scissors to cut the tape which she did. He then pointed to her name sign on the door then offered her the door key. As she unlocked the door Wings said. "Welcome to your office Corporal Macken." When she opened the door she gave a gasp. "It is lovely." Then she saw the flowers with a card which read. 'Welcome to my PA'

"Thank you so much sir and everybody." Then emotion took over, the two men did a quick exit while Barbara comforted her.

"I would never have believed that Sergeant If I had not seen it with my own eyes. I now believe what you said about caring for your staff. That was an eye-opener and thank you for taking me to see it. I have already forgotten that little incident and am now looking forward to working with you all."

After she had left the orderly room, Chris addressed his staff. Do not ever let an incident like that happen ever again. You could easily have turned Corporal Spring into being a martinet with you, fortunately I have saved your skin and managed to win her round and I know you will find her a very nice person to work with."

>>> <<<

Mary Butcher was sat at her desk working when she was startled by the door being flung open and who should appear but her arch enemy Flossy.

"I thought I recognised the name on the door and I was right, it is you."

Mary's hackles were beginning to rise. "You are right, I am the person whose name is on the door and what can I do for you Ma'am?"

"First you will get to your feet in respect for an officer."

"I will get to my feet but not with any respect." She stood up then immediately sat down again.

Flossy was irate not used to being spoken to like that from a SNCO.

"You will do what I say when I say because I am your Officer Commanding and from tomorrow you will vacate this office because then it will be mine."

"By whose authority Flight Lieutenant?"

"I do not have to answer to you, Warrant Officer er…"

"Butcher."

"Ah yes, Butcher. I will report your insubordination to er…"

"Squadron Leader Cody. *He* is my Officer Commanding."

Wings was speaking to Marion on the intercom when Marion's door burst open and Flossy bounced in. Marion carried on speaking to Wings.

"Don't you dare ignore me Corporal and get to your feet when I walk in the room."

"But I was speaking to….she did not finish.

"I don't give a damn who you were speaking to, get to your feet and show some respect to an officer."

"Marion did as she was ordered but did not switch off the intercom, consequently Wings could hear what was going on.

"That is better, it appears that you airwomen need to be taught manners and respect. "Now where is Squadron Leader Cody's office?"

"It is next door Ma'am I will ask if he is free to see you?"

"What did you say Corporal? I do not have to ask your permission to see the Squadron Leader or anyone else. If I was not in a good mood I would charge you for impertinence." Having said that she stormed out knocked on Wing's door then barged in.

"You want to get rid of that disrespectful Corporal who is supposed to be your PA, Bill."

"Stop right there you loud mouthed bombastic bitch. I heard every thing that went on next door. You slag my PA off then bounce into my office, no salute to a senior officer then you have the gall to address me by name. Now get out of my office and return as a civilised person would and that is an order Madam!"

With a face as black as thunder she about turned and began to march out when Wings stopped her. "When you are leaving my presence I expect you to salute me or is that not in your code of conduct?"

She saluted then was given permission to carry on. When she was given permission to enter after knocking she approached him, saluted and said. "Flight Lieutenant Stuart-Nightingale reporting sir."

All this time Marion had been listening to what was going on through the hatch.

Wings buzzed her. "Marion, will you contact Helen Fraser and tell her I would like to see the CO immediately please?"

After a pause, "Sir" said Marion over the intercom; "You can go immediately the CO will see you at once."

"Thank you Marion."

"Sir, Warrant Officer Butcher is here and wants to see you most urgently, she says it concerns the Officer who is with you."

"Send her straight in please. Please wait in my PA's office Flight Lieutenant and do not say a single word to her, is that understood?

"Yes sir." she answered meekly. As she left Mary entered, each glaring at one another as they passed.

"You have definitely got one huge problem Warrant I can see it in your face. What has she been up to with you because I have never seen you look so harassed?"

Mary told him all that had transpired. "I admit I was insubordinate to her rank but that woman is evil."

"I can sympathise with you Ms Butcher we have just had a similar occurrence here and my PA was at the end of it.

Before your arrival I was taking her to see the CO, so if you will excuse me I will proceed with my errand of mercy."

He buzzed Marion, "Send the Flight Lieutenant round please."

"Right Flight Lieutenant you will come with me, we have a date with the Commanding Officer."

"You can go straight in sir," Helen told him.

"Wait here Flight Lieutenant until you are called for."

He saluted the CO.

“Have you got a problem Bill?”

“Not only me sir but the whole station.”

“That sounds very serious Bill, sit yourself down and let us see if we can sort it out. The whole station! It does sound serious.”

Wings told the whole story concerning WO Butcher, his PA and himself.

“My God Bill, what have we got here and which Funny Farm has she escaped from? This is her first day here too; thank goodness we can nip it in the bud before she spreads discontent among the troops.” He then buzzed Helen. “Will you contact the Wing Commander and ask him to come to my office please?”

When he arrived the CO told him. “I want you to sit in on this with us Eric, not only is it similar to the Adams case, but it puts it in the shade. Put him in the picture Bill.”

Wings did so.

“I can’t believe that she would try to go through the station like a steam roller flattening all before her on her very first day. Who is responsible for letting her out of the nut-house? It is obvious she is unstable and a detriment not only to this station but to any other she is posted to. I am ready gentlemen, take up your positions. Send the Flight Lieutenant in please, Helen.”

“You may go in now Ma’am.”

“About time too having me sitting out here like some little sprog airwoman.” She then gave one hard knock and flounced in. “You sent for me sir.”

“Indeed I did Flight Lieutenant and I also expected a salute of respect from a junior officer for her Commanding Officer.”

She flushed as she flung up a hasty salute.

“This is your first official day on my station.”

“Yes sir.”

“I have had a very disturbing report concerning your behaviour towards Warrant Officer Butcher, Corporal (w) Macken who is Squadron Leader Cody’s PA and Squadron Leader Cody himself. What position on your ‘Hit List’ do Wing Commander Pilling and I hold? And have you been posted here to ruin the reputation of RAF March?

“Sir I….

“Do not speak until I give you permission! Where were you stationed prior to being posted here and what was your job?”

“I was stationed at Command sir and was i/c the clerical staff.”

“How long were you stationed there?”

“Three months, sir.”

“Was there a reason you were posted after such a short stay and be careful how you answer because I can check on it?”

“They called it an overbearing attitude, sir”

"You have not learned your lesson have you Flight Lieutenant you carried on here as you obviously left off when you were kicked out from your last posting. Wherever you go you will be a liability, consequently you have no place on my station. You will confine yourself to the Officers Mess until I get orders from Command as to your future. You advocate junior ranks to pay you respect and you are quite adamant about that and you do your best to belittle them so much so it causes them to suspect all officers are tarred with the same brush. Flight Lieutenant Stuart Nightingale you are a morale destroyer, the likes of which I never knew existed.

Before you go I would like to congratulate you on setting up a record. You are the first officer to be kicked off a station on the first day of arrival. That record can be equalled but not beat. Now get out."

Flossy saluted then left without a flicker of emotion.

"There you are gentlemen we have got rid of yet another I will not say bad apple but a rotten apple. I am going to Command Eric, to sort this debacle out, whoever was responsible for her to be posted here will, when I have seen the AOC get a huge rocket, I hope. Thank you Bill for nipping that in the bud, it could have had disastrous consequences."

"She met her match sir when she tried it on with Warrant Officer Butcher, she would never have got away with anything with Ms Butcher guarding her airwomen like a mother hen over her chickens."

"Go and have a word with Ms Butcher Bill she will appreciate the outcome."

Wings saluted and left.

"I am very pleased with our training staff Eric, they have brought young Cody on in leaps and bounds and he is learning from their teaching."

"Yes sir and they think the world of that young man."

"You should have seen WO Barrett's face and heard his reaction when he thought they were losing him. Then when he saw him with his promotion and was told different, they laughed and embraced like a couple of brothers. It was nice to see Eric and I could see the mutual respect between them. We are damned lucky to have such a good and loyal staff Eric, I have never had this experience before."

Wings entered Mary's office on command. She immediately got to her feet but he immediately told her to sit.

"I have come to thank you Ms Butcher for reporting to me immediately about that woman, I cannot address her any differently. You have done this station a good turn because the Commandant in his wisdom has given her the boot."

"Now that is the news I was praying for sir. The CO is indeed a wonderful man and I may add a very fair and understanding one."

"Wings then told her the whole story. "She did not even bat an eyelid when she was dismissed."

"I am not surprised, there is only one person in Flossy's life and that is herself."

"A good name that Flossy, I like it. Well I must go and pacify my PA, in case she is upset."

"Would you like me to do that sir, I have had more experience than you and I have tear stains on my shoulder to prove it, you ask WO Barrett I have his on as well."

They had a good laugh. "I will take you up on that Ms Butcher; I will send her round as soon as I get back to my office. Better still go to her office it is now her domain and she will feel more comfortable sat in her own chair. Thank you."

At lunch Roy told Bill. "Your gut has done you proud again by winning you that bet we had about Flossy. She has been given the boot on her first day, that is all I know at the moment except Mary and Wings were involved."

"I don't know how you do it Bill Barrett," exploded Derwent. "I am going to stop betting against you."

"You'll learn," laughed Bill. "It will be interesting to hear Mary's version."

"This is the first time he has not been involved in getting someone kicked off this station and if you want my advice Derwent do not get on the wrong side of this man or you are doomed!"

"Thanks Roy I will heed your advice. Can I buy you a drink tonight Bill?"

"You bloody creep Derwent Waters," said Roy getting to his feet in mock anger, I don't know why I torralate you."

"Don't you mean *tolerate* Roy?" asked Bill.

"Aw! You know I can't say tolerate."

He left the other two laughing their heads off.

CHAPTER 45

"Sergeant York and his Corporals are in the ops room aren't they Viv?"

"Yes."

"Will you tell Sergeant York I would like a word?"

"You wanted to see me sir."

"Yes. I am going to inspect the accommodation blocks. On my way I will send all the RAF Corporals to you, then you will march them to meet me at their accommodation"

"Yes sir."

Bill went to each of the flights being trained and informed each of the Sergeants to send his RAF Corporals to the office and report to Sergeant York. He then proceeded to the accommodation to await their arrival. When they were lined up facing him he addressed them. "Who is i/c Room 1?"

Corporal Latham answered, “Sir.”

“Come with me. Take me to Room 1.” When he entered he saw the room was in a shambles. “Now show me your room.” The Corporal unlocked his door. Bill saw it was in a mess. “Rejoin the others. Now, Room 2 Corporal, come with me. Take me to Room 2.” That too was in a mess. “Show me your room.” He saw it was also a shambles. “Rejoin the others.”

All the rest of the rooms were in an unkempt and untidy manner, except Corporal Harper’s. His was laid out to the correct procedure.

“Corporal Harper, report back to your flight.”

He then addressed the remainder. “Not a pretty sight is it? Can anyone give me a valid explanation why the dormitories were not laid out as per regulations? When there was no reply he asked. Not even you Corporal Latham, who thinks they could be a millstone round your neck if you played nursemaid? Well I have news for you Corporals they *are* all going to be mill stones around your necks until I remove them. You were warned at the last inspection about your bunks and that a snap inspection would be on the cards which you have chosen to ignore. You have certain privileges as Corporals i/c rooms and they can be withdrawn from you. From tomorrow morning we start the early morning inspections once more and this time you lot will be included. The same rules apply as before and if it does not meet the required standard this time I will have you moved out of your bunks and into that empty dormitory and you will supervise the airmen from there. Is that understood?”

“Yes sir,” was the unanimous reply.

“March them back to their flights Sergeant York and inform the other Sergeants I would like to see them along with this lot after training.”

Bill then carried on and went to see Mary Butcher. “Hello Bill, it is nice to see you, what have you come to tell me?”

He told her the tale of the airmen’s and the Corporal’s sleeping quarters. I have re-introduced the morning inspections and if they do not conform the standard laid down, the Corporals will be moved out of their bunks and into an empty dormitory.”

“That is a bit drastic Bill, think what will happen with no supervision.”

“I have told them they will supervise from their open dormitory. Really Mary, it is just a frightener, I can guarantee I will never have to worry about the state of the accommodation again, Corporal Harper was the only one who came out of it unscathed.”

“You have now got me thinking. You won’t mind if I come and do the very same to my Corporals Bill?”

“Be my guest Mary but I suggest you leave it for a few days they will hear the details from my lot and they will expect you doing the same. After a few days with nothing happening they will probably think it is not going to happen to them.”

"Good thinking Bill."

"How does this office suit you? It is much smaller than your original."

"I am getting used to it with it being compact. Although I was about to be turfed out by Flossy and would have been if she had not got the boot."

"Tell me about it Mary."

She did so and recounted what Wings had told her. "You know Bill, I cannot help but admire that lad, weren't we lucky to have had him posted to us?"

Bill told Viv about the morning events and that Mary was going to do likewise but in a few days when the airwomen have been lulled into a false sense of security. All NCOs will be attending my meeting after training this afternoon; The Sergeants are going to be very happy about it I'm sure. Corporal Harper will be exempt because he was the only one to adhere to the regulations, Bob Dixon will be pleased about that.

I also got the story of how Flossy got the boot, what a bad bitch she was and do you know she was sacked from her job as i/c the clerical staff at Command for her overbearing attitude and some damned idiot posted her here. She did not have a leg to stand on as soon as she opened her big mouth."

"Good old Wings," said Viv. "Our guardian angel."

"Stay here Viv I will go and break the bad news."

As he spoke there was a big commotion in the ops' room. He dashed to the door to see a body on the floor with others bending over it.

"What is going on?" he demanded.

Joe Franks said. "There has been a little punch-up sir. Latham is unconscious we had better send for a medic."

"Viv!" he shouted, "phone Sick Quarters we have an unconscious airman here."

While they were waiting Latham was made as comfortable as possible and first aid was immediately carried out. "He is showing signs sir of coming round."

"Have you any smelling salts Viv?" Bill asked

"Here you are sir I was just coming with them."

"Stick this under his nose," he told the Sergeant who was administering First Aid. When it was applied, Latham gave a shudder then opened his eyes and looked up in a daze. The Medics arrived and took over. After an examination they announced. "He will be alright but we will take him to SSQ for a further examination and then keep him in for observation. Has he fallen down, because he is going to sport two lovely shiners?"

"Summat' like that," said Joe Franks with a grin.

When the Medics had left, Bill asked Joe. "Did you see it happen Joe?"

"I certainly did sir. I was standing right next to him and saw and heard everything."

"Good. After the meeting, can we have a chat Joe?"

He then told the assembled NCOs the story of his inspection of the airmen's accommodation. "These Corporals did not take heed to what they were told the last time this happened. Consequently you Sergeants have the pleasure of making sure your morning inspections are up to the regulation standard. If they are not I shall have the Corporals removed from their little hide-aways and moved into that open dormitory we have and they will continue their supervision from there. The morning inspections will carry on until I decide to stop it. Corporal Harper was the only one who made sure his charges complied with the regulations laid down. The rest of the Corporals have no complaints because they did not comply, consequently they shot themselves in the foot. Now have any of you any questions?"

"Yes sir," said Corporal Pryce. Don't you think that evicting us from our bunks is going a bit over the top.?"

"When you think back Corporal of the warning you got about not complying with regulations plus the fact you had made no improvement to keep your own sleeping quarters clean and tidy. You certainly did not lead by example. Taking all that into consideration I could have evicted you today but you are getting another chance to redeem yourselves. Do you think that is going over the top? Well come on speak up! You know damn well I am right. From now on you have a lot to make up for. Now get out of here you make me sick!"

Addressing the Sergeants he said. "I am sorry it has had to come to this but I had no option."

"No problem Bill, we are here to support you and agree with everything you told them."

"Thanks. Off you go. Joe, can we have that chat please?"

"Latham was niggling Harper as soon as they got in the room with snide remarks and WO's pet. As Harper brushed passed Latham obviously to get well away from him Latham tripped him up. Give Harper his due he got up and well in control of himself told Latham. "Don't be an idiot all your life, take a day off." Latham took offence and pushed Harper hard in the chest. Harper as cool as a cucumber let fly and hit him straight between the eyes then turned away from him. Latham just went down and out for the count. What a punch and what a cool customer young Harper is under pressure. There is no doubt about it Bill, Harper was really provoked and Latham got what he deserved."

"That Joe was all about Harper doing his job as a Corporal and Latham got the hump because he does not know how to behave like one. It is a pity because he is a good instructor but a lousy Corporal and a bad influence on the rest."

"What are you going to do about it Bill?"

"There is no room for him on my staff Joe. Will you come with me tomorrow and tell Wings what happened?

"I certainly will Bill, I have no time for bullies."

"Thanks, I will let you know when we can see him. Are you on your way to quarters now Joe? If so I will walk with you as far as the Airmen's Mess I want a word with our Mr Pryce, pity to spoil his dinner." Joe waited outside while Bill entered the Mess. He removed his headgear and as he entered the noise of chatter stopped and everyone stared at him. "Corporal Pryce" he called.

"Sir" was the reply as Pryce got to his feet.

Bill beckoned him. "A word Corporal " he then retreated to outside the Mess Hall and Pryce followed him. "Sorry to disturb your meal Corporal but until Corporal Latham is discharged from SSQ *you* will take charge of his airmen's dormitory."

"What, besides my own sir?"

"Yes, besides your own. Now go back to your meal before it gets cold."

Joe heard what went on. "You put the wind up him good and proper then Bill."

"Perhaps it will teach him that being a Barrack Room Lawyer does not pay. See you Joe; I am going to pick Tommy up now."

After his dinner he told Tommy. I am going for a pint love to have a word with Roy and Derwent; I will only be an hour or so."

"Take your time pet it has not been a good day for you, it will do you good."

"Do you know something Mrs.Barrett? I luv' you."

"And I luv' you Mr Barrett."

"Hello Bill it is nice to see you, pull him a pint Bert," said Roy.

"Cheers Roy, where is Derwent tonight?"

"Working late, he had to go back in to clear up some mess of one of his Corporals."

"I have had enough of Corporals today. He then told Roy about the accommodation saga."

"These niggling little situations do keep cropping up from time to time to try our patience Bill but nowt' what we can't handle. It is when we get the serious ones like we have just had with Flossy that things get a bit out of hand then we have to call in the big guns to sort it out. Thank goodness we have officers in charge who have some sense and that is a short commodity these days."

"Did you get the full story about Flossy Roy?"

"I certainly did, she certainly was a wicked witch but Wings soon shot her and her broomstick down."

"How are you finding your new Corporal is she settling in?"

"Oh yes and she is a damned good replacement for Corporal Macken. When she arrived some of the staff took the Mickey out of her name. After she gave them a rocket Chris' apologised for their behaviour then took her to watch the inauguration of Marion as Wings' PA. He told her that was the sort of treatment we give our staff, that impressed her. Chris' averted a situation which could have been nasty for the staff. Anyway she has settled in and we are a happy family once more."

"What is her name, Roy?"

"Alice Springs."

That caused Bill to splutter in his beer.

"Exactly," laughed Roy.

Just then Derwent walked into the bar.

"Well done Derwent you are just in time, I was getting a round in." Bill said.

"Thanks Bill I am ready to murder one. Cheers everybody."

"I hear you have been having a rough day Bill."

"All in a day's work Derwent. It is not like you to be doing overtime why did you not delegate it?"

"I have a Corporal who is a bit of a scatterbrain and I wanted to impress on him that he has to change his ways or else. I did not want to load him off on to anyone else and with me standing over him while he rectified his bad work he would know what the outcome was likely to be if he did not pull his socks up."

CHAPTER 46

"Helen, will you tell the Wing Commander I would like to see him."

"Ah Eric, come and take a pew. I did get an interview with the AOC and put my case to him. When he heard the full story he blew his top. Which one of the bloody idiots on my staff is trying to sabotage *My* Flagship I will have his guts for garters when I find out who is responsible and there is no time like the present." He buzzed his Aide.

"Get yourself in here on the double I want a word."

Quick as a flash the aide knocked on the door. "Come In!" the AOC bellowed.

"Yes sir?"

"I want you to find the person who posted Flight Lieutenant Stuart-Nightingale to RAF March brought here and I want him yesterday."

"Yes sir."

A few minutes later Squadron Leader Kingsley entered and saluted, stating his rank and name.

"You wish to see me sir?"

"That is why I sent for you! Are you the one responsible for posting Flight Lieutenant Stuart-Nightingale to RAF March?"

"Yes sir."

"Why?"

"Because of her overbearing attitude to the airwomen in her charge."

"In plain words she was a bully, am I right Squadron Leader?"

"If you put it like that sir, yes, she was a bully."

"Tell me, then why did you post her to RAF March?"

"Sir, knowing that RAF March is the only WRAF Recruit Training Establishment left; I thought she would be ideal for installing discipline into the recruits."

"So you think that the recruits at RAF March are lacking in discipline and the training staff needs a booster?"

"In those establishments sir a good disciplinarian is always welcome."

"If you are an authority on recruit training, where did you learn your expertise, during *Your* recruit training? If that is so Squadron Leader the experts of many years standing will welcome you with open arms they may learn something from you. Come on man you are out of your depth, you off loaded Stuart-Nightingale because you could not handle her. Do you think she is a good disciplinarian?"

"Well, er,er….

"Well, is she or isn't she?"

"Yes sir I think she is."

"So in your wisdom you got rid of her for bullying your staff then sent her to where she could add more power to her elbow. But why did you post her if you respected her disciplinary powers and not made bullying an excuse to get rid of her? I will tell you the reason Squadron Leader. She was a pain in your neck and was the cause of too much hassle and you could not get rid of her quick enough to make the position you held a cushier little number. Unfortunately for you the plan backfired because Miss Whiplash vented her spleen on senior staff at RAF March even going as far as admonishing a Squadron Leader. He immediately saw the danger and stopped her in her tracks. I ask you this. If you had a daughter who had just come into the service and was at recruit training would you have been happy to have that woman in charge of her?"

"But sir that is a hypothetical question!"

"Would you like your daughter to be at the mercy of a bully? And you *will* give me an answer Squadron Leader."

The man was in a spot and there was no way to wriggle out of it.

"No sir."

"You were right Group Captain Wildeman I do have an idiot on my staff."

"How long have you been on my staff, Squadron Leader?"

"Six months sir."

"Were you posted here on promotion?"

"I was sir."

"Then I assume that yours is still an acting rank."

"Yes sir."

"If you had done your homework as you should have done according to your rank, you would have found out that the RAF March staff were all hand picked for their expertise, resulting in it becoming the Flagship of Training Command. Squadron Leader Kingsley, you have given me a load of waffle besides failing in your responsibilities and that has no place here at Command and neither have you. Taking into account all you have said and done I find that you do not even merit the rank of Squadron Leader You will now go back to your office, remove that extra bar from your shoulder, clear your desk and wait to hand over to your replacement which should be very soon, then I will decide on what I am going to do with you. If it is of any consolation, there could be more following you. Dismiss."

"He then apologised to me and said. If only your WO Barrett had taken that commission!"

"So it is goodbye to Kingsley sir."

"He deserved it Eric, there is going to a big shake-up at Command now after that episode and what happened previously, not before time either."

>>> <<<

"Corporal Macken. this is WO Barrett. Can you arrange for me and Sergeant Franks to have an interview with the Squadron Leader please?"

"I will ring you back sir, he is busy at the moment."

"What are your thoughts on it Bill?" asked Viv.

"Latham is the senior Corporal and he is flexing his muscles to prove to the others that he is the top dog. I find no fault in him as an instructor but I am worried about his temperament. I think he has become a little bolshie since the last time I admonished him in front of the other Corporals I hope he has learned from the lesson young Harper gave him that he is not dealing with a patsy. "I want to get rid of him now Viv."

"Flight Sergeant Anderson speaking, Oh hello Corporal, yes he is here. Corporal Macken for you."

"Yes Corporal "

"Sir will see you in half an hour, sir."

Bill was sure he heard a tiny giggle.

"Get one of the Corporals from ops' to ask Joe Franks to report here Viv."

They made their way to Wings' PA's office and waited until they were called in then saluted.

"What can I do for you gentlemen have we another problem?"

"You could call it that sir but it is one you should know about. He then told about the barrack rooms saga and up to when he heard and investigated the uproar in the ops' room. Sergeant Franks will tell you what caused it and what followed."

Joe told his story up to Bill coming on the scene.

"We have here a damned stupid action yet a serious one," announced Wings. "It was only right and proper you should report it because if we let things like that slide we would be making a rod for our own backs. Thank you Sergeant Franks for your account we can now do something about it. WO Barrett and I will now get our heads together to sort it out."

Joe saluted and returned to his flight.

"Sit down Mr Barrett, can I offer you a brew? Shall we call it an office warming? He then spoke through the hatch. "Have you time to make a brew for two please, Marion? What do you make of this Corporal Latham Mr Barrett?"

"He is a barrack room lawyer of the first order sir. He is the senior Corporal and has taken over as boss man. As an instructor I cannot fault him but take him away from the parade ground he has no time at all for the recruits. In his own words he said. "Playing nursemaid to them is like having a millstone hanging round my neck." The incident with Corporal Harper was the result of Harper carrying out his duties as per regulations and Latham ignoring them."

"Your brew sir," said his PA as she handed two mugs of tea through the hatch.

"Would you like a biscuit?"

Wings looked at Bill who shook his head. "No thanks Marion."

"From what you tell me Mr Barrett it appears that Latham is a nasty little sod. That is not going to improve his promotion prospects."

"He has no prospects now while he is on my staff. If he leaves here he has no instructing to go to instead will have to do General Duties and that still involves being in charge of airmen, which he is definitely not good at."

"Okay, Mr Barrett, this is what I intend to do. As soon as he is fit for duty I want him here for an interview then I will make my decision."

"He should be alright by tomorrow sir; a knock-out punch would not put him on the critical list."

"Wings laughed. Right then, tell him to report to my PA for 9:30 tomorrow morning.

Now what news have you got from the Sergeants Mess, when is your next function?"

"We have nothing on the cards yet, although we should be having some games finals coming up soon and the members will be expecting you sir to make the presentations."

"I will be only too happy to do so."

"By the way, the CO has just returned from Command, he has been sorting out who was responsible for posting Florence Nightingale here. I have not heard the details but I understand he really put the cat among the pigeons. I am now going to have to chase you off Mr Barrett because I have another appointment in five minutes. I will send for you after the interview tomorrow."

Bill saluted then left.

>>> <<<

That evening Corporal Latham who had been discharged from SSQs entered the Corporals Club with his buddy Corporal Pryce to be greeted by the song, 'Two Lovely Black Eyes'. To say he was upset by that and the Mickey taking was an understatement it was proved by him bad mouthing the club members as a whole. They bought beer and sat alone at a table. As the evening wore on and after a few beers later he was telling Pryce what he was going to do when he saw Harper.

"Here is you chance," said Pryce, "he has just walked in."

After buying a beer Harper went and sat with Corporal Hermett and his pal they began talking about Hermett's favourite topic, football! They were having a few laughs and Latham getting a bit worse for drink thought they were laughing at him. He jumped to his feet and said. "Come on Arthur lets go and duff the little creep up." He picked up a bottle from the table and as Pryce slunk to the rear of where Harper was sitting Latham confronted Harper and snarled. "Now you little creep it is your turn to visit SSQ." He then swung the bottle at the same time as Price held Harper from the rear he then hit Harper in the face with the bottle. Quick as a flash Hermett grabbed Latham by the hair and smashed his head face down on the table producing a high pitched scream from Latham. Meanwhile, his pal grabbed hold of Pryce who was trying to get away. "You bloody little coward," then he hit him right between the eyes knocking him spread eagled on his back onto a nearby table scattering drinks all over the place.

"Phone SSQ immediately somebody," Hermett shouted as he attended to an unconscious Corporal Harper and over his shoulder he yelled. "Get me a towel quickly and fetch the Orderly Sergeant."

The medics were soon on the scene and gave Harper first aid. He was then put on a stretcher. The Corporal Medic said we will take those two with us too, they need treatment."

"Sod them," snapped Hermett they can walk, get that lad away it looks serious."

"Sorry Roy I can't do that I have to treat them."

"Well treat them at Sick Quarters we will load them in the ambulance for you." With that he grabbed Latham and slung him over his shoulder like a sack of potatoes while his pal did the same with Pryce. "We will come with you," said Hermett just in case these two decide to act up."

The Medical Officer was called out and after examining Corporal Harper he sent him off in the ambulance to the local hospital for an X-Ray while he inspected Latham's and Pryce's injuries. "So you are back with us again Corporal Latham you must be accident prone, besides the enhancement to your eyes your nose is now in a sorry state. How did you manage to do that?"

"No comment."

"I am a commissioned officer Corporal and you will address me as such. I will repeat.

"How did this happen?"

"I was the worse for drink, overbalanced and fell on a table, SIR!"

"Take him into the treatment room," he said to a male nurse."

"Next!" He shouted.

In came Corporal Pryce.

"Ah, we have a strange face and a battered one to boot. Your name?

"Pryce sir, Corporal Pryce."

"Have you two been having a scrap Pryce?"

"No sir we are mates."

"Well it has been known to happen under the influence mates falling out."

"I am waiting."

"Sir?"

"For an explanation"

"Oh, this sir I had a drop too much and as I was walking between two tables some plonker got up and pushed his chair back into me causing me to lose my balance and have an argument with a table sir."

"Well done Pryce, I award you maximum points; it is the best load of bullshit I have heard for years. You are not so bad just ocular contusions."

"Eh?"

"Black eyes Corporal just black eyes and perhaps a jolt to your ego." He then went into the dispensary and returned with two tablets and a glass of water. Here you are swallow these headache pills, you will need these because you are going to suffer a double headache, one for you injury and one for your hangover. Dismiss."

"Now Corporal accident prone Latham let me have a look at that schnozzle, Jimmy Durante would be quite proud of that." He began his inspection and did some probing making Latham squirm with pain. "As I thought Corporal you will need surgery on this nose. I am sending you to the RAF Hospital for treatment. You will need your small pack with things you will need for a short stay, have you anyone who can do that for you."

"Corporal Pryce sir."

"Hmm." He then phoned the guardroom. Is the Orderly Sergeant there? This is the MO speaking."

"No sir he is at the Corporals Club investigating the fight there, but the Orderly Corporal is sir."

"He will do, put him on. Corporal I want you to contact Corporal Pryce and tell him to report at SSQs immediately he is probably in his accommodation.

My Corporal will help you formulate a list of things you will need for a short stay Corporal Latham. You can then tell Corporal Pryce where everything is. We will patch you up for the journey to make you comfortable."

"The orderly Sergeant is here sir asking to see you."

"I will see him in my office."

"Good evening Sergeant you must be here about the casualties."

"Yes sir, I am hoping you can give me some gen for my report."

"Let us start with your side of the story first Sergeant I think it is going to be very interesting."

"Corporal Latham had a personal grudge against Corporal Harper. Tonight he had the Mickey taken out of him by the Corporal Club members about his black eyes which were inflicted by Corporal Harper in a previous dispute. He plied himself with beer, got worked up then while Pryce held Harper, Latham hit him in the face with a bottle. The two Corporals who were sat with Harper retaliated for the attack. Corporal Hermett took full control of the incident by giving first aid as best as he could to Harper and organising the other Corporals in contacting sick quarters."

"Well done Corporal Hermett," said the MO.

"Latham's story was being the worse for drink, overbalanced and fell on a table.

Pryce's story takes first prize. Worse for drink and while walking between two tables a person got up, pushed his chair backwards into Pryce who overbalanced onto a table. I awarded him full points for that one."

The Sergeant grinned. "The charging officers are going to have a field day with those two sir."

"I sent Corporal Harper to the local hospital because it was an emergency. I am sending Corporal Latham to the RAF Hospital because he needs surgery on his nose. As soon as Corporal Pryce returns with his small pack I will be shipping him off. There you are Sergeant the hard work begins now with you writing out your report."

"Thank you sir, it is going to make very interesting reading. I will be placing Corporal Pryce under close arrest, is there any reason medically why I cannot do that."

"None at all Sergeant apart from a headache all he will be suffering from is a hangover."

He waited until Corporal Pryce had collected Latham's small pack and delivered it then he was approached by the orderly Sergeant "Corporal

Pryce I am placing you under close arrest for the assault on Corporal Harper. Further charges may be read out to you tomorrow, now I will accompany *you* to collect *your* small pack and essentials."

When Pryce had been placed in a cell, the Sergeant rang the Orderly Officer.

He arrived at the guardroom in a fluster. When he was told all the details he flew off at a tangent.

"Why was I not informed immediately Sergeant?"

"Because I had everything under control sir, by the time I had arrived on the scene one casualty was on his way to hospital, another was waiting transport to hospital and the third casualty suffered only bruising so I placed him under close arrest and is now sleeping off a hangover."

"But I should have been there to control things Sergeant "

"There was nothing to control sir, as I said, the casualties were whipped off immediately to SSQ where the MO took control. All I had to do was take some statements, see the MO for my report and place Corporal Pryce under arrest."

"You acted beyond your authority Sergeant and I will take this further."

"I acted within the bounds of my orders sir. The Orderly Officer would have had to be called if I could not have handled it as it states on the Orderly Sergeants Orders. Call out the Orderly Officer *only* when necessary. Sir!"

"Ah, well I may have been a little hasty Sergeant and from what you told me you have handled the situation very well. Let me know if there are any further developments."

"Very good sir" he said with tongue in cheek." He spent the next hour writing out his report.

CHAPTER 47

The following morning Tom Bridges entered the guardroom and was informed of the situation by the guard commander who he had to take over from.

When the Orderly Sergeant arrived he showed Tom his report and told him about the brush with the orderly officer.

"Well done you were in your rights; he was upset because he did not get into the act. It looks like a bit of a nasty do, Bill Barrett is not going to be too pleased losing three of his Corporals "

The O/Sergeant reported to the SWOs office to sign off his duty. He showed George his report.

"Well that is certainly nasty, how did you cope with it?"

"Alright, I had no problem until I contacted the Orderly Officer after it was all over, he took offence because I had not called him to the scene but it would have been all over before he appeared. We have to thank Corporal

Hermett for organising everything. He then told George the part Corporal Hermett had played; by the time I had arrived he had the casualties in SSQ, apart from a bit of tidying up by the remaining Corporals everything was tickety boo."

"Thanks, I will have our friend Hermett in to hear his side of the story. Then I will take this report to Wings. Get me Bill Barrett Ian."

"Bill, George here, if you come to my office I will tell you why you are three Corporals short."

"What? I am on my way George."

"Get Hermett in here Ian."

When everyone was present George said. "Now Corporal I want a blow by blow account of what happened last night and do not leave anything out."

Hermett told them in detail what had happened.

"You realise that yourself and Corporal Slinger will be the chief witnesses. From now on this incident is in the Need to Know frame. Got it?"

"Understood sir"

When he left, George remarked. "There goes a damned good Corporal. It was not a pleasant story for you was it Bill?"

"Latham was due to see Wings this morning and I am sure he was going to get the boot. He definitely is now. I am now worried about young Harper, I will get in touch with SSQ and ask them to keep me posted on his condition."

"I will go and report to Wings," said George no doubt he will want to see you later."

"Get me his PA Ian. "Corporal Macken I would like to see the Sqn.Ldr please, tell him it is very important."

"Hold the line sir." After a brief pause. "Sir, you can come right away, go straight to his office."

"Come in Mr Miller, I can only give you a few minutes I have a naughty boy to see in ten minutes."

"I think you will be cancelling that sir, he is in hospital."

"Tell me more Mr Miller what has happened to him?"

"George handed over the orderly Sergeant's report. This explains it sir."

"Sit yourself down Mr Miller while I read it." The silence was broken only with the odd tsk' and oh dear.

"That is absolutely dreadful Mr Miller. I don't suppose you know the extent of the injuries."

"No sir but if you would ring the MO he may tell you something and WO Barrett would be pleased to hear anything to the good because he is worrying about Corporal Harper."

"I will do that right away. He had a lengthy chat with the MO then thanked him.

"Corporal Harper has a broken nose and he needed eight stitches in his forehead and will be returned to our SSQ later today where he will stay for a day or two. On the other hand, Latham came off worse; he is to have surgery to repair the broken bones in *his* nose. He will remain in hospital for some time. I will take Corporal Pryce's charge this afternoon, it will give him time to recover from his hangover and let him ponder over his stupid actions. Shall we say 15:00hrs.then? I will now give Mr Barrett the good news about Corporal Harper. Between you and me Mr Miller I was recommending Corporal Latham to be discharged from the service, this incident will likely save me the trouble."

George saluted and with a "Thank you sir." Then he left.

Wings rang Bill Barrett and told him the gen on Corporal Harper and Corporal Latham.

"Can I come and see you today sir?" asked Bill

"Make it 3:30 Mr Barrett."

"I am taking a walk to have a word with the flights Viv and to give the Corporals extra responsibilities."

He spoke to Joe Franks. How did the inspection go this morning Joe?"

"No problems, everything was as it should be."

"I want one of your lads to take charge of Corporal Harper's room besides his own who do you want to nominate?"

"Corporal Bates."

"Detail him before the end of the day Joe. Corporal Powers has drawn the long straw; he takes charge of the empty dormitory. Corporals Harris and Lucas will take charge of Rooms 1 & 2 besides their own. I am going to enjoy the looks on their faces when I tell them."

He approached Alan Fell. "I would like a word with your two Corporals Alan?"

Alan called them to the front.

"You know we are now three Corporals short, therefore it is essential you Corporals have to double up concerning the barrack block rooms. Besides your own rooms, you will take over and be responsible for Room1 Corporal Harris. You Corporal Lucas will be responsible for Room 2. Be prepared for this situation to last for a little while. Rejoin your flight."

You will still inspect your original two rooms Alan; Ron York will inspect the other two."

Next was Ron York. "How are you getting on with no Corporals Ron?"

"No problem, I can manage alright and I should be able to."

"Between you and me it is a racing certainty you will be getting two replacements."

"Is it as bad as that Bill?"

"It could not be worse. You will still inspect your two rooms even though Harris and Lucas will be responsible for the cleanliness etc."

His last call was to Bob Dixon. "How are you coping Bob, any problems?"

"None at all, Corporal James has taken over Corporal Harper's role as if she has done so all the time and the flight is responding brilliantly to her."

"Bill told him the news about Corporal Harper."

"Thanks Bill that will cheer the flight up when I tell them."

"I have had to detail Corporal Bates to take charge of Harper's room so you will have to carry on with the morning inspections."

When he was some distant away he smiled when heard a cheer come from Bob Dixons's flight.

Corporal Pryce was charged with assisting another person namely Corporal Latham to viciously and brutally attack Corporal Harper whose injuries were serious enough for him to be hospitalised. Pryce pleaded guilty to the charge and was remanded for the Station Commander by Squadron Leader Cody and was to remain under close arrest until he was summoned to appear before the Station Commander.

At 3:25 Bill saw Corporal Macken, "I have an appointment with sir at 3:30.

She buzzed Wings. WO Barrett is here sir."

"Send him in Marion."

"You can go in sir."

Bill thanked her then entered on command from Wings. He saluted.

"Good to see you Mr Barrett, I can't offer you a brew because I have to fly in a few minutes," he said laughing. "That's a good one how do I get this desk airborne?"

"With great difficulty sir."

"Before we start with whatever you came for I want to tell you I have remanded Corporal Pryce for the CO. but he is still being held under close arrest. Now let us start on your problem because I have a feeling you have one."

"I require replacements for two Corporals. It is on the cards that the CO is going to give Latham and Pryce the boot because he will not tolerate that sort of behaviour on his station. With respect sir, I do not want them on my staff, therefore I am submitting a request they are replaced as soon as possible."

"Although your request is presumptuous Mr Barrett I agree with you entirely. Now we arrive at the difficult stage. March is the only recruit training station left, where do we get the replacements? They have been scattered around the service and have not had the opportunity to carry on as drill instructors. There is no-one who we could ask for recommendations, and the ones who are sent us from records will be a case of trial and error and we cannot afford to keep rejecting personnel if they do not fit in with our training qualifications."

"It is a tough one but have you any suggestions Mr Barrett?"

"I have given it a lot of thought and as you say, it is a tough one. I have thought up an idea that I personally think is the only way to solve it."

"Is there a light at the end of the tunnel Mr Barrett?"

"I am hoping there is but it will be up to you to agree and if you do, to put it to the Commandant for his blessing."

"I can but listen, carry on Mr Barrett."

"I want to go to the Records Office taking with me Sergeant Franks; his experience will be invaluable to me. At records I would want to see the records of all RAF Corporals with drill instruction experience. From their records Sergeant Franks and I will pool our knowledge to sort out the wheat from the chaff. Having done so we would want the ones we choose to attend RAF March for a mini-drill instruction course to enable us to assess their proficiency in drill instructing, responsibilities and personality. From that programme I hope to make the right choices."

"Mr. Barrett, you never cease to amaze me. I think that is a great idea and I cannot for the life in me think of anything else to better it. You have my support all the way and when I put it to the CO I am sure he will accept it. I hope to be able to give you his decision tomorrow and if he approves I will get in touch with Records Office for their approval. If they will not play ball I am sure the AOC with a request from our CO will move mountains."

Bill thanked him, saluted and made his exit. He made his way across the corridor to see Roy Shaw.

"Hello Bill, business or a friendly chat?"

"Just come to wind down a little and to have a chat with my best friend."

"It is not like it was in your pre-marital days Bill, at times I did not know if it was your office or mine. We had some laughs and I miss that now. What say we cheer ourselves up with a brew? Two teas please he shouted through the hatch."

"How is your new Corporal settling down Roy?"

"She is a treasure, they think the world of her in there and she is good at her job. Between you and me, I could learn things from her. I believe *you* are a bit short of staff, how are you coping with three of your Corporals missing?"

"Believe it or not Roy, most of the staff accept the extra responsibilities except for the few who are being forced to pull their weight." He then told of the condition of Corporal Harper and Corporal Latham and about Corporal Pryce being on remand and close arrest.

"I have just been to see Wings and we are trying to sort out the Corporal's replacement, which is awkward, with the instructors spread out around the service after they closed the other two stations down. I want to go to Records to look at the records of the Corporals who are qualified and to assess them. The ones we choose, Joe Franks and I, will come here on a course where we can assess their qualities in the field and hopefully chose the right two."

"That is a good idea Bill; I will contact my friend there and ask him if he will make himself available to you if you need any help. Ah, here comes the brew, you have not had one in here for a while have you? What are we doing Saturday any thoughts?"

"Tommy and I are going to my sisters for the weekend, we are taking the photo album for them to make their choice, we have not seen them since the wedding. Well I had better get back to my staff it will be knocking off time soon and I want to be there to see them in case they have something to say. You know I will be glad when this sad business is over and we have some fresh blood on the staff. Thanks for the brew Roy."

Wings saw the Commanding Officer and explained to him Bill Barrett's solution of getting the right type of Corporal instructors and the reason this problem had occurred.

"It is a very sound scheme Bill and I can see no reason why we cannot go ahead with it. You see, closing down two establishments has given us no backup whatsoever for replacements, we have to go searching for them ourselves, as WO Barrett suggests. After we get this problem sorted out I will call a meeting which will include WO Barrett, to find a way on how we can call on reserves as and when needed. Right, back to this problem, I will get in touch with the CO at records and explain the position we are in and our way of trying to sort it out and we would like his support. Stay where you are Bill I give him a call right now."

They greeted each other as old friends do and exchanged news of their families until the subject of the contact was brought about. When he heard all the details he sympathised that it had got to the present state due to MOD not listening to the experts and giving a knee-jerk reaction because of a fall in recruiting. "The records for the search will be put at the disposal of your men but there must be a member of my staff present during the search. If we are forewarned when they are coming that will be fine everything will be laid on for them."

"There you are Bill, everything is settled. Liaise with WO Barrett as to when he wants to go then ring records to inform them. A couple of days there should do the trick don't you think?"

"They could always extend it sir if need be."

"You had better get in touch with him right away then the sooner he can organise it the better."

As soon as he returned to his office he asked Marion to contact WO Barrett.

"You are through sir"

"Mr Barrett? Squadron Leader Cody here. I have just come from the CO and he has approved your scheme. He has been in touch with Records and as soon as you have made your plans for when you want to go, let me know because I have to confirm with them of your intended arrival."

"That is great news sir thank you; I will get things moving at this end and will contact you when we are ready to go."

"Viv, it has been sanctioned. Has Joe Franks gone yet?"

"I will have a look." She went to the door and saw Joe leaving so she shouted of him to return. "You are wanted in the office Joe."

"Sit yourself down Joe this will take quite a few minutes to tell."

He told him the whole story. I want you to come with me Joe because with your experience two heads are better than one and it should only take a couple of days."

"I think that is a good scheme especially running them through the mill here while we make our decisions. I am all for it and looking forward to it. Thanks Bill for taking me along and having faith in me. I hope I can be of use."

"Okay Joe, the first thing in the morning after your Barrack Room inspection we will make our plans."

"Come on Viv, let us get out of here and let the Corporal lock up. I will walk with you to the Mess I have to meet Tommy there."

As they were walking Viv asked. "How long do you think it will take you to choose the Corporals Bill?"

"It will take a couple of days to go through the records and make a short list. Then we have to submit a request for them to attend our selection board. Once they step into this office they will be on trial until they return to their units."

"I am going to be very interested indeed in this project Bill and I know I am going to learn a lot from it."

"How did the inspection go, everything to your satisfaction Joe."

"It was not bad at all but I had to find some little faults just to keep them on their toes."

"How about the other three did they tell you anything?"

"We were all satisfied Bill but we arranged we would find a couple of niggly little things to stop them feeling over confident. It would not do to tell them it was very good when our top marks are "It's not so bad, with room for improvement."

"Right then Joe, down to business, have you any objections if we can go on Monday?

"That suits me Bill."

"Here is what I propose. We spend two days in making a short list. Return here and hand the list over to Wings who will get the ball rolling by applying for the short list bods to attend our selection board which should last a few days if we do the job right."

"Shouldn't we have a panel of selectors who have the final say then informing the final two after they are back with their parent unit?" asked Joe.

"I have thought about that and I suggest, Wings, myself and you. Are you happy with that?"

"Definitely, said Joe with a grin."

"I will go and see Wings then he can get cracking with the arrangements."

"Can you arrange for Sergeant Franks and me to report to Records on Monday sir? we have decided it should only take two days to compile our short list."

"Then what? Mr Barrett."

"We submit the list to you to arrange for them to attend a selection course here at RAF March where we put them through various tests which will culminate in a decision being made by a selection panel consisting of yourself, me and Sergeant Franks."

"You have certainly got it planned out well Mr Barrett and I am impressed. How long do you think the processing will take?"

"I estimate it at no more than five days sir. As soon as they enter my office it starts then."

"Excellent Mr Barrett, I am looking forward to this exercise with great interest and I would like to be involved as much as possible for I have no intention of being just a figurehead. I want to learn Mr Barrett and the only way to learn is to get stuck in!"

CHAPTER 48

Corporal Pryce was standing in front of the Station Commander. He confirmed his number, rank and name. Then he pleaded guilty to the charge. The CO then addressed him. "You assisted in carrying out one of the most despicable and cowardly acts to a fellow service man I have heard and dishonoured the Royal Air Force in which you serve. Therefore I am stripping you of your rank which you have also disgraced and I am sentencing you to fifty six days in detention at Colchester Detention Centre. On completion of your sentence you will be dishonourably discharged from The Royal Air Force. March him out Mr Miller."

When George went back to his office he rang Tom Bridges at the guardroom.

"Tom. George here, Pryce has been stripped will you make sure all his uniforms are stripped and replaced with a Leading Aircraftsman badge before he is shipped off to Colchester? I will contact the clothing stores and the tailor to do a priority one job."

Meanwhile Bill Barrett had got permission for him and Sergeant Dixon to visit Corporal Harper who was in the Station Sick Bay recovering. He was delighted to see the pair of them and tried a smile. "Is that a smile to greet us or a grimace to say, oh no not you two?" asked Bill. They all had a laugh. Bob said. "The whole flight send their best wishes and for you to get back on parade because they are fed up being bossed around by a WRAF Corporal."

"That goes for all the training staff, we all want you back with us but only when you are fit enough. Now is there anything you are wanting, fruit, drinks, a nice young airwoman to come and hold your hand?

"No thanks he said laughing, besides there are a couple of nice nurses in here so don't expect me back too soon and here is one of them."

"Visiting time is over sir, sorry."

"Don't forget Corporal if there is anything you want don't be afraid to ask. See you soon." As they passed the nurse Bob whispered loud enough for the Corporal to hear "He is single and eligible."

"I can hear you Sergeant Dixon." Shouted Corporal Harper as his visitors left, laughing."

>>> <<<

Friday evening Bill and Tommy had a quick meal then set off to spend the weekend with Bill's sister Nessie and husband John after they had forewarned them they were about to set off.

"Don't you dare forget that wedding album," Nessie warned Bill, "or I will turn you round to fetch it without you getting out of your car and Tommy stays with us while you do so."

On arrival they were greeted with outstretched arms with sheer delight on their faces to see them once more.

"And before you ask dear sister, yes, we have brought it."

"Come inside you daft beggar," replied Nessie, I have the kettle on and it will take only a minute to make you your Famous Brew."

After catching up with the family news, Bill and Tommy told them of the happenings at March of how Sam Brown keeps them well supplied with fresh meats, eggs etc from the local farmers and vegetables and flowers from the station's market garden.

"Can we have a quick look now at the wedding album Tommy? asked Nessie because I would like Bill to run us to the shops tomorrow morning. John is paying a visit to the hospital to check on the progress of two of his elderly patients and he will be away for most of the morning. In the afternoon we can go through the album more thoroughly to choose the ones we would like. Is that alright with you Bill?" she asked.

"Have I got an option?" he asked.

"No!" was the answer in unison from both of the women.

John laughed. “You have a lot to learn yet Bill.”

The week end went all too quickly and soon it was time to for Bill and Tommy to be heading home. Before they left they got assurances from both John and Nessie that they would come to RAF March and spend a weekend in their married quarter and meet up again with the people they met at the wedding.

“We will look forward to that,” said Nessie as she kissed and hugged the pair of them.

>>> <<<

At Records, Bill and Joe were made welcome and were given rooms in the Sergeants Mess. They were then shown to the office where they would do their work. A Sergeant was assigned to them and was responsible for bringing the required records and their safety. The two men got down to reading and making notes of the Corporals they were interested in. By the end of the day they had covered a lot of ground.

The attending Sergeant told them. “You have got through most of the names and if you go on at this rate a couple of hours or so tomorrow should see you finished.”

They thanked him for his help and would see him at 09:00 the following morning.

On the way back to the Mess and their rooms, Bill asked. “How many have you got on your list Joe? I have five.”

“Four.”

“That is not bad you have not picked any who had just finished their instructor’s course have you?”

“No way, they have no experience.”

“When we check the remaining records we will ask for the files we want then we go through each one together. I reckon if we finish up with six or eight that should be enough for us to work with,” said Bill.

“I agree eight at the most should be a workable number.”

In the bar that evening they were having a quiet drink and chatting with a few of the Sergeant Mess members when a member came in and introduced himself as Roy Shaw’s buddy.

“I am so pleased to meet you because I have a lot to thank you for over quite a long period. You have been very helpful to me in the past and I want you to know I appreciate it. Roy sends his regards. This is a member of my staff Sergeant Joe Franks; he is my right hand man. Look, can I buy you a drink?”

“No thanks I have to pick my wife up from town, I only popped in to introduce myself. How long will you be staying?”

“We should finish tomorrow.”

"Then I won't see you again before you leave. Give Roy my best wishes and I am glad to have met you at last, your name is revered here for what you did to the Navy and Army." He shook hands with them both, "any time I can help just ask Roy."

By lunch time the following day they had ten names but after a further deep scrutiny they agreed on eight who would be asked to attend the course. After thanking everyone for their help Bill phoned Tommy at the Mess to tell her they were setting off for home and to tell Viv to get the message to Joe's wife. It was too late in the day when they arrived to report in so Bill dropped Joe off at his married quarter.

He then proceeded to his own quarter where Tommy greeted him lovingly saying.

"Get yourself cleaned up, there is a beer in the fridge then dinner should be ready."

"Good morning Mr Barrett, sit yourself down and tell me all about 'Operation Recall' as I have christened it?"

"Very appropriate sir. The treatment and assistance we received at Records was first class. We sifted through the records and short listed eight names, they are all stationed in the UK so there should be no trouble getting them here. Here is the list of names and where they are stationed at present sir."

"Having read their records Mr Barrett what are your thoughts?"

"If their personalities match their qualifications then we will have a hard job on our hands to separate them. It is so close. I would go as far to say I would not put a bet on the outcome."

"My words Mr Barrett, that statement implies the odds are evens. No bets?"

"No bets sir, it would not be fair, I would be wide open to be accused of insider dealings." They had a good laugh at that remark.

"Right then Stage Two. I will get the requests off after I have seen the CO. When do you want them to report?"

"I would like them to be offered the choice of acceptance or not. If they are not interested it would be a waste of time. I cannot visualise them all turning the offer down."

"I cannot agree with you there Mr Barrett remember these Corporals have been trained and given an instructors rank and I will not give them that option. If they think they can get out of it by not trying then they will find themselves in a lot of trouble."

"Putting it like that sir I must agree with you."

"So when do you want them to report here Mr Barrett?"

"I would like them to book in at the guard room on Sunday and to report to the Orderly Room at 09:00 Monday morning, then their course starts as soon as they set foot in my office after lunch. I will make out a list for the

SWO to instruct the duty personnel to escort each one to the empty dormitory."

"Good," said Wings. "The wheels are now in motion."

Bill then went to see George Miller to put him in the picture and gave him the list.

"So you are after new blood to replace those two idiots? If I was you I would consider changing the lot except Corporal Harper of course he is a credit to us all and I predict that he will do well."

"I think you have something there George, I will watch out for the other four and if they start similar tricks as Latham and Pryce they will not know what has hit them.

Well I will be off and have a word with Roy Shaw to put him in the picture."

"Aren't you going to tell him George?" asked Ian Roberts.

"Sorry I forgot. It concerns the market garden and Sam's future Bill."

"Don't tell me it is being closed down George."

"I will give you the bad news first Bill. "Young Bond has been posted on promotion to Gibraltar."

"So that is the end of Sam, he said if he lost Bond he could not carry on because there would be no replacement in the same mould as Bond."

"But all was not lost Bill. When the CO got to know he called Bond to his office and asked what he thought of the posting because he would be very sorry to lose him. Bond said he was not interested in either the promotion or the posting if he could stay here helping with the garden because that is the only way he would stay in the service. The CO pushed a piece of paper towards the lad saying. "Then I would like you to sign this. It means you will stay here at RAF March doing the job you are already doing." Apparently he could not sign it fast enough. He thanked the CO, who replied: "Thank you SAC Bond, you are doing this station a great service."

"Good lad," said Bill, "I bet Sam was a relieved man. There is no getting away from it, that lad has helped to transform that garden and if he left it would have to be closed down. There could be a solution you know, if Bond did leave the service and was still keen to work the garden. He could be employed as a civvy' gardener and rent somewhere in the village. That would be worth considering if and when he has to leave the service."

"Hello Bill," said Roy when Bill entered his office. "How did you get on at records did you see my pal there?"

"Yes and he sends his regards. "If I can be of any help you ask Roy he will get in touch with me."

"He is a good friend and very obliging."

Bill then told him what the arrangements were for receiving the Corporals I want them here to pick up their temporary arrival chits and to be in my office at 13:00 sharp. Can you run me up a few copies of these?" He gave him a rough copy of the stages the Corporals would be assessed on with space for the assessor's marks.

"If you would care to wait for ten minutes you can have them to take away with you that is the speed in which my staff produces the goods."

"I am sorry I can't even stop for a brew Roy I have to get back to the office to sort out their itinerary. If you like you can bring them with you tonight and save me a journey in the morning."

"What if I send them express to your office sir?"

"Now that is a thought."

"Are you coming for a drink tonight? There is a new barman on duty."

"Who is it this time?"

"Chippy, you know, Ray Snell in the Joiner's Shop, he will be a big improvement to the last one, he was pathetic."

"I will have a word with Tommy to get the girls round for a girlie evening."

As Bill entered the bar he was greeted by Roy. "You used to be here a lot earlier when you lived in."

"Sorry for being late but I do have chores to do now."

"Give him a pint quick Chippy he is bringing tears to my eyes. Just look at his hands Derwent, what do you reckon?"

"Definitely housemaid's knees!"

"You what?" said a startled Chippy. "Housemaid's knees? You have only had one pint, what do they put in this beer Roy?"

"Chippy, you may not know it but it is because we are ecctentrics….

"Don't you mean eccentrics Roy?" Corrected Bill.

"You know I can't say eccentrics. As I was saying before I was so rudely interrupted. Because we are as queer as a two pound note we have been christened the Crackpots. So whatever daft things we come out with, take no notice and if it surprises you just raise your eyebrows in sympathy."

"Do you think I will leave this bar as sane as when I took it over?" asked Chippy.

"To be honest," said Derwent. "No! But I bet you would beat Roger Bannister to the door."

"Have the entertainment committee got anything planned for the future Roy?" asked Bill.

"There is talk of a dance and of course the games evening presentations but I have no dates for you."

"Wings is looking forward to doing the honours at the prize giving, he was asking me the other day about Mess functions, he must be getting restless."

"What are we doing Saturday?" asked Derwent. "Anything special?"

“Tommy and I are going to Leeds Saturday morning with the wedding album and the orders. Have lunch and have a shufti round the shops. Then in the evening, what do you two suggest? The March Hare?”

“We have not been there for a couple of weeks I think we should go and pay our respects,” answered Roy.

“Fill em’ up Chippy and put one in for your self,” ordered Bill. “It is good to find a friendly face behind the bar again. Are you enjoying it?”

“I don’t think enjoying it fits the description Bill but it does make a change to get away from the workshop for a little while and if I can put up with you crackpots I can put up with anything.”

“He will do for us; we may even make him an honorary member,” proposed Roy.”

“Sorry Roy retorted Chippy; it would definitely be against my monastic upbringing.”

“Don’t you worry Chippy old lad,” said Derwent who was determined to get his sixpenny worth in. “We will find a cure for that.”

“Well, I must be off, sorry to leave you gentleman, I have enjoyed this little get together, you must invite me again sometime. When is the next HPC meeting?”

“Sod off Barrett, you are worse than us two.” replied Roy.

“What is this HPC?” asked Chippy.

“He hasn’t raised his eyebrows Roy,” Derwent pointed out.

“It doesn’t matter; we will tell him when he is twenty one!”

“Bloody crackpots alright,” muttered Chippy.

CHAPTER 49

Monday morning at 09:00hrs Six Corporals reported to the orderly room. Sergeant Graham read out their names from their arrival chits and handed them out saying they had to be returned before lunch then report to the recruit training office at 13:00hrs. When they left Chris called through the hatch to Roy Shaw.

“Sir, only six of those Corporals have reported in, here is the list.”

“Thanks Chris, it looks like we are going to have fun when they turn up. I will nip across and report to Wings after I have phoned Bill Barrett… Good morning Bill it is I, the bearer of good news, I don’t think. Only six of your eight Corporals have reported in. He then gave him the names of the missing two. I am now on my way to see Wings and give him the glad tidings. No doubt you will be hearing from him very soon. See you later Bill.”

He went to see Marion and asked if he could see sir right away, being of some importance.

She buzzed Wings. “Sir, WO Shaw would like to see you, he says it is of some importance.”

"Send him right in Marion."

"Good morning Mr Shaw I hope you are bringing me good news."

"Unfortunately not sir, only six of the eight Corporals have reported in, here is the list."

"Well, well, well. They are starting off on the wrong foot, looks like it is wrist slapping time Mr Shaw or worse. I will contact Mr Barrett and invite him for a Powwow."

"I took the liberty sir of putting him in the picture."

"Thank you Mr Shaw, can we expect him to appear firing from the hips?"

"Not until he confronts them, then I think they will be lucky to survive."

"Marion, ask WO Barrett if he will come and see me." Thank you Mr Shaw."

When Bill arrived he was told to take a pew. "This was not foreseen Mr Barrett and I take a very dim view of it."

"Me too sir, if they have not got an official reason for not reporting in I shall cross them off the list altogether classing them as unreliable. I cannot understand why they did not phone in to say they would be late or something. My gut feeling tells me all is not what it should be."

"That feeling has never let you down yet Mr Barrett and I will go along with that. When they do turn up I would like you to be here when I question them."

"That will be a pleasure sir."

"Then can I expect to see fireworks?"

"Just rockets sir."

>>> <<<

Joe Franks reported to the office to sit with Bill to help assess the six Corporals

"The six Corporals are outside Bill," reported Viv.

"If you are ready Joe, call in Corporal Anders Viv."

The Corporal marched in smartly and stood to attention as he announced his name.

"At ease Corporal. Have you any idea why you are here?"

"Sir, this is the only recruit training establishment left and I think you are short of instructors. I have been lucky to have been pulled out of the hat and I am here to prove I have the qualifications to fill an empty position."

"Do you think you can fill the post?"

"Yes sir, but you have the last word in that respect."

"There are just two positions to be filled and there are six of you to choose from."

"Then they will have to beat me sir."

"Report here at 09:00 tomorrow and as you leave do not contact the other five until they have been interviewed."

"Thank you sir for giving me the opportunity to get back to doing the job I was trained for."

"What do you think Joe?"

"I am impressed, he is clean, smart and sounds intelligent and he does not waffle, he gets my vote."

"Send Corporal Benson in please Viv."

He marched in and stamped his feet to attention which shook the room.

Bill looked at him, paused and asked. "Name"?

"Benson, Corporal Benson."

"Have you any idea why you are here Corporal?"

"No sir."

"I have two vacancies to fill from you six; do you think you have a chance to get one of them?"

"I don't know sir, I have no idea what will be expected of me."

"You are a qualified drill instructor that is what I want among other things."

"What are the other things, sir?"

"Tell me, what you are like managing airmen away from the barrack square. In the barrack rooms for instance are you in charge of any barrack rooms?"

"Yes sir, I supervise them on a bull night and the rest of the time they are left to their own devices."

"What for instance if there is any kind of bullying in the dormitory, what do you do about it.?"

"I let them sort it out amongst themselves they are old enough."

"And if they have any complaints, do you help them out?"

"No way, I am not a nursemaid, I send them to their SNCO he is in charge overall."

"Thank you Corporal on your way out do not confer with your colleagues until I have interviewed them and report here at 09::00hrs tomorrow."

"Yes sir."

"Well Joe?

"No way will that man fit in here, he may be a good instructor but I think it ends there."

"Send Corporal Deacon in please Viv."

A smart entrance was made by Corporal Deacon, coming quietly to attention as he gave his name.

"At ease Corporal "Do you know why you are here?"

"I surmise sir it is to select a replacement for one of your staff."

"You are right Corporal except I want two replacements and I have you six to pick from. What I have read in your records you are a good instructor. How good an Admin' Corporal are you?"

"My barrack block comprises of four dormitories with a Corporal in charge of each one including myself. As the senior Corporal I am responsible for the whole block and the only complaints I have had on an inspection morning have been minor ones. I pride myself on being firm but fair with the airmen in my charge and I find that they respond sir."

"Thank you Corporal report back here tomorrow morning at 09:00hrs. On your way out do not confer with the other Corporals until they have been interviewed."

"Thank you sir"

"Well?"

"It looks like we have got another potential winner Bill, he too gets my vote. Those two are going to be a hard act to follow."

"Send in Corporal Farrow Viv."

He marched in firmly and without the loud stamping of feet as per Corporal Benson.

"Have you any thoughts on why you are here Corporal?"

"I think you need replacements sir to fill gaps."

"I have read your records Corporal and I note you are very proficient in you job as an instructor. How long have you been qualified?"

"Four years sir."

"Then you must be one of the most senior Corporals in the business."

"I would think so sir."

"What age are you?"

"Twenty five sir"

"Married?"

"Yes sir with one two year old daughter."

"What is your present employment now that you are out of instructing?"

"I am on the Station Warrant Officer's Staff sir and he uses me to drill the airmen when we have a Station Commanders Parade and an AOC's inspection. So I am actually keeping my hand in for what I was trained for."

"Are you interested in filling one of my vacancies Corporal?"

"Indeed I am sir."

"Thank you Corporal report here at 09:00hrs. tomorrow and as you leave do not confer with the other Corporals until they have been interviewed."

"Thank you sir"

"There goes the third contender Bill, the choice is going to be very difficult but at the moment he tops my list."

Corporal Young had very little experience with airmen off the parade ground and was prone to be misled by senior Corporals.

Corporal Norton was of the instant obedience kind who showed little concern for airmen on and off parade.

"That is the wheat sorted out from the chaff Joe. Benson, Young and Norton will get their marching orders tomorrow to return to their units for failing to qualify at the interview. Are you in agreement Joe?"

"Without any doubt Bill, according to their records they all topped the list as instructors but as NCOs, those three were rock bottom."

"Now the hard part is separating the other three, I would like to keep all three. I will go and report to Wings of my findings.

Corporal Macken, I would like to have a word with sir if at all possible."

"Hold the line sir I will give him a buzz....The Squadron Leader will see you right away, go straight in sir."

"Thank you Marion."

"Come right in Mr Barrett and tell me about it."

Bill told him the tale that he wanted three of the Corporals to carry on and the remaining three returned to their units. He explained the reasons and said. "There is no way I could use that threesome sir. To be fair, I cannot question their instruction skills but as NCOs they are rubbish."

"Very well, tell them to report to me at 09:00hrs. tomorrow. I gather you are pleased with the other three."

"I am indeed sir only they have set me a problem, who am I going to reject? Each one meets my criteria."

"I would like to make a suggestion Mr Barrett. To separate them we must find them another exercise which will be foreign to them and I have the very one. Give each one an hour drilling the WRAF flight, after that another hour each drilling the mixed flight. To do the judging I suggest we call on WO Butcher and Sergeant Dixon, he will judge the mixed flight."

"Now why did I not think of that?"

"A word of advice Mr Barrett, take a mini-crash course with my training staff." He then licked his forefinger and drew an imaginary line downwards saying. "That's one up for me Mr Barrett," he said with a big grin on his face.

"I concede sir."

"I would like you to be present when I carry out the interview in case they want to question you on the subject."

"No problem sir, I will be here."

On his way back to his office Bill called at the Barrack Block housing the six Corporals.

On entering he followed the sound of whooping and cheering coming from one of the dormitories. He paused at the half open door to see Corporals scrambling on the floor using a pillow as a rugby ball. A Corporal who was relaxing on his bed with a book saw Bill at the doorway and jumped to his feet immediately. The remainder looked round then jumped to their feet looking very sheepish.

"Corporal Benson!"

"Sir."

"Corporal Norton!"

"Sir."

"Corporal Young!"

"Sir."

"Report to Squadron Leader's Office at 09:00hrs tomorrow morning and for tomorrow morning's accommodation inspection this room will shine like a new pin!" He then turned on his heels and walked out then made his way to see Joe Franks training his flight.

When Joe saw him he came over. "Is everything alright Bill?"

"I came to tell you that there has been a change of plans in the selection Joe. You know as well as me that to try and separate those three by testing their instructing ability would be a waste of time and effort but Wings has come up with an idea. They will each do an hour drill instructing with the WRAF flight followed by an hour drill instructing with the mixed flight with Mary Butcher and Bob Dixon doing the assessing. They will make out a report on each Corporal for us then it will be our job to reject one of them."

"A good idea that Bill it will save a lot of unnecessary drilling and we should be able to pick the odd man out from that."

"Roy, Tom Bridges here, the two missing Corporals have just reported in where do you want them?

"Put them in transit for the time being Tom until we sort them out, they are not the flavour of the month with Squadron Leader Cody and Bill Barrett at the moment, I think they will only be staying the night, tell them to report to the orderly room. Thanks Tom."

Sergeant Graham was in Roy's office when the two Corporals entered the orderly room. Seeing the only NCOs present were Corporal Barton and Corporal (w)Springs they began wolf whistling. The duty clerk went to attend to them but they insisted on the WRAF Corporal attending to them.

"Leave this to me Andy," she said as she saw him rising from his chair.

"What's your name gorgeous?" she was asked.

"Corporal Springs."

"Well spring to it and sign us in," one of them demanded and if you are a good girl I will take you out on a date."

"I don't date slobs... Now let me sign you in then get out of here."

"And who do you think you are calling slobs? One said poking a finger at her.

Quick as a flash she grabbed his finger and bent it backwards causing him to scream with pain.

Roy and Chris heard the scream and looked through the hatch to see what was going on. When they saw the Corporal writhing in agony Chris motioned Roy to just watch.

"Now who is being a naughty boy?" asked Alice in a nice calm voice. Then changing her tone she snarled. "Try that on again with me and I will break your finger," as she gave it another twitch for good measure.

The other Corporal leaned over to try and make her release her grip saying. "Take your hands off my mate."

"Very coolly she released him then quickly grabbed the other guy's arm and dragged him face down on the counter top. Then in an icy voice she spoke in his ear.

"It would take one wrong blink of your eyelid and I could break your arm. Now get up and be good a good little boy because my boss will want a word with the pair of you." As she released him the pair began to bad mouth her.

"You can come in now sir."

When Roy and Chris walked in there was looks of panic on both their faces.

"We saw and heard everything that happened Corporal if you want to press charges I will put them under close arrest immediately."

"Their pride will hurt more sir. I suggest doing what teachers do to naughty children by making them face the wall but I will sign them in first."

There were shouts of approval from the rest of the staff.

She then addressed them. "Your names!?"

"Corporal Ingham."

"Corporal Robinson."

"They are all yours sir."

Roy snarled at them to face the wall, at attention.

"I will now go and report to Squadron Leader Cody."

"I would like to see the Squadron Leader right away Marion if that is possible."

She buzzed Wings. "Sir, WO Shaw would like to see you."

"Okay Marion send him in."

"Mr. Shaw I see a hint of a smile, good news I hope?"

"Yes and no sir. The two Corporal absentees have turned up and I have had them accommodated in transit." He then told him the whole incident that happened in the orderly room.

"Wings curled up laughing. Mr Shaw that is priceless, the best laugh I have had for a long time. It appears your Corporal (w)Springs is not a lady to be messed about with. Well done her, give her my congratulations for sorting out two would be bullies. Marion, ask WO Barrett to report in please. He is going to love this scenario Mr Shaw."

When Bill arrived he was surprised to see Roy there.

"Come on Mr Shaw," Wings said laughing, "Tell your friend the story of the damsel who was definitely not in distress."

Roy recounted the tale to Bill who immediately burst out laughing. "That is unbelievable. We are going to enjoy this interview sir."

"We certainly are but they are not. March them in Mr Shaw I am ready for them and I would like them facing me and not the wall."

Roy marched them in facing Wings as requested. "Do not leave WO Shaw, I would like you to stay." He then addressed the two Corporals "Names!?"

"Corporal Ingham, sir."

"Corporal Robinson, sir."

"You two should have reported for duty here yesterday. You are one day late and therefore you were absent without leave. What have you got to say for yourselves?"

They both had the same answer. "We were told we had to report today sir."

"But you are serving on different stations. I have six other Corporals all from different stations who reported in on time. Why is it that you two should be different?"

"That is what we were told sir."

"Who by?"

"Our orderly rooms sir."

"I want the names of the persons who gave you that order."

They were taken aback by that request and began to splutter and stammer incoherently.

"Now why do I have a gut feeling that you are telling me Porky Pies? Think hard of what I am about to say. You *will* tell me the truth or I will put you both in the slammer until you do and I want an immediate answer. You Ingham, NOW!"

"We palled up when we were on the same unit sir and got very friendly with a couple of the local girls. Last weekend was one of the girls' birthday and we spent the week end with them. It was too late when we realised we had gone past the point of no return and decided that we may as well be hung as a sheep than a lamb."

"That just might be the case Ingham."

"Is that your story too Robinson?"

"To a point sir, I was ready to come away but Ingham insisted on us staying."

"As the old saying goes there is no honour amongst thieves. Yet you still stayed Robinson, the flesh is certainly weak."

"What I cannot understand, you two were chosen along with six other Corporals because all of you according to your records are very good drill instructors. Unfortunately your Admin' ability where airmen are concerned makes you both brain dead. You have just proved that by your loutish behaviour towards a WRAF Corporal in the orderly room. She showed and proved just what you really are; naughty little boys and you will regret tangling with her for a long time to come. Tomorrow morning you will leave RAF March as fast as you can back to your parent unit and do not be surprised when you are called to answer for your actions here. If you do not understand that I will simplify it. Charge sheets will be forwarded to your respective units. Have you anything further you would like to add WO Barrett?"

"Only disgust sir."

"WO. Shaw?"

"Only to thank Corporal (w) Springs for proving how to turn these so called Macho men into whimpering slobs."

"Have you two got your own transport?"

"Yes sir."

"Then do not delay you departure until tomorrow, I want you off this station right NOW. Get out!"

Marion, get me the guardroom please."

"Guard room Flight Sergeant Bridges."

"Flight Sergeant Bridges? Squadron Leader Cody here. Corporals Ingham and Robinson who are in transit I have ordered them off the station with immediate affect. Please will you ensure they do leave without delay?"

"It will be my pleasure sir."

"Well gentlemen, that was a pleasure to do, I hope someone follows up my report in the charge sheets and get rid of those two bad eggs."

"You did fine sir," said Bill, "there was nothing else I could have added you said it all."

"I am learning Mr Barrett, I am learning."

"I have a gut feeling you are also learning to pinch other peoples quotes as well, Squadron Leader," said Roy.

That remark caused a laugh.

"I am sorry Mr Barrett but it just slipped out."

"I don't mind, they might earn you a pint in your Mess."

"That was a good day's work gentlemen, thank you for your support; it is comforting to know it is always there."

09:00hrs the following morning Bill Barrett marched into SHQ to see the three Corporals lined up outside Wings' office. "Good morning sir," they chorused upon seeing him.

"Good morning. "You are chewing Benson, get rid."

"I have nowhere to put it sir."

Bill asked Marion Macken for a scrap of paper.

"Here you are put it in this and you ought to have more damned sense. Now smarten yourselves up and who gave you permission to slash those peaks? Do you fancy yourselves as guardsmen or summat?"

"It helps to show more authority over the recruits sir."

"It makes you look more like bloody idiots. Besides, you do not drill recruits any more so who are you trying to impress, your mirror?"

He knocked on the door of Wings' office.

"The three Corporals are here sir."

"Wheel em' in Mr Barrett"

Bill marched them in. "Corporals Benson, Young and Norton sir."

"Stand at ease. I do not know if you will be disappointed in what I have to say but you have not been accepted as one of our replacements. Therefore you will return to your parent units after being cleared from this station. To put you in the picture and a view for you to do something about it I will tell you the reason for non-acceptance. From your records each of you was chosen to attend this interview because you are good instructors and I find that commendable but we are not looking for just that. We want NCOs who can act and carry out all NCO's duties especially with airmen in their charge. In your job your rank as a Corporal is known as a protection rank to give you some authority over recruits. All the same you are still classed as NCOs but it does not stop there you still have responsibilities to airmen whatever their trade when you are in charge of them. It is sad to say but each of you come nowhere near to reaching that criteria and if you want to make a career of the service then you have a lot of thinking to do otherwise some of these lowly airmen will pass you by on the promotion ladder.

Have you any questions you would like to ask of me or WO Barrett?"

"Yes sir," said Corporal Benson. We have had no chance to show our skill on the parade ground."

"As I said at the beginning Corporal, if you had paid attention. Your skill as instructors was never in question it was your mental attitude towards airmen away from the parade ground that failed you and here at RAF March the well being of our recruits is paramount."

"Any other questions?

"Good, now go to the orderly room to collect your clearance chits. Dismiss."

"I hope that is the last we see of any more undesirables Mr Barrett. You know I keep thinking of that young female Corporal taking on those two lads, she certainly has guts."

"Excuse me asking sir but have you put WO Butcher and Sergeant Dixon in the picture as to what you want them to do regarding those three Corporals?"

"Thanks for reminding me Mr Barrett I had forgotten. Marion, tell WO Butcher I would like to see her when it is convenient."

"I will be off now sir, it is time for my brew, I am getting withdrawal systems. Do you want me to send Sergeant Dixon to you?"

"Sorry about that Warrant, we do not seem to have time these days for an informal chat with a brew. Don't worry, when you hear the call, hit the ground running and you can put Sergeant Dixon in the picture."

Bill left laughing.

CHAPTER 50

The selection committee was in situ in Wings' office and the three Corporals were outside in the corridor waiting a little nervously for their fate.

"Shall we have them in all together to tell them gentlemen or would you rather they were heard individually?"

Bill and Joe both agreed on them being together.

"That was my decision too," said Wings. Bring them in Sergeant Franks."

The three marched in very smartly and saluted.

"At ease gentlemen," ordered Wings.

"We three want to congratulate you on the way you have presented yourselves during your stay with us. You are a credit to your rank and a credit to the service and you have given us one big bloody headache trying to separate you." That brought smiles and a laugh from the Corporals.

"It is unfortunate that we can only take two of you on our staff but to the one of you who we cannot take at present I will tell you this in front of these witnesses. You have my word that the first opportunity a post needs to be filled on my staff you will be at the top of the list. I cannot be fairer than that and I hope you will accept that in good faith. You will all receive a notification of your result."

Wings then got up from his chair, walked round to the Corporals and shook each one by the hand saying. "Well done."

Bill and Joe followed suit. Bill told them to report to the orderly room for clearance.

The Corporals saluted Wings and said their thanks.

"There go our replacements gentlemen. Our final reports clinched it for us because we each voted for them in the same order Farrow, Deacon and Anders. Is that going to put a smile back on your face Mr Barrett?"

"It would have been a bigger smile if I could have had all three sir."

"Patience Mr Barrett is what I was taught at drill instructor training! When I get a problem concerning my training staff I look at my little statuette for inspiration and say to myself. 'Wings' that is why you were awarded this trophy. You both look gob smacked gentlemen. I have known about 'Wings' for quite some time and I would like to thank you because it could have been a damned sight worse."

They had a good laugh about it and Joe said. "That is the respect we have for you sir and you have well and truly earned it."

“The next stage is to get the applications in for the transfer of Farrow and Deacon. Farrow is a married man and will need a married quarter Mr Barrett.”

“I will go to see WO Shaw and arrange that and with the co-operation of Mr Hardcastle a quarter will be ready for him to sign for when he arrives.”

“Excellent. Thank you gentlemen.”

They saluted then left the office.

Joe returned to his flight while Bill went to see Roy.

“Nice to see you Bill, are you ready for a brew?”

“Aye, I am always ready I am getting as bad as George Miller for brews.”

“Two teas and bickies please,” Roy shouted through the hatch.

Bill told him about the selection of the Corporals and the applications for their posting.

“He would like you to get a married quarter organised for Corporal Farrow.”

“That is no problem,” replied Roy.

“I will tell you summat’ else Roy. That crafty young devil has known for some time we call him Wings and he is quite chuffed about it.”

“How the heck has he found that out? I mean no-one has slipped up when he has been present at anytime as far as I know but you can bet he won’t tell us.”

”Why is it Roy that when everything is running smoothly we suddenly we get a run of spanners being thrown in the works?”

“That is just the way that fate treats us Bill, one minute we are up and the next minute we are down, life gets cruel and I suppose it is a way of telling us to not take things for granted and over confident. Now that we have had a purge forced upon us by bad apples are we going to fall back into the way of thinking that things surely cannot go wrong now and then get kicked in the teeth again. We may not get kicked in the teeth Bill but we had better protect our backsides.”

“Roy, you amaze me I had no idea you were a student of philosophy. When it comes down to the nitty gritty you are certainly no dum-dum.”

“Bill please you are embarrassing me, that is just one of my many accomplishments!”

“Roy, I bow to your knowledge but I must leave you before I puke.”

“Get out of here you miserable cretin, no more hospitality for you my lad. Are you coming for a drink tonight?”

“If I am allowed after finishing my chores,” he said laughing.

“HPC” retorted Roy.

Bill saw that Jackie was on duty when he arrived at reception in the Sergeants Mess to have a word with Tommy.

“Hello Bill I have not seen you for a day or two have you been busy?

"More likely frustrated Jackie. I am hoping I may get out tonight for a drink with the boys."

"I heard that Bill Barrett," spoke Tommy as she arrived on the scene. I suppose I am to stay home twiddling my fingers while you go out enjoying yourself with the boys. As a matter of fact I have just had a phone call from your partner in crime asking me, "Can your Bill play out tonight Mrs Barrett?"

"What is that man like?" asked Bill. "I told him only if I was allowed after finishing my chores."

Jackie could not stop laughing.

"That Jackie is why they are called the crackpots. Why don't you come home with me when you stand down I will rustle up something to eat and then run you home when you want to go."

"That would be nice Tommy thank you, I can keep you company while Bill is playing out."

"Well spoken Jackie," laughed Tommy, "That is a good one."

"Wait while I see that Roy Shaw I'll give him playing out!" Bill said pretending to be angry.

>>> <<<

As Bill walked through the ops' room he called Sergeant York to come in his office.

"Ron, be honest with me, can you manage for another week or so on your own without Corporals? Because I can get one from one of the other flights to step in for the time being."

"I can manage quite well Bill and personally the ones we have left would not fit in with my methods. I am doing fine and I have no problems with my recruits."

"Now for the good news Ron, we have made our decision with the Corporals we are keeping and they both will join your flight and I can tell you that you have got a couple of crackers. We could not fault them in any way. One of them, Corporal Farrow will be moving into quarters when he arrives. The rejected Corporal will definitely be filling the next vacant post."

"I will be looking forward to meeting them Bill it could be the making of a great team."

When Ron left, Viv came in. "I have just seen a happy smiling Sergeant come out of your office, what have you done given him a pay rise?"

"Better than that Viv, he has got two excellent Corporals joining his flight in a matter of days. Corporal Farrow who will move into quarters and Corporal Deacon who is single and will live-in. Corporal Anders will fill our next vacant slot."

“I have some news for you,” said Viv, Corporal Harper is reporting sick tomorrow morning to ask if he can come off light duties, he wants to get back to his flight.”

“It will be nice to see the lad back Viv; I reckon Bob Dixon has missed him. Talking of news, you will never believe this. Our beloved Squadron Leader has known for some time that we call him Wings.”

Viv gave a gasp. “How on earth has he found out Bill?”

“Dunno’ and I don’t think he will tell.” He then proceeded to tell her how it came to light. “It came right out of the blue, Joe and I were speechless. He intended to give us a shock I’m convinced on that and he succeeded. When we call him sir now, you can see a twinkle in his eye. Come on Viv, it is time to shut up shop, I will walk you to the Mess because I have to pick Tommy up.”

>>> <<<

A signal was received at RAF March from the RAF Hospital stating that Corporal Latham was being discharged and returned to his parent unit. Wingco’ Pilling informed the Medical Officer that Latham would be sent to SSQ under escort on arrival for an immediate medical examination to ascertain if he would be fit enough to be accommodated in the guardroom under close arrest. He then contacted Flight Sergeant Bridges of the RAF Police and told him to provide an escort for Corporal Latham to the SSQ immediately on arrival and to stay with him until further orders from me through the M.O.

The driver of the transport carrying Corporal Latham reported to the guardroom, as he was doing so Corporal Latham left the vehicle and was walking away but was spotted by Tom Bridges. He called after him. “Where do you think you are going Corporal?”

“To my billet Flight.”

“In here! and be quick about it. Why have you not booked in?”

“I thought the driver was doing that Flight.”

“You know damned well you have to book in personally, the driver came for a signature to hand *You* over to *Me*! Don’t you come the old soldier with me Corporal or you and me are going to fall out with each other.” Tom then gave the grinning driver his signature then he drove off back to his unit.

“Pick up your small pack Corporal we have a date with the MO.”

“It is not necessary Flight I was discharged fit for duty.”

“I am very pleased to hear that Corporal because that means you and I are going to see a lot more of each other. Now pick up your small pack and consider yourself a very lucky lad because you have got me as an escort. Now Quick March to SSQ.”

Tom Bridges reported in to SSQ and the duty Medic informed the MO that Corporal Latham had reported in under escort.

"Take him into the examination room and I will be with you directly." He asked Tom Bridges had he any instructions appertaining to Corporal Latham.

"Only that I had to stay with him and wait for further orders from the Wing Commander via yourself sir. Incidentally, Latham said your examination was not necessary because RAF Hospital had discharged him fit for duty."

"Thanks Flight Sergeant I will go and see if his looks have been improved.

Welcome back Corporal accident prone Latham and how are you feeling? Any aches or pains?"

"No sir I feel fine, they did a great job of re-setting my nose."

"Let's have a look at it then." He did a very thorough examination and was satisfied with it. So you are now looking forward to getting back into harness are you?"

"I certainly am sir."

"Well from my examination I can say you are fit for duty.

"Thank you sir that is a relief."

"Stay there for a few minutes and relax."

He then rang the Wingco' and told him the result of his examination and that he was fit for duty.

"Excellent, inform the escort."

"It is Flight Sergeant Bridges sir."

"Better still, put him on I want to speak with him."

"Flight Sergeant Bridges sir."

"Flight, I want Corporal Latham putting under close arrest, will you accommodate him in one of your suites in the guardroom? He will be charged with causing grievous bodily harm to Corporal Harper. He will be attended to tomorrow."

"Very good sir"

"I have to place him under close arrest sir." he told the MO.

"Come on then Flight I want to be there when you tell him the good news."

"Corporal Latham," said Tom. "Under direct orders from Wing Commander Pilling you will be charged with causing grievous bodily harm to Corporal Harper and I am instructed to place you under close arrest." He then gave him the official caution.

"I should have really done the little creep over while I was at it, he won't get away with it I will see to that. They might sling me out but I have got friends still serving."

"Flight Sergeant Bridges I am witness to that outburst. Get him out of here!" exclaimed the MO.

Corporal Latham was duly placed in a cell to wait being called on to answer to the charge.

"If anybody wants me," said Tom Bridges to his Corporals, "I will be in the SWO's Office."

"Hello Tom, we don't often see you over here, what can we do for you?" asked George Miller.

"I thought you might be interested in our new occupant in suite one. Corporal Latham!"

He then told the tale and also the outburst in SSQ.

"He is a nutter," said George, I can see him getting banged up and the key thrown away. I do not know what gets into these lads nowadays Tom. Everything was running smoothly for Bill Barrett then as soon as he reminds them of their NCOs' responsibilities they cannot accept it. They just want the rank but not the responsibilities that go with it. If Latham had ideas of making a career in the service he has definitely waved that goodbye. This station will soon be getting a bad name after sending five bods to Colchester in just over a month and Latham will be the sixth."

"When all is said and done George, we have got rid of a lot of wrong uns' which has done the service a good turn and I applaud those responsible for their dismissal. Well I will get back to the guardroom and see if any tranquilisers are needed."

"You can borrow my size nine boots to give him a good kick up the backside Tom."

"I can do better than that George, mine are size ten! I will be seeing you," he left laughing.

"Bill," said Roy over the phone. "I have some good news for you, Corporals Farrow and Deacon report in on Monday."

"Thanks Roy that is good news I will start making arrangements to receiving them."

He went into the ops' room and told Viv. "If I am wanted I will be in the SWO's office."

George welcomed him with. "Hello Bill, have you come on business or is it social?"

"Official business George, I have two Corporal replacements coming on Monday and I want Corporal Latham's bunk for one of them. I hear he is in close arrest and it is a pound to a pinch of.... he will end up in Colchester. Is there a chance he can be made to move his gear to the empty dormitory which will be only temporary and also made to clean the bunk thoroughly before he hands over the key?"

"That should be no problem Bill; I will see Tom Bridges who will see to that. What about the other bunk which was ex-Corporal Pryce's? That is empty as well."

"Corporal Farrow will be moving into Quarters within a few days so it would be pointless him moving in there, I suggest he may as well stay in transit it would only be for the odd couple of nights at the most."

"Yes, I see your point. I will speak to Tom it will please him to give that nutter summat' to do. I will let you know when it has been done Bill. I had better get on with it right away because his charge will be coming up very soon and we want that bunk cleaned before he goes off to his Holiday camp."

"Some Holiday Camp. He won't know what hits him because as you know once he puts a foot inside the gates he will start doubling up and will not stop until he steps back out through those gates on his release. Anyway, thanks George I'll be seeing you."

Tom Bridges told his Police Corporal. "Get the prisoner out here, give him his belt shoe laces and tie. I want to see him properly dressed."

When this was carried out it he addressed Corporal Latham. "I have a little job for you Corporal I am sending one of my Corporals with you and I want you to clear all your belongings from your bunk then you will give it a very good clean for the next occupant. You will clean it because I shall inspect it and if it is not cleaned properly you will continue to clean it until I am satisfied it is fit to live in. You will then take your gear and use a locker in the empty corridor in the next barrack block to store it. Do you understand?"

"Yes Flight."

"Yes what?"

"Yes Flight Sergeant."

"That is more like it. March him away Corporal "

After Corporal Latham had completed his task to the satisfaction of the Corporal escort and deposited his gear in a locker in the empty dormitory he was being marched back towards the guardroom at the same time as Sergeant Dixon was marching his flight off the parade ground. When the escort realised this he diverted his prisoner away to avoid Latham seeing Corporal Harper. Latham had other ideas, as soon as he saw Corporal Harper it was like seeing a red rag. "Harper," he screamed out loud and ran towards him. The escort chased after him shouting, "Harper, Harper, watch out its Latham." Harper turned and saw a furious Latham running towards him mouthing obscenities. He waited until Latham was almost on him then calmly side stepped, stuck out his foot tripping Latham who fell sprawling to the ground. The escort leaped onto Latham and put him in an arm lock while he was still on the ground mouthing to let me get at him as the escort kept telling him to calm down. Sergeant Dixon halted his flight to see if he could help the escort. At the same time George Miller who had been going to SHQ saw what was happening and came running over.

"Okay Sergeant I will see to this you march your flight off." Then as he helped the escort to get Latham to his feet he saw that he was bleeding from the grazes to his face and hands. "Right it is to the Sick Quarters for you m'lad. Prisoner and escort Atten…shun! Quick March!"

When the M.O. saw who it was he said, "Welcome home Corporal accident pro Latham, what is your excuse this time?" When he got no answer he thrust his face close to Latham's and repeated his question in a commanding voice. I said, what is your excuse this time and I do not want any more of your fairy stories."

"I was tripped up on the parade ground sir."

"Who by?"

"Corporal Harper sir."

"That figures, you will never learn Corporal you will never learn." He then told a medical orderly to take him into the treatment room and "Treat this poor Tommy's wounds."

"Stay with him," George told the escort.

"What happened Mr Miller?"

George told what he had seen. "I don't think he will be troubling us for long now sir he has dug himself a big hole he cannot get out of."

"I'm afraid you are right Mr Miller and because of his behaviour I can foresee a psychologist being called in. I will have a word with the escort and find out what triggered it off before you saw the incident. I want to report to Wing commander Pilling with a full story."

"I will go and relieve him in the treatment room and send him to you sir."

The Corporal escort gave the M.O. the details of what happened.

When Corporal Latham had been treated, the M.O. told George he had got what he wanted from the escort. "You can now take him away Mr Miller."

"Prisoner and escort fall in outside. To the guardroom Quick March." On arrival there Latham was deprived of his belt, shoelaces and tie then shown to his cell. George told Tom Bridges about the incident and the quick response by the escort.

"The M.O. reckons Latham will end up seeing a trick cyclist and if he does not end up on a funny farm I will be very surprised."

The M.O. went to see the Wingco' and told him what had happened and gave his thoughts on the subject.

"From your account Doc' it certainly looks like he needs treatment. We had better see the C.O. and get his ruling. Barbara, will you get myself and the M.O. an appointment to see the Commanding officer right away please?"

"You can go immediately sir."

"Come in Eric, Doc', sit down and tell me what the problem is."

Wingco' began. "You know we have Corporal Latham under close arrest sir, I will hand over to Doc' to tell his side of the story."

Once again Doc' told his story and his thoughts on the subject."

"I agree entirely with you Doc' the lad needs an intensive examination and until we get a report on that we cannot proceed with any disciplinary action. Get in touch with the RAF Hospital and state your case they will then take over. I suggest an escort of two to transport him to the hospital in case he becomes unstable. Then gentlemen we have to just sit back and wait for their verdict."

Within an hour of the M.O. ringing the hospital Corporal Latham and his escort of two RAF policemen were on their way.

CHAPTER 51

Corporals Farrow and Deacon booked in at the guardroom and were given transit accommodation for the night. The following day being a Monday they reported to the orderly room. They were handed arrival chits and they began their tour of the station to receive signatures from the sections which were applicable. They were greeted warmly at the training office by Bill Barrett.

"Corporal Deacon, you will move into No1Cpls. Bunk after handing in your arrival chit. Corporal Farrow report to WO Shaw in the orderly room he will arrange for you to take over a Married Quarter. Just a minute, I will find out the arrangements for you." He then rang Roy. "Roy, what is the gen on Corporal Farrow getting a quarter?"

"Tomorrow morning, I will get the time from Tom Hardcastle. How is that for service?"

"It is only what I can expect from the one who controls from the hub of the station. Thanks Roy, I owe you one AGAIN! You can take over a quarter tomorrow Corporal. When you return to the orderly room with your chit, see WO Shaw and he will give you the time for the take over. When that is completed you have my permission to take a few days off to bring your wife and family to their new home and I want you back here for duty next Monday morning. I suggest you tell your wife to inform MOD you want to hand over your present quarter."

"Thank you very much sir, the wife will not believe it when I tell her."

Bill then signed their arrival chits. "You Corporal Deacon will report here for duty tomorrow morning. I will see that the bunk key will be left inside for you and you will be in charge of No.1 dormitory."

"Excuse me sir, but dormitories one and two do they accommodate Sergeant Yorks' flight?"

"Yes."

"Then Corporal Farrow would have moved in there had he lived in."

"He would Corporal Deacon, what is on your mind."

"Corporal Farrow, myself and the occupants of dormitories one and two make up Sergeant Yorks' flight. If I took over the two rooms there would be no interference from the Corporals of the other flights therefore giving me full responsibility of them away from the parade ground."

"Are you volunteering to take on that responsibility Corporal?"

"I am sir, and could I hold the key to that spare Corporal's Bunk?"

"Why would you want that Corporal?"

"I can use it to store the cleaning materials for the airmen. I have experienced rooms running short of materials prematurely while others have not got that problem. It's called 'raiding parties' sir."

"You certainly know the ropes Corporal and I am impressed."

"It comes with experience sir."

"Good, you have my permission to become NCO i/c Rooms one and two and I will see you get the other key."

He called Flight Sergeant Anderson. "Viv, will you get one of your staff to tell Corporals Harris and Lucas to report to me?"

When they arrived he told Harris to go now and open up No.1 bunk and to leave the key inside. "You are now relieved of the responsibility of the dormitory, our new Corporal Deacon is taking over but I want you to fill him in about the morning inspections and I don't want you to get any ideas that because he is new here he is a new Corporal. Both he and Corporal Farrow are senior to any of you lot by a long chalk and you may learn something from them such as the responsibilities of a Junior NCO. You Corporal Lucas will hand over the key of No.2 Corporal's bunk to Corporal Deacon because he is also relieving you the duty of dormitory 2. I thought that would bring a smile to both your faces. Off you go and try to make him welcome you will find he is a very decent chap."

Corporal Alfred Deacon was satisfied that his Bunk was up to standard and had been cleaned thoroughly. After the evening meal he gathered the airmen from room 2 into room one where he introduced himself and told them what he expected from them. "You will find that I maintain a high standard both on and off the parade ground. I will personally inspect your rooms prior to the morning work parade and the Sergeant's inspection. Finally, any time day or night if you have a problem or want advice just knock on my door and I will do everything I can to ease your problem or if it is very serious I will take you to a person who will be more qualified than me. If you want to question me, go ahead, I am also a good listener. Thanks for your time."

As he made his way back to his bunk he met Corporal Lucas coming down the stairs. "Hello there I am Ron Lucas and here is the key to the other bunk."

"Thanks I am Alf Deacon," he said as they shook hands.

"There is a darts match in the Corporals Club at 8 o'clock, do you fancy coming over for a drink and a chat, I am not playing but you could meet some of the other Corporals "

"I don't mind, thanks."

"Good I will pick you up when I am ready, Sam Harris will be coming too he is the other Corporal upstairs."

The Station Medical Officer reported to Wingco' Piling. "It is not good news about Corporal Latham sir. I have been in contact with RAF Hospital and they tell me that Corporal Latham has been examined by a psychiatrist. He is now receiving treatment in a psychiatric ward and is expected to be in there for some time."

"Do you think that we will have seen the last of him Doc?"

"I should think so sir but we will know definitely within a few weeks if he is responding to the treatment."

"Thanks Doc. I will relate what you said to the CO."

When Corporal Farrow reported back for duty he thanked Bill Barrett for the help he got with this Married Quarter. He was even more surprised to receive a bouquet of flowers from Bill on behalf of the training staff to welcome his family to RAF March.

When the orderly room staff received the news of Corporal Marion Macken being promoted to Sergeant there was great rejoicing. Flight Sergeant Barbara Page escorted her to the clothing stores to collect her chevrons and to the tailor for them to be sewn onto her uniforms. After congratulating her, Wings told her to take time off to move into the Sergeants Mess. Roy Shaw asked Corporal Springs to assist Marion in the move over to the Mess.

"Report to reception and you will be shown to a room Marion, everything is laid on for you and Barbara will escort you into dinner and show you the ropes." He rang reception who confirmed a room was ready for the new Sergeant(w).

When Marion reported to reception she was warmly greeted with congratulations from Tommy, Jackie and Jill.

"I will show you to your room Marion," said Tommy. Marion and Alice Springs followed carrying the kit. "This corridor is for our WRAF SNCOs and your neighbours are WO.Mary Butcher, Flight Sergeant Viv Anderson,

Sergeant Margaret Roper and Sergeant Dot Dean. Now commence sorting your things out and I will be back presently with a cuppa' for you both."

>>> <<<

Mary Butcher rang Bill Barrett. "We are having a very important committee meeting in the mess tonight Bill and I would like you to attend.

It concerns the preparations for Christmas, I have already notified Roy and it could be quite a long session, we have a lot of ground to cover."

"No problem Mary I will be there." He then contacted Tommy and explained the situation and suggested she asked Barbara over for the evening because Roy will be tied up too.

"We have a big meeting tonight Viv, it appears we may be in for a long session."

"We have to make a start Bill, Christmas will be here before we are ready for it and there is so much to organise."

"I will just nip down to the public phone and ask Ann how the list is coming on for the senior's party; it should give us a good idea of the numbers. Hello Ann, Bill Barrett here, yes she is fine and so are the rest of us. We have a big meeting tonight to discuss the Christmas festivities, how is your senior's list coming on?"

"It is looking good I do not think there will be many more to add to it but at present it totals twenty eight, that should give you an idea of what you will have to work on. I will put a closing date on it say for in a week's time, how does that sound to you?"

"That is good, thanks Ann that is a big help."

"Will we see you all on Saturday? Because the natives are getting restless and keep asking after you all."

"We will be there thanks Ann, see you Saturday."

On the run-up to Christmas life was hectic in the Sergeants Mess especially for the entertainments committee. The party for the seniors of the village was a huge success; they were fussed to the extreme by the young men and women of the station who volunteered their help much to the delight of the elderly people when they were being made such a fuss of. Wings became very popular as he chatted and mixed with the seniors. Captain Bligh (Bill Barrett) and his party were in great demand by the March Hare Pub regulars. A very happy crowd of seniors left the station each carrying a small gift parcel in chauffeur driven private cars ferried to their homes by volunteer SNCOs.

The usual chain of events followed. Officers and Senior NCOs waited on the other ranks at their Christmas dinner. Although plenty of humorous banter was exchanged nothing got out of hand and when it was all over the Officers were invited back to the Sergeants Mess for a winding-down drink.

Bill and Tommy played hosts to Roy and Barbara, Derwent and Viv, George and Betty Miller, Sam Brown and Mary Butcher, Tim and Ann Wilson from the March Hare pub, at a pre-Christmas dinner in their married quarter, with a stipulation of no presents and no bottles just an exchange of Christmas cards. Sam supplied the Turkey and vegetables ordered of course by Tommy. George Miller got a nice surprise when he saw Ann; they greeted each other as old friends. "I will never forget that day you won that drill contest at RAF Chatsworth. I, along with so many of the staff were so proud of you and your girls."

"You were our hero George when you ordered that obnoxious Chambers-Jones off the parade. Have you still got half that swagger cane you almost tickled his fancy with," she said with a laugh."

"I don't know about that but I do know it would have brought tears to his eyes and yes, I still have it and Mary still has the other half."

"Who is taking my name in vain?" asked Mary.

"Calm down Mary we were just reminiscing about Chambers-Jones' swagger cane."

"Well be careful what you are saying George Miller! My half can still be put to good use." That comment from Mary brought lots of laughter from the rest of the guests.

"She is still the same hard woman Ann as she was at Chatworth."

"I agree with you George," said Bill. "She is the same old battleaxe."

"I have told you before about that Bill Barrett."

Bill and George joined in with her saying. "And less of the old," which caused more laughter.

After dinner when they were sat relaxing with a drink the topic arose as to what each couple were doing over the holiday period.

Bill said. "Tommy and I are going to my sister's."

Roy said. I am taking Barbara to meet my parents and staying over Christmas."

Derwent said." I too am taking Viv to meet my parents and staying over Christmas then Viv is taking me to meet her parents and staying over the New Year."

Mary said. "Sam and I are going to the Algarve and staying in the hotel you stayed in, we will then see if it is as good as you said."

This brought applause while the girls came to her and gave her a kiss and the men shook Sam by the hand.

"That will be wonderful," said Tommy. "We are all delighted for you both and we know you are going to like it there. We will be thinking of you."

George said "My Christmas is not going to be so exotic I will be Orderly Officer over the Christmas period." That announcement brought Ahs' of sympathy from the ladies.

"We will be keeping the flag flying and the doors open for our merry makers and believe me we will be rushed off our feet," said Ann. "After seeing the New Year in *we* will need a holiday on the Algarve."

After toasting each other they all made their way back to their homes saying they were looking forward to meeting up and enjoying the New Year together.

>>> <<<

Corporal Roy Hermett and Senior Aircraftsman Bond were summoned to the Station Commander's Office. In the presence of Wing Commander Pilling and Squadron Leader Cody he presented Corporal Hermett with the Air Officer's Commendation (AOC) certificate for your NCO qualities in attending an injured comrade by administering on the spot first aid and comfort and being responsible for the quick turn out of the Station Medical Team. "Well done Corporal," the CO said as he shook him by the hand. "You are the type of serviceman the RAF needs."

He then presented a similar certificate to Senior Aircraftman Bond. It read. For your unselfish duty to RAF March by voluntarily working many hours beyond the call of duty to make sure that all the Station Messes were always supplied with fresh produce from the Station garden. The CO shook his hand. Congratulations you deserve this SAC Bond, very few people know you turned down a promotion and a good overseas posting to make sure the Station garden would not be closed down, because as sure as eggs are eggs that is what would have happened. On behalf of all the RAF March personnel I thank you."

After the presentation the Wingco' and Squadron Leader came to offer their congratulations to them both.

>>> <<<

Prior to the Station stand-down, the Commanding Officer addressed the Station personnel.

"I would like to thank each and every one of you for your efforts in maintaining the reputation of high quality that has come to be expected from Training Command's Flagship. During this year we have enjoyed good times and unfortunately some bad times. We are leaving those bad ones behind and my forecast is we are going to have a New Year we all will be proud of but only if we all pull together and make it happen.

On behalf of all my Officers I wish you and your families a Happy and Joyous Christmas and a Very Happy, Healthy and the Best New Year yet. God Bless you all."